Sharpshooter *in* Petticoats

SOPHIE'S DAUGHTERS

Sharpshooter *in* Petticoats

MARY CONNEALY

BARBOUR
PUBLISHING

© 2011 by Mary Connealy

ISBN 978-1-60260-148-2

All scripture quotations are taken from the King James Version of the Bible.

This book is a work of fiction. Names, characters, places, and incidents are either products of the author's imagination or used fictitiously. Any similarity to actual people, organizations, and/or events is purely coincidental.

For more information about Mary Connealy, please access the author's Web site at the following Internet address: www.maryconnealy.com

Cover design: Lookout Design, Inc.

Published by Barbour Publishing, Inc., P.O. Box 719, Uhrichsville, OH 44683, www.barbourbooks.com

Our mission is to publish and distribute inspirational products offering exceptional value and biblical encouragement to the masses.

ecpa Member of the
Evangelical Christian
Publishers Association

Printed in the United States of America.

Dedication/Acknowledgment

You know what I had in mind when I wrote Mandy's shooting scenes in *Sharpshooter in Petticoats*? That scene near the end of *True Grit*, when John Wayne goes charging across that open meadow, two rifles firing, twirling them to cock them. I loved that scene. And I like to think my heroine Mandy McClellen Gray Linscott has true grit.

And I'd like to dedicate this book to Aaron McCarver. This book ends a saga, nine books: the Lassoed in Texas series, the Montana Marriages series, and the Sophie's Daughters series all intertwine. Aaron helped edit them all. Keeping it all straight was a big job and Aaron's help was a Godsend. Thank you, Aaron. God bless you, and I love your skill as an editor and as an author.

★ One ★

Tom Linscott slid backward five feet before he caught a slender rock ledge and clawed at it to stop himself from plunging a hundred feet more.

The rock was nearly sheer. He felt blood flowing from his fingertips. His grip was shaky already, and now it was slippery. He clung to that ledge like a scared house cat, afraid to move, fighting to slow his slamming heart and steady his breathing. He'd been climbing a long time, and he had a long way to fall if his grip didn't hold.

Then he did what any thinking man did when something scared him. He got mad.

So, he clung to the side of that stupid mountain, gathered his strength to go the last twenty-five or so feet, and fumed. He was a rancher not a mountain goat. He should *not* have had to climb up here.

No woman should be this hard to get.

His handhold felt solid; his footholds were all of three inches wide. He needed a minute of rest before he went on to a more precarious spot. And while he hung there, dangling over a dead drop that ended in jagged granite, he looked up and saw her.

7

The woman he'd come for. Lady Gray.

She lived in a fortress, cut off from all the people she considered beneath her. The rumors about her were legion and harrowing. Ruthlessly dangerous, some said. A witch, others had called her. She'd put a curse on the land she ruled over.

Tom hadn't told anyone of his plans until just before he left home. But he'd listened for any whisper of her name, any passing reference to the legendary Lady Gray.

She was the most dangerous woman in the West. As fast and deadly with her rifle as any woman alive.

That last part Tom suspected was true. The first, well, he hoped she wasn't dangerous to him, but he was minutes away from testing the theory.

He'd had to admit he was coming right before he left because there were arrangements to make. That's when one of his cowhands told Tom with dead seriousness that he'd lived in this area and it was widely repeated and believed that to approach Lady Gray meant certain death.

But Tom knew something none of the rest of them did. He knew what had brought her to this place. He understood the roots of her reputation. He knew who she was before the legend had been born. And he knew she was no witch.

That didn't mean she might not blow a hole in him with that blasted Winchester if he wasn't real careful.

Right now she stood motionless, looking up, clearly visible in the starlit night. He watched her and stoked his temper while he hugged this stupid cliff that he should *not* have had to climb. The fool woman should have invited him to come right up to the front door of her fortress.

As he watched, a mountain breeze billowed her dress and cloak and scarf in the night, and in the moonlight it was as if living power swirled around her. Everything she touched was more alive, more vital, more beautiful. A half moon glowed in the cloudless eastern sky, while she faced the west.

As her dark cloak and light hair danced around her, Tom knew exactly why her reputation had reached the level of the mystical. Back when Tom had last seen her, she'd been beautiful and wounded and sweet.

No one put those words to Lady Gray now. Untouchable was more often repeated. Untamable certainly, as if anyone would consider trying to tame a witch. She was called cold, but Tom had seen the warmth. Life might have forced her to hide that away, but Tom would never believe the warm, intelligent, vulnerable woman he knew wasn't there somewhere. Merciless. That might be true. Tom was sneaking in after all. He didn't want to risk finding out she had no mercy. Unbeatable, too. A warrior with nerves as steady and strong as the stones of her castle.

But all of that reputation wouldn't keep friends nor enemies away. She had a large supply of both.

A rifle, now, that made people fight shy. But even the rifle wouldn't keep Mandy Gray's family back. They were a salty lot. But the danger of knowing her was so intense that she'd begged those she loved to stay away, and they'd let her alone.

Tom had heard the grumbling, had done some of it himself. Her pa had come and tried to pull her out of her mountain fortress, one of her sisters, too, and some faithful old friends. She'd run them off to save their lives. And Tom knew, even if no one else did, that her coldblooded rejection was rooted in love. Or maybe he just believed that because he'd been run off, too.

Her cloak stormed and twisted around her. Her hair, loose in the wind, danced white, like living smoke curling around her head. It went with the gray of her clothes. It was said she always wore gray to match her name and her castle and her mood. But in the night, who could say what she wore? Everything about her looked gray, even her eyes, which Tom knew were a flashing sky blue.

It gave Tom grim pleasure to know he was dressed in pitch black. That suited his mood.

A desire to yell at her, tell her he was coming, coming to rescue her from this self-imposed exile, clogged in his throat as he saw the butt of that deadly accurate long gun poking up at an angle by her left shoulder. She always wore it that way. The rifle and her lightning-fast reflexes were as much a part of the legend as her beauty and isolation.

She'd be real glad to see him. He was sure of it. But she had a reputation for shooting first and asking questions later, so he didn't want to startle her.

Mandy Gray and that rifle. Tom bit back a growl that she'd made it so hard for him. He fully intended to own Mandy, and he'd use that rifle on her backside if she didn't come along quietly.

But he'd tell her all that a bit later, after he had her disarmed. The element of surprise increased his chance of survival.

Since she was right where he wanted to be and there was no way to gain that high ground as long as she was there, Tom settled in to his precarious perch to watch her and pick his moment to stake his claim. Considering she was the most beautiful woman Tom had ever seen, watching was no hardship.

As he waited, a long tube appeared over her head as if she were taking aim at the sky. A thrill of fear raced up his back as the irrational thought flickered through his head that Lady Gray was having a showdown with God. She'd declared war on the whole world, why not God, too?

Tom followed the line of the tube and saw a falling star streak across the sky, then another. As if maybe God was shooting back.

Shaking that madness away, he knew she hadn't made a move toward her rifle. Tom was watching too closely to miss even Mandy Gray's wicked speed.

She pointed upward and held the tube to her eye, riveted somehow, completely unaware of her surroundings. Tom tried to figure out what had caught her attention until he realized that her utter focus on the sky gave him his chance to move.

Wiping his bleeding fingertips on his black shirt, to make them less slippery, he resumed his stealthy climb, glancing every few seconds at Mandy and that tube and her frozen fascination with...something.

He'd never seen anything like it before.

★

The sky is falling.

Mandy's heart trembled and she enjoyed it—the fear.

For so long she'd feared nothing. Felt nothing. Not joy, not fear, nothing. She loved her children, so she felt that to some extent, but her love translated into protecting them, and to do that she needed to remain in control.

Beyond the love of an angry mama grizzly, her heart was as dead as her husband.

She didn't fool herself with romantic notions that her heart was dead *because* her husband had died. No, she'd been finished with feelings long before Sidney had assumed room temperature. The men who'd shot Sidney had hardened what few feelings she had left.

So now the sky was falling.

Maybe the end of the world. Maybe Jesus coming again.

That suited her.

White lights shot across the sky. She lost count. She stood and watched through Sidney's telescope and *felt*. For the first time in a year she wasn't ice cold all the way to her soul. It was as close to free as she could be in the stronghold of her home, Gray Tower.

Logic told her that the world probably *wasn't* coming to an end. That would be too easy. She hadn't had an easy day in her life. West Texas wasn't what anyone would call easy, and certainly there'd been no ease since she'd come to Montana.

She pulled the telescope away from her eye and watched white slices of heavenly light. Content with the goose bumps of fear, her spirits rose. Assuming the world wasn't ending, she'd come to a good place out here. Her children were safe. She was safe—bitterly lonely but safe.

And at night she looked at the stars and dreamed of being far away. And dreamed of making sense of that map Sidney had left, a map that would take her to a gold mine and give her a way out of her troubles.

But the map with its odd star markings as a starting place made no sense. And the gold and the freedom it could buy might as well be as far away as those slivers of slashing light. But the stars changed. She'd learned that since she'd begun studying them. And every night the stars were out, she looked and hoped Sidney's map made sense.

Tonight, here she stood again and watched the sky and stayed safely in her tower. The Shoshone people who lived around her had made this land impenetrable. And she hadn't had a report of someone trying to gain access for months.

A few reported deaths weighed on her. And there was one nightmarish night when they'd gotten through the watching Shoshone and come upon her. She'd survived that life-and-death fight on a moonlit night, but with a scar on her soul—the knowledge that she had killed another human being.

What choice did she have? Running her thumb over the little callus on her trigger finger, she knew she could fight or she could die, and her children with her. When evil men preyed on a woman, they had no right to hope for mercy, and neither the Shoshone nor she showed them any.

Another star shot a streak of white light, and she shivered in that lovely fear, the first real feeling she'd had since the cold had sleeted through her veins on the night she took a man's life. The fear gave her hope.

Maybe, finally, even without Sidney's gold, she could believe she was safe. She could dare to believe the men who hunted her had finally given up.

A hard hand clamped over her mouth. She went for her rifle to find it locked between her body and whoever held her.

"Hold still," a voice hissed in her ear. "I won't—ouch!"

Mandy struck hard with her telescope, going for the kill. She slammed her attacker in the nose. Even as she landed the blow, she knew it wasn't hard enough. His arms never relented. His grip on her trapped rifle never wavered. Then somehow her telescope was gone, thrown aside. She heard glass shatter as it landed against the rocks. Then it bounced and clattered over the cliff. The telescope she needed to study the stars and save herself.

With a sickening twist of her stomach, she knew she'd failed her precious babies. That thought made her desperate, and she twisted, fighting the iron grip. Her hard boots stomped but missed the man's foot. With a sinking stomach, she knew this man was tough.

Her elbow rammed his stomach. He grunted and his grip tightened, pinning her arms. She could get no force behind the blow. He lifted her off her feet. She kicked with her heavy boots. Grunting in pain, he wrapped one leg around both of hers and they fell backward.

The grip knocked the wind out of her even though she landed on top.

"Stop! Mandy, quit." The man still whispered.

Mandy instantly knew he was aware of her Shoshone friends and was careful not to alert them. Where were they? They were so diligent.

"Will you please—"

Writhing against him, panic drowned out his words. She didn't need to hear to know the man would spew threats and gloat with pleasure at her sure death.

13

Her children! What would become of them? What plans did this evil man have, all because of Sidney's filthy gold. She sank her teeth into the hand over her mouth and clawed at the muscled wrist.

"Mandy! Will you stop that?" The voice was deep. "Ouch!" Raspy. "Get your teeth out of me." Familiar.

She froze. She knew that voice.

"Are you done trying to beat the stuffing out of me yet?"

Tom Linscott.

Mandy's taut muscles relaxed. She opened her clenched, attacking jaw and sagged back against the hard length of him. She wasn't going to die today.

Looking toward the heavens, she saw yet another streak of light. The sky wasn't going to fall after all. Her world wasn't going to end.

Tom's hand lifted from her mouth. "I knew I had to quiet you down before I tried to talk to you." He rolled sideways, tipping her off of him.

She kept moving and gained her feet, ignoring an almost instinctive need to go for her rifle.

Standing, dusting his backside, Tom gave her, and her rifle, his full attention.

"Get out of here. You need to go. I'll signal the Shoshone people so they'll know you're coming out the gap." Mandy frowned and looked over the ledge. "Did you climb up that cliff?"

Taking his hat off and slapping it on his leg, Tom said, "Yep."

"How'd you do that? Wise Sister's family would have seen you. They know this is the only other way in."

"Not exactly a 'way in,' Mandy. It took me two hours of hard climbing in the pitch dark. My fingers are bleeding." Tom scowled at his hands, black tipped with blood.

Mandy noticed some teeth marks, too. "Well, you're in." Mandy took an uncertain step forward when she said those words.

He was definitely.

In.

Then she, who thought everything over and had complete control of her actions and complete death in her emotions, launched herself into his arms.

He caught her and lifted her onto her tiptoes and kissed the living daylights out of her. A moment stretched to a minute, then two. Her arms tightened on his neck.

He pulled back. "Mandy, I've been—"

"Shut up." She tilted her head to deepen the kiss and put an end to his ridiculous talking for long minutes more. He cooperated fully, and Mandy realized she could feel so much more than just fear.

When she regained her senses, she found her toes dangling about three inches off the ground, not quite sure when he'd lifted her. He pulled away and, even with his face shaded by his Stetson in the dark, she saw him smile.

"Hi." His white teeth flashed as pure as shooting stars.

She dove for his lips again but he ducked. "We're going to talk now. I've come to get you out of here."

In one second, with one poorly chosen sentence, Tom cleared Mandy's head of nonsense.

"I can't leave." She pushed against his shoulders. "I'll be killed."

"I'll protect you." He ignored her pushing.

"You can't." Her shoving hands turned into fists. "You'll be killed."

He lowered his head and kissed one of the fists that was curled upon his chest. "I'll hire enough people to guard us."

"No!" Her struggling paused as she watched his soft mouth touch her taut fingers. She shook her head to clear it. "They'll be killed."

"I've got tough men. We'll protect you and your young'uns."

"I can't take the children out." Shaking her head frantically,

15

Mandy knew they'd come to the real reason she stayed trapped in here. "They'll be killed."

"Will you stop saying that!"

"No, because—"

"Will you shut up, or do I need to gag that mouth again?"

Mandy frowned but didn't speak the obvious. He'd clearly heard her already.

"There is no reason on earth you have to stay up here."

"Yes, there is. I'll be kill—"

An extremely rude snorting noise cut her off. "There have been other rich people, Mandy. Many of them have lived to an old age."

"They didn't make enemies of the Cooter clan. There doesn't seem to be any end of them. And they all have a grudge, aimed straight at me."

"The Cooter feud against you is famous, no denyin' it. But the solution isn't to hide up here for the rest of your life."

"Yes it is." It was a stupid solution; even Mandy knew that. But it seemed to work, and the alternative was death. "If I go out in public, they'll come for me."

"Then they'll be stopped, arrested, and hung."

"You can't arrest them all. They're like cockroaches. They keep coming. I've already been shot at twice. Hit once." Mandy rubbed her arm, long healed but not forgotten. "Sidney is dead."

"No great loss."

"Buff was shot."

"That was before the feud."

"Luther was shot."

"I know. A bunch of Cooters have been arrested. Several are dead."

"But there are always more of them. There's no end to it."

"Buff and Luther weren't hurt badly."

Sidney sure had been, but Mandy didn't mention that. "In the last few months there've been no attacks." That she did mention. A tenuous peace, but the best she could hope for. "They seem satisfied as long as I stay up here, like they've got me in prison, I suppose. But every time I try to leave or someone tries to get in, they come and keep coming. The Cooters and their kin will hurt anyone who gets in their way."

"Then they'll have to go through me."

"That's exactly right, Tom." The night wind tossed Mandy's gray cloak around, whipping it, lifting it until it floated around her like smoke, drifting and tossing her hair. "They'll come through you. I'm not risking anyone else. I'm here. I'm safe. I hope the really spiteful members of the Cooter clan will die out by the time my children need to leave. Until then I stay."

"Then I'll stay with you."

Shaking her head, Mandy said, "You've got family, a sister and nephew, a ranch."

"Two nephews, now. My sister had another son."

"My family is all in Texas. The Cooters haven't gone that far to bother them, mainly because they've gotten the notion I've cut my family off."

"Wonder where they got that idea?"

From Mandy herself. She'd started the rumors about her family begging for money. All nonsense and a blow to the McClellen family pride. Ma and Pa would never have accepted the lie she put about. But then Luther was shot trying to get in to see her. He was lucky to survive. After that Mandy's family had respected her wishes and left her alone.

Tom wasn't leaving.

"I'm not staying." Tom crossed his arms and planted his feet as solidly as if they were rooted to the ground. "I've got a ranch to run. Let's get packed. We can be well away from here by morning. The way through the gap is clear tonight."

"We can't be sure of that."

"I'm sure of it." Tom reached out and grabbed her so hard his fingers bit into her arm. She'd have bruises tomorrow. Fair enough, she'd punched him in the face. He'd have a few bruises, too.

"I'm not going." Mandy yanked against his grip.

Tom jerked her forward so suddenly she stumbled into his chest. His arms went around her waist, and he lifted her up to eye level. Mandy didn't think of herself as a short woman. But then she was mainly surrounded by toddlers, so compared to them she was quite tall. Tom was a big man, though, and he made her feel tiny and very feminine. Just look how he'd grabbed her and kept her from getting to her rifle. It was galling.

Now he lifted her straight off her feet. His muscles were the iron hard bands a man earned fighting nature to run a ranch. He dangled her there with no apparent exertion and stared straight into her eyes. "How about we do it this way, Mrs. Gray?" Tom swooped down and kissed her until she didn't have much left in her head, surely no sense.

He pulled back, only inches, his intense eyes and stubborn jaw filling her whole world. Made her want. Made her feel. "I'm taking your children out of this fortress tonight. You can come with me or stay behind."

Made her crazy. "I won't let you."

"You can't stop me." He fell silent and waited. A big, tall stack of pure stubborn.

Going for her rifle wasn't really an option since she'd just admitted keeping him alive was her first reason for not going. Still, her fingers itched to grab for the barrel.

When she didn't respond, Tom set her on her feet, turned, and stalked toward the house, as if he planned to pack the three children up and take them without her permission or company.

She reached for her rifle and grabbed. . .air. Looking down by her right hand where the muzzle was always waiting, she realized it was gone. Looking up, she saw Tom carrying it.

"Looking for this?" He raised his arm high so the gun was silhouetted against the starlit sky.

The growling noise in Mandy's throat surprised her. Yes, she was definitely feeling again. Rage, terror.

God forgive me, I feel attraction, caring, desire. Worst of all, hope.

Shaking her head to dislodge that ridiculous notion, she couldn't wipe away the hope. And really hope was the worst because she *knew* better. Tom letting her believe there was a way out was the cruelest thing he could do.

Running her thumb over her trigger finger, she liked it better when her emotions were dead. Going back to that thrilling fear that the sky might be falling would be wonderful.

He reached the house, that stupid gray monstrosity Sidney had named Gray Tower after himself. Sidney Gray. He'd named his son after himself. He'd have named the whole wide world after himself given half a chance. It was a wonder he hadn't tried to pay the state of Montana to change its name to Gray.

She glared at her home. It looked like a castle out of a fairy tale. All they needed was a moat and a fairy godmother.

Tom grabbed the knob and went in, slamming the door behind him. He'd never find the children in there. Too many rooms.

She dashed after him...not to help him find the children...to get her long gun back.

★ TWO ★

"We're not setting up camp for the night. Not this time." Cord Cooter jerked his reins so hard the horse reared up and fought the bit.

"Eight of us dead." Cord stayed in the saddle but not without some difficulty. "The Grays have killed eight of our kin. I'm ready to settle accounts."

He wheeled his temperamental horse around and looked at the six men with him. They were barely visible in the dim light of the heavily wooded trail.

One of his cousins, rattlesnake-mean J.D., rode up beside Cord. "I ain't gonna ride into that gap. She's got it staked out by ghosts. I swear we've lost men without hearin' 'em die nor findin' their bodies. There's somethin' ain't right about the mountains around her. They're cursed. The woman's a witch. And that place is surrounded by haints."

"She ain't no witch. I've talked to her. I've had my hands on her." Cord had touched her one time. One time only. And he could still feel her slender shoulder. . .and her fear. It made him hungry to feel both again. . .and more. "She's human enough."

One hand, for one second, two years ago. He didn't tell his

20

family that. Cord's fingers clenched into a fist, and only the memory of a broken nose and two black eyes—barely healed from the last fight with one of his cousins—kept him from swinging a fist at his cowardly, superstitious cousin, J.D. He was an old man more interested in sitting on a rocking chair than avenging their family.

"I'm content to stake out the trail to Helena in shifts and wait to pick her off if she rides to town." J.D. looked around and nodded.

Cord heard a lot of agreement in the grumbling.

"You're gonna let that woman kill all those Cooters and not pay? Grandpa'd skin you yellow bellies alive if he could hear you now." They were about five miles from the gap that led to Lady Gray. Mandy Gray—Cooter didn't like thinking of the reputation she'd earned up in these parts. They could be there in an hour, and Cord was tired of waiting. They should strike tonight and be done with it. He'd given up on having Mandy and the gold and had a plan that would let him be done with the rugged life he'd been living for the last two years.

"Grandpa set it down that we'd back each other." J.D. snarled like a hungry wolf. "Cooters stick together. We done that, Cord. But corralling Lady Gray in that gap is good enough. She can't enjoy all her gold. She can't get out. No one can get in. I don't have a belly for killin' a woman anyhow, and what happens to her children if we kill her? I think blasting that gap closed is worse than killing her without getting blood on our hands. You've seen her standing on that cliff, late at night, aiming her gun at the stars like she's aiming to shoot God right out of heaven. She's in league with the devil. We've got her trapped, and I say as long as she stays trapped, we're getting our due for our cousins. Getting more of us killed ain't gonna make nuthin' better."

Cord looked at the men. The faces were different, but no one would look twice and not know they were family. The white shock of hair was mostly covered by their hats and concealed by darkness, but their stocky build was the same. They all had a few weeks' worth of grubby dark whiskers on their chins. And the set of their jaws and the cold eyes were of a kind. He was mighty proud of his family, but he was by far the youngest. The rest of 'em were getting soft.

"More Cooters should be drifting in to Helena soon." Fergus turned his horse so he stood side by side with Cord. They were brothers. Two of a kind. And even Fergus had no belly for that gap and that witch woman. "Cord's right that we've gotta make her pay for what she's done." Then Fergus turned to Cord. "But not till there's more of us, brother. Let's keep the trail covered and wait for the train. There's something ain't right about that gap and the land around it. We've lost too many men."

"It's Old Nick, I'm telling you," J.D. shouted. "She sold her soul, and now she's under the protection of the devil hisself. We've lost men right while we could see her. We know it ain't her what killed 'em because we could see her standing all the way up there, her rifle aimed at heaven, with her out of range so she couldn't'a shot any one of us anyway. And if she did, there was no crack of a rifle. And never a body found."

A chill went down Cord's back. J.D. had the right of it. His cousins had vanished as if the ground had opened and they'd been sucked right down into the brimstone. But Cord didn't believe in God, so that meant there was no devil neither. Couldn't have one without the other to his way of thinking. His cousin was just a superstitious fool. Chances are those no-account cousins had picked their moment, slipped away, and run off. Their horses were gone, too, weren't they?

"We know she's not shooting anybody." Fergus urged his horse a step closer to Cord. "But we're down to five of us. If this is a blood feud, then we're losing too much blood. Instead of a head-on attack, let's wait for more help and go at her hard."

Cord appreciated his brother standing by him physically even if he didn't support Cord's plan.

Fergus went on, now looking at Cord. "Until then, she's stuck in that fool's house. Judging by the way she stands up there, every night, and aims her rifle at God, I'd say she's lost her mind. And we're the cause. I like your idea of trapping her behind a pile of rock where she lives. Make it her tomb. We'll as good as kill her without drawing the blood of a woman. But we need to wait for more Cooters."

"But this is different than when we've tried to get through that gap and take her. We don't have to go far in. We just dynamite it shut. We wouldn't have to stay around to put a bullet in her." Cord almost agreed that the gap was haunted. He'd felt a hot brush on his neck a time or two like the breath of the devil, as if someone was out there, watching, ready. Rushing at his back. But he'd whirled around and there'd been nothing.

Fergus's eyes flared. "Dynamite would do the trick."

Cord and Fergus had ridden into Helena for it a few days ago, but now no one had the belly to plant it.

"If we slipped in quiet and set it off," Cord said, trying to sway his stubborn family, "we'd be done with this."

"Last time we rode in we lost two men, and that was long before we got to the gap. Why're you so sure we can even set the dynamite?" J.D. groused.

"We'll do it because we're Cooters, and when we stick together we can't be stopped." Cord nodded.

His cousins did, too, grudging but tempted to do this and be on their way. They'd been stalking this woman for too long. Cord and Fergus had been at it for two years, though they'd waited awhile for their family to come at first. None of the men here tonight, except for Fergus, had been in on the start. Those men were all gone. Somewhere.

Lady Gray was proving to be mighty hard to kill.

"This time we all stay together. Before, when we've lost men, it happened when we got separated." He looked at his cousins and saw the stubbornness, but they wanted this done. They wanted to go to town and forget the woman holed up on that mountaintop.

Shifting his horse around, Fergus clapped J.D., the oldest of the Cooter cousins, on the back. "We'll set the charges. Then we'll blow that gap and leave that woman in there." Fergus looked at the cousins one by one and added, "Buried alive."

They all nodded.

With grim satisfaction that they were doing something instead of standing watch on a trail, J.D. said, "This is gonna be over before the rest of our clan even show up."

"We'll do for that woman what she done to us." Cord jerked his chin, satisfied. "And people'll learn the price they pay for hurting a Cooter. The family's pride will be upheld." He wasn't all that eager to ride into the teeth of that witch woman's gunfire. The dynamite suited him fine.

Cord reined his horse in a circle and led the way for the old codgers. This group was so motley he was almost ashamed to be a Cooter. But this would restore their name and show that Cooters were men to be reckoned with. Strange to be ashamed of his family at the same minute he was ready to kill for their pride.

With Fergus galloping at his side, Cord knew that, finally, tonight was the end of this. There'd be no gold for him, and he'd never get his hands on her again, and that chafed. But it was almost enough to picture Lady Gray buried alive.

The vicious pleasure told him they were doing the right thing.

★

"Tom, you get out of my house." Mandy rushed up behind him and caught his arm as he grabbed for the doorknob on the second room down her entry hall.

Tom purely liked her hanging from him, so he didn't protest.

He just dragged her along. "Quiet, woman." Tom had decided before he'd started this he wasn't going to discuss any of it with her. He was *telling* her, and that was that. "I'm hunting for your children so I can save them. I'm getting them out of here and taking them to my ranch, with or without your cooperation."

She held on as he kept walking, and he heard the heels of her boots skidding along on the stone floor.

"This is the dumbest house I have ever seen." Tom reached the next door and swung it open.

"Try living in it." Mandy threw herself in front of Tom as he pulled his head out of the store room he'd just checked. "Try heating it."

"You can't stop me." Tom glared at the stubborn female. "I'm taking your children and, just like a wild mama longhorn, I'm betting you'll traipse along behind them. If you're real good, I won't make you stay in the barn when we get to my ranch."

"You did *not* just compare me to a cow."

"If you're *real* good, I'll let you live in my ranch house and be my wife."

"Wife?" Mandy's throat moved as if she were swallowing hard.

"It's about time, don't you think?" Years past time, Tom thought.

"It is never going to happen." One pretty little hand, rough with calluses, caught his arm as he tried to go around her.

"It's already happened." Tom peered down into her eyes in the shadowed hallway. "We've been meant for each other from the beginning."

"We have not!"

Remembering the day he'd come to her home to visit the foal born out of his stallion and Belle Harden's mare, Tom could still feel the connection that had sprung up between them. He refused to believe a word of her denial. "Why do you think I've stayed single?"

"Because no woman would have you?"

Tom shook his head. "Nope."

"Because there are no women in Montana?" She might have actually growled when she said that.

"No women wouldn't have stopped me. I'd have gone and hunted one up if I'd've wanted someone else. Nothing much stops me once I've got my mind set on something."

"To—o—om!"

A single lantern burning in the long stony hallway barely dispelled the gloom enough so he could see her face. He saw a lot of defiance, but he also caught a glimmer of hope. This was no time to be a pessimist, so Tom refused to believe he imagined it.

But, being a man of action, just in case the defiance outweighed the hope, he picked her up and kissed her again. That seemed to have a persuasive effect on her before, at least in the sense that she quit trying to punch him.

By the time he was done being a man of action, he was tempted to just grab ahold and tote her off to a preacher-man. From the way she kissed him back, he was hopeful she'd cooperate. . . eventually.

But first he had to find those children. Setting her on her feet like a bucket of fresh milk, he said, "Tell me where they are. With or without your help, I'm finding them and taking them. So you might as well help. Getting out of here in the dark is a lot safer than waiting till daylight. You want your children to be safe, don't you, Miz Gray?"

Taunting. He knew it. He was so disgusted with her for marrying that worthless Sidney Gray he could hardly keep from turning her over his knee. Knowing she'd probably find a way to shoot him if he did helped keep him from acting on that impulse.

"But they won't be safe if you take—"

Tom walked around the little road block.

"Come back here."

He went on down the hallway. "I'm gonna start yelling pretty soon, Mandy girl. That'll wake 'em up, and I'll just follow their cryin'." He stopped and looked back.

She was dogging his heels, still yapping like an ill-tempered hound. Convincing her wasn't part of his plan. Who had time for that?

"Are these rooms all full of furniture?"

"Of course. Who has a house without furniture?"

"It's coated with dust and looks like you've never been in the room." Tom kept moving.

Open the door. "Kitchen." Slam.

Open. "Pantry. Not much food." Slam.

Open. "Closet." Slam.

"I'm getting a sense that the kids are upstairs." Tom wheeled and headed back toward the front door, where he'd seen a flight of stairs. He almost ran over Mandy while he walked.

She jammed a shoulder into his belly.

"That does it." He hoisted her and tossed her over his shoulder.

"Tom Linscott, you can*not* come in here and just take over my life!" Her yelling near to raised the rafters.

And Tom heard a thin cry of "Mama" from overhead.

"Shame on you for waking your babies, Miz Gray." He almost swatted her on the backside, it being within convenient swatting distance. But the thought of how much he'd enjoy that convinced him it was sinful. "By the way, we're changing all the children's names to Linscott."

"Put me down." She pummeled him in the center of his back.

She had a good wallop, but nothing he couldn't handle. He held her legs real tight though. She could do some damage with those feet.

He was glad he'd tucked her rifle into the first room he'd searched and she'd been too busy scolding and fussing to notice and go hunt it up. If he'd have slung it over his shoulder as he'd originally planned, she'd no doubt be unloading it into his backside about now.

Dealing with Mandy Soon-to-Be-Linscott, the sharpest shooter and fastest draw anyone in the West had ever heard tell of—male or female—was a powerful sight easier if she was disarmed.

He trotted up the steps, shaking her a bit more than was absolutely necessary. When they reached the top, he needed his hands to carry the young'uns, so he swung her back in front of him and caught one of her flying fists with the hard slap of flesh on flesh. She took another swing and he caught that hand, too, just as she'd have slugged him in the nose.

Again.

"Mama!" A new voice, tearful but a bit more mature than the squalling baby, was added to the racket. A little girl. Probably Angela—she'd be four years old by now. Tom was partial to her because she'd learned his name the last time he was here. Nearly two years ago. He fancied the notion that she might remember him, though he knew it was unlikely.

Didn't matter anyway. She was going to have to start calling him pa.

"You can't take three little children out of here, Tom. You don't have enough hands."

"I've got it planned." He smirked. She was so cute in the dim light of another long hallway. "The oldest can ride piggyback, and I'll carry the two younger ones in my arms. I also intend to steal a horse."

"Now you're a horse thief?"

"That's right, Miz Gray. I'm planning to steal the two horses I sold to that fool you were married to. They deserve better than to live stuck away up here. So it's more like I'm rescuing them. Get the sheriff if you object. Except, whoops, you'd have to leave your fortress to do that, now wouldn't you? Well, since you're runnin' to the law, maybe you'll carry one of the youngsters for me. I can get by without any help, but I wouldn't refuse it."

"How did you get in here anyway? How could you have slithered past all the guards?"

"I had Wise Sister talk to her Shoshone family and convince them to look the other way whilst I climbed that mountain." Tom relished telling her that. Her trusted guardians had betrayed her. By letting him in, they'd as much as said they were picking him for her.

"She did not!" Mandy sounded horrified and also loud.

A new voice added to the mix. "Mama!" An outburst of tears followed the word.

That must be the three-year-old, Catherine. "You know a decent mother wouldn't stand here yelling, scaring her babies. What is the matter with you anyway?" Tom frowned and gave her one more chance. "You want to carry one? Or do I have to handle them all while I turn horse thief?"

"That is kidnapping. A worse crime that horse thievin', Tom Linscott!"

"That's right, practice your new name."

"That's not my new name you big, dumb—mmphf."

Tom yanked her hard against his chest and kissed her until she forgot about yelling. He slid one hand into her wild white hair and tilted her head back so he could pour all his loneliness and eagerness to have her into one single kiss.

With no ability to yap at him, she turned into a full partner in that kiss. Her arms wound around his neck, and he knew, whatever words came out of her mouth, this was truth. She wanted him. She was meant for him. This was the destiny God had laid out for the two of them.

She calmed and went along so enthusiastically Tom tried to figure out a way to speed up their wedding vows to tonight.

Since they were about two days' ride from the nearest preacher, nothing came to mind, so, when he quit, he wheeled toward the first door. All the crying was coming from there. "A house this big and the children don't even get their own rooms."

Mandy's hand landed hard on top of his as he gripped the knob. "They don't *want* their own rooms. Guess what. I sleep in there with them. I don't want *my* own room. This place is spooky. Worse yet, it's cold. If we stay together, then we only have to heat up one room to survive the winter."

Tom looked down and smiled. "You're coming, aren't you, Mandy girl?"

All the defiance and temper melted from her expression, replaced by fear. "It's not safe for you, for any of us." She had her mind stuck clear in a deep old rut.

"I know. But I can't help it. I need a wife and you're the only woman I can imagine being such." He considered kissing her again if she kept arguing. He decided that when she went to nagging it was almost like she was begging him to kiss her.

"I will *never* be your wife. I'd just as well sign a warrant for your death."

She was worrying about him; that seemed like a good sign. "I gave you a year since that worthless husband of yours died, but you never came nor mailed me a letter asking me to come."

"That's not my place."

"Figured you might see it that way, seein' as how we've only met twice before. But I knew how it was meant to be between us right from the start. And I'm sure you did, too." Tom flipped his hand over, off the knob, to grab hers. "Didn't you?"

There was a long moment of silence. Well, silence not counting three crying babies.

Finally, with a frown so fierce it hurt Tom's heart, she said, "I was a married woman."

"That was a big old avalanche blocking the trail between us, I'll grant you that." Tom smiled at her confusion.

"And now trouble comes riding with me." Mandy shook her head, and in the dim light of the hallway, he saw her eyes, so light blue they looked gray, fill with tears. "Terrible trouble. I won't bring that to your door."

"Finally figured that one out, too." He interlaced his fingers with hers and held on, hoping she got the message soon that he was planning on holding on forever. "That's why I quit waiting for you and came to fetch you home."

One more kiss, then he opened the door and went in to meet his children for the second time. He approached the oldest girl, Angela, such a pretty little thing with long, wispy blond hair half escaped from a braid.

Behind his back he heard his stubborn almost-wife snarl, "I *am* home."

Tom sighed but kept a smile on his face for the little girl's sake. Someone around here had to think of the children's best interests.

"And I will *never* marry you."

Smiling, he lifted Angela into his arms and said, "Hey, little girl. Call me Pa."

"Pa?" Angela tilted her head and the tears slowed.

"Yep. I'm your new pa. We'll practice it until you learn it well."

"Tom, don't you dare tell my daughter to—"

"We've got plenty of time, because with your ma bent on talking me to death, this is shaping up to be a long night."

★

Sidney Gray had tried to level a mountain. Pure stupid.

Cord had figured him for a halfwit from the first, but a halfwit in possession of a fortune. Cord was able to take orders from the man who was paying his salary. The money had been good, and he'd seen no way to separate Gray from that fat pot of gold he had tucked away in a Denver bank. So Cord had handled dynamite

31

for one long summer, learned how to run a long fuse and get clear and how to pick a spot that would do the most damage quickly. Even back then Cord had seen how easy it would be to bring that whole gap right down on a man's head.

The way it worked out, Sidney had paid Cord by the month to learn exactly what he needed to know to trap Mandy in this place forever.

There were cracks all over the walls of that gap, torn there by the blasting. Toward the end of the summer, they'd quit drilling holes for the dynamite sticks and just used the cracks that were already there. Some of the crew of skilled blasters had pointed to specific spots and warned Sidney that the wall was weak. They'd warned Gray that his gap would someday come tumbling down. Not could. . .would. They'd been sure the stone lining this gap was undermined and had warned the high and mighty Lord Gray that he was courting trouble.

Gray had just scoffed and said if the gap collapsed he'd blast it open again.

Cord had listened and watched, and in the dozens of times he'd passed through that gap, he'd located the exact spots where he could plant explosives. He'd have that gap closed in minutes.

Fergus rode up alongside him. "I've told the men to stay tight together. You may not want to believe in haints, Cord, but there's for sure somethin' in these woods. Wolves'd howl. A grizzly bear would kick up a ruckus if it attacked. Both of them critters would leave plenty of blood behind. We've seen no sign of Indians or outlaws. And that witch woman is usually up there where we can see her, pointing her gun at the sky like a madwoman. She's not down here picking the men off."

A cold chill crawled up Cord's spine. It was the honest truth that men had disappeared. "Gotta be Indians."

"There ain't no Indians around here, Cord. The army moved 'em off years ago."

Cord saw the gap in the distance, the rocks black and threatening. The other Cooter kin rode so close behind that Cord was ashamed of their cowardice. He was also glad to have them near to hand. They approached the gap. Cord saw the tall, narrow opening yawing in front of him and felt like it was a huge, gaping mouth, waiting to swallow them whole. Where had all Cord's kin gone?

"Pull up." Cord refused to admit it was because he was losing his nerve and needed a few seconds to build his backbone up. "I want to get the blast rigged and ready so we just ride in there, plant it, and pull out fast, running the fuse until we're clear. The second we're out, we detonate the sticks of dynamite and then we hightail it. We'll be in and out in a few minutes. So fast no ghosts nor curses are going to have time to stop us."

He reined his horse off the trail and felt the woods surround him. Cord swung to the ground and pulled the dynamite from his saddlebags and began cutting the fuse.

"Use plenty," J.D. said. "I want to do this once and be done for good."

Cord curled his lip in contempt, without telling his cousin that he'd already pulled out about double what they'd need. Cord wanted out of here, too.

"Did anyone see that woman up there tonight?" Cord paid attention to the dynamite but not so raptly that he failed to notice that no one rode away to check. They all studied the top of that gap from where they sat on horseback. There was no witch woman silhouetted as she took aim at heaven with her long gun.

The men were well and truly spooked.

"Nope, no sign of her. Bright night, too." Fergus had stayed on his horse.

Only Cord had dismounted. It made the woods close in, and he felt that odd warm breath on his neck. The devil breathing on him.

Working faster, Cord stuck a fuse on plenty of dynamite. And he gave each stick plenty of fuse so they could be well away before they lit it.

Cord was a coward, too. That thought sneaked into his head before he could stop it. He shook it off the best he could, but it stuck to him like a burr.

He felt eyes watching him right where he stood. The eyes of a crazy woman. A crazy woman he'd touched and wanted. A woman who was no witch. She was warm and beautiful, with eyes that looked straight into his soul and found him wanting.

He hungered to crush the contempt he'd seen in her eyes. Drag her down until she was thankful for a man like Cord Cooter.

But tonight he gave all that up. It was lost to him and it chafed, but there was no other way. They couldn't get in, so tonight they were going to bury her alive.

Three

Mandy was going to be buried alive. They rode toward that gap, and her throat closed, and her breath battled to squeeze through her clenched jaw.

The gap stood between her and death. Inside it she could survive. Outside, death roved and snarled and snapped like a pack of rabid wolves.

And not just her death, but the deaths of any she'd be called upon to kill. A shiver rushed up her arms and shook her spine. Cold. She needed the cold to face what lurked outside the gap.

More than the cold, she just plain needed to stay inside. She rubbed on that callus she'd grown by keeping her rifle always to hand. Hating the bit of hardened skin, she knew her heart was just as hard and just as terrified of what was waiting for her outside that gap.

But Tom was leaving, and he was taking her children with him. So now here she rode straight for death with no way to get control of the situation. And that made her crazy.

Being crazy probably described her pretty well as she headed for that gap like she wasn't afraid to die or nuthin'.

"I can't believe that idiot husband of yours didn't manage to do harm to my horses." Tom was riding one of the horses Sidney had bought from him two years ago.

They were beautiful animals. Mandy had cared for them with utter devotion, hoping Sidney never noticed how tenderly she watched over them because she knew they were a little piece of Tom.

Now they rode away from Gray Tower on the matched team of blacks Sidney had bought from Tom, leaving the huge house and all its lavish furniture behind without a second thought to its value. She'd also abandoned closets full of stupid gray clothes. The furniture had just been more to dust for Mandy. The clothes, she and her children wore because she had no others.

Tom had Angela in his lap and nearly two-year-old Jarrod in the pack strapped on his back. The little tyke was chunky and given to running wild. He was dark while his sisters were fair, and Sidney had proclaimed the boy his spitting image. Mandy thought Jarrod took after her pa.

Mandy had taken the bare necessities with her. Diapers and Sidney's map. She ran her hand over the map she'd slipped inside the bodice of her dress and fretted to think of her shattered telescope. That telescope and this map were what she'd always hoped would lead her to freedom.

Right now Jarrod was settled in that pack and acting contented, waving cheerfully at Mandy, almost as if he wanted to taunt a smile out of her when she was feeling so grim.

Tom carried the chunky little boy in that pack without a sign of effort, though he loaded Mandy's arms or back down heavily these days. Mandy stared at her wriggling, grinning son, who yelled, "Bye-bye, Mama."

Bye-bye Mama indeed. God protect me. Protect us all.

She slid her hand to where her rifle should be on her back and wanted to go pound on Tom because she felt so helpless without it. If she had possession of it, they had a chance. Besides, she needed to touch the muzzle to bring the chill rushing through her veins, the cold that helped her pull the trigger.

Tom and two of her children were riding straight into the teeth of the Cooter family's gunfire. Mandy followed along, knowing she should somehow run Tom off with her Winchester. But the man was canny enough to have possession of her children. Even as sure a shot as Mandy was, she couldn't be sure of not hitting one of them. And even if she could be sure, none of that was possible because she didn't have her gun.

In near despair, she admitted to something even worse than that. Her heart wasn't in killing him. Confound it.

★

"Hurry up. I hear something." J.D.'s whisper sounded loud as a rifle shot. Cord heard the man draw his six-shooter and cock it.

"Shut up." Cord would have said more, but he was rushing through the job. This was the last stick of dynamite to place. The fuses where ready to be doled out and attached to the plunger. Cord fastened the last blasting cap to the stick of dynamite and began backing out of the gap.

He thought he heard something, too, but he ignored it. His imagination was running wild in this pitch black pass with his brother and cousins as jumpy as spit on a red hot skillet. The gap pressed on Cord until he could hardly breathe.

Fergus held a lantern, but it barely cast enough light to work. It did nothing to push back the weight of these high walls, looming, threatening to collapse and bury them all.

"Bring my horse." Cord eased the fuses out hand-over-hand, careful not to pull on them and maybe loosen the connection so they wouldn't detonate.

They neared the mouth of that gap, and Cord hurried toward it, eager to breathe deeply again. He fed out the fuse.

His family was slower, and they'd strung out behind him as he stepped out of the black pit those gap walls created.

"Move faster. I'm going to blow that thing. Can't you keep up?"

He rounded a pile of rocks well out of range and dropped to his knees. Immediately he fastened the fuses to the plunger, so hungry to bury that woman alive he was drooling.

★

"Can you keep up?" Tom snapped at her like she was a private in the army and he was the almighty general.

"Let me have my rifle back." Resuming the argument she'd already gone through ten times, she reached the inside edge of the only way out of this place—unless she turned mountain goat like Tom—and nearly turned and galloped back to the house.

To keep from doing just that, she kicked her horse into a trot, forcing the beautiful thoroughbred to enter that narrow gap. The stupid place Sidney had blasted out with dynamite—barely wide enough for a small wagon to squeeze through. All because he wanted to live atop a mountain. The gap snowed shut all winter. Though it melted open in the short Rocky Mountain summer, it didn't matter because there were Cooters outside that gap trying to kill her.

The gap was easy to guard against the whole, back-shooting world. . .but it hadn't stopped one pest of a rancher who wasn't afraid to scale a cliff. It was all wrong that she found that appealing.

"I'll give it to you when you catch me." He had the nerve to look back, and even in the black belly of that gap, she knew he was gloating.

The gap was too narrow for them to comfortably ride two abreast. The steep sides cast them in deep shadows as they rode farther in, until it cut off even the starlight—which reminded Mandy again that she'd lost her scope.

She needed it to study the night sky. She'd been doing it ever since she'd found Sidney's map and the stars he'd used to lay out a direction to his treasure. She'd never made sense of the map, but staring at the heavens night after night reminded her of her place, her low humble place in God's creation.

Sidney had been fascinated by the stars once his fortress was finished. Mandy didn't think he was in awe of how small he was. Instead, she suspected he resented the heavens for daring to be above him. And maybe the moron was looking for a way to build way up there.

Sidney had hauled home books about the stars. Mandy had listened when he talked of constellations and the North Star and the phases of the moon. And after he'd died, she'd found peace in the night and the stars.

Now she'd lost her telescope. She'd have to remember she was lowly without any help.

Except Tom would probably remind her.

And she'd lost that one tool that might help her find Sidney's gold. Gold that would help her buy freedom.

The sides of the gap rose to a dizzying height. Mandy could see her rifle in the boot of Tom's saddle. He'd also scrounged through her house and taken four pistols, a shotgun, and a Bowie knife.

It had been left to Mandy to remember to bring diapers for Jarrod.

Men!

Instead, mainly because Catherine was on her lap and Jarrod was watching her from the pack on Tom's back, Mandy said, "I'd like it now, please, Mr. Linscott."

A far more earthy phrase full of dire threats and insults was pressing to escape through her lips. But the children were close at hand.

"Call me Tom." Then Tom tilted his head and in the dark seemed to look down at Angela. "And you can call me Pa, little girl."

"Pa!" Angela kicked her feet, which stuck out almost straight on both sides of the broad-backed black Tom rode. Mandy could just barely see her little moccasins.

"Do *not* call him Pa." Mandy could not sit idly by while that travesty occurred.

"Pa!" Catherine, on Mandy's lap, twisted around and grinned up as if the order were a joke.

Jarrod's legs were encased on that papoose-like pack on Tom's back, but the little boy's arms were free, and he waved them wildly and yelled, "Papa!"

"That's right. I'm your pa. You might as well call me that right from the start."

"My other pa is dead." Angela's high-pitched voice carried back to Mandy.

Tom bent down and responded, but Mandy couldn't hear what the coyote was saying to her daughter.

Shaking her head, Mandy couldn't believe the actions of this night. If things continued to progress as they were, maybe her order was a joke. Maybe she was destined to marry Tom. And maybe Tom and Mandy's children were all destined to die under the blazing guns of the Cooter clan.

Tom had announced they probably would never come back, and he'd picked the horses he'd sold Sidney and let the others loose. He handled the long-legged black spitfire mare so easily, Mandy wondered if the horse remembered him. He hadn't offered to bring a pack horse or let Mandy bring any extra clothes, and she hadn't asked. There was nothing in that stupid fortress she wanted.

The gap wasn't all that long, and she could see gray against the pitch black past Tom's broad shoulders. She swallowed audibly.

"You all right?" The varmint sounded kind, like he was reading her mind. Or maybe he'd noticed that Mandy hadn't corrected Catherine when she'd said, "Pa," and from that he judged she was either ready to stop arguing or in a complete mindless panic.

She was neither. She was just resting up to start all over again nagging until the man saw sense.

"I—I just haven't been outside this gap in—in. . ." She was whispering, and so was Tom, as if they were in church. At a funeral. She hoped it wasn't their own.

"In over a year. I know. I've talked to Luther and Buff and to a few of Wise Sister's guard dogs."

"They're not guard dogs!" Mandy hissed this time. Now she was turning rattlesnake. Well, it was bound to happen as upset as this had made her. She had an Arkansas toothpick in a sheath in her skirt, and it would stand in nicely for a set of fangs.

"They are the finest, bravest, most generous people in the world."

"You don't have to tell me." Tom laughed softly. "I meant guard dog as the highest compliment. It's a fine thing to be able to protect someone from harm."

The laughter seemed unnatural. It wasn't his usual state of mind. He seemed more comfortable being a bad-tempered grouch. "They let me past, didn't they? I love those folks. How'd you get a tribe of Shoshones to protect you?"

"I own the land all around here. Sidney bought it for miles in all directions."

"Your husband bought a mountain's worth of wasteland? He was an idiot."

Mandy didn't argue. "So now I own it, but it's really their hunting ground, always has been and, to their way of thinking, it always will be. So they don't respect the fact that I own it one bit."

"Neither do I, but for a completely different reason." Tom's horse neared the exit to the gap.

"Wait." Mandy's soft cry of fear made Catherine jump and Tom pull his horse to a quick halt.

★

"Did you hear something?" Fumbling with the fuses, Cord froze.

Fergus had stayed at his side. The others had eased back behind a bigger pile of rocks. Cord intended to follow them the minute he hit the plunger.

"Haints, called up here by that devil woman." Fergus knelt at Cord's side.

"There's no such thing as ghosts, nor the devil neither." Cord didn't believe in that because he didn't believe anything survived after a man was dead. And it made no sense to believe in the devil if one didn't believe in God, and Cord didn't. But still, he felt the blood thundering in his ears. Which was probably what he'd heard.

He turned back to his fuses, just a few more seconds. He'd set three blasts. He'd blow the gap closest to the house first, so the fuses closer to him didn't get torn loose by falling rock. But they'd all go almost at once. He intended to detonate all three of them as fast as he could.

"Fergus, here's the first one." He handed the plunger to his brother.

Fergus lifted it and grabbed the handle to shove it down.

"Not yet!" Cord worked frantically now, wanting this done. "Wait until we can blow them almost all at once. I go first. You hit yours after the second explosion I set off."

"Hurry it up then. I'm eager to turn that woman into the walking dead, leave her alive inside her own tomb." Fergus laughed with ill-concealed greed. "She's killed her last Cooter."

★

"What?" Tom jerked his horse to a stop so hard it reared up, but he brought it instantly under control and kept the children safe. He turned to Mandy with his Colt six-shooter in hand, aimed upward, as he scanned the gap.

"Don't you feel it?"

He felt nothing but irritation. "Feel what?"

"There's someone out there." Mandy rode close enough that her horse's head drew even with Tom.

"No, there's not. What is the matter with you?"

"I'm afraid for you to go out the mouth of that gap." The gap was so narrow Tom could block her from passing him simply by turning his horse sideways.

"Don't go out there. Please. We can turn around." She tried to push past.

Tom would have to move for her to get ahead of him, and he wasn't budging.

Leaning forward, she caught Tom's gun arm. "Let me go back. Then you climb back down that cliff. Don't go out that entrance. Just leave us."

"I'm not going back, and I'm not leaving these children. You can come if you want." Tom jerked against her grip.

"We can't." Her nails bit into his forearm through the fabric of his shirt and he flinched. Her voice dropped even lower. "Tom, they're out there. I can almost hear them breathing, waiting. You'll die. We'll all die."

"No, they're not out there. Wise Sister's friends made sure there's no one near abouts. They went all over the area to make sure. Now they've dropped back to let us pass. We're safe, Mandy." He wished she'd believe him, but it didn't matter. They were going out.

"We're *not* safe. If they're cleared out tonight, then they'll be back tomorrow. If I'm gone from here, then they'll find out and come to where I am."

"How'd this start anyway?" Tom asked.

"Sidney's bodyguards shot two Cooters. You remember Cord. He was Sidney's bodyguard when Sidney bought these horses from you."

"Yep, I met him. Never cared for the man."

"No one did but Sidney—and that only lasted until I convinced him Cord was after his gold."

"Convinced him? What do you mean? *Wasn't* Cord after the gold?"

Mandy shuddered, and Tom was glad she was holding his arm or he might have missed the telling reaction in the dark.

"What is it? What did Cord do to you?" Tom figured out enough from that one little shiver.

"I had to convince Sidney Cord was after gold, but Cord didn't really *do* anything. He was a man with bad things on his mind. The reason I didn't like him was the way he spoke to me. I knew he was dangerous."

"Which means"—Tom's disgust for Sidney deepened, which Tom hadn't believed was possible—"if Cord bothered you, that wouldn't have been enough to make Sidney fire him?"

"He did nothing except frighten me. And even that was mostly what I sensed. I knew it wasn't enough to make Sidney fire him. So I lied. I made up a threat to Sidney's precious gold, which wasn't a lie. Cord wanted the gold right enough. Sidney sent the man packing almost instantly. He made a trip to town then fired Cord in Helena so the man was well away from our cabin. Sidney hired a new bodyguard and ran for home, hoping to beat Cord here. I warned Sidney it might come to shooting trouble."

"That's where Sidney was when Jarrod was born. I remember. And Luther and Buff and Wise Sister and Sally ran afoul of Cord, along with that painter greenhorn."

"That greenhorn is my brother-in-law now. Be nice."

Tom snorted. "I remember them talking about Cord teaming up with a brother of his. When Luther and the rest of 'em got to your house they were pushing hard, sure the Cooters were on their way straight to you. But they never came."

Mandy nodded.

"Your worthless husband was in town. He'd left you alone to have his child and came straggling back in after you'd had him all alone."

"Not alone, Tom." Her claws relaxed, and Tom felt her gratitude. "You were there."

It had been the finest experience of Tom's life. He could barely speak past the feelings that recalled themselves when he thought of how he'd been there when Jarrod had come into the world. This boy was Tom's regardless of who had fathered him. No one would ever convince him otherwise. And since the boy was Tom's, it figured his sisters were, too. He was the father of three. And he was coming to the job a lot later than suited him.

"I remember your husband getting all excited about his longed-for son and ignoring the girls who were begging him for attention." Tom had thought Mandy could've used some attention, too, but he didn't see any reason to point that out. "I wanted to stomp the man into the dirt right then."

"Luther did it for both of us," Mandy said. "But firing Cord wasn't what caused the worst of the trouble. That started when a Cooter died."

"Before that, Cord and Fergus teamed up to get the gold."

"Yes, and brought in some cousins. They attacked us, but we had a lookout at the gap by that time, and a couple of those cousins died. Turns out they've got a passel of cousins and a taste for vengeance against anyone who does their family wrong. I heard someone say that Cooters really stick together."

"Then they're fools. They think they can attack honest folks and if those folks fight back they've got good reason to start a feud over that?"

"So it would seem," Mandy replied. "And Sidney hired more guards. I didn't like them either, but they fought for the brand while they were here. They ended up in shooting trouble with the Cooters, and a couple more Cooter cousins died. There have been several clashes, and Sidney was killed in one of them. That was before Wise Sister's Shoshone family moved into the woods around our house. Killing my husband wasn't enough for 'em. I'm alive, and to their way of thinking, I still need to pay."

Tom had heard the rumors. A blood feud. "What kind of polecats turn their blood feud on womenfolk?"

"The Cooters have made it clear all of Sidney's family would die."

"Even the women and children?"

"Everyone. That's what I heard, and hard as it is to believe, I got a bullet lodged in my shoulder one time, and another shot missed. The hate in those people makes me sick. It's obsessive, murderous." She let go of Tom, and he had to stop himself from checking to see if her nails had drawn blood. The woman had herself a grip.

"If I could give them all my gold to buy peace, I'd do it, though it galls me to pay the Cooters for their brutality." Mandy ran her hand over the front of her dress in a way that drew Tom's attention. "But their hate is a deadly thing."

That got Tom's eyes back where they belonged.

"Cooters died at the hands of Sidney Gray's guards. It's a blood feud that they've sworn will last until the last Gray or the last Cooter is dead. There seems to be no end of the Cooters, but there are very few of us Grays."

Tom was quiet, watchful in the dark. Mandy wanted to scare him off, but he knew better. He knew deep down she was terrified he'd leave her. She did want to be saved. But she was so unselfish, so honorable, so brave, so sweet, that she'd chosen a life of pure loneliness rather than endanger someone else.

He cupped her chin, leaned in, and kissed her.

Half expecting her to fight him, knock him back, his heart burned with pleasure when she kissed him back.

When the kiss ended, she whispered, "They're out there." She sounded just this side of crazy. But Tom suspected anyone who had survived what she had would be right on the ragged edge of losing her mind. But she'd held on. And now he was here to take over all her worrying.

"No, they're not." Tom flicked the tip of her nose.

"Yes, they are. I can feel them."

"You can't feel nuthin'."

"They're out there."

"No one's out there."

"They're waiting."

"You're making up something to worry about." Tom went straight back to kidnapping her children, knowing she'd follow along.

"You sound loco, Mandy girl. I'm purely worried about you."

She made a sound that made him glad he hadn't given her the rifle back. She was a crack shot, he'd heard. Chances are she could pick him off and not harm either of her youngsters.

"I'm telling you to get back here."

Tom turned his horse and headed out of the gap. "Quit yapping and let's move out."

"You're going to die, Tom. I know they're out there and ready."

F o u r

Are you ready?" Cord set both his plungers on the ground and took a grip on both handles. In the dark, Cord could just make out Fergus's nod and his own hand on a third plunger.

"Ready."

"On the count of three, I go. One." Cord leaned his weight forward. "Two." He braced himself for the blast.

"Cord! Fergus! We got trouble."

Cord jerked his hand away from the detonator like he'd been struck by lightning. Fergus pulled back, too. Both were kneeling. Cord didn't stand. He whirled around and looked through the underbrush.

J.D. was scrambling forward with Dugger on his heels.

"What?" Cord tried to penetrate the darkness but could see no danger.

"Two of the men're gone." J.D. tripped and fell on his belly, breathing hard like he was scared to death

"What?" Fergus's voice dropped to a deadly whisper.

"You heard me." Thrashing forward, J.D. got to his knees, facing Cord and Fergus. Dugger stood back, leaning over them like the halfwit he was. The three of 'em on their knees might well

48

be attending a prayer meeting.

"I thought you were going to stay together." Cord realized as he'd said it that the men with them hadn't stayed together at all. They'd left Fergus and Cord to wire the dynamite and faded back into the woods. Cord had forgotten all about what his cousins were doing.

"We were together, all four of us. Keeping low, waiting for the blast. My brothers were right behind me." J.D.'s eyes were as wide and round as a spooked horse, and Cord didn't blame him. They could look for the brothers, but Cord knew it was a waste of time. They'd never find a trace of them. "And now they're gone, without a sound, no trace of them anywhere. Just like the others. I tell you these woods are haunted."

Cord did not believe in ghosts. But there was something out there. There had to be.

"Let's blast that hole and get out of here." Fergus reached toward his plunger.

★

Tom rode on with two of her children.

The big, dumb kidnapper.

She watched and waited for one of those awful, vicious Cooters to shoot Tom right out of the saddle. Her eyes burned, and she fought it, but there was no stopping the tears. She could not believe she would pick a moment like this to waste her time with such nonsense. "Tom, don't ride out there yet." No gunfire split the night. "You've got to give me that rifle back. I want to be able to fight." She'd have said more, but her voice wasn't working.

"Come on up and get it." Tom rode straight on out.

There was no shot. Only silence, broken by quiet hoof beats and the sounds of the forest at night.

Mandy stopped the tears by getting mad. "You're an idiot."

"I'm marrying a crazy hermit with three children. I reckon

that makes me an idiot all right." He just kept on riding. And he was still alive. "But Sidney was an idiot, and you married him. You've shown a bent for that. So why not do it again?"

"Maybe I learned my lesson."

"Doubt it." Tom turned to the south.

"And you have no survival instincts."

He was out of the gap, still riding.

Mandy goaded her horse and caught up to Tom in seconds.

Without looking at her, he pulled her rifle out of the boot of his saddle and held the gun out straight at his side.

She snagged it. She felt more in control when, with economical motions, she slung it across her back, butt side up by her left shoulder, muzzle down within grabbing distance of her right hand. She could breathe again.

"I've got my stallion picketed off this way. We've got to stop for him."

"Let's move fast. If you want to get away from here, let's not dawdle." She kicked her horse and didn't even threaten to shoot Tom but rather listened and smelled and opened herself up to the land around her, watching for trouble.

"So, the Shoshone like you, huh?" Tom asked, catching up to her and matching her blistering pace.

"Yep, there was some trouble between them and Sidney."

Tom snorted. "No surprise. There was trouble between Sidney and everyone."

"But they've forgotten him, I guess," Mandy would probably have hit Tom if she hadn't been busy looking for two-legged predators. "Because they work well with me. They live on that land. My title to it keeps others away—except those vermin Cooters—so the Shoshone can have the land to themselves, and I get some credit for that in their minds. They know the Cooters mean me harm, so they watch out for me. It's as simple as that."

"They're mighty fierce protectors."

Mandy knew that to be the honest truth. It was a blessing pure and simple, and she owed it almost entirely to Wise Sister, Buff's wife of two years. "They haven't set up a regular village because the government might send troops and move them if they realized they were here. They live quietly in the woods, and I stay on my side of the gap. We have peace between us."

Mandy and Tom rode side-by-side, though he was picking their trail. She remembered Belle Harden had lived quite a ways from Helena. She'd mentioned the town of Divide, and Mandy had learned vaguely where that was. Belle's mare had unexpectedly given birth to a foal bred to Tom's stallion. Which must mean Tom lived near Belle. Mandy felt her throat close with the thrill of getting to see Belle again.

They found Tom's stallion exactly where it was supposed to be. The horse did his best to fight Tom every second while Tom saddled and bridled the big animal. Then Tom swung on its back. Their three horses were a matched set—black and strong with beautiful lines. Mandy's pair so obviously offspring of Tom's stallion.

Tom led the second horse as they headed out. With every step, Mandy remembered death rode with her. She would be bringing it straight to Tom. It wasn't a possibility; it was a certainty. She had to get away, get back to her fortress. But for now, with her baby strapped on Tom's back, she had to follow.

The silence was eating at her, giving her too much time to worry. "Where do you live anyway?"

"Southeast of Divide." Tom picked up the pace, as if he meant to run away from her questions.

Well, let him try. "How close to Belle Harden?"

"She lives a long way to the northwest, but I run across her once in a while."

Something moved in the woods.

Mandy's hand was on her rifle before she was aware of the motion.

51

"Careful, it's one of the—"

"I know." Mandy cut Tom off, furiously. "Part of being good with a rifle is knowing what I'm shooting at. Did you think I'd just start unloading bullets into the underbrush?"

Mandy's heart pounded because she'd come perilously close to doing just that before she recognized the slender Shoshone brave, riding his horse, shadowing them in the woods. The horse's unshod hooves barely sounded on the soft forest floor. The man emerged, long and lean, dressed in buckskin pants and no shirt, carrying a spear and riding a pinto pony bareback.

The trail widened, and they were riding down a smooth meadow, sloping away in the moonlight. Mandy knew this land well and knew they could make good time for the next hour in this direction.

"Let's put some space between us and that gap." Tom's voice was hard, commanding. And he didn't wait to be obeyed. He kicked his horse and began a steady, ground-eating gallop.

Another Shoshone appeared silently as a ghost from the woods. The hoof beats became a steady drum like the rolling of distant thunder as more and more of her friends rode out of the night. They drew nearer until they were riding, surrounding her, flowing with her over hills and down swales, around rocky outcroppings between wooded areas.

"What's that?" A deep rumbling from behind them caused Tom to pull his horse up and wheel back toward the direction they'd come.

"Thunder?" Mandy looked over her shoulder into the night sky. Starlit, no sign of an approaching storm.

"That's all this night needs is rain." Tom turned and rode on.

"An avalanche, maybe." Mandy's skin crawled for no reason she could understand, and she rode quickly after Tom. Whatever that was, it was far behind them and made no difference to this journey. The only difference it might make was if that gap had collapsed, something Mandy used to worry about when she passed through it.

Now, she turned her attention to the far more likely possibility of being cut down by gunfire.

★

Cord stood from behind the sheltering rock. The air was still full of dirt, but all the rock had settled down. In the darkness, he could see that they'd turned the gap to rubble.

"Now let's hunt for my brothers." J.D. was a tough man, but he couldn't keep the tremor out of his voice.

Cord wanted to go out and holler up to that overlook where the witch woman lived, make sure she knew who'd locked her in. Whether it was the explosion or his own pleasure at finally taking action against the woman, Cord felt none of that spookiness that had plagued him almost from the beginning.

The woods felt safe, empty. Even the night critters were scared back into their holes by that explosion.

"Start hunting."

J.D. knew better than to hunt.

"We've never found a single man, J.D." Cord would have hunted, though, if it'd been his brother.

"This time I'm not stopping until I do." J.D. whirled, like he was going to storm off on his own. But he didn't. No one wanted to be alone.

"This'd be a good time to remember Cooters stick together. Let's not go off alone." Cord wouldn't have gone along except for the faded sense of spookiness.

Maybe they'd driven off the evil spirits with the dynamite. "First light will be coming soon. Then we'll keep looking until we piece together what's happened."

J.D. jerked his chin, satisfied with the decision. They went as a pack to study the place where J.D.'s brothers were last seen.

★

There were four or five Shoshone riders in front of Mandy and as many behind her. It was the whole family, children, women, young men and old.

No one talked as they galloped along. She'd certainly spoken to her friends and protectors in the last year. But they were a quiet people, and she wasn't even sure of their names, though she recognized faces.

They weren't even really her guards. And they were good-hearted, peaceful people. But they did walk the woods all around her home. And they could defend that land if forced to. Their very presence kept the Cooters back. She rarely spoke to them or even saw them, but a few times one of them would come to the house for some reason. She'd heard stories in their broken English of Cooters being stopped, but she didn't ask how. She did know the villains had chosen to leave her alone as long as she stayed in her mountaintop home, and she gave these people credit.

They reached a narrow spot in the trail that wound sharply downward. Tom, who kept the lead, slowed his horse to a fast walk along the treacherous path. The trail dipped lower and widened.

Mandy rode up beside Tom to check on the children. Both were fast asleep. Catherine was dozing on her lap.

The trail wound back and forth across the face of the mountain. Jagged peaks rose high over their heads as they descended.

"Let's stay to a walk for a while. The horses are blowing hard." Tom glanced at her, his face weathered, his expression determined, as if he expected her to start fussing at him again.

Like a nagging woman rather than one of the straightest shooters in the West.

"Why did your husband build up there anyway? Stupid place for a house."

Mandy sniffed. "Isn't it obvious?"

"Reckon I'm not quite dumb enough to figure out what Lord Gray was thinking."

"Lord Gray, that's about right."

"And you're Lady Gray. That's why you dress as you do, right?"

"I dress in gray because it was one of Sidney's quirks. It seemed like he came up with a new one with every sunrise. Gray clothes, gray like his name."

"And he dressed you?"

"No, he went to town. I didn't."

"Never?"

"I had three small children, and Helena is a brutally hard day's ride. Why would I go to town?"

"So you wear gray because. . .?"

Mandy saw clearly he didn't get it.

"Because if any clothing or fabric was purchased, Sidney bought it, and he bought gray. I could make my clothing and the children's clothing in gray, or we could go without. I'm lucky the man didn't make the children wear gray flannel diapers. I suspect it's hard to find, or he'd have done even that."

"I've mentioned this before." Tom arched one eyebrow. "But your husband—"

"Was an idiot." Mandy cut him off. "I know."

"And is that why he built his home all of gray stone?"

Mandy almost laughed. It ended up being more of a snort. A cranky snort. "Well, Tom, stone is gray almost all the time, in case you haven't noticed."

"So the color of Gray Tower is just a coincidence?"

"Actually it is mostly. Although he could have just built a log cabin. But Sidney loved building himself a castle, and castles are made of stone. It probably is what set him on his gray clothing obsession. Gray for his name, Gray Tower for his house, gray suits. And he built up there because it suited him to be above everyone. He could play at being a king."

"It's a wonder he bought my black horses."

"He wouldn't have later on, after he became obsessed with all things gray."

"All on top of a gray mountain. And why'd he build it up there, so far from everything?"

Mandy sighed. "For the simple reason that Sidney had a thirst for looking down on people."

"But he was an idiot; everyone thought so. There's not a man in these mountains that doesn't consider him a fool and look down on *him*. They laughed when he died and asked how the no-account managed to survive as long as he did. How could he look down on anyone?"

"I doubt you said to his face you thought poorly of him."

"Well, no, of course I didn't."

"The answer is simple then. He didn't know. He thought highly of himself because of his money and assumed everyone else felt the same." Mandy shrugged. "I'm not sure Sidney was completely rational toward the end. He couldn't have noticed anyone who disagreed with his delusion. It made no sense to imagine being high up in some far-off place made you important. Someone had to see you showing off to be impressed. And someone has to speak to you, to tell you how powerful and important you are. I think in his calmer moments he knew that. He never even stayed in that house much. He'd go to Helena at least once a month, often twice. And he'd stay away a week or more. The shortest trips he made were six days. He took longer trips occasionally."

"You said Helena was a hard day's ride."

"Yes, and Luther always made it in two days. Once in a while it would take three. But Sidney didn't care much for roughing it. He preferred leisurely two-day rides in. Then, once he was in town, he stayed and conducted business. Lived in the best hotel, ate good food."

Spent time with dance hall girls. Mandy didn't say that aloud.

"Leaving you up here alone with the children?"

"Like I was when Jarrod was born."

Tom had come to deliver horses and ended up next thing to delivering her baby. She'd known back then how things were between Tom and her. A bond had formed that day. It was the kind of shared experience that made a man climb a mountain to get to a woman. And made Mandy ignore common sense and ride out into the dangerous world with him.

"Sidney's trips to town usually lasted a week or two. Sometimes he stayed away more than a month. He told me he rode to Denver on those occasions to have a visit with his gold." That hadn't been true, as Mandy found out much later.

She'd given Sidney the bad news, after Jarrod was born, that she'd never share a bed with him again. There would be no more babies born between them. He'd kicked up a fuss, but Mandy hadn't been able to stand the thought of his touching her. She'd blamed it on Sidney's behavior, but now she wondered if it wasn't at least partly because of how she felt about Tom.

"After Jarrod's birth, Sidney stayed away even more. I. . .I strongly suspect. . ." Mandy hadn't meant to start this. She did a lot more than suspect. Sidney had flaunted it.

"That there was another woman?"

Mandy nodded. "I wasn't going to risk being alone with another baby to birth, and I told him so. He got difficult. He seemed to no longer care what anyone thought of him, as if everyone was beneath him, and that most definitely included me. I suppose that means he did care for me, at least a little, if I could hurt him that way. But I was too angry to be swayed, and he had his son. That was enough for him.

"He'd gotten self-indulgent and sullen. He gained an amount of weight that should have been impossible in the West, with it taking so much work to provide food. But Sidney lived high when he was away from home. Or so I assume. Lavish meals, not a minute's worth of hard labor. His appetite for food was as large as his appetite for grandeur. He completely quit paying attention to me or the children, even Jarrod. When he was home, he sequestered himself in a huge room in his stupid fortress, with a masterful view of all that was beneath him." Mandy hesitated. "And he began watching the stars."

"The stars?" Tom's brow furrowed.

Mandy realized she could see him quite clearly. The night was waning, and the sun was pushing its way toward the horizon. Another day began. How many did they have before the Cooters came?

"Yes. When he spoke at all, he spoke of constellations and comets and planets. I think he begrudged anything that was above him."

"Even the stars?" Tom laughed, but there wasn't much humor in it.

"Yes. I was watching the stars when you jumped me."

"A scope? Was that what you held? I thought at first it was your rifle."

"No, it was Sidney's telescope. I've taken a liking to stargazing. The scope went flying over the cliff when you tackled me. It's the one thing I'll miss from that fortress."

"Because now *you* begrudge anything that is above *you*?"

"No." She controlled the urge to punch him as they moved along side-by-side in the dampness of dawn. "Just the opposite. To remind me of how small I am. How alone. How completely I have to depend on God who could create the heavens."

"Nothing like the Montana Rockies to remind a person of God." Tom looked around and saw that they had a clear stretch ahead. "My horse isn't breathing hard anymore. Let's try and make some time."

He kicked his horse into a gallop, and Mandy fell in behind him again, glad that the talk had ended. Glad to think of something other than her wretched marriage.

★

"Cord, over here. I found two sets of tracks." J.D.'s voice brought everyone running.

"Your brothers didn't come riding out of that gap." Cord studied the ground, and those tracks were clear. And enough debris had settled on them that it was undeniable that someone had ridden out of that gap shortly before the dynamite had gone off.

"She got away!" Fergus howled like a wolf with his tail in a crack.

"But she broke from cover." Cord suddenly had a chance at what he'd thought he'd lost. Like a bird that'd been flushed from the scrub brush, Lady Gray had run. That meant she was away from this awful haunted ground. Maybe there was still a chance he could have everything he wanted. The lady and the gold. He faced the direction the tracks led and almost smelled the running prey. "We can get her now."

His cousins and Fergus all got it the first second he spoke out loud. Lady Gray had left her fortress, and she'd left this spooky, cursed woodland.

"Let's ride." Cord swung into the saddle and kicked his horse into the fastest gallop the trail would allow.

Five

The ride went on, slow in spots, faster when the terrain allowed. Occasional breaks when one of the little ones had to be seen to in some way or other.

Mandy noticed several of the Shoshone braves pick up speed and ride ahead as if Tom had ordered it. But Mandy'd been watching, and Tom had given no order. How long had he been planning this?

Catherine slept in Mandy's lap, and she saw no sign of the children being active on Tom's horse.

The sun began to show itself. Mandy knew she should be exhausted, but she was exhilarated. She was free.

And the Cooters were now free to come for her.

God, forgive me. I'll bring trouble with me to Tom and anyone else who tries to protect me. But it feels so good to be free. Thank You. Protect me. Protect my children. Protect Tom and these wonderful people who have guarded my home and all the new people that I will brush up against.

Mandy knew she needed to get away from everyone who mattered to her. But how? How could she protect her children away from the fortress?

The land grew more civilized, at least compared to where Mandy had been living. There were open valleys, pastures full of cattle. They startled a herd of elk and, as they forded a stream, scared a mama grizzly bear and her two cubs.

Enough of the land was rugged that the horses walked and had a rest from time to time. The Shoshone people stayed at her side like a human barrier from attack, and it tightened Mandy's throat to see their loyalty. Though she'd tried to be a good neighbor to them, mainly their loyalty came from the love of these people for Wise Sister. That love and loyalty might well get them killed.

The burden of that had kept Mandy sequestered for this last year. And now, to be out, to be free. . . The guilt and the longing were so powerful she was reduced to following Tom's orders. Like a brainless sheep.

★

Standing idly by while a man came courting Emma was killing Belle Harden, and when something went to killing Belle, her very first instinct was to kill it right back.

It was in that spirit that she kept an eagle eye on Emma's beau.

It was the longest night of Belle's life. And she'd had four wedding nights, given birth to six children, and married off a daughter against her will. Belle's will, not Lindsay's. Lindsay had been all for that wedding.

But none of it had been this bad.

Marrying off Lindsay had been bad, but it had been quick. This could drag on for a long time. It'd better.

But that meant it was awful to watch.

Silas had rounded up the young man, and Belle hadn't been quick enough on her feet to prevent the meeting.

"She's not old enough for a beau, Silas," Belle hissed in his ear, feeling for all the world like a rattlesnake. She had fangs, too, and she wasn't afraid to use them.

"She's a woman grown, Belle. What was I supposed to do when Linscott asked if the young man could meet my daughter?" Silas stood beside her on the tidy porch of the house he'd built for them right after their marriage. He'd added on a bedroom since then. Good thing with the family growing.

"You could have shot Linscott. That man has been a thorn in my flesh for years." Belle thought of the beautiful black stallion that had been born to one of her older mares from Linscott's runaway stud and almost forgave the varmint.

The varmint being Linscott. She forgave his stallion easily enough.

Linscott had shown up and tried to make Belle pay the outlandish stud fees. They'd both known he was wasting his time, but it had given Belle a chance to gloat, so she'd let him stay and complain for a while. The gloating, combined with that beautiful foal, now one of her top horses and earning her stud fees of her own, had been enough fun that she'd almost forgiven Linscott.

But not quite. And now she could draw on that old grudge to stir up her temper into a wicked storm complete with lightning bolts coming out of her eyes and stabbing right into Mark Reeves.

Belle's eyes slipped to where Emma and that whippersnapper walked, a good three feet of space between them, along the corral, talking horses, Belle hoped. They neared the corner of the barn, and to keep the young couple squarely in sight, Belle leaned sideways and conked her head on the post that held up the roof of their porch.

Silas rubbed her head and grinned.

Which made Belle mad. "Mark Reeves, what kind of name is that?"

"What kind of name is Belle Tanner-Svensen-O'Rourke-Santoni-Harden?" Silas caught her arm and turned her to face him. Then he slid one strong arm around her waist and pulled her close.

"That's not my name." For a change she didn't have a big belly to hold them apart. The baby was almost two months old, her second son. She didn't bother trying to shake off Silas's grip. She liked his hands on her. She hadn't felt them on her in quite this way since before the baby was born. In fact she did the exact opposite of trying to shake Silas off. She surprised both of them by shivering and taking a quick peek at Silas's lips.

"It sure enough isn't your name. It's Mrs. Belle *Harden* and nuthin' else." Silas smiled and rubbed his hand up and down her spine. "So, feeling rested up from childbirth yet, Mrs. Harden?"

She was suddenly feeling rested up to beat all. But she forced herself to frown. "I'm staying right here on the porch to watch that young man court my daughter, and you know it."

Without his smile slipping an inch, Silas said, "I'm not going anywhere either, ma'am. For now." He glanced over at the young couple. "But there is always later."

Silas's sideways glance reminded Belle she'd quit keeping her eye on Mark and Emma.

The couple had vanished behind the barn.

She gasped and turned.

Silas turned her right back and kissed every thought right straight out of her head.

Every thought but one. And that one had her wrapping her arms tight around Silas's neck.

He eased away from her, his brown eyes—more like her hazel ones than any husband she'd ever had—glittered in the setting sun. "And later, Mrs. Harden, I might be interested in going somewhere. With you."

"We. . .uh. . .we need to—"

Silas's arms went around her waist. He yanked her forward and shut her up. Then, much, much later, he pulled away. "Shame on you, Belle. You're supposed to be checking on our daughter.

He released her and helped her let go of him. He'd kissed

enough starch out of her knees that they failed her. She sank down hard and sat on top of the porch railing. Good thing Silas had built it sturdy.

"Stay put." He jabbed a finger right toward her nose.

Sighing, she obeyed him. She obeyed far too often lately, confound it. But still she stayed put and smiled up at her cantankerous husband.

"I'm going to go see if young Mark needs any help checking out the backside of our barn." Silas tugged his Stetson low over his eyes and turned to walk at a very fast pace toward where Emma and Mark had disappeared.

If Belle hadn't been so bemused from that kiss, she'd have been shocked at the complete confidence she had in Silas being fully capable of pinning back Mark's ears. And it wasn't that she didn't trust Silas. It's just that when it came to abusing suitors for her girls, Belle enjoyed seeing to that chore personally.

★

"Thanks for agreeing to coming out for a walk with me, Emma." Mark was having trouble pulling in a deep breath. Here he was standing next to the prettiest girl he'd ever seen, and she didn't seem opposed to the idea of his being here.

"You really asked Tom Linscott to talk to my pa to get permission to call?" Emma sounded flattered.

Mark should have let that stand, but he was having trouble thinking of things to say—which wasn't like him. So he could hardly ignore the only thought in his head, now could he?

"I didn't really do it to be proper and respectful, Emma."

"You didn't?"

Maybe Mark hadn't put that right. "What I mean is I saw you in Divide, and you were so pretty. I asked the boss about it, and he told me to stay as far away from you as I could because your folks were the orneriest parents he'd ever known. He said your pa would beat me into the ground then run a herd of stampeding cattle over me, and your ma would shoot what was left of me and bury me under a tree on your ranch that even now was surrounded by the graves of worthless men who'd come calling."

"Linscott said that?" Emma surprised Mark by smiling.

Shrugging, Mark smiled right back. "Actually I'm prettying it up quite a bit."

Emma laughed.

Every minute he spent near her was pulling him down deeper. "But I did get the message loud and clear that I'd be unwise to just come riding out to your place and bang on your front door and expect you to come out and ride off with me."

"So you saw me walking down the street, and that was all it took." Emma's smile faded. "I happen to know there aren't all that many women in Montana. I suppose you'd have come chasing after any female you clapped eyes on."

Shaking his head, Mark said, "Nope. It wasn't seeing you that did it. Although once I saw such a pretty woman, I was definitely watching you close, or I probably wouldn't have seen what it was that caused me to hunt up Linscott and ask questions."

"What was it?"

Was Mark supposed to talk about another woman to Emma? Mark liked women. Liked talking to them, liked looking at them. But he was a restless man, and he had a lot of building to do before his thoughts turned much to women. But when he'd seen Emma— "You went up to your horse, a fidgety roan mare who was pulling at her reins against the hitching post and looking hard at Tom Linscott's stallion."

Emma's eyes widened. "She was a lot more interested in that stallion than she was in letting me load my saddlebags. But what of that? Why'd that make you ask about me?"

"She was fighting the reins, and you waded right in there next to her stomping feet and jerking head and ran your hands down

65

her neck." Mark stopped and swallowed hard. The way she'd touched that horse, her hands so strong and gentle. It'd hit Mark hard, and he'd been transfixed. "And you talked to her."

So much like one of the McClellen girls. Beth, especially with her gentle touch, though Beth was older than Mark. Sally was Mark's age, and she'd been a better cowhand than most men, certainly better than Mark, and Mark thought he was pretty good. He'd seen Emma Harden and almost felt her hands touching him, almost heard her voice talking to him, gentling him. He'd stared until his eyeballs had near to gone bone dry.

Then he'd headed straight to one of Tom's hired hands and been laughed at.

Threatened with Belle Harden and, almost as an afterthought, Silas.

It hadn't deterred him. He'd gone to Tom and been warned. Belle Harden again.

When Mark'd persisted, Tom had gone to Silas. And Tom had ridden off to do some chore with someone named Lady Gray. There hadn't been much talk of what exactly. And Mark had been given a day of freedom and directions to the Harden Ranch.

Seeing Emma handle that horse with such skill had made Mark homesick so bad it'd taken all his will to not just ask Tom for his pay so he could ride home to Texas. Instead, he'd filed on a homestead and come calling.

"I talk to horses. Don't you?" Emma gave him a narrow-eyed look as if she expected him to make fun of her.

"I do. But I—I just—there was a family of girls back near my home. Blond girls who were good with horses and cattle." Mark reached out and caught Emma's hands just in case she didn't like him talking about other girls and tried to make a break for it.

"So I remind you of someone?" That didn't sound like it suited her much.

"You remind me of a kind of woman I respect." He turned

Emma to face him. "The kind who's tough enough to work alongside a man and strong enough to tame a hard land without ever being anything less than beautiful and gentle."

Emma's eyes widened, her lips softened.

Mark shouldn't be looking at her lips, but he'd accidentally taken a peek—or two.

A very gentle tug brought her closer to him than he'd ever been to a woman. Which wasn't saying he was so honorable, really, though he liked to think he was. He'd certainly done his best to charm a few women, but they just hadn't been much interested.

Another quick glance at her lips—which weren't frowning at him one bit—made him hope that maybe, just maybe, Emma *was* interested. He pulled her toward him and, hallelujah, she came.

"So, you finding what you're hunting for back here?" Silas Harden's voice made Mark drop Emma's hands like he'd gripped the business end of a red-hot branding iron.

He had his back to Silas, and Emma was blocked from her pa by Mark's body. They exchanged one long, lingering look before Mark turned to face Silas, not touching his daughter in any way.

★

Tom kicked dirt over the fire and rose. "We'll be in Divide by mid-afternoon today."

Mandy had thought the journey would never end. But now it would. And she'd stop. . .and the Cooters would find her.

She turned to the Shoshone people who had stayed by her side for the last year, women, men, old, young. "Thank you so much for your protection."

Swallowing, she said what was very likely the truth. "I'll never come back to that house on the mountaintop." Most likely she'd be dead, and she had no wish to be buried there.

An older woman who looked much like Wise Sister, stout and silent and strong, bounced Jarrod on her ample hip and listened, as did all her people. Mandy held Catherine. Angela ran in circles, singing quietly, on the far side of the smoking campfire.

"That house is yours if you want it." Of course they wouldn't want it. "And anything in it, though it's full of such foolish things I doubt much of it will interest you. There's some food and blankets. Take anything you want."

"Thank you." Tom spoke to Mandy's guardians. He acted as if they'd done something for him. Or as if they'd done something for his woman. "We'll let you return to your home now." He lifted Jarrod out of the Shoshone woman's arms and settled him into the pack on his back.

The Shoshone people immediately mounted up and rode off in their quiet way.

Fighting the urge to cry out with fear at being alone here in this dangerous world, with only Tom and her children to pay the price for the Cooters' vendetta, Mandy remained silent. There was no reason to believe the Cooters would be here. They'd come soon, but not right now today.

Tom caught Angela when she ran too near the fire. He growled like a grizzly bear while he hoisted her high then nearly dropped her.

Angela screamed then laughed and yelled, "Again."

"Say, 'Again, Papa.'" Tom hoisted her up.

"Again, Papa."

"That's my good girl." Tom hugged her tight and scratched his whiskery face on Angela's neck.

"Tickles, Papa." She giggled and squirmed and hugged onto Tom's head, right under his Stetson.

Mandy wanted to pound her head against something hard.

The drum of hoof beats drew Mandy's head around, and she reached for her rifle.

"Don't shoot, Lady Gray." Tom stepped in front of her as a group of cowboys rounded a bend in the trail. "These are my men." Tom set Angela on his hip, raised his hand, and waved.

The cowpoke in the lead waved back.

So, they weren't to be on their own. Tom had arranged protection for the whole journey.

A dozen trail-hardened cowboys rode up with a thundering of shod hooves. And in with them Mandy saw a woman, her hair flying free, long and blond and snarled.

Mandy knew with one glance that the woman rode like one of the Shoshone. She had no saddle on her horse. Her back was ramrod straight but leaned forward until her body was almost a perfect line with the horse's regal neck. She moved with a stallion—that had to be another offspring of Tom's black—as if she and the animal were one. It was a nearly perfect match for Tom's horse.

"We've been watching the trail. No sign of trouble." The first cowboy spoke to Tom, but he smirked at his boss holding a toddler in his arms and carrying another on his back.

"Let's go." Tom didn't seem to notice he was being laughed at. Or if he did notice, he didn't care. He hugged Angela tight, then, with her in his muscular arms, he mounted up with no extra effort due to the two extra people he carried.

Mandy was on her horse a second later, with Catherine in her arms. She kicked her horse forward, riding into the midst of the Linscott hands.

Her eyes focused on something that could not be. A young cowpoke wheeling his horse to head for Tom's ranch was undeniably familiar. Mandy guided her horse toward the blond man. "Are you one of the Reeves boys?"

He turned when he heard the name.

"You are." Mandy pulled up beside him.

The man's face widened into a huge smile.

"Mandy McClellen." He moved his horse until he rode side-by-side with Mandy.

Ahead, Tom noticed and turned to glare, as if he was ready to give his cowhand an order.

"Which one are you?" She could barely say the words through the lump in her throat. Someone from home. Someone left from the childhood that seemed so long ago it had never existed.

"Mark." He smiled and that rascally Reeves charm was clear to see. "I work for Tom Linscott, and so does my cousin Charlie." Mark jerked a thumb at his saddle partner.

"Mark, it's so nice to see a familiar face." Mandy remembered all the trouble this scamp and his brothers had gotten into back home.

"He said he was going for Lady Gray and someone would ride in for us when it was time to meet him." Mark shook his head as if he still expected it to clear and she'd vanish or maybe turn into a stranger. "He never said your first name, and I wouldn't have known Mandy Gray anyhow."

Without really even knowing she planned to do it, Mandy reached across the small gap between her. She wanted to launch her whole self into Mark's arms. He was a man now, strong enough to catch her. But she had Catherine on her lap, and all she could spare was one arm.

"I've missed you," she whispered into his neck. She didn't miss Mark Reeves. Honestly, she'd never been able to stand Mark Reeves. But she missed home, her parents, her old life where she was safe and respected and loved. And suddenly she felt as if she had missed Mark Reeves desperately.

It was all too much. Mandy broke down and cried.

"Mama cwy?" Catherine slapped her cheek gently. Then Catherine was gone.

Mandy grabbed for her, afraid the little girl was falling. She looked and saw the woman on the black stallion settling Catherine on her lap. The baby was safe, at least until the Cooters found them.

Knowing it was shameful, Mandy wept harder, and both her arms went around Mark, who held her in arms so strong they couldn't belong to the skinny, half-grown boy Mandy had seen years ago.

Then, just like she'd lost her grip on Catherine, she lost her grip on Mark when she was lifted, gently but firmly, away from her old nemesis.

Mark had made school a nightmare at every opportunity with his antics. He'd tortured teachers, tormented girls, gotten into trouble, a ringleader with the other boys—his brothers especially—but he had a knack for talking other boys into nonsense, too.

Mandy had spent a good portion of her growing up years wanting to strangle Mark Reeves. She'd never been so happy to see anyone in her life.

Clawing to hang on, Mark pried her arms loose. She looked at him, wondering why he was betraying her.

He had his hand on his gun as if ready to fight for her. Then the fierce expression cleared, and he shook his head as if to joggle his senses back around to sanity.

That's when Mandy realized Tom had her. Tom had pried her arms loose, not Mark. Tom had Jarrod on his back, but Angela was sitting in front of a dark-haired man with green eyes who rode alongside the blond woman.

"Lead her horse, Reeves," Tom snapped and rode forward holding Mandy on his lap. "Make yourself useful."

"Yes sir, Boss." Mark's deep voice shocked Mandy. Even more, the obedience in it. No boy could change that much. Mark had never obeyed an order respectfully in his life.

Mandy needed someone to hold on to so she looked up at Tom, who was watching her with kind blue eyes that did not go with such a cranky man and his brusque orders.

"I'm sorry I'm crying." She thought of her pa and how much the man hated tears then threw her arms around the big jerk who'd just stolen her from Mark Reeves, the terror of Mosqueros, Texas.

"Me, too." Tom sounded resigned.

At least he didn't cringe and run like Pa would have. Of course she was hanging on really tight. And to be fair, her pa wouldn't run. But Mandy would know he wanted to.

The tears were nowhere near spent, so they broke free again and Mandy, barely aware they'd started riding again, soaked the front of Tom's shirt while she cried out a year's worth of tension and fear. . .knowing she couldn't really cry it out. It'd still be right there waiting for her when the foolish tears were over. As surely as the Cooters would be waiting.

And that made her cry all the harder.

★

"Get off the trail, fast!" Cord had ridden ahead to scout. Now he raced toward the three men. There were only four Cooters left, until the next pack of 'em showed up.

All three men scattered. Fergus to the uphill side of the trail, J.D. and Dugger, J.D.'s last living brother, to the downhill side.

Cord went with Fergus.

"What's going on?" Fergus had dropped back a long way and now he waited for Cord to explain himself.

"Shoshone coming. A war party. Let's ride forward so we're away from where you left the trail." Cord looked out and saw it had been a rocky stretch. Add in that they'd been following a big group—probably including these Shoshone—so the trail was torn up enough to conceal new tracks.

Cord hissed loud enough that J.D. let himself be seen across the trail. Cord waved his arm forward to let J.D. know to keep moving. They'd been riding for about five minutes when the Shoshone came through. The group, women and men and a few youngsters, were moving fast. Cord stopped and held his breath as the party rode straight past the stretch of trail where J.D. and

Fergus had ducked out of sight.

As soon as the Shoshone wound around a curve, Cord and his kin returned to the trail and set a fast pace to put distance between them and that band.

"Those Indians will eventually see we rode along behind them." J.D. was such a complainer that Cord was wishing whatever happened to his brothers had also happened to J.D.

"They might not," Fergus growled.

"That's who's been haunting the woods around that gap." Cord knew he was right.

"But we looked for Indians. We saw no sign."

"Usually they'd have a village, and we'd find signs of teepees and fire. But they were laying low. Careful. Probably watching us the whole time." Cord felt a shiver of fear race up his back. "We're lucky that witch woman left that fortress of hers. She don't have no protection out here."

"Good, because we owe her." J.D. scowled.

"Are we gonna have to get even with all them Indians, too, J.D.?" Dugger was none too smart, but he took orders well and talked very little. "They must've killed our brothers when we were blasting that gap. Does Granddaddy's rule about sticking together mean we've gotta take on a whole village of Shoshone?"

Cord wished like crazy Dugger'd stop talking.

There was something wrong with Dugger. He'd stayed childlike in his head while his body had grown into a man. Mostly he was quiet, and when he did talk Cord always had a powerful wish that the fool would stay silent.

"I think Granddaddy will understand that we can't start a war with the Shoshone. That's just too big a fight." J.D. looked at Cord nervously.

Truth be told he was none too fond of his cousins, and honestly he'd never even met his big brother, Fergus, until a year ago. Or he'd been a baby when Fergus had taken off, so it was as if they'd never met. What kind of stupid rule was it that they all had to fight to defend family?

"Then let's make tracks." Cord pushed hard, glad of an excuse to stay ahead of J.D. and Dugger. No sense admitting out loud that Cord didn't want to start a war with the Shoshone neither.

S i x

This is wrong, Tom. All wrong." Mandy grabbed a handful of Tom's soggy shirt front and got a hunk of skin while she was at it.

"Ouch!" The leaky woman had finally quit crying and commenced to scolding. Sighing with relief, Tom'd gladly admit to the whole world he preferred scolding to salt water.

"I've got to get into that gap and back to my house where it's safe."

Scolding got old, too, though. Why couldn't the woman just ride quiet? He started looking back fondly on the last half hour or so. Sure it had been filled with sobbing and his shirt was soaked through, but at least it had been quiet sobbing.

"We're almost to the Double L. Another hour or so until we get home. We'll get married. Then tomorrow we'll ride into town and get you and your young'uns some new clothes. Gray is an ugly color." Tom waited for her to thank him for rescuing her.

She frowned so deep Tom braced himself to get walloped. But he didn't let her go. He liked holding her close in his arms. Idly as he cantered toward home, looking at his future wife's cranky expression, he wondered if he'd ever get to hold her when she wasn't shedding tears or being kidnapped.

Well, he'd kissed her a time or two with her full cooperation. Right at the beginning. Of course that might have been before he'd announced his kidnapping plan. Or at least before she'd believed him. "If you didn't want to marry me, you shouldn't have come home with me."

"You kidnapped my children, you big dumb—mmmph."

Tom kissed her to shut her up. The woman'd marry him, whether she knew it or not. In fact, she was so stubborn that they'd probably be married and have three young'uns, in addition to the three she already had, before she quit squawking about it.

He had no doubts about his ability to get her to say "I do," though. He hadn't faced up to much in his life that he hadn't gotten squared away to suit himself. Why should marrying an unwilling woman be any different? He was sure, despite her definite statements to the contrary, she was planning to marry him. The fact that she was letting him kiss her right now was a really good sign.

Which made him think of Mandy launching herself into Mark Reeves's arms. Tom held Mandy closer just in case Reeves hadn't gotten the message that Tom'd staked his claim on the woman. Mark was to keep his hands to himself.

He pulled back from the kiss, his stallion carrying both their weights without breaking a sweat. He loved this animal.

"I'm not going to marry you, Tom." Her lips were swollen, and she was staring right at his mouth. He decided that outweighed her words. "It would be a death sentence for you. I might as well just pull the trigger myself."

"I appreciate you worryin', but I'll be fine." Tom sped the horse up, and his men fell in until the pounding hooves and fast pace made talking impossible. He contemplated exactly what he'd say to get her to come around to his way of thinking.

Poetry, flattery, bribery?

Nope, none of that would work.

He needed to kidnap one of her children again. He mulled over just how to arrange that. How did a man hold a child on the far side of a wedding vow and force the child's mother to come on across the line?

Tom glanced down and saw a little spitfire in his arms, shooting daggers with her eyes, arms crossed, completely trusting him to keep her on his saddle. He wondered if she realized what that trust meant. No sense pointing it out.

With an effort he kept the grin off his face. He contemplated getting all that fire into his life, into his cabin, into his heart. He was determined to do it before the sun went down. Just because she said no was no reason to change his plans.

Mandy McClellen wasn't going to spend one more day. . .or night. . .not being his wife.

★

Mark Reeves controlled himself when he reached for his gun. But he was shocked by that sudden reflex to protect his Mosqueros nemesis, Mandy McClellen. He'd never felt such a thing before. For anyone.

He was raring to protect Mandy, and her children to boot. He noted, even though he could only see Linscott's back, that the man was kissing the livin' daylights out of Mandy.

Mark'd have his hands real full stepping in there and taking Mandy back. Then he saw Mandy's arms go around the boss's neck and suspected Mandy wasn't going to cooperate if Mark went to saving her right at this time.

"It don't look like she's being hurt at all, Mark." Charlie Cooper smirked.

Mark would have never made this trip out west without company. He'd had a herd of boys around him all his life. When none of his brothers would come, he'd ridden to see his cousins and talked Charlie into heading for the frontier. His aunt Hannah had almost skinned him for making off with one of her children.

Mark had done a good job of getting around Aunt Hannah and persuading Charlie. They'd signed on with Tom Linscott early in the spring.

"I see that look in your eye, Mark. If you mess with Linscott and get yourself fired and run out of the country, can I have Emma?"

Mark whirled to face Charlie and saw him fighting not to laugh.

It calmed Mark down some. "You stay away from Emma Harden."

"But we're a team. You as good as dragged me away from Sour Springs, right when Ma and Pa were fixing to have another baby. Now you're gonna up and get married and leave me alone." Charlie sounded like he was teasing, but Mark wondered if there wasn't a spark of truth about it. Charlie was crazy for family, having lived the first ten years of his life without one.

Which reminded Mark of a very simple solution to Charlie's worries. "You know Emma's got a sister, right?"

"Really?" Charlie lost the teasing gleam in his eyes. "I wasn't in town the day you saw Emma. You never mentioned a sister."

"Guess I've been mostly talking about Emma, huh?"

Charlie's blue eyes flashed mischief. "That's a fair statement."

"Well, she's got one. A woman grown, too, though young. Her sister wasn't in town. I found out about her when I went calling. I barely saw her when I was at Emma's house. But Sarah Harden is about the most beautiful thing in the whole world next to Emma. Red hair that looks like it'd be hot to touch. Green eyes that I noticed even though I only saw her for a few minutes and was only thinking of Emma. You could marry up with her and stake a claim, and we could settle here and build our ranches side by side."

Charlie smiled. "You always were one for making a plan, Mark. I need to be careful or you'll talk me into marrying some woman I've never even clapped eyes on. I'd never even heard of Belle Harden until you started talking about Emma. Not too many women out here."

Mark slapped Charlie on the back. "Better get a look at her before you make any wedding plans. But you're going to be real interested."

Mark's eyes slid back to Mandy, and all his pleasure in teasing Charlie faded. "I've got to find out what's going on."

Charlie nodded and Mark kicked his horse to ride over to Abby Sawyer, carrying the bigger of the little blond girls in her lap. The tyke reminded him of one of the McClellen girls from back in the day.

Looking down, Mark saw the front of his shirt was still wet from tears. Mandy was powerful upset. What if she didn't welcome Tom's advances? What if she was so vulnerable she couldn't stand up for herself and she grabbed onto whoever was closest?

"That's Lady Gray?" Mark asked Abby, Tom's sister.

Mark had been working for Tom Linscott since the spring branding. He'd learned that Tom's sister was almighty tough. She'd come over for a visit and found out Tom wanted a group of his hands to ride out to meet him on this trail and escort him back to the ranch, riding shotgun to protect Lady Gray.

Abby had decided to come along. When Linscott's foreman told her no, she'd taken to sharpening her knife until the foreman said yes. The woman didn't take orders worth spit. She reminded him a lot of Belle Harden. And Emma for that matter.

Riding her horse with a grace and ease Mark had rarely seen before, Abby kept an arm wrapped around the little girl with dandelion wisps of white hair. "I understood my brother was going to fetch Lady Gray," Abby said. "So that must be her. The woman has a reputation as wide as these mountains, but I've never seen her before."

"No one's ever seen her." Mark had heard talk, too. "She lives in seclusion on that mountain in a fortress. The bits I've heard made it sound like she was loco. Crazy."

And it was Mandy.

Mark felt sick wondering what had brought one of the toughest, smartest young women he'd ever known to such a place. The McClellen girls were impossible to tease or torment. A boy learned soon enough that doing it only brought pain. Mark knew that from personal experience.

His big brother, Ike, had been sweet on Mandy for a few years, but Clay McClellen was a scary man, and Ike hadn't been enough in love to risk his neck.

"I've heard she's deadly with her rifle. I admire that." Abby patted the little girl and smiled down at the upturned face. "I've never been so good with a firearm."

Mark wanted to know more, but he hesitated to even speak to Abby Sawyer. He hated calling her Abby. It felt improper. But she took to sharpening her knife when anyone called her Mrs. Sawyer, so Mark didn't dare do that.

"Not loco," Abby went on, "not according to my brother. He spoke of her only in passing. A few words in a few years' time, but enough that I thought he knew more than most."

Riding up beside Abby came Wade Sawyer. Wade Sawyer was the largest rancher in the area since his pa's death. Silas and Belle Harden were second. Tom's Double L was a close third.

Mark had filed on his modest little homestead in a valley he'd scouted out in the mountains, not all that far from Belle Harden's spread. He needed to have a cabin built on it before snow fell so he could set to proving up on it. Between now and then he was earning his living with Linscott, who had promised to pay him in cattle instead of cash money.

Mark knew Abby Sawyer lived in a teepee in the woods near Wade's huge ranch. Rumor had it that sometimes when it was really cold she deigned to move into the house. But mostly Wade lived in the teepee with her, or so Mark had heard. It was some cock-eyed deal Wade had made with her when they'd moved to Wade's ranch.

Wade had a slightly older girl in his lap. Mark swallowed hard at the sight of the two girls. They were the image of those little girls he'd known from school and church. They were Mandy McClellen's children through and through.

He opened his mouth to tell Wade and Abby what he knew then closed it. Maybe Mandy didn't want everyone to know where she'd come from. Why did she live up there like that? How had she become Lady Gray? Mark knew he had to talk to her alone before he ran off at the mouth.

"I heard someone call her a witch." Wade spoke quietly, their words not for Mandy's and Tom's ears.

All three of them stared as Tom pulled farther ahead. Mandy's arms were still tight around his neck.

"They said she put a curse on the hills around her mansion. A curse that would swallow up anyone who came to bother her."

"It looks like my brother got through." Abby sounded smug.

He did indeed appear to be through whatever defenses Mandy had built around herself.

Tom twisted in his seat and yelled, "Let's get home. Pick up the pace."

The dark-haired baby boy on Tom's back jumped and hollered. The little girls started squirming and fussing, too. The girl on Wade's lap looked up and behind her. She took one long look at Wade and squalled.

"Better go let her see that her ma hasn't run off." Wade patted the baby with the big hand he rested on the girl's tummy. Wade grinned at his wife, who also had a fussing little girl.

Mandy was looking around Tom's shoulders, a furrow on her brow.

Wade kicked his horse gently and picked up speed. Abby fell

in and left Mark behind. Full of questions. Twisted up inside with worry for his old friend.

Tom Linscott was a tough boss. The man was quick with a fist, and he'd sent a few no-accounts down the road since Mark had signed on. But the ones he fired deserved it. Tom rewarded hard work with decent pay and good food. They had a clean bunkhouse, Sundays off if there wasn't trouble, and Tom treated them with respect, something Mark was grateful for beyond everything else.

With a grim clench of his jaw, Mark knew he wasn't going to just let Tom sweep Mandy off her feet and plunk her into his house, not if it wasn't Mandy's wish. If it meant losing his job, Mark was going to make sure Mandy was safe and happy. He'd even take her back to Texas to her folks if that suited her.

Except what about Emma? How was he supposed to get to know Emma better, get himself a cabin built, and earn enough money to get a start on a ranch, if he was traveling half the country to get Mandy and three children home?

And yet right now, he knew that taking care of Mandy was something he could not shirk. Shaking his head, Mark picked up the pace just as he was told.

They came into a valley that was part of Linscott's vast range, and Mark saw the herd of prized Angus at the far end of this pasture. They were beautiful. Mark had never seen a black cow such as these before. A few Herefords and plenty of longhorns in all colors, including black, but these cattle of Linscott's were famous in this corner of Montana. And his name was rapidly spreading. Mark had come to this ranch particularly because of Tom's reputation.

As they rode past them, Mark spotted the old bull that had started all of this. He stood proud and watchful on land a bit higher than the herd. A mean old beast Mark had been warned to steer well clear of. Mark had heard the same warning about the boss's old black stallion.

Tom's Angus cattle, his thoroughbred stallion. The boss was a strong man, but he had brains, too, and no one could deny it.

Mark studied the massive shoulders on those Angus, the deep bellies, the wide backs and hindquarters. Linscott had found himself a goldmine without lifting a pickax. Mark had heard enough about Linscott's ideas and the financial risks the man took. . .and the amazing wealth he'd amassed in a few years because of the sleek black cattle and the stunning thoroughbred foals ranchers were willing to pay a premium for. There'd been plenty of talk about Linscott's success as Mark roved around the West, working cattle drives, hunting for a place to put down roots.

Finding the Linscott ranch felt like going to college, which three of his brothers had chosen rather than do the respectable work of ranching. Mark could have been a doctor like Ike or aimed for lawyering like John or studied business like Luke. Mark knew he was uncommonly smart, and his ma, a teacher, was all fired up about education.

But Mark wanted the land.

When Abe decided to stay on and ranch with Pa, there just wasn't anywhere for Mark. The Reeves ranch would support two families, but not three. Mark struck out on his own, looking for a likely place and saving money for the day he found it.

He'd lived for a while near his aunt Hannah and uncle Grant and their passel of kids. Mark had been sweet on their daughter Libby, but Libby'd had other ideas, and Mark had moved on.

He thought he'd found his place here in Divide, Montana. He'd scouted out a likely valley and homesteaded. And he'd met Emma Harden. He could picture his life laid out tidy before him.

Except here was Mandy McClellen. Mark could no more deny his need to protect her than he could stop breathing.

He could figure out a way to do everything he wanted. If he just had a plan.

★

"I seen 'em, Cord." J.D. came riding in, back from scouting the trail. "There's a passel of 'em, though. The four of us can't take 'em all on."

"How many?" Since the Indians had left off guarding Lady Gray, Cord had been sending out the men to find an overlook, a likely spot to finish this. They knew a crowd rode with her, but they'd been pushing to catch up and hadn't taken the time to sort out all the tracks.

"Twenty and they're all armed. A salty-lookin' bunch."

No overlook was good enough for the four of them to kill twenty hardened men.

"Now what?" Dugger asked.

They rode along while Cord pondered. Wait for more cousins? It didn't suit Cord to attack directly even if he had Lady Gray's men outnumbered. But he sure as shootin' wasn't coming straight at her where the Cooter clan was so short on men. Attacking head-on wasn't Cord's way anyhow. He preferred to have the odds in his favor. The cousins seemed to come in two or three at a time. They'd be awhile collecting twenty men.

And that's when a sight greeted Cord's eyes.

"Look at them cows." Fergus spoke first.

"They're beauties." Cord stared at the heavily muscled animals. "That bull is the biggest I've ever seen.

A huge, shining black bull stood to one side of the herd, back a ways as if standing guard. His head lifted, and he looked straight at Cord with the arrogance of the biggest, meanest critter on the land. A beast who had never met an animal to best him. The sun shone down on that bull, and his coat gleamed like a black jewel set down in the middle of the mountains.

"I've heard there's a rancher in these parts, Tom Linscott who breeds black cattle and horses like the one leading the group with Lady Gray," Fergus said. "Reckon that's Linscott?"

"Seems likely." Sweet satisfaction lightened Cord's dark thoughts. "What if there was a stampede? Any rancher would take his cowhands after the runaway cattle, 'specially if he thought they were being rustled. That'd leave Lady Gray to us."

Of course they'd have to split up. He'd send J.D. and Dugger to run off those cattle with as much noise as they could muster while he and Fergus finished things for the Cooters with that witch woman.

Cord would have preferred to scout out the land, learn who he was dealing with, figure out all the back trails in the area, and pick the best route to run off the cattle. But there wasn't time for any of that.

"Don't figure on getting away with the herd." He caught J.D.'s eye and knew the fool wanted those cattle. Well, let him try for 'em, but Cord doubted they could sell those black beauties anywhere without Linscott finding out about it. "Just get 'em moving. Make sure those cowhands are after you, and then cut and run, get back on the trail Lady Gray is following, and try to catch up with Fergus and me and back us in the fight."

"I wouldn't mind me a few beeves to sell, Cord." Dugger was always the first one to complain. "There ain't much money in chasing after that woman." And he had a rare knack for saying the absolute truth, right when it irritated Cord the most.

"If this lot is as salty as you say it is, you decide if you want to try and get away with that herd with them on your trail."

Dugger's stubborn chin weakened fast.

"Tom Linscott looks to me like a knowing man. We don't want him or his cowhands on our back trail, Dugger." J.D. gave his halfwit brother a slap on the back. "We'll just stampede the herd and circle around."

J.D. was the only one of them who had gotten a good look at Linscott and his cowhands. Whatever he'd seen must have really scared him.

If Cord could have gotten his hands on Granddaddy, he'd have shaken the old man until he changed his mind about Cooters sticking together. But for now, Cord didn't see as he had much choice. "Give Fergus and me some time to get in position; then start the stampede."

★ Seven ★

Tom should give his horse a breather.

Not that the black stallion seemed to get tired, but he was carrying double. Triple if he counted Jarrod in the backpack. . .and Tom *didn't* count the little guy. And the trail was a hard one. Still, Tom felt so pushed to get home it was almost like an itch in his shoulder blades. The kind of itch that made a man look around for men aiming their guns.

Tom's eyes slid over his prized herd of Angus. Before long there'd not be a cow left on Tom's place that wasn't shining black. He kept this herd close to his cabin mostly just to be able to enjoy looking at them every day. His eyes paused on the massive black bull that was the kingpin of his herd. He'd added bulls, bought 'em, and raised a bunch.

Not one single one of those black cows had a rifle aimed at him or Mandy, though, and his shoulder blades still itched. Most likely, thanks to his soon-to-be wife, he'd be having that feeling pretty much all the time—maybe for the rest of his life.

"Wade," Tom barked at his brother-in-law and realized that he'd started to get used to Wade. The man let Abby push him around, and that galled Tom. But then Abby was a feisty little woman. She pushed Tom around most of the time, too. Tom just put up more of a fight. Wade seemed to *like* taking orders from his wife.

Wade galloped up, and Tom asked, "Did you send word to Red that we'd be in town?"

"Yep, and it's Saturday, so I expect he'll be close to hand." Wade carried Angela in his arms. The four-year-old was fussing, and when she got this close to Mandy, she started hollering in earnest.

"Good, go in and get him. Bring him out to my ranch." Tom caught Mandy's arms as she reached for her child. "I need to ask you something before we take Angie back."

Wade hesitated, giving Mandy a chance to decide whether to go along with Tom's orders.

"Give her to Mark." Mandy looked around for that blasted Mark Reeves, which stuck in Tom's craw. "He's got a lot of little brothers. He can keep her happy for a few minutes."

Wade tugged on his hat brim and turned his horse back toward his wife, probably to get her permission before he rode off.

Tom was too slow and didn't get a chance to sneer at Wade. He looked back with regret to see Wade hand the little girl off to Reeves. What was that kid doing riding alongside Abby as if he was a friend of the family? And now he got to take one of the young'uns?

"I can't believe how nice it is to see Mark." Mandy stretched her neck to see around Tom and stare at that young whelp.

"How do you know him?" Tom had meant to ask right away, but he'd let Mandy finish her crying first and then gone to kissing her witless, and he'd forgotten about snatching her out of his cowpoke's arms.

"We grew up together in Texas. He was my mortal enemy in school. Always in trouble. I had to practically run that school single-handed for years while every teacher tried to make Mark and his brothers behave."

"So you hated him then?"

"Couldn't stand him, nor any of his brothers."

"Then why were you sitting in his lap?"

With a wobbling smile that Tom was terribly afraid would bring on a new bout of tears, Mandy said, "It made me homesick is all. Reminded me of Ma and Pa. I wish I could see my mother." Her lip quivered as she stared at Mark, now holding her daughter and teasing a smile out her.

Tom had to fight down the urge to stop the tears with a kiss. It would be no hardship. Although at the rate his woman shed tears, if Tom didn't think of some other way to put a stop to all the crying, he might end up kissing her almost constantly for the rest of his life. Tom shifted restlessly in his saddle as he enjoyed the thought of being saddled for life with that sweet chore.

Wade took off galloping toward Divide, and with a suppressed grin, Tom figured out exactly how to distract Mandy from a new bout of tears. "Wade is going for the preacher so we can get hitched before nightfall."

"What?" Mandy's head snapped around so she was only looking at Tom. There was plenty more yelling to come, and that was why Tom hadn't wanted Angela in Mandy's lap.

"That's more like it." He had her undivided attention now.

"I am not going to marry you."

That troublemaking Reeves kid came riding up just as Mandy made that announcement. Tom had seen the kid's eyes, and he'd seen the young man make a quickly aborted move for his gun. Mark wanted to protect Mandy. Tom respected that. At the same time it made Tom want to plant a fist in the youngster's face.

The kid was a good cowhand, but he was given to dumb stunts and reckless behavior that had brought Tom right to the brink of sending him down the trail a few times. Tom had held off, though. The kid knew cattle, and he was a worker. The nonsense always came during his spare time.

Tom had been a stubborn kid, too, refusing to come west with his family, staying behind in the East, hoping to win the favors of a foolish young girl. Tom's selfish decision back then had left his family to die and Abby to be raised by the Flathead Indians. Regret over that still saddled Tom with guilt, so he had a little bit of patience with young men and their nonsense.

He'd given Mark Reeves a chance. Most young men grew up. But now Reeves saw a lady in need of rescue. Saving Mandy would appeal to him.

Tom sullenly admitted it appealed to him, too.

"You don't have to do anything you don't want to do, Mandy." Mark had Angela in his arms.

"Mama, pick me up!" Angela fussed and reached across the space between the horses.

"Reeves, drop back. We're talking and we don't want the young'un to hear." Tom didn't want Mark to hear either, but yelling at the whippersnapper wasn't a smart thing to do when Tom was trying to lure Mandy into a wedding. Well, trick her into it was more like it. Threaten her into it. Bully her into it. Yeah, he wanted Reeves to drop back bad.

Punching Reeves in the mouth wasn't a great idea. But Tom didn't rule it out completely.

"No, I'm not dropping back." Reeves squared his shoulders and looked Tom right in the eye. Tom had to give the kid credit. He knew Reeves was as good as begging to be fired.

"Mandy. . ." Tom looked down at the bundle of cranky woman in his arms. Her eyes were only for her fussing daughter.

"What?"

"Tell Reeves it's all right."

"I think I should see to Angela. She might—"

"Not yet," Tom cut her off. "Tell him we need to talk."

Mandy arched one blond brow at him in a way so threatening

Tom felt a little curl of fear. Surprisingly, the fear was a pleasant, tingly feeling. He was fully prepared to be scared to death by his wife for as long as they both shall live.

And Tom intended for that to be a very long time.

"And tell him you aren't one to be pushed into doing anything you don't want to do." That part was true enough, which was why Tom was going to have to push real hard.

Tom took a second to wonder why he couldn't have chosen a more easygoing woman. Then he thought of Abby and that wicked knife. Belle Tanner Harden and her long line of dead husbands. The West didn't breed too many easygoing women, and that was as it should be. The strong survived out here.

"So, if I don't shoo him off then I'm a coward?" She sounded so sweet. "Is that what you're saying?"

Tom almost smiled at the gently asked question. He already knew Mandy well enough to suspect he was about one wrong word away from being assaulted. Looking at Mark, he said, "Drop back."

"No." A stubborn look on Mark's face impressed Tom at the same time it made him want to punch the young pup. "Mandy needs to know she's got a choice. I don't know what's going on, but Mandy is one of the toughest women I've ever known. She was already that in grade school."

Looking down at his sweet almost-wife, Tom said, "Really?"

Mandy nodded with a dangerous kind of smirk.

"And if something has upset her to the point she'll hug up against me—who she's never been able to stand—and cry—which I've never once in my life seen her do—then it's not fair to push her into any decision right now."

That struck Tom as being wise, sensible, and fair. But this was no time for nonsense of that sort. He needed to crush Mark Reeves like a bug. Tom decided to appeal to Mark, man-to-man. "If I don't next thing to force her to marry me when she's overwhelmed with all that's going on—"

"What is going on?" Mark interrupted.

Ignoring him, Tom went on, trying to make the little pup see reason. "Mandy wants to marry me something fierce."

"I do not."

Tom resisted the urge to gag his woman. "But she's got a lot of trouble on her back trail. She's got a band of outlaws looking for revenge for something her idiot of a dead husband did, and they've been after her for a long time."

"I never said I wanted to marry you something fierce, you big dumb ox." Mandy jabbed Tom right in the chest with a finger that was almost as sharp as Abby's knife.

"And anyone who gets close to Mandy comes under the guns of the pack of coyotes who are hunting her." He glared down at her. "Don't they?"

"That is the absolute truth. That's why I can't marry you."

"And that's the *only* reason you won't marry me, right?" Tom forgot Mark and focused completely on Mandy.

"That's right." Mandy slapped her hand over her mouth. From behind her fingers she said, "No, that's *not* right. I don't want to marry you for a whole lot of reasons."

Tom looked at Mark and arched a brow.

Mark's belligerent expression had eased and his focus had shifted from confronting Tom to understanding why Mandy was saying no—and being on Tom's side. Mark saw clearly that Mandy wasn't trusting Tom to protect. An insult to all men.

"I helped deliver Jarrod." Tom jabbed a thumb over his shoulder at the little boy he carried on his back.

Mandy lifted her hand off her own mouth to slap it over Tom's. "Don't tell him that."

"Are you calling me a liar? Did I help or not?" Tom noticed Mark Reeves's eyes grow wide. To deliver a baby, a man that was neither Mandy's husband nor her doctor, was shocking. There were few people in the world who could imagine something that intimate passing between an unmarried man and woman.

Mark looked at the baby. "You've got to marry him then, Mandy. If your pa gets wind of this, he'll come up here and kill Tom before those outlaws get within a hundred miles."

"He's welcome to try," Tom snarled. "But I'll bet your pa will side with me and help me drag you in front of a preacher."

"It's not like that." Mandy's eyes narrowed and threatened certain death.

"It's exactly like that." Tom looked at Angela, glad he'd carried her and coached her most of yesterday. "You remember me, don't you, sweetheart?"

"Papa!" Angela's little fingers quit reaching for her ma and stretched toward Tom.

"Are you—I mean—no, you're not really—you can't be the older children's—pa—too?"

From close behind them, Catherine squealed from where she sat on Abby's lap. "Papa!"

The little angel was copying her big sister. Tom hadn't gotten a turn with Catherine. He intended to have plenty of time with all three of his children.

Jarrod said, "Papa," and bounced against Tom's back, waving his arms. "Papa, Papa." The little boy yelled it every time he bounced. Tom had noticed Jarrod calling the horse papa and his supper and his toes, but no sense pointing that out to Mark right now.

"All three of them? And you're not married?"

"Tom Linscott!" Mandy made a fist. It was cute. As long as he watched her Winchester, he thought he could take her. "You stinking—"

"I'm your pa, aren't I, Angie?" Tom thought this was going nicely. He reached over and tickled the little girl under her plump chin.

"I love you, Pa." Angie giggled.

A few more seconds of this, and Mark would pull out a shotgun and force the marriage. And that was good because Tom figured it might take both of them.

"We need to get your pa married to your ma right quick, don't you think?" Tom asked Angie, while shifting his grip subtly on Mandy to keep her from getting to her shooting iron, always handily strapped on her back. And it was blasted uncomfortable carrying her with that thing.

"Papa," Jarrod hollered, getting into the spirit of the thing.

Abby rode up beside them, scowling. "These are your children, and you've never seen fit to bring the woman home?"

Lucky for Tom no one knew much about Mandy's life. She'd managed to get those who knew her to leave her alone. And to everyone else, she was a legend. Some even doubted she existed up on that mountain. He held a legend right in his lap.

"Mandy McClellen, is this true?" Mark had changed sides fast.

Tom smiled down at Mandy.

Who swung a fist straight at Tom's nose.

Tom grabbed her fist in his bare hand and pretty much had her pinned down. "For you to say no shames you and labels me for a coward who would leave you up there alone because I didn't want to face your enemies."

Turning to Mark, Tom gave him a man-to-man look.

Mark jerked his chin.

Angela screamed, "Papa!" and reached for Tom again.

"You have no honor, Thomas Linscott." Mandy tugged at her captured fist.

Tom had a firm hold, though.

"What enemies?" Mark asked.

Tom ignored the youngster. "Say you'll marry me. Restore my honor." Tom didn't smile. This was too serious. If he couldn't marry her with her cooperation, he'd use underhanded means and cheer her up later. "Whatever you say doesn't make one speck of difference. You're marrying me. That's that. You know we're meant for each other. Say yes, Mandy honey. Say you'll marry me."

She lay there, fuming, her arms pinned, her gun out of reach, her fist enclosed in his big hand.

Angie yelled, "I want Papa."

And the toughest woman Tom had ever known crumbled right before his eyes. Tears brimmed in those confounded, always-leaking eyes. She whispered, "Yes."

Before she could say more and muck it all up, Tom kissed her quiet. He raised his head and realized they were getting close to the Double L.

He looked at Mark Reeves, who didn't seem pleased. Like maybe he was torn between drawing on Tom to rescue his old friend Mandy. . .and drawing on Mandy and taking part in a shotgun wedding to restore the honor of his boss.

Deciding not to give the kid time to think, Tom hollered, "Let's get home." He spooked his stallion—that wasn't hard, the feisty animal was always ready to bolt—and the horse took off running.

Which suited Tom just fine.

★

Mandy was dizzy from the changes of the last days. That's the only excuse she could possibly give for what she was about to do.

Condemn Tom Linscott to death.

Herself, too, certainly. But she'd known that ever since she'd stepped foot through that gap.

If it was just her, she'd take her chances, rely on her speed and toughness and live as she pleased away from that fortress. But her *children*, Tom, Luther, all the people who'd side with her would be at risk. And yes they were tough. They wouldn't die as easily as Sidney. But a bullet could cut someone down from cover, and that was the Cooters' way. That's how they'd wounded Luther.

The Cooters were a pack of treacherous, back-shooting coyotes. Would they really kill children? The first Cooter was killed shortly after they'd started posting a guard over the gap to their home. The Cooters had tried to rush the gap, apparently believing they'd find gold or the information they needed to go on a treasure hunt. There'd been a gunfight. Sidney's guard had held the Cooters off and managed to kill one of them. Shortly after, they'd gotten word that the death of a Cooter began a blood feud and the Gray family had to die.

But children? Toddlers? What kind of animals were these people? Deep in her heart of hearts, Mandy could not believe these villains really intended to kill children. In fact, she thought they weren't all that bound and determined to kill a woman. That explained why they'd left her alone, as long as she stayed in her fortress.

But now she was out. And she was on the verge of getting married. Whatever scruples the Cooters had, they wouldn't hesitate to kill Tom. And yes, Tom was tough, and he had a salty bunch of cowhands. But the Cooters just kept coming and coming. There was no end.

The dread of what she was bringing about by marrying Tom twisted in her gut. The honest, soul-deep desire to be married to him lured her, enticed her. . .caused her to be willing to risk his very life. The longing for him and the terror for him combined to leave her frozen with indecision.

Not so Tom. He was the king of decision making.

He rode into what must be his ranch yard, swung down from the saddle with her still in his arms, and tossed his reins to Mark. "I want half of you men to ride out and check the herds and be on the lookout for trouble." Tom strode straight toward Wade Sawyer.

She'd never heard of the man before, nor seen him, but she'd learned his name when Tom had sent him for the preacher. Wade was another man who would most likely be at risk if he worked here for Tom. Mark, too, might die, and his cousin Charlie. Maybe the blond woman.

Mandy reached to push Tom's arms away so he'd set her down. Before she could get loose, she noticed a redheaded man holding a Bible in one hand and a baby in the other standing next to Wade.

Tom's cowhands rode out in small groups of two or three, in different directions, while Tom carried her around like a parcel.

Beside the redheaded man stood a pretty, dark-haired young woman, not much older than Mandy, with children of a similar age. There was an older girl with braided hair that hung over her shoulder and dropped nearly to her waist. A little boy with out-of-control red curls clung to the young mother's skirts and looked like the image of the Bible-toting man, who held a carrot-topped infant.

Without setting Mandy down, Tom paced straight toward Wade and the others. He stopped a few feet ahead of them. "We're getting married, Red. Let's get on with it."

"Let me go." Mandy felt herself blush, and she was tempted to take a swipe at Tom, but the parson was watching.

"Are you going to put that rifle down for our wedding?" He ignored her order to release her.

"No." Narrowing her eyes, Mandy dared him to disarm her.

"How about for our wedding night? Will you take it off then?" Tom's eyes held heat that had nothing to do with temper.

Mandy found herself totally disarmed. Literally.

Because while she was bemused by Tom's statement, her gun—and her gumption to resist him—both vanished.

He extended her rifle to the blond woman who'd been holding Catherine for so long. The woman—Abby—Tom's sister—Mandy was losing track of everything—swung down off her horse with Catherine tucked comfortably on her hip. Abby grabbed the Winchester and tucked it into the boot of her saddle, then came to stand beside Tom.

Like she was the best man?

For some reason that made Mandy fall a little in love with her possibly unless-she-could-get-control-of-her-life-right-this-minute sister-in-law. Mandy had missed her sisters something fierce.

Wade stepped close and lifted Jarrod off Tom's back and stood beside his wife. Another witness for the groom.

As always, Mandy had no one. She glanced at Mark, who came up beside her holding Angela. Which made Mark Reeves her. . .bridesmaid?

With a jolt, Mandy realized she had no children in her arms. In fact, someone else had cared for her children for hours. Something that hadn't happened in a year. She'd been all her babies had, day and night, for everything. Food, clothes, safety, teaching—*everything* they had came from her hand or it didn't come.

The Shoshone had helped. They'd brought in food on occasion from a good hunt. But they left it quietly, often without Mandy seeing them, sometimes with a few words in broken English about rumors that had reached their ears about the Cooters.

Mandy was fairly certain her children didn't even know there'd been any other adults in the world.

"I'm Red Dawson." The preacher touched the brim of his Stetson. "I'm the preacher in Divide."

Mandy wanted to gather her children into her arms and run. She held off for just a few seconds thinking God might not approve of her being blatantly rude to a parson. "I'm Mandy Gray."

"Not for long." Tom took her arm and faced Red. "Let's get on with the ceremony."

"You'll be killed." Mandy tugged on her arm, but Tom had her well and truly caught.

"He'll be killed if he marries you?" Red narrowed his eyes.

"I'll be fine." Tom nodded at Red. "Let's go."

"Tom, there's no rush." Red sounded reasonable. Like a really nice man of God. Like a strong, wise friend. Mandy liked the looks of his wife, too. "If Mandy doesn't want to get married, I'm not going to perform the ceremony. We need to be certain of God's will in something this important."

"God wants us married. Mandy's got her doubts, but God doesn't."

"Listen, you big—"

Tom bent down and kissed her.

From Abby Sawyer's arms, Catherine yelled, "Papa."

Giggling, Angela reached from Mark's arms for Tom. "Papa kissing Mama."

Jarrod, bouncing in Wade Sawyer's arms, waved his hands, giggled, and yelled, "Papa, Papa, Papa, Papa!"

The kiss ended, and Mandy had forgotten what they were talking about. And where she was. And she wasn't all that sure of her name and if it was winter or summer. And for a second even she wasn't all that sure Tom Linscott *wasn't* her children's papa.

Vaguely, she did notice that Red's brows had arched almost to his hairline. "What is going on here, Tom?"

"I'm trying to marry the mother of my children."

The parson's face darkened into an expression that seemed to promise fire and brimstone. "Now see here, Linscott. I want to know—"

Mandy was so distracted by Tom's kiss that she didn't even find the grace to blush. In fact, she didn't even find the wherewithal to listen to the parson.

"And she's being stubborn about it." Tom leaned close until his cheek rested on hers, and she forgot all about her children and Red and her Winchester.

"I'll not have a member of my flock carrying on without—"

The voice of the local holy man was like a faint buzz she couldn't quite understand because of Tom's sliding one strong arm around her waist.

"You will—" He caressed every bump in her backbone while he whispered into her ear.

"Mandy, you don't have to get married today if you don't want to. I'll—" Mark patted her on the shoulder while Angela yelled, "Papa." But that barely penetrated her ears after Tom's kiss.

Each whispered word Tom spoke sent a little tingle straight into her brain, which made thinking sensibly impossible. "Marry me."

That was no proper proposal.

"Tom," Mandy heard Wade throw his voice into this mess, "you need to let Mandy have time. A day or two to decide."

A day or two? Mandy couldn't imagine things getting better in a day or two.

"Mandy girl, say yes." There was that voice, that touch, that strength drowning out everything even though he whispered.

"I want some answers. Who are these children, and why are they calling you—" The parson yammered on, but Mandy didn't quite have the gumption to go into a long explanation. Not when her bones were melting as she listened to a man order her around.

In the normal course of things, Mandy never followed orders unless she got ordered to do something she fully intended to do anyway. But now disobedience wasn't so easy with shivers running down her neck, spreading far and wide.

"You've been coming to my church for a long time now, and you've never said a word—" Red waved the Bible at both of them as if he was prepared to beat the sin right out of their lives.

"My brother will do as he wishes and—" Abby was talking now.

Mandy took a moment to truly and deeply appreciate that the dark-haired woman standing next to the cranky preacher remained quiet.

This was the strangest wedding ceremony Mandy had ever seen. Her first one had been tidy and proper, though, and what a dumb move that had been.

"Now, Red," Wade broke into the preacher's rant. "Tom wouldn't do a thing—"

But really, who could pay attention to all the talking when Tom was so close and her bones were liquid? All the voices just a steady roar, like the wind blowing, easy to ignore.

"Say yes, sweetheart." Tom brushed his lips across her ear and nodded his head, slowly, gently.

Mandy found her own head nodding right along.

"It's time." Tom eased back, still nodding. "Finally, it's time for us."

Mandy nodded right along.

And what reason could she possibly have for not marrying Tom anyway? She'd wanted him for years. Shamefully, sinfully, she'd known he was a much better man than Sidney. She'd kept all of that to herself when it was such a dreadful betrayal of her wedding vows. She'd denied it so completely she'd not even admitted it to herself.

Well, maybe she'd admitted it a few times—for a second or two each time—but there was no reason to deny it now. Sidney was gone. Tom was here. Her chance for a life with a man she respected was within her grasp.

Why not? Why not reach out and grab this chance at marriage to a good, strong man?

Because Tom was going to die.

"Now, Tom." Wade broke into her thoughts. He sounded reasonable and sane. But since when did sanity have any place in her life? "I think Mandy needs time to—"

"I love you, Pa." Angela just would not stop.

"Where did three children come from that call you pa?" Red interrupted. "You will answer me now, Tom Linscott. There are three innocent, impressionable children involved, and I—"

"Let's talk"—with a glint of annoyance, Tom quit tempting her and turned to Red—"about *your* wedding for a few minutes, shall we, Preacher-man?"

Mandy looked between Red and his wife and saw them both blush just a bit. Red went so far as to quit scolding. The wife, with her china white skin and pure complexion, got very busy wiping her perfectly tidy baby's chin while the palest hint of peach darkened her cheeks. Red, with his Irish coloring, red hair, and freckles, turned a far more vibrant shade of red and he clutched his Bible a little tighter. What had happened to these two?

"How Cassie and I got married has nothing to do with this." Suddenly Red sounded a lot less like he was holding a revival meeting demanding sinners repent and a lot more like a young awkward rancher.

"Sure it does."

"No, it doesn't."

"You married a woman you didn't know."

"I knew her a little." Red moved closer to his wife's side.

"You said your vows while you were both standing on the freshly dug grave of her husband."

"We didn't *pick* that spot." Red frowned.

"And you"—Tom turned to Wade—"traipsed your horse over the grave and kissed Cassie in front of a throng of men and tried to take her for yourself."

Abby scowled at her husband.

Wade smiled at her, which struck Mandy as very brave. "Things were different back then, Tom."

"And you"—Tom glared at Abby—"spent more time pulling a knife on Wade—"

"And me," Red spoke up, looking a bit relieved that Tom wasn't talking about him anymore.

"And me," Tom added.

"Your sister tried to stab you?" Mandy was liking Abby better all the time.

Through all of this, Tom's strong hand remained on her back, holding her close. Her children took turns yelling "Pa."

The chaos and Tom's gentle touch almost distracted Mandy from the fact that she was bringing certain death to the man she wanted to marry. And wasn't that what it all came down to?

Mandy made her decision. "It doesn't matter."

God, protect me.

She turned to Tom. "You're a fool to do this."

God, protect Tom.

"I'm probably evil, certainly a weakling, to marry you."

God, protect us.

"We're putting my children at an even greater risk outside that fortress, and I hate that."

God, protect them.

"But you're determined and I—I—" She reached her hand out to run her fingers gently down a face that she adored. "I want to be your wife more than you want to be my husband."

God, protect this marriage.

"That's not possible, Mandy girl."

"Yes. May God protect us, *yes.*"

Tom's expression altered from determination to satisfaction.

"I'll marry you."

Red looked worried.

"It's about time." Tom's satisfaction turned to pleasure.

Wade looked resigned.

"And God forgive me for it."

Abby looked like she'd gladly pull her knife right now if need be.

"God's going to bless you for it." He kissed her quickly, lightly, but with a kiss that promised a lifetime of more. "No forgiveness required, darlin'."

Angela yelled that Pa was kissing Ma.

"You're sure, Mandy?" Mark's hand rested on her back. "I'll see you get home to Texas if you want me to. I'll take you."

Angela waved at Tom from Mark's arms and said, "I love you, Pa."

Before the whole storm could fire up again, Mandy said, "I'm sure, Mark."

Sighing, she looked at Tom. Shaking her head at the foolish, foolish man, she let her hand slide from his face, down his arm, until she held his hand. And he gripped hers as if he'd never let it go.

"I hope and pray you're right about God blessing us, Tom Linscott, because we're going to need Him to survive."

Eight

Dearly beloved. . ."

Tom almost choked when he heard the words. Crazy as it seemed, he really hadn't given much thought to the fact that he was actually getting married. He'd been too focused on bringing Mandy around to saying yes. And heaven knew that was a big enough job.

He hadn't pondered actually *being* married. Much.

He'd been a bachelor for a long time.

"We are gathered here today to join this man and this woman. . ."

Of course he'd planned this day up to this point down to the last detail. That included plotting with the Shoshone, picking a day Red would be handy, arranging for the Shoshone to protect their escape, and making sure his cowhands met him and took over their protection. And that didn't mention kidnapping his woman and dragging her to his ranch and using every trick, threat, and bribe he could think of to force her to stand up here and say, "I do."

Sure, he'd done all that to bring about getting married, but that wasn't exactly the same thing as *being* married. He had a little trouble paying attention to Red and listening to his wedding vows, and that was no doubt a Rocky Mountain–sized sin.

His feet turned to pure ice. He had an itch between his shoulder blades that told him the Cooters would be coming plenty soon. And he had a soon-to-be wife who could outshoot him, out-yell him, and had knocked him in the head with her telescope not all that long ago. He probably had a black eye to show for this twisted courtship.

"Do you, Tom Linscott, take this woman—"

Abby jabbed Tom in the ribs.

He looked at her.

"Say, 'I do,' white man." Abby hadn't drawn her knife, though, and Tom took that to mean he hadn't acted in any way that was truly offensive.

But the day was young.

"I do."

★

Mandy couldn't believe he'd said it. Even more, she couldn't believe she was about to say it right back.

Red turned his attention to Mandy. "And do you, Mandy Gray, take this man to be your lawfully wedded husband, to have and to hold from this day forward, for as long as you both shall live?"

"I"—gunfire exploded in the distance—"do"—Mandy whirled around to face the trouble, reaching for her rifle. . .which wasn't there—"need my gun."

"You do need your gun?" Red shook his head, took one lightning quick glance at his Bible as if trying to remember where that part of the wedding vows came from, then turned toward the gunfire and produced a Colt six-shooter.

A different kind of preacher, no denying it.

The shooting came from the direction they'd just ridden. Right where Mandy had seen that herd of all black cattle.

"Rustlers!" A cowhand came riding into sight, leaning low on his horse's neck. Even from a distance, Mandy could see bright red blood on a scalp wound. "They're running off the herd. They've shot Tex and Lefty."

All thoughts of getting married obviously fled Tom's mind as he sprinted for his stallion.

Mark shoved Angela into Mandy's hands and ran.

The cowhands all followed.

Tom vaulted into the saddle and turned to look straight at— Abby.

That bothered Mandy some. The man should have looked at her.

"Get everyone in the house and make sure Mandy has her Winchester."

Mandy decided Tom was showing some sense at last.

"Wade, Red, you protect the woman and children. And Red!"

The preacher-man turned to look at Tom's thundering shout. "What?"

"You finish this wedding." Tom jabbed a finger straight at Red. "I don't need to be here to hear the pronouncing." Tom wheeled his horse and raced toward the rolling gunfire.

Mandy had known she'd married a man of action, but honestly, even she was a little overwhelmed. And a wedding certainly didn't count if her not-quite-husband wasn't around to hear it.

"Let's get inside." The preacher caught her by the arm.

Abby slapped the rifle into Mandy's hands.

Mandy slung it over her shoulder, almost conking the preacher in the head, and felt safer than she had ever since she'd been disarmed.

Red ushered Mandy and his wife and all the children to Tom's house.

Mandy saw that it was almost a stockade. Solid log walls with opening slits just wide enough to use for gun sights. Those inside could shoot out, but it would be mighty hard for those outside to get a bullet in.

Before they'd gone ten steps, Mandy felt a bitter-cold chill rush up her spine that she'd felt only a few times before, and every time it had meant—

"Cooters." Mandy broke from Red's grip. "This is staged. Everyone, in the house now."

Mandy remembered who she was in that moment. She wasn't the weak-spined critter that had agreed to marry Tom Linscott for the stupid reason that he made her pulse race and she respected and maybe even loved him. And she wasn't that mysterious witch woman, Lady Gray, with the cursed forest. And she certainly wasn't the woman who had tried to win Sidney's respect by twisting herself around to suit him during their marriage.

She was Mandy McClellen, the fastest, surest gun in Mosqueros, Texas. And maybe in the whole West. And if she wasn't the fastest, she was still almighty fast.

She had six children to protect, two women, a rancher, and a preacher-man. Maybe the rancher, Wade Sawyer, would be some help. Except she saw that Jarrod was in Wade's arms, and Abby had Catherine. Which left Wade out of the shooting.

Red had his infant in one arm. His wife had the redheaded toddler and was running with her hand holding the little dark-haired girl.

"Let's go." Mandy waved a hand at the preacher. "Faster. They'll be coming from a different direction than the gunfire. That's a diversion." A bullet whizzed past Mandy's head seconds after she spoke.

Angela howled in fear and set the other children off.

Mandy caught Red and shoved Angela into the hand that held his Bible. "Inside! Now!" She rushed the house, whirling to move backward as fast as she could and still bring up the rear.

Her blood took on the feel of the Rockies in January. She

aimed and fired, aimed and fired. There was no thought involved. She didn't look down her gun sight. There was no time. She didn't need to anyway. She could feel where those bullets were raining from. Two gunmen, both with rifles, high on the hill south of the cabin. She used her own body to shield the preacher and her son and the other little one the preacher had.

Prodding the rest of them ahead of her with her voice, her eyes picked out the puff of smoke curling from the guns firing at her. With deadly accuracy, she unloaded her Winchester, whirled it in the air one-handed to cock it, fired again, cocking and firing faster than the eye could see.

In the way of every fight she'd ever been in, the world slowed. Mandy had time to aim and fire. Time to reload. Time to look side to side and behind her back and over her head. Time to plan her next shot and figure where she might need to aim next.

Glancing back, she saw Abby, with Mandy's daughter in her arms, look at Mandy's rifle and understand the skill, the speed, the deadly aim. Mandy read all of that without missing a shot.

Abby turned away and ducked inside as a bullet cut a chunk out of the door inches from her blond head.

Wade had a drawn Colt revolver, but it was useless at this distance. Besides, he was carrying Jarrod. He had to get to shelter, and he did, disappearing inside.

Two of her babies were safe. Mandy snapped shells out of her ammunition belt and reloaded almost as fast as she could fire.

"Go! Get inside!" Mandy saw Red turn back to her, worrying about her, his eyes wide as he noted her speed and accuracy and frigid control. "I'm right behind you. Move!" She had complete awareness of everyone behind her, the outlaws firing on them, where the door was, where her rifle would hit.

She heard a shout of pain from up on the hill, and one of the shooters' guns fell silent. The dry-gulchers moved, ducking sideways. She followed them with flying lead. They crouched behind a pile of rocks. Both gunmen were firing again. She knew exactly where they were by the sound of their thundering guns and the sheer cold calculation she was capable of.

Gunfire caromed off the ground behind Mandy's running feet. Red picked up speed, thank the Good Lord. Her rifle exploded steadily. Angela cried only a few steps behind Mandy, but even that didn't penetrate the cold in her veins.

Red's wife was in. Then Red, Jarrod, and Red's own child in his arms were swallowed up by the door and those heavy log walls.

Mandy had five steps to go. Three. A bullet buzzed so close to her ear Mandy felt the heat. And she was inside. The door slammed behind her, and bullets peppered the sturdy slit logs of the door.

The gunfire continued from outside, steady, lethal.

Red set a massive brace across the door.

Abby had a knife in her hand and was watching through one of the rifle sights.

Wade pulled guns down from a rack in the large room, one side half-covered by a stone fireplace. He loaded guns as fast as his hands could move.

"There's a crawlspace under that rug." Abby pointed at a bearskin rug in the center of the living room. "Cassie, get the children down there."

Red's wife stood her toddler on his feet and scooped both children out of Red's arms.

Mandy watched all of this while she reloaded her Winchester with hard, quick movements.

With a jerk of a strong arm that didn't really seem to go with being a preacher, Red opened the trap door, lifting rug and all, and waved Cassie inside, with all six children.

It reminded Mandy sharply of the crawlspace under her home in Texas. She'd been forced to go in there for cover once. It was a good position. Red dropped the door shut, and the rug settled over it so no one would even know it was there.

Mandy could turn her attention to the fight knowing her children were safe. "What's in the back of the house? Can they come in that way?" Mandy, rifle in hand, moved to peer out the gun portal on the south side of the room. She could tell from the direction of the gunfire that their attackers had moved.

"The shots all came from the front," Abby shouted over the sound of blasting lead.

"They're a pack of back-shooters. They'll come at us from behind if they can."

The gunfire stopped as suddenly as it had started. The Cooters were cold-blooded and smart. They'd probably hoped to finish this in a single hail of bullets. When that failed, they knew to save ammunition.

"I'll go keep an eye on the back of the house." Red strode that direction, shouting orders. "Wade, get upstairs and see if you can get an angle on where they're shooting from."

"They're on the south," Mandy yelled. "But they're on the move, too."

"Tom will hear the shots and come running." Red rushed out.

Wade jerked open a door and vanished up a stairway.

A second later, Red popped his head back in the living room and his steady gaze nearly pinned Mandy to the log wall. "By the way, I now pronounce you man and wife." He turned those blue eyes on Abby. "You're the witness."

Abby nodded.

"That does *not* count," Mandy called after him.

The only response was Red slamming the door on his way out.

"It doesn't!" Mandy glared at Abby.

Who shrugged. "Talk to the preacher, not me."

Mandy scanned back and forth, high and low. She saw no sign of movement, no outlaw to draw a bead on. Once she decided there was no one to shoot at, she had a chance to think.

That running cowhand had shouted that they'd shot Tex and Lefty. "Death." It had already begun.

"What?" Abby leaned a rifle against the log wall but kept her knife in hand as if that was her weapon of choice.

"I brought death to your brother."

The blond woman's brow furrowed.

Mandy wouldn't blame Abby if she threw that knife straight at Mandy's heart. In fact, that might be best for everyone. Surely they'd leave the children alone once she was dead. Surely they'd leave Tom alone if she never married him. Then he wouldn't risk his life every time he stepped into the open.

For a second Mandy's stomach roiled and the muscles in her knees wavered until she thought she might drop right to the floor from the thought of Tom, even now, running straight into the teeth of evil guns.

"What do you mean by that?" Abby peered through the narrow slit in the front wall of the cabin then moved to the far side of the room to look out. She was restless, watchful, careful. . .furious.

Mandy couldn't help liking her. "The reason I've stayed up in those mountains alone. . .well, alone with my children. . .is because a family named Cooter has declared a blood feud against my family. My husband's bodyguards killed a couple of Cooters when they attacked us, and the whole Cooter family came running to take up arms against us."

"Feud?" Abby shook her head. "Against a woman and children? What sort of cowards are these?"

"The sort that come and come and come." The sort that could talk family and feuding but would probably leave her alone if there weren't a fortune in gold. "There seems to be no end. A group of Shoshone lived in the woods around my home and kept them back. The Cooters seemed content to leave me alive as long as I was trapped in my cabin. When Tom came, I told him the Cooters would come with guns blazing. I know that's what's going on now. They ran off Tom's herd as a diversion so they could attack the house and try to kill me. They've probably already killed some of Tom's men. They won't stop."

"So why did you come to him, then? Why didn't you send him away when he asked you to marry him?" Abby looked at her knife. Sunlight, through the slit in the wall, glinted on the blade.

"He didn't *ask*." Mandy deserved to have Tom's sister hate her. Mandy would hate anyone who brought danger to her family. "He *told* me we were getting married. When I refused, he kidnapped two of my children. Then he spent the whole ride here teaching them to call him pa."

Abby stared at Mandy for a long moment. Then a smile quirked her lips. "That sounds like something my stubborn, know-it-all brother would do." She turned back to keeping watch.

"But I need to go back. I need to leave here and take the trouble with me."

Abby kept her eyes straight forward, alert, listening but not distracted from her lookout post. "Here's what I think."

For some reason, Mandy felt as if this was important, epic even. Abby was a tough woman, and she obviously cared about her brother.

"To stay in hiding to protect your children is a wise thing, if that is your only hope to save them."

Exactly as Mandy had thought. Her stomach sank. The wise thing to do was to go home. Back through that gap. Back to seclusion. Her throat seemed to swell as if the idea of going back to that bitterly lonely life would choke her to death.

"But that *isn't* your only hope." Abby's blue eyes blazed like the heart of a flame.

Even from across the room Mandy felt the woman's strength, and Mandy, who considered herself as strong as any woman alive, wanted to lean on Abby Sawyer.

"My brother is a strong man. My husband is strong, too, in his own way. Strong in kindness and decency. A stronger man in many ways than my brother. My husband is wise, and he recognizes that true strength is inside, in a man's soul, in a man's faith in God."

"Tom isn't a believer?"

"He is. But even God doesn't seem to be able to control Tom's red-hot temper."

Mandy had seen that temper a time or two. It didn't bother her. Mandy could handle a cranky man.

"You shame my brother by living away from him, not giving him the respect he deserves to protect his family."

"We are not his family." Mandy left her gun sight and moved to the far end of the living room. She saw no movement outside. Not the least whisper of activity that would give her a target.

"You are." Abby roved between the two sides of the room. "You spoke your vows before God. I'm the witness. But even without the vows, my brother has claimed you in his heart. That isn't a gift he gives easily. To turn your back on that gift marks you as a weakling and a coward. You give these Cooters the power to decide where you live and with who."

"A weakling? A coward?" Mandy's spine stiffened. She was reminded forcefully she had a temper of her own.

"What would you call it?" Abby turned from her vigilant watch to look Mandy in the eye.

From the length of the wide living room, it occurred to Mandy that they looked alike in general ways. Long blond hair, blue eyes. Abby was taller, leaner, burned brown from the heat of the Montana summer. But Mandy bet, even with that gleaming knife, Abby *wasn't* tougher. "I'd call it keeping my children alive."

"I say you're the rabbit and the coyotes have driven you into a hole. The speed that you had when you leveled that rifle tells me you're *not* frightened, defenseless, and cowering. You're *not* a rabbit. So why do you let them rule you? Get back out into the world. Face these coyotes. Give my brother the respect of letting him protect his woman and children. If he can't do it, then you do it yourself."

"I've already—" Mandy's voice broke. She didn't know if she could say what she wanted to. The words had never passed her lips. Her heart picked up speed, and her throat tightened, telling her to keep quiet. And yet Abby's steady eyes and challenging words dragged the words out. "I killed a man, Abby."

Mandy was sick to admit it. She'd never spoken the words aloud to anyone. But in the early days, shortly before Luther was wounded, she'd been standing watch and a man with that white thatch of hair had jumped her, gun drawn, and Mandy had killed him. He'd been no match for her speed and accuracy. He'd been no match for the cold-blooded way she fought.

"It's a scar on my soul." Mandy looked into Abby's eyes, begging the woman to understand. "No matter how much evil a man does. No matter how much he may deserve to die. No matter the danger to me and my children if I *don't* fight back. No matter that I had no choice but to pull that trigger—" Mandy realized in a flash that her true cowardice and weakness was buried behind these words. "It's a terrible thing to take a human life."

She never wanted to do such a thing again. Did the fact that she'd killed put her beyond heaven?

"Thou shalt not kill."

It was stated as clearly as anything in the Bible.

When she thought it all the way through, Mandy knew God could forgive anything. But it shouldn't happen.

The worst of it was knowing she'd cut off a man's chance for eternal life if he died, unrepentant, by her hand. Because the man coming after her was evil, she had very likely, with one twitch of her trigger finger, sent a man to eternal fire.

It made her sick to think it might happen again at any time. Today.

"I was safe from this." Mandy lifted her Winchester. The

weapon fit her hand as comfortably as her fingers. "I was safe from having to kill again."

"I saw the way you shoot. I've never seen more accuracy, more speed."

"I'm too fast." Mandy looked at her rifle. "I've always been greased lightning, fast and cool and deadly. When there's trouble, I get cold inside, calm, cruel. I'd kill again to protect my children. And I can't let them kill me and leave my children with no one. I *can't*."

Abby looked down at her knife. "And you don't want to kill again?"

"No, never again. As long as I was up there, hiding like a scared rabbit"—that's exactly what it had been like, quivering and frozen in her dark hole of a mansion—"I didn't have to kill. Now, out here, I'll have to. And it's not just me. Because of me, your brother will have to kill, or his men will have to. Some of your brother's men may be dead already. I brought death to Tom's door, even if he always wins against the endless stream of Cooters."

"I see." Abby nodded. "Yes, maybe you're not a coward then, nor a weakling. It takes strength not to kill with all the force at hand when danger comes." Abby's gaze lifted from her blade and smiled. "No wonder my brother wants you."

To her surprise, Mandy felt a smile curl her lips. She really did like the idea of having a new sister.

"You said your vows."

"But Tom left in the middle of it. We aren't married."

"Red says you are. He's a man of God. He's probably right about it."

"I can't do it to Tom."

"You think he'll come riding back in and say, 'Forget the whole thing. You're more trouble than you're worth?'"

Mandy had no such hope. "I'd decided to say yes, just because—selfish as it is—I *want* him." Mandy's eyes rose again to Abby's. "I want him so badly. We met years ago, when I was married. Even then, sinful as it was, I wanted him, wished for him. I fought dreaming of him but failed too often. We never spoke of it, but I knew it was the same for him. That's true weakness."

"Stay with your decision to say yes to my brother, Lady Gray. And let the Cooters come. We'll all protect you. Besides, you're already married to him."

"I am not!" Mandy thought of Tom out there chasing those back-shooting Cooters. She thought of the preacher, then of the preacher's pretty wife cowering below the house with all the children. "So many people called upon to risk their lives, to fight and maybe die, all for me."

And all for gold, which was at the root of this. If Sidney hadn't found gold, none of this would have happened. Mandy needed to get her hands on that gold. She'd use it to put such a high price on the head of every Cooter they'd have to leave her alone.

Mandy turned back to her gun sight. She saw nothing, but she didn't expect to. These were Cooters. They wouldn't come straight at her. They'd play coyote. They'd shoot her from cover. And Tom and Abby. Anyone who got in their way.

And if Tom won today, it would mean he'd killed a few Cooters. And the blood feud would expand to include him, married to her or not. He'd put a target on his own back.

Mandy couldn't let this happen. In one blinding instant, as if she'd broken from all her worries and guilt, she knew what she had to do. She'd declare her own feud. Her blood chilled as she thought of it.

Dare she risk hunting for brutal men? To protect her children and the man she loved, could she choose a path that would separate her forever from God?

Tears cut at her eyes. These she didn't even worry about. If a woman deliberately chose a path of murder—deliberately turned from the most fundamental of all commandments—surely that was a decision that warranted a few tears.

She'd always prayed, *God, protect me.* She wasn't even sure when she'd picked up that habit. About the same time she'd realized just how deadly she could be with her rifle. And Mandy knew that the deepest desire of her heart, God's protection, was for this moment. Protection from the decision that would set her on a path that led straight away from God. But it was the only way she could think of to protect her children and all these people she loved.

God, protect those I love.

But she didn't say that prayer for herself. If she set out on this course she would no longer deserve such protection. Truth be told, she would no longer need it. With her rifle in hand, it was the rest of the world that needed protection from her.

She raised the Winchester in front of her eyes, and it felt as if it were welded to her hand, burned into her soul. Her course would leave her forever marked as a killer.

She already was one, but that killing had been forced on her. Now she would choose to kill.

God would not protect such a woman, but it didn't matter.

"I'll protect myself."

★ Nine ★

Tom leaned low over his horse as he saw his purebred Angus bull disappear over a far rise, leading the rest of his herd.

The animals flowed like black water. Two men pushed them.

Tom knew even as his horse thundered up the trail after the beeves that this was a diversion. There were more Cooters, and even now they were closing in on his ranch house, coming for Mandy.

He knew how strong the walls of his cabin were, how well laid out the Double L. No one could breach the walls. There was no good place for an outlaw to lie in wait.

He'd only built it a couple of years ago. By then he'd lived out here long enough to have learned how to make his home safe. And he'd already pictured Mandy in his house, though he'd held out little hope that she'd ever really be there, what with her being a married woman and all.

So, she was safe back there, and he'd picked right to leave her with Red, Wade, and Abby. But still, it ate at him. He wanted to be at her side. But the real way to make her safe was to round up these stinking, yellow-bellied Cooters and lock every one of them away. No matter if there were two of them or fifty.

He urged every ounce of speed out of his stallion. The horse had put in days of hard work with precious little rest, and now Tom was asking more of the magnificent animal. The horse didn't disappoint him, but the Black had to be worn down.

The stampeding herd raced up a crest and were visible again. Tom saw the outlaws drive the cattle up a trail Tom knew all too well.

Mark Reeves came alongside Tom on one of the Black's offspring.

Tom snapped at him, "The trail they took is the long way around. We can cut them off if we take that trail between the aspens."

Mark leaned low over his galloping horse's neck, intent on keeping up with Tom. He yelled to be heard over the hoof beats. "I know the one."

The outlaws had just made a mistake that gave Tom the advantage. Except—

"But a lot of my cattle will go off the cliff overhanging the river if they're moving too fast. We've got to cut the herd off before they reach the narrows at the peak of that trail. Plenty of the cattle won't survive that fall."

Rage went all the way to the bone as Tom pictured his beautiful Angus cattle plunging to their deaths. Tom would be starting his own feud if that happened. "We've got to stop them." Tom turned and yelled at his twenty or so cowhands, all riding close behind him, fighting for his brand. "Half of you follow me."

He felt pride in the men who'd thrown in with the Linscott ranch. He liked a lot of them almost as much as he liked his black stallion. "We can cut through that low valley and come around. Mark, take half the men and go up after them. If we stop them in time, those yellowbellied Cooters will turn and try to run. That'll bring them right at you. They're cowards so they might surrender without a fight, but be ready in case they try and shoot their way through your line."

Tom hadn't meant to put Mark in charge, but the kid was closest. It made sense to give him the order to pass on. Tom veered his stallion toward the lower but less visible trail tucked between the trees. He urged every drop of speed out of his powerful thoroughbred in a race against time to save his cattle, put a stop to the Cooters, and get back to his wedding.

The aspens slapped Tom in the face as he dashed through the woods. The trail went straight toward the end of that high, climbing trail. The Cooters were going to be taken out of this fight before it ever started.

Tom reached the point where the curving high trail met up with the low trail and turned to race upward. He finally heard the thundering hooves of his cattle. "We've got to stop them," he yelled over his shoulder. "Turn them back."

Tom's stallion blew from the fast ride and the steep climb. They had to get to the cattle and turn them back before the narrowest part of the trail, and it would be close. It made Tom sick to think of it, but he might have to kill a few of them in the lead to stop the rest.

The men came up beside him on the trail, still wide enough to ride four abreast, and two more rows of nearly that many men rode behind Tom. The hill reached its peak ahead. On the right, a mountain soared overhead. On the left, it dropped off for a hundred yards to a fast-moving river. A man might survive such a fall, but it would be a chancy thing. If Tom's herd plunged over that drop, many would die.

They closed in on that crest. The sound of those pounding, runaway cattle, laced with an occasional wild bawl of fear, drew nearer.

Tom glanced to the left and right and saw some of his best men. They might well die today, thanks to Tom's determination to have Mandy Gray. He was well and truly married to her now, so there was no going back. This was the bronco he'd saddled, and his drovers rode for the brand. Any one of them was free to turn around and ride away right now. It did his heart good to see their loyalty.

They reached the crest. The cliff was only yards away. Dust kicked up by a hundred head of runaway cattle was visible ahead.

Tom charged forward, and at last his herd came into view. He drew his gun, mindful that he'd sent men up behind the herd, and fired into the air, shouting, his cowhands firing and waving, creating as much racket as they could to halt the terrified Angus.

Tom and his men raced ahead. The Angus came on. A few at the front twisted and skidded along, pushed by those behind. Reining back on his stallion, Tom watched the herd shove toward him, to trample him and his cowpokes. Tom reared his stallion up, hoping to make himself and his horse as big a barrier as possible. His men did the same, shouting, firing into the air. His big bull stumbled and went down. Cattle from behind him shoved on ahead, bawling.

Looking at the crowd of slowing cattle, Tom saw his own men down the trail. Mark Reeves had gotten into the middle of the herd somehow and was turning the farthest cattle back around. A few were already trotting downhill. The pressing mill of animals slowed. The gap between Tom and the beeves narrowed.

His bull reared up, still alive, but Tom knew he had to be injured. Then the old guy was lost in the dust.

No sign of the rustlers who had started this. Tom holstered his revolver and pulled his hat off, waving it, hollering.

Reeves got between more of the tightly packed animals and turned them aside. The bunch that would hit Tom and his men was smaller now, a few dozen head. But they were propelled forward, the front cattle unable to stop. Tom braced himself for the impact.

In an instant he was swallowed up by the herd. The roiling dust blinded him. He felt a steer collide with his stallion, and the horse staggered but stayed on his feet.

He could lose his most valuable animals today—his stallion and his bull. What a wedding present.

Tom slapped his hat in the faces of the black, bawling critters who surrounded him and pushed him and his horse toward that cliff. Battling for each foot, Tom resisted being pushed back, wondering what was happening to the men behind him.

Then, as suddenly as he'd been surrounded, all was still. Tom could barely make out where they were, and that death drop might be one wrong step only inches to the side. He held his horse in place.

The cattle shoved, and he saw the big heads turning, mooing, packed too tightly against each other to move.

Mark Reeves emerged from the haze. With a coiled lasso, he slapped at a single steer, turning him and heading the big brute down the hill. Tom's Angus bull came into view in the middle of the herd, and Mark went for the big guy next. With soft, soothing noises meant to move the animals without startling them into another run, Mark hazed the bull until he turned and headed back the way he'd come.

Tom breathed a sigh of relief knowing his bull had survived this mess. The bull moving broke the logjam of cattle, and they followed the bull. Tom saw the cattle walking placidly away. The big lugs looked exhausted from the stampede.

The dust cleared enough that Tom could dare to move. His horse was so close to the edge, a chill of fear raced up Tom's back. He quickly put space between himself and that ledge. A few cattle had gotten past Tom, but his drovers had turned them and sent them ambling after the rest of the herd.

"What about the shooters?" Tom turned to Reeves. "Did you get 'em?"

Mark shook his head. "We saw the trail they took. Once they got the herd running fast, they turned off and left them to stampede on their own. I watched close, we all did, but there was no likely spot for them to dry-gulch us."

"I reckon that's the only reason they didn't. This had to be set up to draw us away from the cabin. But once they all got inside, they'll be safe. No one can breach my cabin."

"As long as they managed to get inside." Mark's eyes were sharp for such a young man.

Tom nodded and said, "Let's make tracks for home."

★

"They're gone." Red emerged from the back room, and Wade came downstairs. "I caught a glimpse of them riding away. Two men are all I saw."

"Two shooters." Mandy checked the load on her rifle then felt in her pocket for bullets. "Where were they headed?"

She strode toward Tom's rifles, mounted on the wall beside the fireplace, and helped herself to a bandolier, dropping it over her head to cross her chest. She added a second and tucked two boxes of shells in the pockets of her gray dress.

"I saw them running over the rise to the southwest. There's some mighty wild country up there."

"Show me the trail they took."

"Let me get the young'uns out of the cellar first, Mrs. Linscott." Red walked for the bearskin rug.

Mandy caught his arm so hard he flinched. "The trail first, while it's fresh in your mind." Mandy directed her attention away from Red for a second. "Abby, you take care of the children."

Abby arched a brow as if no one gave her orders and lived.

Mandy ignored her. "And I'm not Mrs. Linscott. My almost-husband ran off before you made the pronouncement. It doesn't count."

"It counts," Red said easily.

"You're sure we're married?" Mandy thought of that for a long second and realized that now, if she died, someone else would be responsible for her children. If she could stop the Cooters—even if she died trying or even if she didn't die but ended up in prison. She felt the heat of shame and wished for the comfort of her usual icy nerves. "Shouldn't we have a marriage certificate of some kind?"

Red produced a sheet of paper from his pocket. "I made it up before you and Tom rode into the yard. I'm signing it now in front of both of you." He looked around the room and spotted an ink pot on a desk, with a pen beside it. He strode to the desk, dipped the pen, signed it, and then gave the certificate to Abby. "You sign just below."

Abby swiftly signed it, giving Mandy a defiant glance. "There. You're my sister."

"You're sure this is legal?" The man was a parson. Why would he lie about such a thing?

"It's legal." Red showed not one speck of doubt. "He said, 'I do.' You said, 'I do.'"

Mandy had actually said, "I do need my rifle," but this wasn't the time to quibble.

"That's what matters." Red thrust the paper and pen toward Mandy. "Sign."

"I'll swear to that." Abby reached down for the bearskin.

Making her decision, Mandy grabbed the pen, dipped it again, and signed boldly. Then she dragged Red into the kitchen. "Which trail?"

Red pointed.

"Okay." She stared hard, memorizing the way, checking landmarks so she could find whatever trail must be up there.

"I'm going to go make sure my wife is all right. You might want to come and comfort your children." The preacher-man sounded like he was chastising her.

Mandy controlled the urge to give him a butt stroke across the back of his head. That said more about her current state of mind than whether he was an annoying man. Instead of slugging him, she handed him back her marriage license.

Red seemed to sense her violent attitude. He gave a little shake of his head, rolled his eyes heavenward, and then left the room.

Which suited Mandy just fine. She sure hoped Abby got her meaning when she told the woman to take care of the children. She was now legally their aunt.

Mandy jerked the door open and within minutes was on horseback, riding one of the beautiful offspring of Tom's stallion, rushing after those mangy varmint Cooters. She'd end this by killing every mother's son of them or dying in the attempt.

Either way it would be over.

If Red said she was married, and Abby said she was married, and Mandy had signed the paper swearing she'd made her vows, then that was that. Tom was her children's father. Tom was free to raise her children, should she not survive this madness.

Her Winchester hung heavily on her back. The weight of the bullets threatened to drag her to the ground. In the end she was afraid today's choices and this load of deadly ammunition would drag her right down into Hades. But it was the price she'd decided to pay to protect the people she loved.

God, protect me.

That old prayer came to her, but Mandy shook her head and spoke aloud to the sky. "I don't mean it, God. I don't deserve Your protection on this path of killing I'm on. But protect my children, Lord. And my husband. Reckon I took my vows before You and meant every word. But when he finds out what I've done, he may just tell Red to rip up that paper and forget the whole thing."

At a ground-eating gallop, she aimed her horse for that trail Red had pointed out. While she rode, she wondered if a woman could be hanged for stealing a horse from her own husband.

Ten

"She stole my horse?" Tom's voice rose to such a high pitch it hurt his ears.

"I don't think a woman can rightly steal a horse from her own husband." Red shrugged.

"And now you can't find her?" Tom clenched his fists and stormed straight toward Red and the worthless man Abby had married.

"I think she took out after the men who were shooting at us." Wade stepped in front of Red. It was his brother-in-law's way to draw a fist to his own face to protect someone else. He might even have thoughts of Tom's soul, not wanting Tom to slug a parson.

"She can't have gone far." Red came up to Wade's side. Calm, strong, wise, a hard man to thrash for a lot of reasons, confound it. "We just realized she was gone a few minutes ago."

"She took enough bullets with her to start a war," Abby added.

The whole lot of them had realized Mandy was gone and gathered outside by the time Tom came riding into the ranch yard.

"She left her children behind?" Tom couldn't believe a woman would do such a thing.

"I reckon they're your children now, too, Tom." Red lifted his shoulders as he stated the obvious. "Just like your horse is hers."

"So we're married for sure?" Later, Tom intended to beat the tar out of both Red and Wade for losing Mandy. But right now he had a missing wife to track down.

"You oughtta sign it, too." Red handed Tom a piece of paper with a neatly written record of the marriage, signed by Red, Abby, and Mandy, all three. "But even if you don't, you're still married."

Red said that as if he expected Tom to argue, but being married to Mandy, the little horse thief, suited him right down to the ground. Tom grabbed the paper. Red produced a pen and a bottle of ink. Tom scrawled his name and thrust pen and paper toward Red.

"It's yours." Red refused to take it.

Tom folded it roughly and jammed it into one pocket.

"Abby, tell me what went on around here. Sawyer, pack me some grub."

Abby talked while Tom led his stallion to the barn.

When his sister paused to take a breath, Tom jerked his chin at the stallion. "Will you take care of him? Everyone else on this ranch is scared to get near him."

Abby agreed and kept talking, letting him know all that had unfolded. She made a point of talking about the way Mandy handled her rifle. Tom had heard a similar story years ago from Belle Harden, who had met Mandy when she was a new bride.

He'd asked too much of the black. He strode toward the corral where Tom's second favorite horse was held. The most perfect colt to ever come out of his stallion, and that was saying something because his stallion bred true.

Tom stumbled to a halt when he reached the corral. A dozen horses grazed in the pen, none of them the one he wanted. "She stole my *best* horse?" Though it was no time for such a thing, Tom laughed. He had married himself one beauty of a woman.

"Borrowed, Tom. Not stole." Red had tagged along to the corral.

Tom remembered well his plan to beat Red within an inch of his life. Right now time was too tight. "Which way did she go?"

Red pointed to a trail in the distance Tom could only see because he knew his land so well. "She asked me where I saw the men riding, the ones who shot up your house."

"And you told her?" Tom wheeled to face Red head on. Maybe he'd take the time for that beating after all. "Why would you do a stupid thing like that?"

Red shoved his face right up into Tom's, which reminded Tom that Red wasn't just a sky pilot—he was also a rancher who'd come out here and tamed a mighty mean stretch of land. "I *told* her because it never occurred to me that a woman would abandon three children and a man she'd just married to go hunting a pack of killers. What kind of woman did you marry anyway? She's acting crazy."

Tom shrugged. He couldn't really argue Red's point, though arguing came real easy. "I married me the sharpest shooting woman in the West, I reckon."

"That you did, Tom. I saw her in action." Abby bridled Tom's second choice for a horse while he saddled.

"I saw her, too." Red shook his head in wonder. "I've never seen anyone shoot like that. Why do you want a woman who appears to have a taste for killing? What are you thinking to pick a woman like that?"

Tom looked past Red and saw Red's wife, sweet little Cassie Dawson, quietly tending all six children, both the Dawsons' and Mandy's—

Tom caught that thought. They were his children now, too. He liked the sound of that.

Tom's temper would have crushed Cassie like a bug the first week of their marriage. Shrugging, Tom felt a little sheepish, but this was a man of God. It'd be wrong to lie. "Honest, Red, that's what I like *most* about her."

Tom got a notion that would make things safer for *his* children and threw a few orders at Abby.

"Good idea. I'll do it." Abby would obey him because it was a good idea, and for no other reason. The woman didn't submit to a man worth spit.

He grabbed the bag of grub from that jelly-spined Wade Sawyer—the perfect man for Tom's sister—then he set his horse to galloping before he left the ranch yard. He was in a hurry to drag his gun-slinging wife back home and get started on his honeymoon.

★

Mandy caught up to them at sunset. She could read sign like the written word. She'd seen where the two men shooting at Tom's ranch house had met up with two others. Now she was almost within shooting range of four Cooters, and she intended to leave them all dead in the dirt before she slept tonight.

The sin of what she planned rattled at her like a longhorn bull dodging a branding iron.

She ignored her conscience. Ignored a lifetime of teaching. Ignored the hurt she'd cause her parents and sisters and children. She couldn't tackle four armed men head-on. So she'd unload her gun into their mangy hides as they sat around their campfire. She'd dry-gulch them and keep firing until they were all dead or she was.

Then she'd sit back and wait for the next Cooters to come, and the next. She'd left honor and her children and any claim to decency behind when she'd set out on this path. And she knew it.

She edged her way up the dirt, on the ground above where they were settling in for the night. An inch at a time. She wanted no motion to draw the Cooters' attentions, no sound to stir their suspicions.

She heard the crackle of a campfire and knew the lazy coyotes were settling in for the night. They hadn't run as far as she'd expected when she'd seen the far trail they were on. Of course they hadn't. Because, though today's attack had failed, they'd now begin their planning for the next one, and the next.

It was why they had to die.

She had only another inch to go and they'd be visible. Then with equal slowness, she'd aim her trusty rifle. Four shots. A hot hunger in her gut had her hoping she could kill them in four shots. It was evil, the greed to kill.

It was the path she'd chosen, but still, the pleasure that came with her willingness to kill surprised her. Good and evil weren't far apart in a woman's soul.

She smelled their fire, clean and crisp from dry wood and leaves. Not like the sulfuric fires where she'd spend eternity.

Her mouth watered as her hand tightened on the trigger. The one thing she hadn't been able to summon was the cold. For some reason it eluded her. And killing the Cooters flooded her with heat straight from the heart of the devil.

★

"I'm done waiting, Sophie." Clay felt his spine crawling for some reason he couldn't imagine. But he'd felt it a few times before and he trusted it.

His wife looked at him, and their gazes locked. She knew exactly what he meant. "Why now?"

Shaking his head, Clay couldn't explain it, but then Sophie was pretty good at figuring his thoughts, so he usually didn't need to. "It's riding me, and I'm not going to sit quiet anymore."

"She's a grown-up woman, Clay. She made her wishes known, and we should respect them."

Clay didn't think even his stubborn wife sounded quite as sure as usual. They'd had this fight a dozen times. He wanted to get to Montana and fetch his daughter home, and he was going to do it. If he had to fight off some mob of men to get to her, so be it. If he had to fight Mandy, so be it.

The boys were sitting quietly at their studies. Smart sons, good ones. Clay took a hard minute to realize he was riding into danger and might well not come back. But to sit here safe while his daughter was in trouble went against every bit of his grain.

"I'll go along, Pa." The most talkative of the twins, Cliff, spoke up. He'd be of some help. His boys were tough and savvy, no denying it. But he wasn't going to put them in danger.

Although from Mandy's letters, the very few there had been, Clay knew getting involved in this stupid feud could draw those Cooters down on his whole family.

"Nope, your ma needs you here." His eyes went to Laura. She was grown up enough that she'd be the next daughter he had that would come dragging some idiot husband home. A half crazy doctor for Beth, a painter of all things for his rough and tough Sally, and for Mandy, that worthless Sidney Gray.

Alex Buchanan had gathered his wits and ended up being a solid husband for Beth. Sally's husband, Logan McKenzie, was not what Clay would have picked. Clay's eyes went to a huge painting on the living room wall of a spectacular mountain scene that reminded Clay of his childhood in the Rockies. Truth was Logan adored Sally, and the nomadic life they lived seemed to suit them. They came through the area and stayed for a month about twice a year. There was a baby on the way now, and Logan had promised to settle somewhere once there was a family to think of. Clay believed him.

Sidney Gray. There was no explaining that. Although to be fair, he'd seemed like the most solid and sensible of the three men when Mandy had picked him. Of course Clay had loathed him, but that was the normal state when a man came bothering one of his girls. A lawyer, solid, educated, prosperous. It had all been lies. At least the lunatic doctor and rootless painter had been honest.

Clay vowed there and then to just shoot any man who got near Laura and be done with it.

"You need someone to ride with you, Clay." Sophie had that look in her eyes, the one that said she was about to take the bit in her teeth.

"I'll send a wire to Luther and tell him to meet me. I'll need someone to guide me to that mountaintop where Mandy lives anyway. Maybe Buff will come, too. I'll ride careful, check with the law when I'm in the area." Clay held Sophie's gaze.

After far too long, she jerked her chin. "Fine. I have the feeling it's time for us to go, too."

"No, not us. Me. First light. I need to go talk to the men."

"I'm going, Clay." He heard her muttering, "Help me, Lord. Help me, help me, help me," as she turned to begin packing a sack of food.

When his Sophie started praying that prayer, there was no stopping her. So Clay didn't try.

"Boys, come on along so you'll know what's going on." Clay plucked his Stetson off a peg by the door and went out, his sons, sturdy boots clomping on the porch, falling in behind him.

He wondered how he'd go about running off the women when they came hunting his sons. How did that even work?

★

Sally threw off the covers of her bedroll with a quiet growl of frustration and reached for her broadcloth pants.

In the dim light of morning, she saw Logan's eyes flicker open as she dressed.

When he focused on her, his brows rose nearly to his hairline. "You haven't worn those in a while." He sounded scared.

She would have grinned if worry wasn't eating at her. "I've got to go see Mandy." One moment of indecision had her running her hand over her slightly rounded stomach. She had a baby to think of now. Her hand drifted upward to the bit of ribbon on her chemise, then she turned to drag her favorite cowpoke shirt over her head.

God, have mercy. On my sister, on my child, on me.

"It's dangerous." Logan got up and began dressing. He knew her very well. Protest all day long, but he knew how this had been riding her, and he knew she'd just snapped. "You know I want Mandy to be safe, but we can't just go diving into the middle of a feud with—" Logan gestured at her belly.

"I want this baby to be safe more than I care about my own life." Sally slung her rifle across her back even before she put her boots on and felt a fraction safer. She still wore it all the time, but honestly, life was pretty safe with Logan. Painters just didn't draw trouble, thank the good Lord.

"I've hung back and stayed away as long as I can." She continued to dress. "But I can't do that anymore."

She'd enjoyed the summers in Yellowstone after splitting the winters between New York City and Mosqueros, Texas. Logan had produced some of his most beautiful work. As summer drifted past and Sally's belly got round, Logan kept finding new wonders. Sally could be content with this life forever. Their children would have to learn to live a rugged life and travel back and forth across the country, but with Logan, Sally had found that to be fun.

"Your ma said we should respect Mandy's wishes." Logan was dressing as quickly as Sally. "She's an adult woman, and she asked us to let her be. Told us she was handling her own problems and had no wish to bring them raining down on the rest of us."

Sally cooked and hunted and saw to a shelter, and lately she'd done it all wearing a dress, or a split skirt if she was riding. She'd found she preferred it to pants. Discovering just how much being feminine appealed to her was embarrassing, but with Logan she felt safe admitting she liked pretty things. In fact, she felt wonderful admitting it.

She'd found Logan had a talent for hunting and was better at Western life than she'd first thought, so he helped with the running of the house, especially since they'd found there was a baby on the way. But mostly, he painted. Sally looked at his work stacked against the flimsy walls of their tent. She respected it as much as she respected her pa riding herd.

As she finished dressing, she knew a riding skirt had no place in what lay ahead of her. "I'm going to talk to Wise Sister and Buff. See if they'll ride along." Sally jammed her foot into her boot and stomped it on the ground to get her heel inside.

The boots thudded as she took two long strides before Logan caught her arm.

She turned to him, glaring. It was hard because she loved him with all her heart.

"*We're* going."

"No, you stay here. You've only got a few more weeks before the snows close up Yellowstone. This is your only chance to catch the leaves turning color and the elks with full racks of antlers. And I heard you talking about that big geyser almost due to blow. If you ride with me, you'll miss it."

"And if I don't come along, I'll miss you."

"Logan, no."

He rested his beautiful, graceful, brilliant hands on her slightly rounded stomach.

Sally had fully planned to stay in Yellowstone as long as possible. Then they'd ride the train to Texas, Beth would deliver her baby around Christmas time, and then they'd head toward New York to see Logan's parents and brothers and introduce the McKenzies to their newest grandchild before heading back west for another summer of painting.

Sally adored her in-laws, especially when she saw that, though they were just as baffled by Logan's strange inclination to paint as she was, they accepted it and respected his talent. Though they were city people, at heart they were more like her than they were like Logan. A fact that bonded her tight to them.

"Sally, yes. I'm going." He raised one of those talented hands to rest it on her chest and caress her concealed pink ribbon, the feminine bit of fussiness that he understood better than anyone. "I'm not letting my increasing wife ride into a gunfight while I stay safely behind painting pictures. Either I go or you stay."

"I've got to go."

"Then it's settled."

Scowling, Sally said, "I'll go saddle the horses."

"I'll ask the man running the park to ship my paintings home. We'll ride out of here, but then we're taking the train. It's a long, rugged ride to your sister's home. We're going to be careful. I won't let you exhaust yourself or harm our baby."

"My ma rode horseback right up to the day her babies were born. A long hard horse ride won't hurt me."

"Please. . ." Logan's arm snaked around her waist.

The usual weak-willed agreeableness that flared up whenever she found herself in conflict with her husband took over. "I think there's a shorter way if we ride horseback. Remember how we had to go way north of Mandy's on the train the last time we went there, then ride a long way south to see her? I think if we skip the train we can cut a couple of days off the trip. But I promise I won't ride recklessly."

Logan kissed her soundly. "You are such a good, obedient little wife."

The confounded man knew she hated it when he talked to her like that. He grinned as if daring her to blow up.

Since she was getting her way about the trip, she didn't get too mad at him. But the mad was there, simmering.

He kissed her again as if to dare her to let her temper go, as if he liked it.

Her annoyance turned into something else, something warm and passionate. Throwing her arms around his neck, she kissed him until she almost forgot what she was about. When she let go, she was satisfied to see the friendly look in his eyes. "Finish getting dressed while I saddle our horses."

"Yes sir, ma'am." He sounded like an obedient soldier. Then she heard him laugh as she shoved back the tent flap and stormed away.

★

Mandy was good in the woods. Not as good as Beth, her little sister, but almighty good. She could sneak up on anyone, and no one would ever take her by surprise.

The next inch would give her the first view of the Cooters. Her hands tightened on her rifle. She could do this. She had to.

Something stopped her, something inside. She fought it. To let these men go was stupid. This was her chance.

Don't do it.

Was that her conscience speaking to her? Or her cowardice?

She had to do this, or they'd be right back. Her children could have died today. She felt those bullets so close to her, so close to everyone, all running because of her. Some of Tom's cowhands already had died.

Do it.

Her heart was beating, her blood running hot through her veins. The cold she felt when she was going into action needed to come. She paused, rubbed that callus on her trigger finger as if it were a genie in a magic lamp and she could get the icy calm to come out if she just rubbed enough.

She wondered if she could shoot without it. Even hunting for game, she'd always felt that chill. But she'd never had time to think before, just react. Leastways not think about shooting a man. She'd never consciously tried to bring that cold.

Don't do it.

I have to. I have no choice.

Do it.

Was that wisdom and courage emerging? Or was the devil on her shoulder luring her into sin? It didn't matter. She knew this was sin. And she had to do it anyway and live with the consequences. She gathered her muscles to rise up, come out of hiding, and fire. She'd do it.

A hard hand slapped over her mouth. Weight like a collapsing mountain crushed her into the ground. She knew in that second that she'd failed. She'd given up everything she believed was right in the hopes of ending this feud. All she'd really done was put herself at risk, abandoned her children, and all for nothing. She hadn't even thinned out the pack of coyotes who wanted her dead.

"You are the most contrary wife a man ever had."

Tom. He knew exactly what was going on.

Her gun was wrenched out of her hand, which was annoying, but it didn't stop the surge of relief and even joy she felt to have Tom with her and to have this deadly choice taken from her.

She turned her head, and he let loose of her mouth and only eased his weight for a second as he flipped her over onto her back.

She smiled.

He kissed her witless.

When she could think again, she pointed toward where the men, still blocked by the woods, were camping. "Cooters." She barely breathed the word.

Tom eased down the hill on his hands and knees, dragging her along, as if she might not follow. The man had her rifle for heaven's sake. What was she going to do up there without it?

He had a hold of one arm and pivoted her so her head was turned downhill. Then he dragged her along on her back, like she was a deer he'd brought down.

It took her a second to get over the pleasure of seeing him. Then she scrambled to her feet and fell into step with him. He had her wrist in one hard hand and her rifle in the other, and he strode with ground-eating steps toward where she'd left her horse.

They reached the horses, now grazing side-by-side; then Tom said, "Mount up. We can't talk this close to them."

He let go of her, possibly because he trusted her but more likely because he knew she needed her Winchester and figured she'd come along until she could retrieve it. Swinging up on his horse, he glared at her. She experienced a little thrill of fear at his fierce expression.

Feeling unusually obedient, she mounted up and had to move fast to keep up with him as he headed down the trail. They were too far to get back to the Double L tonight, so she expected him to stop riding at some point and yell at her.

Mandy had to admit that at least part of the light spirit she felt was because she'd been stopped from unleashing lead at those Cooters.

They'd put several miles behind them when they reached a trail that turned off. Tom followed it to a rock wall that curved into a perfect shelter.

"Tom, are we—"

"*Do not talk to me*, woman." His shouted words practically took a bite out of her hide. "I'm about one wrong word from turning you over my knee."

No one talked to her like that.

Tom had his horse unsaddled before Mandy could get her mouth shut. She wanted to dare him to manhandle her but was just the least bit afraid he might be serious, so she went to work stripping the leather off her own horse. Tom had a small fire crackling by the time she'd finished with her horse and put it on a lead rope to graze.

And now finally it was time to talk.

"I've made my choice." She stalked over to Tom. "I'm not going to sit like a frightened rabbit and wait for those Cooters to come for me and my children and you."

Tom looked up from the fire, where he was feeding in sticks, with eyes so blazing hot Mandy felt burned.

"So you headed out to kill them, is that right?" He threw in a bigger stick. "You were crawling up that rise to murder those men in cold blood—"

"They deserve to die!"

"Because you don't trust me to protect you, *is that right?*" Tom shouted the last three words.

"I did it to save your life. I know you'd protect me. I know you'd *die* for me. I understand all of that. But I can't let you."

"The one thing you don't seem to know, woman"—Tom surged to his feet—"is that you can't *stop* me."

His arm whipped out quick as a striking rattler, and he yanked her hard against his body. "You're mine." He grabbed a hank of her hair. "You're mine, and I'm through waiting for you." He sank his heavy hand deeper into her hair and tilted her head back. "We're married. I *will* protect you. I *will* die for you."

He kissed her until her knees went weak and her arms wrapped around his neck to keep from falling. Long moments later he raised his head, his blue eyes burning into hers.

"Better than that. I will *live* for you. That's all you need to understand." He swooped his head down, and Mandy had one flash of a moment to think she was still prey, this time to a diving hawk.

She understood. At last she finally and completely understood that she was Tom's, and he was hers.

As he lifted her up in his arms, she accepted it. Tom had just saved her from doing something beyond the pale. He'd stopped her from breaking her covenant with God. God had surely seen to it that Tom arrived in time. God had protected her.

His lips never left hers as he lowered her to a blanket and came down with her to hold her hard against him. She clung to him. His iron muscles, his iron will.

The Cooters would come and come and never stop. But if she'd destroyed them, she'd have destroyed herself.

Then she forgot all about the Cooters. Tom drove them out of her very thoughts, and all she knew was she'd done it right this time.

She'd married herself a strong, smart, decent man.

★

He was married to a lunatic. Soft skin, beautiful eyes, passionate nature, crazy as a rabid swamp rat.

Tom pulled the loco little vermin closer. She murmured but didn't wake up.

It made him sick to think how close it had been. Mandy had clearly planned to unload her Winchester on those men. Maybe she wouldn't have gone through with it. He hoped and prayed she couldn't have. But she'd considered it. Left his cabin contemplating it. Come close to doing it.

To become a back-shooter, a cold-blooded murder, was the kind of choice people couldn't recover from. It broke their minds, scarred their souls. Tom had never killed a man, and he hoped he never had to. He reckoned he'd do it to protect his life, his herd, and definitely his wife and children. But killing when a man was pressed into it was different than planning ahead to kill, no matter how evil the men.

That was the woman he'd married. There was no way to explain it other than she'd gone completely loco. Hiding up in that mountain fortress for the last year might well have pushed her clean over the edge. He wondered if he'd have married her if he'd known she needed to be strapped into a straitjacket and locked in a cell.

Mandy shifted her weight and rested one of her work-roughened hands on his chest.

Sure he would have. She was a mixture of strength and softness that made Tom a little dizzy when he thought that she was now his. He had the signed papers to prove it.

"Tom." In the still-flickering firelight, he could see her face, see her lips move to form his name, though she barely breathed the word. But she sighed, and her breath was warm on his skin. He moved his arm slowly, to tuck her even closer without waking her, and she flowed against him like warm rain.

Aw shucks. Even now, knowing what kinks she had in her head, he'd marry her again. He'd have to get a net. Keep his eyes peeled. Chase her down and drag her home when she went berserk.

But so what?

He kissed her forehead, and she feathered a kiss across his jaw. He looked down and saw her eyes flicker open, heavy lidded with sleep and contentment.

Though he hadn't meant to wake her, he couldn't really get too upset that he had. Especially when she stretched up to meet his lips with her own. He didn't make her stretch far. As he kissed her, he decided to hire a few more cowhands. That'd give him more spare time to cope with the madwoman he'd married.

And that was the last rational decision he made for a long, long time.

★

Much later, Mandy lay in her husband's arms, staring at the stars, and saw a comet zip across the sky. She'd been watching these same heavens. . .how many days ago?

Could a woman's life change so much in such a short span of time.

Another streak of light reminded her that the night Tom had

come for her, she'd wondered if the sky was falling. "Tom, have you noticed all the falling stars lately?"

"Hmm?" He was almost asleep.

She lay with her head on his shoulder, one hand resting on his broad chest.

What would Tom have to face to survive being married to Mandy McClellen, Lady Gray?

"I watch the stars. I told you that. Look up there. Maybe you'll see a falling star. They're raining down. It's. . .almost. . .scary."

Tom pressed a kiss to her forehead. Then Mandy felt him shift, and a glance at him told her he was staring up. "It's a beautiful night to be camping out."

A star streaked across the sky. They were in an open area surrounded by woods, so they didn't have a wide view of the sky, but straight overhead they could see. "So strange that there are so many. I wish I'd brought my books with me from Sidney's house."

"Books about what?"

"The stars and planets and meteors. They were fascinating. I read about how sailors found their way all around the world using the stars. Can you imagine?"

"Sure, I can find the stars and get my bearings, know north, south, east, west."

Mandy nodded.

Tom's arm tightened around her. "So you're scared when you look at the stars? How do you have time to be scared of falling stars when you've got Cooters to worry about?"

"The book—one that Sidney got just recently—names all these meteors and comets and says they come again and again. The unusual rain of falling stars is caused by a meteor shower called the Perseids."

"Perseids?" Tom pulled her so close she had a hard time remembering they were stargazing.

It was actually a romantic thing to do, Mandy decided. Lie in her husband's arms and stare at the sky, with no moon tonight but blazing with stars and the occasional streak of light. She'd talked about the stars with Sidney. Or more correctly, she'd listened when he talked. And out of sheer boredom she'd read the books and papers he'd amassed, using his wealth to gather them from far and wide. But she and Sidney had never gone out together. And *nothing* between her and Sidney had qualified as romantic.

"Yes, a meteor that passes close to Earth once a year, during the first weeks of August. The comet has a long stream, a tail following it. With rocks I guess. And some of the rocks in that tail get close enough to Earth and come plunging down, and they leave a slash of light when they do."

"But not the main comet? It doesn't come down?"

Mandy shrugged. "I don't understand how it works. I just know from Sidney's papers that it does. And I can look at the sky and see the truth of it." Another comet left a burn of light.

"I think, woman, that once I've got you back to my ranch, you're going to be too busy at night to do much stargazing."

Tom moved and blocked out the sky. His face, shadowed by the night, filled her vision, and his lips indeed distracted Mandy from the stars. Mandy was certain Tom didn't give the stars a single thought for quite a while. She was certainly thinking of other things.

Later, as she was lying, relaxed, in his arms, she saw yet another comet leave a stripe of white in the sky. Mandy's stomach growled, and she wondered how long it'd been since she'd eaten. Tom, too, for that matter, but she was too content to move. Too happy to be in Tom's arms. He'd regret soon enough that he'd chosen her to love.

Mandy paused. Love?

Tom's words had all been about possession. He'd said she was his. They were meant for each other. They belonged together. And tonight he'd claimed her as clearly as a man could claim a woman. But he'd never spoken of love.

Did she even want his love? Did she want to love him? Loving a man was such a stupid thing to do. Because if she loved Tom, then she'd want to depend on him.

True, her pa had been dependable. But her real pa, the man who'd been married to her ma when Mandy had been born, had proved unreliable, and Mandy had adored him. And Sidney certainly hadn't been a man to depend on, and Mandy had been madly in love with him at first. Thinking of love seemed dangerous, risky.

She thought of her actions today, how she'd tried to call that cold-bloodedness to herself and hadn't been able to and had planned to kill those men anyway. . .maybe.

It made her sick that she might have done it. It made her just as sick that she'd left those men alive.

Could a woman who wanted to kill love? What man would want that kind of woman in his life?

Terribly glad she hadn't committed murder today, she still wanted the Cooters dead. Her mind chased itself around until she thought she'd go crazy. . .crazier.

Tom pulled her close, and that broke off the circle of worry. Foolishly she felt safe. And she decided to let exhaustion win for now. As she dozed off in the strong arms of her husband, her last waking thought was that she felt a little sorry for the man.

He'd spoken marriage vows with a lunatic.

★ Eleven ★

"Wake up, you crazy woman."

Mandy jerked awake and saw Tom crouched a few steps away, across an open fire, holding a coffeepot that boiled almost as hot as his expression. In the firelight, he looked grim and dangerous and worried. It was still dark, though Mandy thought she saw a bit of lightness to the east.

As always she looked up and studied the stars. Always the stars. Then she looked back at her ferocious husband. His tone and the grim scowl on his face was not in keeping with the man she'd spent the night loving, but it was a pretty good match for the man who had dragged her bodily away from where she was drawing a bead on the Cooter clan.

"Want some coffee before we talk about what in the name of heaven you think you were doing yesterday?"

Mandy sat up in bed, and when the blankets fell away, she quickly caught them and pulled them to her chin.

Tom didn't seem to notice. It was a shame really because she'd very much like to *not* have this conversation with him.

He poured her a tin cup of coffee and brought it to her. She had to fumble to grab the cup and the blanket both. He went back to the fire and threw some bacon into a red-hot skillet. He went to work on the bacon with his back to her. Deliberately, she was sure, so she'd have a moment to make herself decent.

She came up to the fire, putting the finishing touches on braiding her hair just as he was scooping the bacon out. It irritated her that he'd packed so well for the trip. He'd been just in the nick of time to stop her after all. He handed her a tin plate with bacon and a corn cake on it. This is what they'd eaten on their way from her home to his. Maybe it had all been in his saddlebags already.

"So, you were planning to back-shoot those men, is that right?" Tom settled onto the ground, his back resting on a fallen log. He held a plate in one hand, a cup of coffee in the other, obviously ready to have a calm visit about the fact that he was married to an almost-murderer.

"I was planning to." Except maybe she wouldn't have gone through with it. "I wanted them dead. I don't know. I was tempted."

Tom's eyes slid to her rifle, close beside him on the far side of the fire. Making herself decent included going armed. All that was left was strapping on her Winchester. They were married now, so he might as well know she went armed all day, every day and slept with her long gun on the floor within easy reach. She saw it lying beside Tom and decided, just for now, to leave it there.

"We're going home today. Maybe you remember what you left back home. Your *children*, who need their *mother*." He left off staring at her rifle to glare at her. Fury like she'd never known flashed out of his eyes. The flickering fire made them even more savage.

Husbands didn't really turn their wives over their knee, did they?

"You know they've had no one but you for the last year. Think they might be a bit *upset* that you took off yesterday and left them with *strangers*?"

147

Mandy stood, her breakfast half eaten. "I've got to get back to them."

"Good idea, except they're gone."

"Gone? You said we had to get back to them." Mandy thought of the Cooters. Had they taken them?

"No, I asked you if you remembered them. They're small. You went through childbirth. Probably changed a lot of diapers. There are three, two girls and a—"

"I remember my children," Mandy snapped.

"Okay, good to know. So when you went haring off it was with them firmly in mind, then. You planned to ruin your life and probably hang and never be near them again. That was all planned out. A deliberate choice. Good to know."

"Just tell me where they are so I can go get them. The Cooters didn't—"

"Abby and Wade, along with a few of my cowhands, took them to Belle Harden's house."

"What?" Belle Harden, the toughest woman Mandy had ever known. Mandy wanted to go to Belle's house, too.

"They're safe. Belle lives in a mountain valley with two ways in. I sent enough drovers they can post a guard day and night. It's a lot like where you live, only her husband, being of sound mind, built her a cabin not a castle. And they've got thousands of acres of rich pasture land around them to feed their cattle instead of a few yards of solid rock like you had."

Mandy couldn't leave her children there for long. She took the last bite of her last corn dodger and set her plate aside to scrub her face with one hand. "I snapped yesterday."

Tom made possibly the rudest sound of disgust Mandy had ever heard. "If you'd've killed those men, you'd have deserved to hang. Then who was going to raise your children?"

"You." Mandy looked up from her hand. "You're their father now."

Tom rolled his eyes. "Yeah, they won't even notice you're gone.

Is that what you think?"

Mandy had done a lot of thinking yesterday. Frantic thinking, laced with fear and panic and hate. "How many of your men were killed or hurt yesterday? I know they wounded that cowhand that came running in, bleeding. He said more were down."

"Didn't you notice he turned around and rode back out with us? He was barely scratched. It wasn't even a bullet. The bullet hit a tree, and a chunk of bark ricocheted and hit him."

"He yelled two names. The Cooters shot two more of your men."

"Both dove off their horses when the Cooters opened up. One of 'em knocked himself insensible on a rock. The other took a bullet in the leg. Just grazed him. They're going to live. They were already up and on horseback when we got out there."

"I brought death to you."

"The Cooters, not you."

"Well, I brought the Cooters. They'll never stop coming. I just snapped. I wanted to stop them, hurt them, wipe them off the face of the earth."

"And you remembered just how good you are with that stupid rifle. Abby told me she saw you in action."

"I can barely remember it." Mandy looked up and locked her gaze on Tom's. "I've got a reputation with that rifle, Tom, but you don't know—"

"Don't know what?"

Mandy remembered how she'd fought to make herself cold. But her hate had all been red hot. "I don't even like people to know just how good I am. I probably shouldn't tell you now, except Abby saw."

"She was mighty admiring of your skill. She's more comfortable with a blade." Tom said it like he was admiring of a woman who preferred a blade. Well, too bad for him he had a sharpshooter for a wife, and he was stuck with her.

Because of last night, there was no going back. They were well and truly married. There could even now be a baby on the way. Another fragile life in desperate need of provision and protection.

In the clear light of day, Mandy was amazed that she'd so recklessly and eagerly seen to her wifely duties.

"If I don't know the half of it, why don't you tell me?"

"Abby will tell you I'm faster'n greased lighting, but what she can't see is what's going on inside me." Mandy lifted her coffee, clutched the tin cup with both hands as she thought of the cold, and tried to put it into words. "I'm fast and accurate, but there's more."

Glancing at the shining stars overhead, something called to her. She longed for her scope, but more likely she just didn't want to go on talking. "It's as if—as if time slows down. I don't feel like I'm moving fast. I get—calm, deadly calm. So calm it frightens me when I think of it later. I'm firing and aiming, cocking my gun and reloading."

"That's not so unusual. I've talked to men who've been in the Civil War. They say it's like that."

"But I'm thinking, too. I'm figuring angles, moving to get a better shot if I need to move. All of that and so much more is going on, and the gun keeps firing, keeps hitting what I aim at. I—" Mandy broke off her telling and stared at her boots, not wanting to see what Tom thought of his wife.

"You're what?"

"I'm cold." She shoved her toe in the dirt. "Ice cold."

"Keeping a cool head in an emergency is a good thing. Abby said you did that."

"It's more than a cool head. I don't feel—sane—" She took a quick glance at Tom then looked down again. "I'm so detached, ruthless. I do whatever I need to do. I feel no guilt, no remorse. And since this last year, hiding from the Cooters—"

"Abby told me you killed one of them," Tom said quietly.

Mandy glared as she raised her coffee cup in a salute. "For a man who was in a hurry to catch me, you sure had time to do a lot of talking and a lot of packing."

"Abby talked while I saddled my horse. Wade loaded a saddlebag with provisions while I worked. I ordered her to go to Belle's, and she obeyed me because it suited her. Red shoved that marriage paper in my hand and assured me we were legally married. I did all of that and still managed to be on the trail five minutes after I heard you'd lit out."

Mandy shuddered to think what would have happened if he'd taken ten minutes.

"So now we go get the children?" Mandy missed them desperately. When she'd set out yesterday, she'd felt as if she were giving them away. If she'd killed those Cooters, she'd've hanged most likely, but her children would be safe. And her death would end the feud. The Cooters would quit coming if she was dead, Mandy was sure of it. Now that it looked like she'd dodged the noose, she could hardly bear the fear and love she carried for those little ones who were her whole life.

"No, now we go home, and we face the Cooters without having the children to worry about. They'll be safe. Abby's good. She'll make sure they aren't followed. And Belle and Silas will make sure their valley isn't breached."

"While we wait for the next attack?" Mandy felt it again, that sick need to destroy, to fight, to kill.

God, protect me from this ugliness inside.

It was the first time she'd prayed since she'd made her decision to hunt down the Cooters. She hadn't felt that she deserved the help of the Lord, not even the ear of the Lord. Praying now flooded her soul with the life she'd nearly wiped out of it yesterday.

"God, protect us," Mandy prayed aloud.

Tom nodded. "We want God on our side for this, Mandy. How could you be so dumb as to choose a path without any hope of His blessing? It's an act of insanity."

Those blue eyes leveled at her. Asking her a question that she was afraid to answer.

"You brushed aside what I said about the way I feel when I'm shooting, Tom. But insanity might cover it. I had little sisters growing up."

"I met Sally, your sister who dressed like a wrangler."

"We were all good shots. None of them was as good as me, though Sally was mighty close. Beth always thought she was second best, but I'd say she was third—though no one was as good at sneaking around in the woods as Beth." Mandy missed her sisters with the stabbing pain of a bullet wound.

"We talked about it a lot, worked on our strengths and weaknesses. What we figured out was that none of them reacted like me. None of them knew quite what to make of that crazy coldness that came over me." Mandy tossed the dregs of her coffee onto the dying fire and watched it sizzle in the flames.

Then she looked up at her husband and confessed the depths of her ugliness. "I've always believed that I have it in me to be a murderer. I think what happens to me when I shoot is what happens to a hired gun, a professional killer. I'm terrified of that part of myself, and that man I killed. . ." Her eyes fell shut.

"What about it, darlin'?"

"I was too good at it. It haunted me later. But when it was happening. . ."

"You liked it."

Unable to speak, she looked at him, and he looked back until she got control of her tightened throat and clenched jaw. "I felt proud. Proud that I'd beaten him, proud that I'd brought him down hard and fast. It's a feeling, that pride, that is a terrible sin. God speaks of the sin of pride, and I know it to be true."

Tom shrugged. "I'm proud of my Angus herd, proud of my stallion. Proud of my pretty wife and the three beautiful children I have. I'm proud I built a house strong enough to keep you safe from the Cooters. Is that all a sin, too?"

With a shrug, Mandy said, "I guess it's a sin if God convicts you of it. And He certainly convicts me. I felt it again yesterday when I was creeping up that rise to get those men in my sights. I don't know if I'd have done it, but I might have. Worse yet—" She fell silent.

"Worse yet," Tom went on for her, "you might have enjoyed it."

"I might have, at least right at that moment." Forcing herself to turn to her brand-new husband and face him with the truth, she said, "I have this callus on my trigger finger."

She took Tom's hand and rubbed her finger against his. His were so strong and work-hardened she wasn't sure he could even feel it, but he ran his finger gently, carefully over her index finger. In the dark, she knew when he found the right spot. He paused and rubbed the rough skin slowly.

"What of it?"

"It's a reminder to me of what I am."

"You're a beautiful woman, a loving mother, an obedient wife."

Mandy thought Tom didn't sound all that sure of the last part and smiled despite the deadly serious topic. "I'm a sharpshooter. As good as anyone anywhere, I reckon."

"Your hands have calluses other places. Why worry about that one?"

"It's like living proof that I'm dangerous, to myself, my children, my parents and sisters, you. I never want to forget that, because it's who I am."

"It's part of who you are, but not the biggest part." Then Tom said, "You're part of me now, too. Anytime you want to run your hands over me to remind you of that fact, I'll be glad to allow it."

Mandy laughed, but it didn't last. It couldn't last, not while the cold inside her existed. Except this time, she hadn't been able to bring the cold, and that made her wonder what it would have done to her to pull the trigger in the heat. Maybe instead of enjoying it, she would have hated it. Loathed it. In fact, been unable to do it.

Tom shook his head and drew her attention. He looked mighty sad for a man who'd just spent the night in the arms of a woman he claimed to have wanted for five years. "Mandy, honey, I think it's best for the two of us, just privately here, to admit that you are as loco as a rabid swamp rat."

Mandy agreed with him, but she wasn't all that crazy about hearing him say it out loud. "Tom Linscott—"

"What, Mandy Linscott?"

"Good grief, I have a different name. I hadn't even thought of that yet."

"What were you going to say?"

"You should make a point, if you're gonna call me a rabid swamp rat, of always having a firm grip on my Winchester."

"Already thought of that." Tom raised it above his head with one hand while he tossed dirt on the campfire with the other.

Mandy let him keep the rifle while they broke camp. She glanced upward again and tried to figure out what was drawing her eye skyward.

They were half a mile down the trail when they reached a clearing in the woods where the sky opened wider. The soft gray of dawn was winking out the stars.

The wide heavens above drew her eye, just as they had earlier. She slowed her horse then slowed it more as she stared and wondered and suddenly knew. The stars!

Could it possibly be? Could she have, at last, found the key to turn this maddening lock?

Tom was stretching out his lead, but because they'd been riding single file, not talking, he didn't notice he was leaving her behind.

Her eyes darting between the stars and her husband's receding back, she carefully eased Sidney's map out of her pocket and unfolded it with terrible care so the paper wouldn't give a single crackle that might draw Tom's attention.

The map was as familiar to her as her own face. Hours upon hours of studying it, wondering about it, looking through Sidney's books to decipher this stupid map, told her the truth before she looked. With a rush of pleasure so powerful it felt sinful, she compared what she held in her hand to what she saw in the sky. And they matched.

Which meant that at last she'd found a way to escape the brutal violence of the Cooter clan, without using her Winchester.

The clearing ended, and the trees swallowed Tom whole. He couldn't know, not yet. Not when he was still so stubbornly insisting on protecting her. She folded the map as silently as she'd unfolded it then tucked it away without saying a word.

This plan, well, she'd include him. It wasn't likely he'd fail to notice when she disappeared. But he didn't need to know everything, not until it was too late for him to protest.

She ran her thumb over that little callus on her trigger finger and hoped that this madness could end without a blaze of gunfire and the death of her soul.

And she wouldn't even have to tell a single lie. Which wasn't the same at all as telling the absolute total and complete truth.

★

"Beth, I'm going to get Mandy."

Beth looked up as her pa slammed her door open. Her eyes snapped with satisfaction. "It's about time." She rose from the table where she was eating breakfast with her husband and two children. "Is Ma going?"

"I tried to leave her, but yes, she's going. She's buying supplies right now and sending a telegraph to Luther."

Beth went straight for the rifle she kept hung over her front door.

"Put that gun back. I'm just asking you to watch out for the young'uns."

"I won't be able to, because I'm going with you. Get Adam and Tillie to mind them while you're gone." She looked over her shoulder at Alex. "They'll help you out, too."

"You're not going, Beth." Pa yanked his hat off his head and slapped his leg.

"Fine." With a snort of disgust, Beth wheeled away from her pa and headed for her satchel and the supplies she'd need to pack. "You and Ma go by yourselves to get her, and I'll go by myself."

"I declare I have the most stubborn bunch of womenfolk." Pa rammed his hat back on his head with fierce disregard for the beating the Stetson was taking.

Beth headed for her bedroom, but Alex erupted from the table and grabbed her arm before she could get out of the room. "You're not going without me, Beth."

Turning, she saw that he was concerned for her, not afraid of being left. There was a time that the idea of staying here, doctoring the folks in Mosqueros without her, would have sent him into a panic. Resting her hand on his wrist, she felt the slow, steady beat of his pulse. His heart was tied to hers. But she had to help her sister. She couldn't bear to think of Mandy locked away from them. She'd been chafing to go to Mandy for a long time. Now the waiting was over.

"Somebody's got to watch the children." She looked at her sweet little blond-haired daughter and her sturdy little son who looked so much like Alex.

"Now, honey—"

The door snapped shut, and Beth saw that her pa had left. He wasn't getting away with that. She shut Alex up by kissing him senseless.

When she had his full attention, she unwrapped her arms from around his neck and said, "I've got to go, Alex. I don't want Pa and Ma facing down an army of feuding gunmen alone, not even with Mandy at their sides. There's no way to get hold of Sally, wherever she is."

"I don't want you walking into a gunfight, Beth."

"There's not going to be a gunfight." Beth felt the weight of her rifle on her back and had the good grace to be embarrassed. "I promise to be careful."

Alex's brow lowered. "Fine, if it's going to be so safe, then there's no reason for me not to come along."

Her stomach pitched when she thought of Alex getting mixed up in shooting trouble. It might be too much for him, considering the scars, both physical and emotional, he still carried from war. Beth shook her head. "You're not going."

"Why if it's not dangerous?"

"Because I said so." Beth jammed her fists on her hips.

Alex proved right then and there that he'd come a long way from the deeply traumatized man she'd married, the one who avoided any sort of trouble. He proved it by smiling right into her gritted teeth. "Not good enough."

"You need to stay and watch the children." There, that was a solid reason.

"I'm bringing them along." Alex had the nerve to smirk.

"You're not taking my children to a—" Beth stopped herself before she said—

"Gunfight?" Alex scowled. "Is that what you were going to say?"

"No." Maybe. "Of course not." Probably not. They could probably just grab Mandy and haul her home, and those awful Cooters would get tired of looking for her.

"Well, if the children come with us, then we'll be sure to avoid a gunfight at all costs. Right?"

Beth couldn't really come up with a good enough reason for him to stay. Not without lying, and she respected him too much to lie. She might possibly not respect him too much to keep from slugging him, but she'd never lie. "You're not going."

"Fine. You go see Mandy and the children, and I will go see Mandy and the children. If we happen to take the same train, you don't even have to sit with us."

She decided that when he'd been so upset, when they'd first met, and not pushy at all, those had been good days. "Come then. If you can keep up." Beth headed into the bedroom while Alex wiped the mouths of Beth's precious children.

Good grief, she was taking her children to a gunfight. Well, maybe she could convince Alex to stay to the side and just doctor the wounded.

Alex came in before she had her satchel packed and began shoving diapers into a gunnysack.

It was worse than before. She was taking a *baby* in *diapers* to a gunfight.

"I'd sure like my little sister watching my back. She is pure lobo wolf mean with that rifle of hers. Almost as fast and accurate as I am. Though neither of us can hold a candle to Mandy, of course."

God, give me strength to do what I have to do. Give me strength.

As they swiftly and silently packed, she took a moment to lay her hand on his shoulder, and when he turned to face her, braced for the next round of the fight, she kissed him. When she was done, he held her gaze, and she saw the peace and courage and strength of the man she'd married and couldn't resist kissing him again.

"I'm glad you're coming, Alex."

"Me, too. It'll remind you of why you need to be very, very careful."

Give us both enough strength to take care of Mandy. Give me strength.

★ Twelve ★

Belle Harden saw a woman top the rise that led through the low gap into her valley. More riders came behind her.

As soon as the first person became recognizable, Belle smiled. A visit from Abby Sawyer was always welcome. It was a good chance for Belle to get her knife sharpened. No one had quite the knack Abby did.

Then her eyes slid to the others in the group. Two little children. Then one of the riders with a child in his arms twisted in his saddle, and Belle saw a baby slung on that rider's back. Three children.

Wade was along of course. He tagged after Abby everywhere. Strange man. Abby seemed to adore him, and despite a few years of worthlessness in his youth, he'd turned into a decent man.

Belle had a hard time hating him, but she did her best.

There were six men riding with the Sawyers and those children. The Sawyers had only had two children, didn't they?

Then her eyes landed on Mark Reeves. Her smile turned hard and fast downward. What was that polecat doing here?

Belle turned and strode toward the house to have a little talk with Emma.

Silas met her before she'd gotten anywhere near.

"I already spotted the Reeves kid and said my piece, Belle. Emma knows how we feel."

"That she's too young, and Reeves is a no-account pup who needs a whip taken to his hide?"

"Yep, of course Emma knows you'd never take a whip to a pup's hide. But I think she's very sure you'd do it to Mark."

"Good, then you've saved me some time." Belle turned back to the approaching group.

They were setting a good pace and were in the yard before long.

Belle noticed Emma come outside. Betsy came next. Then Tanner tagged after Sarie, jumping and yelling like always. The child had more energy than ten regular people. It was naptime, or there'd be an even larger group to greet the Sawyers and that polecat Reeves.

"What's going on?" Silas asked Wade as the man swung down from his horse.

Abby alit next carrying a three-year-old.

And Mark, the polecat, had the pack carrying one child and held a four-year-old who jerked awake with a little cry when he dismounted. The little girl threw her arms around Reeves's neck and sobbed for her mama. Mark rested a hand on the little one's back and bent his head to talk with her. Except for one annoyingly welcoming smile in Emma's direction, Mark was focused completely on the child, talking sweet nonsense, holding the little one gently.

Emma went to the child as if she'd been lassoed and dragged. Belle frowned, but she could fault neither Mark nor Emma for the unhappy child. And as much as she wanted to hate Mark Reeves, the youngster was doing his best to comfort the little girl.

"These are Mandy Gray's children." Wade helped Mark swing the pack off his back. "Tom sent us here because there's trouble, and he wanted to get the children out of the line of fire."

The little boy in the pack had his lip stuck out, quivering, as he watched his big sister cry.

"Shooting trouble?" Belle lifted the little boy out of Wade's pack while Wade held on to the leather contraption. "With children involved?" Then another thought struck her. "Shooting trouble Mandy Gray can't handle?"

Belle turned to Emma. "You remember Mandy Gray, don't you?"

Emma reached for the crying girl, and the child shrieked and buried her face in Mark's neck.

Mark gave Emma an apologetic look, then rested one of his big hands on the flyaway white hair and crooned to her.

"Sure. I felt like I'd met a woman after my own heart." Emma looked worriedly at the crying child, inched just a bit closer, which put her that much closer to Reeves. Emma and Reeves exchanged one more of those blasted understanding looks. "Mandy could swing a rifle into action like nothing I've ever seen before."

Sarah came and stood behind Mark's back and started talking to the little one over Mark's shoulder.

Another one of the cowpokes came up slightly behind Mark—right next to Sarah in fact—and nudged him. "Need any help there?"

Mark turned to Emma and said, "This here's my cousin, Charlie Cooper. Charlie, this is Emma Harden and"—Mark looked over his shoulder—"her sister Sarah."

Belle couldn't have been watching her daughters much closer, so she noticed clear as day the way Charlie reacted when he looked at Sarah.

And if Belle wasn't mistaking it, Sarah looked right back.

"Howdy, Emma." Charlie touched the brim of his hat then reached out a hand to Sarah. "Pleased to meet you Sarah."

Sarah took his hand and smiled in a way that made Belle want to reach for her shooting iron.

Angela let out a squall that drew Sarah's attention and probably saved Charlie's life.

"I've got about a dozen little brothers and sisters," Charlie said.

"A dozen?" Sarah actually looked away from the child, and that was unusual. Sarah had always had a special heart for the little ones. "A dozen or so?" A smile bloomed on Sarah's face.

Belle had to admit that comment caught her own interest.

Charlie laughed. A great laugh. So great it made Belle a little sick to her stomach.

"My ma and pa adopted me when I was about ten, off an Orphan Train."

"What?" Sarah's brow furrowed. "I've never heard of such a thing."

Nodding, Charlie went on. "I've never rightly counted, but Pa said I was about the twentieth child he'd adopted. And he kept on doing it all his life."

"Your pa adopted children? Not your ma?"

"Yep. He started before he and my ma got married. Then they kept doing it afterward, and they had a few children of their own."

"How many were adopted, and how many were their real children?" Sarah seemed overly fascinated.

"We're all real." With a brief frown, Charlie said, "I don't rightly remember which are their own and which are adopted. But I reckon we're all real enough. I've got two little brothers with sort of strange speckled greenish brown eyes, though. They look a lot like my pa. I'm pretty sure they were born to my parents."

Then Charlie reached a hand out, and for a second Belle thought he was going to touch Sarah, but instead he tapped Angela on the chin. Looking at Angela, but talking definitely to Sarah, he added, "My parents are wonderful people with a heart for children without homes. I'd be glad to tell you all about them."

Which would give him time with Sarah. Which wasn't going to happen.

Charlie touching Angela turned Sarah back to the unhappy little girl. With skill far beyond her years, Sarah cajoled Angela out of the crying, but the little one didn't quit clinging to Mark until Tanner ran into Mark Reeves's leg and sent him stumbling forward into Emma. Emma caught him, and the two shared a smile.

Belle decided then and there she needed a horse whip. And no horse was in a bit of danger.

"Thanks, Em." Mark stayed far too close to Belle's daughter.

The collision distracted Angela from her tears, but it had almost the exact opposite effect on Belle. She thought Mark took way too long apologizing and asking if Emma was hurt, as if the girl was made of spun sugar or something. And Charlie reached out a hand to rest it on Sarah's arm as if she'd almost fallen in a heap.

"Anyone want a molasses cookie?" Sarah had the knack, and no one could deny it. Though offering cookies to little children was no stroke of genius.

Angela rubbed at her eyes. Emma went to relieve Abby of the child she carried.

The little girl, younger than Angela, screamed, "No! I want Mark."

Abby rolled her eyes, but Mark came over, and Abby passed the child to him.

Shaking her head and smiling, Emma said, "Maybe this one will let me hold him." She took the stout little toddler from Belle.

Even the baby boy stared at Mark but allowed Emma to carry him. They headed for the house with Tanner running between them hollering. Betsy tagged along. It usually fell to her to ride herd on Tanner. Belle had a moment to praise the Lord that Betsy had been able to keep her roughhousing little brother alive all these years.

Charlie didn't go with them—which kept Belle from dropping

him with a butt stroke—but he was looking way too long after the little group, and his eyes didn't seem to be stuck on his cousin.

Though her arms remained tight around Mark's neck, Angela now looked between her sister, in Mark's other arm, and Tanner. The racket Belle's son made seemed to drive all thoughts of crying out of Angela's head.

Belle needed to keep an eye on Emma and Mark, but first she needed some answers. "What's going on?"

Abby did the talking as usual.

"Of course they can stay." Silas gave the house a concerned look.

Belle wondered if he was considering building on. "And we appreciate the cowpokes to help guard the gaps. We don't keep drovers, so we'd have our hands full posting a guard around the clock on both of them. And it sounds like we'll need to do it."

"We need to get on home," Wade said. "We've been gone from our own young'uns for too long. But with the six men from the Linscott place, you should have plenty of help."

"Five men," Belle said. "Only five are staying."

"Why only five?"

"Because that no-account Mark Reeves has to go."

"Mark's my cousin. He's a top hand," Charlie assured Belle.

"Four, I want you out of here, too."

"What did I do? I know how to keep watch."

"Don't matter if either of you can lasso the moon and break it to ride. Mark's sparkin' Emma. He can't stay here. If I had my way, I'd post a guard at the gap to keep *him* out. And I saw the way you just looked at my Sarie. You're leaving, too."

The drovers laughed.

"I'm not joking." Belle had long ago perfected a glare that shut most people up. It didn't fail her now.

Except with Abby. "My brother insisted that Mark ride along, and you can see why. The children took to him more than anyone else. Tom's their pa now, and he said Mark had to stay with the little ones. They're a sight upset by all this commotion around their ma when they're used to just living in that house with her alone. Tom would never have sent them here if he didn't think the danger was serious. And you'll need six men to stand shifts on two gaps. You can't do it right with less."

"Mark's had one or more of 'em on his lap the whole time," Wade added.

Belle thought of her own girls and how completely she'd raised them alone. They'd have been devastated if she'd died and left them with strangers. And the older girl especially had clung to Mark. All of them had looked to him. No denying it.

"I suppose it'll upset the children if I have to beat Mark over the head, too." Belle glared at the house. Then she looked back at Charlie. "But I doubt they"ll mind over much if I carve a notch out of you."

She thought Charlie got the message, judging by his wide eyes and respectful silence.

Silas went to the drovers and discussed where to put up their horses while Belle said good-bye to the Sawyers without even getting an edge put on her knife.

Then she turned to her house, bulging at the seams with children, and one polecat.

She strode to the house. She didn't think all those little ones and Sarie combined were quite good enough as chaperones.

Besides, getting those children to trust her and her girls was now top priority. The second job on her list, as soon as she'd earned that trust, was booting Mark Reeves out of her valley.

★ Thirteen ★

Emma, if you come stand right beside me and talk to Catherine and Angela, with Jarrod in your arms, I think they'll calm down. See, Catherine is already watching her brother." Mark tilted his head so he could look little Catherine in the eye. "Aren't you, honey?"

Mark looked up and smiled at Emma, who'd come right on over. Mark had a passel of little brothers, and he'd learned a long time ago that a man carrying a baby was a lure to a woman. He'd used it many times in his earlier years. Before Emma he'd never been serious about women, but he'd always liked their attention. Now he used these little ones as tasty bait.

"I only had brothers growing up." He looked at the girls in his arms. Sure he was baiting an Emma-trap, but he sincerely cared about Mandy's little tykes. "My folks only had boys."

Emma kept her eyes on Catherine, her voice gentle and sweet, her hands stroking Jarrod. "Hi, Catherine. I only had sisters until Tanner was born. There were four of us girls."

"Four?" Mark looked around the room, blond Emma, redheaded Sarah, black-eyed Betsy. "Who'm I missing?"

"I've got an older sister who's married."

166

Mark smiled and Emma seemed caught in the smile. Jarrod in her arms, Catherine and Angela in his. He could see them as a family. Children of their own. Blue-eyed and blond-haired, Mark reckoned, though obviously Emma came from a family that could churn out children of all descriptions.

"So, you've got a lot of little brothers?" Emma was a tough Montana cowgirl. Mark knew that and it suited him. A woman needed to be strong to settle the West. Mark figured if he touched her hand he'd find calluses as tough as boot leather. And he almost reached out to check but thought better of it. Having two children in his arms slowed him down, too.

She was close to him now, and she'd stay here if he didn't make any false moves. She was as pretty as a spring rose, and her voice washed over him like warm rain.

The thought of having children with her was almost more pleasure than Mark could take. "Yep, five when I left home. But my folks have one every onest in a while, so who knows? Ma's getting older now. She has to be almost forty I reckon."

"My ma's almost forty, and she just had a new baby." Emma tipped her head toward a crib where a little one slept. "Your ma must've been young when you were born."

"She's not my real ma. My ma died having me and my two brothers."

Emma's brow knit with a frown. "Three babies at once?"

"Yep, triplets. We're the only ones I've ever heard tell of."

"I didn't even know babies could be born three at a time. And it killed your mother to have you?"

"Yes." Mark had been having fun until now, luring Emma closer, flirting a bit, acting like a hero because the children took to him. But it hurt to think that his birth had done his ma in. "Pa raised us for the first five years alone. Then he remarried."

Thinking of his pa's second wife helped him shake off that strange guilt. "She was real young. Seventeen when they got married.

I have twin brothers who were ten when Pa married her, so she's closer to their age than his."

"Twins, too?" Emma shuddered. "Did the rest of your little brothers come in batches like that?"

Mark shook his head. "Nope, and I'm glad, because Ma is a good'un. I'd have hated to lose her."

Angela picked that moment to rest her head on Mark's shoulders and fall asleep as if someone had switched off a light. Mark smiled down at her. He'd seen his little brothers do this.

Emma reached up and ran one work-scarred finger across Angela's cheek.

Catherine snuggled closer to Mark and looked to be the next one to nod off.

"You're good with them," Emma whispered.

"I've had my share of practice. And I like little ones." Mark looked down at the little girls.

Angela's eyes, closed in sleep, were still rimmed with tears where her lashes lay white and spiked from all the salt water. Catherine sighed and leaned her head on Mark's shoulder as if the weight of it was more than her neck could bear.

Forgetting his flirting for a second, Mark said, "They're powerful lonely for. . ." He looked at Emma and arched one brow. "Ma."

"It must have been bad for. . .her. . .to leave them. A. . .person. . . doesn't leave little ones easily. I remember when we first met her. She was just in the country from Texas. A young thing to be married. Though a sight older than Lindsay, my big sister."

"You met Mandy when she first came here?" Mark felt the stirring of excitement. If they knew her, it must be all right to tell them he knew Mandy from way back.

"We helped her and her first worthless husband build a cabin. A great little cabin not that far from Helena. There was no need to move up there where they went and build what I've heard called a castle. Ma wrote a letter to her folks back in Texas letting them know Mandy was safe and settled for the winter."

"So you know she was a McClellen, too?" Mark's tone finally pulled Emma's attention away from the children.

Emma leaned closer and spoke in a sharp whisper. "Too? How do you know her? Do you know these children from before?"

Mark might well be imagining it, but he thought he caught just a hint of something from Emma that could count as jealousy.

"I've never seen her children before, but I know Mandy." Mark kept whispering so Emma would have to stay close to hear. Besides, Catherine needed quiet to sleep, now didn't she? "I grew up with her in Texas. We went to school together."

"Did you come up here to see her?" Again that little bite of annoyance.

Mark had to fight to suppress a smile of satisfaction. "Nope, I had no idea who Tom was bringing home. I mean, I heard Lady Gray. I heard the rumors about her being a hermit."

"A witch. Which was ridiculous. She was a nice woman. Ma and all my family took a powerful liking to her from the first."

Mark nodded. "Then when we rode out to meet Tom, I couldn't believe my eyes when he had Mandy. And she recognized me, too. I think the children took to me partly because I felt the connection to them 'cuz I knew their—" Mark stopped himself from saying "ma" and looked down at Catherine, whose eyelids were nearly closed. "I knew Lady Gray."

"Connection?" Emma still sounded a bit tart.

"She's married, Em." A smile just would not be held back.

"Widowed you mean."

"No, I mean married to Tom Linscott. They saw to it before all the trouble started. Mandy was my mortal enemy when we were kids. I was always up to some nonsense in school, and she was the bossiest, most scoldingest girl I've ever met. But I haven't seen anyone from home in a while. And then knowing what I knew about Lady Gray, then seeing Mandy. . .well, I know her and her family, and they're good folks. I can't stand by and see Mandy come to harm."

Emma's fair skin, even burned brown by the summer sun, showed a tinge of blush.

"Why, Em? Would it bother you if I had a connection to some other woman?"

Emma scowled, but she stayed close. . .very close.

"Because the only woman I want a connection to is you, Emma Harden."

"You do?" Emma whispered. Her scowl faded, replaced by the sweetest smile Mark had ever seen.

Which made Mark very aware he was looking at Emma's lips. "Oh, yes, I want that real bad."

He'd thought it through and logically decided that Emma was the woman he wanted to marry. She was everything he wanted, strong and pretty and smart and a God-fearing woman. But until right now his plans had all been made in his head. He'd marry her and be happy with her and build a ranch with her. It made perfect sense.

But as her sweet smile grew wider and her eyes filled with interest in a way that made Mark feel like a king, Mark figured out the difference between logic and love. Because right at that instant he fell headlong in love with this pretty woman with the baby in her arms. Mark had never felt anything so right in his life.

And Emma needed to know that he was more than just mildly interested. He'd come close to stealing a kiss out back of the Hardens' barn when he was here before. But Emma's pa had interrupted before he could work up the nerve.

He was full of nerve now.

"Emma?" He glanced at her lips again and decided to take the little girls out for a walk behind that same barn. Lure Emma along.

"Yes?" Almost as if she'd read his mind and was agreeing. And once she started agreeing, who knew what she might say yes to.

"It's crowded in here and hot."

"It sure is." Emma patted Jarrod on the back but kept her eyes locked right on Mark.

"Maybe we could take the children for a little walk."

"But they're sound asleep. Should we put them to bed?"

"A little fresh air won't hurt them, will it?" He leaned closer as if fresh air was a big secret that only he knew, and ignored the fact that the children had been out in the fresh air through the whole long ride to the Harden ranch.

"No, I don't suppose so." She sounded grateful that he'd shared the idea.

"So, let's you and me—"

"I'll be glad to take those children off your hands now, Reeves." Belle Harden's voice had the effect of the tip of a blacksnake whip cutting a slit in his skin.

Mark straightened away from Emma fast, only now aware of just how close he'd been to her right here in the middle of Belle Harden's kitchen. In about five more seconds, he'd have had that kiss, even with all these people around.

He turned to face a very cranky, heavily armed woman. A woman he hoped would one day very soon be his mother-in-law.

If she didn't shoot him first.

★

"We're gonna make that woman sorry she left her house." Fergus mounted up beside Cord.

Cord led the way as he always did. He was hopeful that some more cousins would show up soon. They were running purely short.

"Why'd Grandpappy make this rule about Cooters sticking together?" Dugger asked in his childlike way.

"Family pride, that's why," Cord snarled. "You oughta get some."

"The most of our family I know ride the outlaw trail," J.D. grumbled. "Where's the pride in that?"

"We're hard men and we fight for the brand. That's the Cooter way," Cord said. "Nothing wrong with letting the world know that they're steppin' into a buzz saw when they hurt a Cooter."

Cord felt his chest swell with pride. He'd been raised by his pappy, a mean old codger, but with pride in family and a powerful sense of loyalty. The old man had loved feuding.

Even more so, Grandpappy did. Cord was one of the few of the cousins who ever knew the old man because Grandpappy spent his whole life working long hours. Cord had come along later, when Grandpappy had finally slowed down, against his will.

"You never knew Grandpappy, and I did. You remember the family rules, but I know *why* he made those rules." Cord looked back at Dugger. The man was pure dumb, but this was simple; maybe Dugger could learn it better than all of them.

"Our real name is Couturiaux. You all know that, right?"

Dugger looked lost.

J.D. shrugged.

"Sure. We all were raised hearing that. Stupid long name. I like Cooter better," Fergus said.

Cord preferred it himself. A man would be all day writing his name if it was Couturiaux. "I was raised by Grandpappy Cooter, and he loved to tell stories of the old country. I heard all about how he came to America and got his name chopped up by the only man who'd give Grandpappy a job."

"I always thought the long name sounded stupid." Fergus shrugged.

"Well, Couturiaux was a respected name in France. To be forced to shorten it by a pompous rich man, the only man hiring when Grandpappy got off the boat from Europe, nearly choked him."

"Yeah, well, try getting someone to spell that name. I don't blame the guy for wanting it shorter," J.D. said from where he rode behind Cord and Fergus. "And try getting a poor man to give you a job."

Cord decided then and there his cousins were pathetic. "Look, Grandpappy had his family pride ripped right off his back when his name was changed. And he had to accept the name change in order to feed his family. By the time he got ahead and could start his farm, his sons were grown and started families of their own. All of 'em were used to calling themselves Cooter. Grandpappy knew it was too late to get anyone to change the name back, but it burned him, and he made it a point of family pride to demand we all support each other. He couldn't have the name he wanted, but he could mold the family tight together in other ways."

"Makes sense to me," Fergus said. "When I rode off from our place, I didn't like leaving you behind, Cord. I reckon a lot of that is the family pride you're talkin' about. I know my pa was a harsh man, and I knew you'd have a hard life. It ate at me that I should have taken you along, but you were just a baby and me a young man alone." Fergus frowned.

Cord looked at his older brother, feeling some dismay to think he'd most likely end up looking like Fergus, because Fergus was stout and wrinkled and ugly. Cord might feel family loyalty, but that didn't mean he didn't know a homely man when he saw one. Right then, Cord decided he'd finish this mess with Lady Gray, then leave his family behind and hope to never see a one of them again. He didn't want to end up alone on the outlaw trail. He wanted a soft bed, a soft wife, and maybe a few babies with streaks of white in their hair. But he did appreciate that his big brother had wanted to take care of him. "Thanks, Ferg. I'm glad I caught up with you out here. I'd been looking for a while."

The foursome crested a distant hilltop and looked back. They'd come a long way.

Cord had felt cold for a while last night, like someone was taking a bead at his backbone. He'd decided to put some distance between his family and Lady Gray for a few days.

"Well, will you look at that." Dugger said it, but all of them immediately realized what had happened. They'd found the perfect lookout.

"The Double L brand belongs to Tom Linscott for sure." Fergus had been in this country longer than the rest of them. And that house of his is built like a fort.

"What do you think that cowpoke is doing with Lady Gray anyhow?" Cord saw how impenetrable the house was. He'd learned that well when their first attack had failed. Now, looking down from this far distance, the whole ranch looked well fortified. It was laid out so the few overlooks could be defended well.

"Linscott's a known man. A big rancher with a reputation for raising a top herd of cattle, like those big blacks we ran off." Fergus pulled a chaw of tobacco out of his pocket.

Cord had heard of Linscott, but he'd never ridden these trails nor met the man. He suspected that a man savvy enough to lay out this ranch and build a big spread knew enough to post a lookout. They'd never get as close to Mandy Gray as they had that first day. Not while she was living in Linscott's house. It chafed him that they'd missed that chance. He glanced at Fergus and the red scratches on his neck where rock had exploded under Mandy's gunfire.

Taking one second, Cord let himself remember the way that woman had moved with her gun. It shrank something in Cord's stomach, and that fear made him mad and made him determined to give her a taste of that fear.

"Why did he drag her out of her fortress and take her to his ranch?" Dugger scratched at his neck.

As he considered the Double L, a memory came back to Cord. "Years ago, I was with Gray in Helena, and Linscott was in town with a herd. I remember now Gray bought a matched pair of horses from Linscott, and Linscott agreed to deliver them. Maybe Linscott met Lady Gray back then. Maybe something more was going on between him and Lady Gray, and he came to get her and take her for his own."

Cord had touched Lady Gray exactly once, and his fingers still felt the heat of it. He'd wanted her. He'd wanted that arrogant fool, Sidney, dead, and Cord planned to step in and claim Mandy Gray for his own. He'd have the woman and the mountain of gold Sidney was always bragging about. With heated satisfaction, Cord thought of the dark, streaky-haired children Mandy would give him. A passel of them in fact. Boys. A new generation. Cord had decided long ago his children would bear the name Couturiaux.

Now Tom Linscott had her, and her gold. Any children Mandy would have would be light-haired instead of dark with a white streak. The hungry jealousy almost sent Cord into a rage. It also gave him bitter satisfaction to decide that Linscott had bought into this feud. The Cooters now had someone else to settle with.

"It's miles away, but we can see them coming and going from that ranch." Cord looked at the forest around them and saw ground covered deep in soft pine needles and the nearby trickle of spring water. It was a likely place to camp with a perfect overlook of the ranch, though far out of rifle range. "We can bide our time here, just like we done by Lady Gray's gap. We'll wait and watch and pick our moment to strike."

Cord swung down from horseback and tied his horse to a scrub pine. "Let's set up camp. Then let's start scouting to see if we can find a lookout that's within rifle range. I don't want to wait too long to let Linscott know he's made a big mistake."

★

Mandy rode into the Double L at a fast clip.

Tom kept up. If he hadn't, she'd have taken a stick to his

backside to hurry him along.

Every few yards, without slowing her pace, Mandy turned around to study the trees and hills around them, looking for likely places for dry-gulchers to hide out.

She noticed full well that Tom did the same. At least he was taking the threat seriously. All Sidney had done was hire bodyguards and leave his protection to them.

They cantered into the ranch yard, and Mandy's skilled eye saw that Tom had posted a lookout on every high peak near his cabin.

And what a cabin it was. Sidney had built a castle. Tom had come very close to building a fort. Most people didn't live in such intense security. Since she was the only thing Sidney and Tom had in common, Mandy took a second to wonder if she somehow made men feel endangered.

"What are we going to do about the children?" It was burning a hole in Mandy's belly to think of them, so far away, so cut off from her.

"The first thing we're going to do is talk to the law. I want a U.S. Marshal to know what's going on."

"The law can't stop them, Tom." Her horse sidestepped, and she realized she had a death grip on the reins. Relaxing her hold, she said, "They keep coming and coming and—"

"I know." He cut her off. "You've told me that about fifty times. But I'm going to give the law a chance." Tom nodded toward his oversized log cabin at a tall, lean man wearing a star, leaning on the hitching post right in front of Tom's door. "And there's just the man I want to see. He's the toughest man in the territory."

Tom hollered at a nearby cowhand.

"All I see is a man with a target painted on his back. You. If that man throws into our fight, then there'll be a target painted on him, too. I think I should go to the children, Tom. Belle would see sense and let me go back to the mountain."

Tom turned to Mandy, "You can't go to the children. Sending them away keeps them safe. I don't think any man is a low enough varmint to kill a little child, so I'm hoping they won't even chase after the young'uns. But they might come after you, and if the lead starts flying, I want the children tucked far out of the way."

Tom swung down and handed the reins of his horse to the bowlegged old man who seemed to mosey along but covered the ground fast enough.

Tom took Mandy's reins as she dismounted, and the drover led the horses away.

"Thanks for coming, Zeb. Mandy, this is Zeb Coltrain." Tom shook the man's hand. "He's been chasing bad guys since before you were born. Zeb, this is my wife, Mandy Linscott."

She wondered if the children were Linscotts now.

"Howdy, ma'am." Marshal Coltrain wore a Stetson, but what hair Mandy saw was dark, and his face, half covered by a huge, drooping mustache, had the weathered look of a man used to living much of his life outdoors fighting the elements. However, he was by no means old enough to have been chasing bad guys all that long.

"I been hearing rumors about you, Tom. What kind'a trouble have you stirred up now?" The lawman tucked his thumbs in his gun belt as if he didn't have a thing to do but jaw with Tom, but Mandy saw the sharp awareness in the man's eyes. He had two six-guns, tied down, a knife in his belt, and the coldest black eyes Mandy had ever seen.

She had a terrible mix of hope and dread. Hope he could somehow protect her.

Dread that she'd get him killed.

Pretty much the same things she felt toward Tom. Except she felt a few more things toward Tom. Wifely things. She thought of those things and glanced at him. He caught the look and winked at her in a way so intimate she couldn't help remembering how well she'd liked being in his strong arms. Tom went back to talking to Zeb Coltrain.

Mandy saw a smile quirk Marshal Coltrain's lips, and knew the marshal hadn't missed that little exchange. Surely a lawman learned to watch everything. He stayed alive by picking up subtle clues.

Mandy felt her cheeks flush and decided she very much hoped the lawman couldn't read her expression with perfect accuracy. "Can we go inside and talk about this? I feel like someone is lining up a rifle right at my back."

Tom rested a hand on the small of her back, reminding her that he'd stand between her and any gunfire.

She hated knowing that.

They went inside, and Mandy noticed the bullet holes in Tom's front door. She walked through Tom's main front room, where Mandy had already drawn gunfire, and went through a wide doorway into Tom's tidy kitchen. She filled a coffeepot from a bucket of water near the dry sink.

Tom and Zeb followed her, already talking.

"These Cooters"—Zeb sat at the table in Tom's kitchen—"the rumors about them and their feud have done some spreading. I've heard bits and pieces. But except for your husband, it seems to me the only ones that've been dying are Cooters. That's a stupid way to conduct a war."

Mandy didn't want to tell them about the one she'd personally blown a hole in.

"My little wife here killed one personally that came at her while she stood watch one night."

She glared at her overly talkative husband, but he didn't even notice.

He was too busy throwing wood into a potbellied stove and lighting a match to some kindling. He brushed his hands together.

She crossed her arms so Marshal Coltrain wouldn't see her

hands tremble. "I did what I had to do. It was self-defense. I didn't go out hunting—"

"Any man coyote enough to attack a woman deserves whatever happens to him." For a lawman, Zeb here seemed uninterested in hearing about a killing.

Tom sat down across from Zeb. "I had one of my hands ride in and send word for the marshal. I didn't expect you here so fast, Zeb."

"I was in the area. I had yesterday to send a couple of wires, and I already got one back. These Cooters are like lice the way they've spread."

"Well, they sure as certain make me itchy." Tom leaned back in his chair as if he didn't have a care in the world.

"Mrs. Linscott, ma'am, you're right about there being a passel of cousins. We're trying to get to the bottom of why they're really coming after you. It don't make no sense. One man in town said he'd heard that the Cooters were just crazy for feuding and the granddaddy of the clan kept them all whipped up about sticking tight together."

"But against a woman and children?" Tom shook his head. "Never heard the like. And who started this whole notion of the Cooters sticking together no matter what? Where is this granddaddy? Is he still alive? I'd like to plant my fist in his face for being behind this."

"I've asked a few questions, and like I said, I'm expecting to hear more. But the good part is that there are some Wanted posters on this crowd. I heard tell of a few Cooters back East, in Tennessee and Kentucky, who are honorable, prosperous men. I've got a telegraph to them to ask if they're connected to this mess. I can call in a few more lawmen because there's some reward money on the head of a Cooter or two."

"But which Cooters?" Mandy asked. "How do we find them? They all have that streak of white in their hair." Mandy could still see the man she'd shot. His hat had fallen off, and there he'd been, dead in the night, that stripe showing like a skunk.

Mandy started opening the few cupboard doors in Tom's utilitarian kitchen. Her kitchen now. But she needed to learn it.

Tom rose from the table. "Let me help you." He went straight to a small door and opened it. "Coffee's in here and most food stores."

He looked over his shoulder and smiled at her. "A wife oughta learn her way around her husband's house, now shouldn't she?"

Mandy was sorely afraid she was blushing again, which was ridiculous for a woman with three children. But being with Tom as his wife was an all new experience, and the dreadful blushes kept surprising her. For the moment, she diligently kept her back to the marshal.

"I think we need to hear how this all started, Mrs. Linscott. Between the Cooters and this strange feud business and all the mystery that surrounded the witch woman, Lady Gray, about half of what I've heard is probably exaggerated or outright lies."

The coffeepot made a sharp clink of metal on metal as Mandy set it on Tom's squared wood-burning stove in his kitchen, which had the same strange slits in it rather than windows. Mandy should have found it smothering, but those thick log walls felt like the strong arms of God to her. Safety. "I've kept to myself for a long time, marshal. I'm out of the habit of trusting folks or leaning on anyone."

Tom's strong hand settled on her lower back. His fingers slid up her back slowly, touching each bump in her spine. Beth called them vertebrae, and somehow, when Tom did that, it was like he was sharing his strength with her, offering her his protection, lending his strong hands to help her find her backbone. "Time for new habits, then. Come on." He urged her toward the table.

Though she felt panicky at the thought of talking through

the troubles, she wanted Tom's hand to support her enough to go along.

Dragging out a wooden chair, Tom waited for her to sit straight across from the marshal. Then he sat at the head of the table.

Mandy thought of the majestic wooden table in the formal dining room in her mountaintop home and much preferred this rustic rectangular one, clearly made by hand from split logs.

"It didn't start out as a feud. The Cooters wanted Sidney's gold. Cord Cooter worked as his bodyguard, and I always thought he had a sly, cruel look. But then so did the other bodyguard, and he was loyal to Sidney."

"I met 'em both, Zeb," Tom interjected. "One time in Helena when I sold Sidney a team of horses. Both tough men. Didn't care for 'em myself." Tom leaned back in his chair, watching Mandy in a way that told her he'd protect her from hard questions as surely as he'd protect her from gunfire.

"Sidney fired Cord, and there was a run-in between Cord and my sister, who was coming to visit. Which led him to find a brother. They teamed up with it in mind to get their hands on our money. I heard—" Mandy's throat seemed to quit working, and her eyes shut.

A warm touch brought her eyes back open. Tom had leaned forward and clasped her hand.

It settled her enough to go on. "Cord intended to kill Sidney and force me to marry him. I know his main goal was to get his hands on Sidney's gold. Sidney heard something like that when the Cooters ambushed him and his bodyguards shortly after my sister's visit had ended. Sidney lived, thanks to his guards, a Cooter died, and shortly after that we found that guard dead, shot in the back. A note was pinned on his shirt telling us we'd started a blood feud by killing a Cooter and that every Cooter in the country would come boiling up out of their Tennessee hills to wipe the Grays off the face of the earth. We had incidents that came hard and fast after that. Luther was shot."

"Who's Luther?" the marshal asked.

Mandy explained about the mountain man who had helped raise her pa and been like a grandfather to her all her life.

"But he survived the attack?" Tom slid his hand from hers and went to fetch the coffee.

Distantly, Mandy realized that should have been her job. "Yes. Then there was an attack on the men who were building our house. It was as good as done, which was for the best because the whole work crew quit. We were safe in our gap because there was only one entrance and Sidney kept a lookout posted. But when people would go through it, to town or for any reason, they were at risk."

"You said you shot a man?"

Tom poured her a cup of steaming liquid, and the curling steam helped keep Mandy's shivers away. Even so she rubbed her hands up and down her arms. "Yes, another Cooter. He had the look of them, but I'd never seen him before, so I knew they were telling the truth about the feud." Her fingertips touched the ugly scar on her shoulder. "I was shot myself, but it wasn't serious."

She'd cared for her three children with her arm in agony, because by then Sidney had almost completely cut himself off from her. He sat in his regal office by day and watched the stars by night, and he took every excuse he could think of to ride into town and stay away as long as he could. A risky business considering the Cooters, but Sidney couldn't stay home. In the end his restlessness killed him.

"Sidney was shot down in the streets of Helena. A man was arrested, also a Cooter. Sidney's guards rode out to tell me. I guess I went a little crazy at this new attack. I convinced Luther to leave. He didn't want to, but he knew I was about at the breaking point, and his leg was healing so slow he just made one more person for me to guard. I sent a letter with him to tell the rest of my family to stay away."

"And the Shoshone people who helped you?" The marshal took a long drink of his coffee, which still had to be boiling hot.

Thinking of Buff's new wife made Mandy smile, though her heart was heavy. "Wise Sister is the wife of another good friend of my family, Buff. The Shoshone are Wise Sister's family and friends. She figured out a way to keep me safe. The Shoshone consider the land around my house their ancestral hunting grounds, but the government had moved them off. They came back, but very quietly. They made themselves known to me and occasionally brought in food and a few reports of Cooters who had tried to invade. And they didn't set up a regular village, mainly to keep the government from knowing they were there but also because the Cooters were just as evil to them as they were to me. Since it was my land, private property, no one much cared who lived there. And all my problems stopped. The Shoshone kept the Cooters back, though there were run-ins with them."

Mandy frowned over the trouble she'd caused those fine Shoshone folks. Well, their trouble ought to be over. . .since it seemed to be following Mandy. "With Sidney dead and the gap and land near it guarded, as long as I stayed close to home, I was safe."

Tom and the marshal nodded in nearly identical motions. They were quiet, thoughtful as they drank their coffee.

Mandy joined them, thinking of what it meant now that she had left her fortress. The Cooters had already attacked once. But even while she dreaded what was to come, she looked at these two men.

Tom, much better looking but cut from the same cloth. Western men, forged by harsh elements. So like Mandy's pa. The kind of man she loved, respected, and wanted in her life.

What in the world had she been thinking to marry Sidney?

It was a wonder God didn't strike her dead with a lightning bolt for her stupidity.

★ Fourteen ★

It's a wonder God didn't whack you with a lightning bolt for being so dumb as to marry that sidewinder, Mandy honey." Tom meant it kindly. He'd added honey at the end, hadn't he? How much sweet talk did a woman need?

Mandy's eyes flashed a lightning bolt or two of their own. Tom decided maybe calling her dumb hadn't been the right thing to do. But for heaven's sake, she was as smart as any woman he'd ever met. And she'd done a mighty dumb thing. Pointing it out shouldn't get him in any trouble.

"But he's dead, and now you're married to me. I won't be wandering off to town for weeks at a time. You just leave all this Cooter business to me and the law and don't worry your pretty head about it." Tom expected a smile and a thank you.

"This is my problem, not yours."

He was doomed to disappointment. Women were a mystery. Looking at Mandy's beautiful, flashing eyes reminded him that they were a wonderful mystery.

Tom ignored her foolishness. "So, Zeb, what do we do next?"

"I'm going out to where you saw those Cooters camping.

I want to read their sign and get an idea what kind of men I'm dealing with."

"They'll shoot you down from cover." Mandy got up and fetched the coffeepot.

The tinkling of the coffee into the tin cups as she gave them a refill warmed Tom's heart. He'd gotten himself a good little wife, except for her stubbornness. . .and her preference for shooting people. And the pack of killers on her trail. And—

"I'll ride careful, ma'am." Zeb interrupted Tom's dark thoughts, which was just as well. Zeb tested the coffee then took a careful sip.

"I hear you're mighty good with that shooting iron, Mrs. Linscott." Zeb gestured at Mandy's rifle with his coffee cup.

That's when Tom noticed she was wearing it across her back, in the kitchen. Partly it amused him to realize he'd gotten so used to her and that always-handy rifle that he barely noticed. Partly it irritated him that she didn't feel safe and trust him to protect her, not even inside his home.

"Why don't you hang that rifle up?" Tom was tempted to disarm her. He'd done it before.

"I never do. Even at night, rocking the babies to sleep, I keep it on the floor close to hand. It's a good habit to have it close."

Tom reckoned she was right, but it pinched to think of how self-sufficient she was. He wanted his woman to trust him to protect her.

Zeb finished his coffee and set the cup down, then swiped his hand across his moustache and rose. "I'm going to do some tracking. If I think those four Cooters are ones from a Wanted poster, I'll bring 'em in."

"Be careful." Mandy's brow furrowed.

Was she just nervous after years of being hunted? Or did the coyotes really deserve this level of caution from Tom's sharpshooting wife?

"Appreciate the concern, ma'am. And maybe by the time I get back to Divide I'll have some answers to those wires I sent about the Cooters." Zeb headed for the door.

Mandy met Tom's eyes. He could see she was holding back more words of caution.

"He's good, honey." Tom stood and followed Zeb out, Mandy trailing along. Since it wasn't her nature to follow, Tom decided she was hanging back to keep her mouth shut.

Zeb rode off, and Tom came back inside.

"We'll give him a few days and see if he can iron this all out." Tom slid his arm around Mandy's waist. She moved before he could get ahold and remind her how much fun it was to be married.

Snatching her Stetson off the nail where she'd hung it, Mandy slapped it on her head.

"Where are you goin'?" Tom blocked the door or she'd have stormed right out.

Jamming her hands on her hips, Mandy said, "I've got two choices."

"You've got one choice." Tom grabbed her hat. "You stay inside where it's safe and let the law do its job."

"Two choices and neither of them include staying inside."

Sighing, Tom regretted even asking but knew he might as well get it over with. "What are your choices?"

"I can go to my children. They'll be so worried. They've never been away from me."

"And maybe bring gunfire down on them."

"Except you seem to think the Cooters have ridden off so no one's around to follow me."

"What's the other choice?" Tom knew he wasn't going to like this one either.

"I know in my gut that the real reason the Cooters won't quit coming is that gold. They may not even have a notion of getting their hands on it, but they sure enough let it push them into the crazy way they've been acting."

"You don't know that for a fact." Though it sounded pretty reasonable to Tom, unfortunately.

"So, my other choice is to ride to. . .Denver and get that gold out of my life."

Why had she hesitated when she'd said Denver? "What are you going to do? Throw it into the streets?"

"I might. I just might."

"We'll be days riding to Denver."

"Not we, me. You stay here and defend your ranch. I'll go deal with that gold."

"You're not going anywhere without me, and I can't be away that long. It'd take two weeks going there and back. Are you going to leave your children for that long?"

Mandy flinched, and Tom figured he'd just stopped her in her tracks.

"So, you're saying I can go to the children, then?" The expression on her face almost tore Tom's heart out. She could go there, and her location might remain secret, at least for a while, maybe for long enough to let Zeb straighten this whole mess out. But if the Cooters got wind of it, they could come at the Harden clan, and turning a pack of back-shooters loose on the Hardens wasn't Tom's idea of being neighborly.

"You're staying here, woman." Tom stalked up and leaned over her. He was nearly a foot taller and outweighed her by close to a hundred pounds, he figured. That put him in charge. "You heard those wedding vows. Love, honor, and *obey!*" He jabbed his finger right at her nose. "You're obeying me, and that's the end of it. I gave you *one* choice, and you're taking it. Stay inside."

"I'm not going to sit around inside a log fort while men hunt and kill you and anyone else they think has a connection to me."

"Instead you'll go traipsing off and hope when they dry-gulch you that rifle will be able to settle things your way?"

"Which gives me an idea for a third choice." Mandy stepped closer to Tom. Not backing down and agreeing sweetly like a woman had oughta.

"What's that?" He shouldn't ask. He knew it before he opened his mouth.

"Instead of going to Denver or my children, I can take this rifle and head for those Cooters and finish what you interrupted yesterday. I can hunt them down like rabid skunks."

Well, he'd known what he was getting into when he set his sights on marrying the fastest riflewoman in the West. He didn't expect her to be all that easygoing. Still, in this instance, she was going to mind her husband. She'd do things his way or he'd know the reason why.

"You're staying here." Tom put his hands on her waist and lifted her right off her feet until she was eye-to-eye with him. What was she going to do about that? Whatever else her skills were, she couldn't beat him in a wrestling match, and he wasn't about to change his mind.

Mandy's arms went wide, and Tom braced himself for an attack. Then those arms wound around his neck, and her lips near to swallowed him up.

★

Mandy tried to stay mad at Tom as he brought up the rear on the trail to Divide. She managed it mainly because the man would not stop complaining.

"This is the most ridiculous plan I have ever heard." Tom pulled his stallion up beside Mandy and glared. "We need to stay at my ranch."

Mandy wasn't so much leading the way as making a run for it. True, Tom had agreed to this madness, but only after three straight days of nagging. And she was deliberately riding so fast he had his hands full keeping up. It gave him less time to think.

It also made them harder for a hidden gunman to hit.

She'd heard Tom send men out to scout ahead. The main trail to Divide was the one Tom had chosen. He'd said there was only one spot on that trail that made him nervous. One narrow stretch, lined with trees so thick they would have their hands full turning around if needed. There was a rocky overhang on that trail that would be a perfect position for a shooter. But the Cooters weren't from around here, and Tom assured her they'd need to do a lot of scouting to figure out just how Tom rode to Divide. There were several routes, and if they picked the best way then they'd have to scout for a solid lookout spot. There was one. But though it was well-known to Tom, he also said only a knowing man would be able to get to it. It was encouraging, but still, Mandy didn't ride easy.

She'd spent three straight nights doing her best to persuade her cranky husband to see things her way.

Not even her best persuasions had worked until this morning when Tom had come storming in from riding herd to announce one of the herds had been run off, some of them injured, many missing, all exhausted and turbulent and threatening to stampede again.

"Those varmints are just going to keep coming." Mandy threw him a furious look. "And we didn't see a thing until it was too late to do anything but clean up the mess. That's just the way they operate. We have to do something. We can't just sit here like big fat targets waiting for them to hurt us."

Tom glared at her, the fire in his eyes mostly for the Cooters and the damage they'd done, but Tom's grip on his temper was always shaky. "We can handle this, Mandy. I'll hire more hands. We'll bring the herds in closer."

"How much will that cost you, Tom?" Mandy snapped her fingers in front of Tom's face and made sure he heard the sarcasm when she said, "I've got an idea. Why don't we go to Denver and get the gold I have in the bank? We can use it to put a bounty on the Cooters' heads that will run them off for good."

Grabbing her wrist, Tom shook his head. "This means they're back. They're watching the ranch. I've got men combing the hills, and they'll eventually find this bunch and bring them in. We're not leaving. You're safe here."

"You're not safe." Mandy tugged on her captured wrist.

"I'm fine." Tom held on tight.

"Your cattle aren't so fine, are they?" Mandy wrestled against his grip. It was hopeless to try and get him to let loose, but she was in the mood to fight with him, so she went on with it.

"Stand still." Tom jerked her forward.

"Let me go." She crashed into his rock-hard chest and nearly knocked the breath out of herself. "Not just my arm. Let me go to Denver."

His arm came around her waist, and they stopped arguing. Stopped wrestling.

"Tom, please." Mandy's fist opened and pressed against his shoulder. "I can't stand to think of all I'm costing you. I can't bear to think cowhands and lawmen might die trying to settle my troubles."

"No one's died."

"Yet. And now you've lost some animals." Mandy went on her tiptoes. She couldn't be this close to him and not want to be closer. "You might die. I survived it when Sidney died because I'd quit caring about him and I blamed him for so many of our troubles. I don't mean I wanted him dead. I just. . .what I felt wasn't the grief a wife should have for her husband. All of that had died over the years."

"Thank God it wasn't you." Tom bent down and kissed her.

"And what if—it was you—Tom?" She broke her words up between kisses.

"Would you grieve for me then, wife?" Tom's eyes flashed humor now, rather than the rage when he'd come in to tell her about the stampede.

"Terribly." She slid her free arm around his neck. "Forever."

Tom let go of her wrist and slid his arms around her waist. He lifted her clean off her feet in a way that always made her feel delicate and feminine. Truth be told, she didn't feel like either of those things very often.

"Please, I don't want to sit here and let the Cooters run our lives. I've done that for too long. I want to fight back."

"And you think you can do that with your gold?"

Nodding, Mandy said, "I've seen what people will do for gold, Tom. I think I can make life so hard for those feuding outlaws they'll quit the country and leave us in peace."

"I can make my own ranch secure, Mandy. You should trust me." Tom met her eyes with a solid, studying look.

"But your land is sprawled out enough that you can't hire enough men to cover it all."

"We can't just sit there at the ranch and wait for them to cause trouble, that's for sure." He had the temperament of a grizzly bear most of the time.

Mandy found that suited her. She really was fond of her cranky new husband. More than fond, honestly. "You won't let me go to the children, and as it happens, I agree with you. No sense leading these coyotes to them. But we have to do something, and that gold is like an itch I've been needing to scratch for a long time."

"But what are you planning to do with it? You can't put a bounty on a man's head unless he's wanted for something."

"I'll use it to get rid of them even if I've got to give it away. If I didn't have any gold, they'd never have been harassing me. I don't care what they say about Cooters sticking together."

"You're not seriously going to just haul it out of that bank in Denver and set it on the street and holler, 'Come and get it,' are you?"

"I've given it a lot of thought, and I need to give it just a little more. If nothing else, we'll use it to hire more hands."

"Bodyguards like Sidney hired?"

"No, tough men. Picked by you. Then we really could secure your range." Except no matter how tough those men were, the Cooters would do damage. Men would be hurt or killed because of this feud.

She just couldn't quite decide, but it had become like a burr under a saddle to think of that gold, and the facts she knew of it that no one else did. Somehow that gold meant safety to her.

Finally, with a single jerk of assent, he said, "All right. We'll go. I'm ready to do something to drive those varmints off my land."

Before another hour passed, they were in the saddle heading for Divide, to see the sheriff. "We need to be seen leaving Divide." Mandy urged her horse a little faster.

"So the Cooters will quit the country and come after us?"

"It'll get 'em away from your ranch and my children."

"*Our* ranch and *our* children."

Mandy looked at him and smiled.

"Just ride." Tom's growling went on, but Mandy decided it wasn't even really growling. Not when it came to her husband. This was just normal. When he really started growling, there'd be big trouble. "Wanting them to come after you is even more loco than wanting to ride to Denver and give away all your gold. You're as crazy as everyone said you were when you lived up there in that fortress."

Mandy came to a wider spot in the trail and pulled up for just a second so Tom's stallion could ride side-by-side. They each led a second horse. If they pushed hard, switched saddles, and rode long hours at a fast pace, it wasn't impossible for a rider to make a hundred miles a day. But that was on a good trail. There was nothing good about the route they were taking.

Her heart ached to think of how long she'd be away from her children. To think that maybe she'd never see them again.

And they weren't going to Denver either. Another of Sidney's lies. This one Mandy had maintained. She'd break that news to Tom a little later, just before she led him northwest of town instead of east. He was a bit too knowing of a man to fail to miss that little detail.

When they reached Divide, Mandy went to the general store. There were a few things to buy for the trip, but mostly she knew the Cooters seemed to have a knack for finding her. So, if she let it slip that she was riding out, that word would draw the Cooters toward her. That would protect the ranch and send the Cooters off in the wrong direction, toward Denver. Meantime she and Tom would be riding hard for Sidney's gold.

Mandy gathered the supplies while Tom left to talk with Marshal Coltrain. When he was out of sight, she ducked out the back door of the Bates' General Store and ran for the telegraph office. She needed to warn a few people, because if this went bad on her and she died, she needed someone to raise her children. Tom would probably do it. Belle Harden, too, but it wasn't their duty. Besides, she hadn't sent word to her family in so long it was heartbreaking.

Her days of protecting everyone by keeping them away from her were over. Not by her choice. Tom had dragged her out of her mountain hideout, and now she was forced to stand and fight, and Mandy was in the mood.

She'd find that gold and use it to buy harassment against the Cooters. Or an army of tough cowhands for Tom's ranch. Or, if that didn't work, she'd use the gold to lure those Cooters into a gunfight and have it out with them once and for all. She didn't care how many of them there were. She had lead enough and was savvy enough to win this fight even if it took her the rest of her life.

She was glad now that Tom had stopped her the other night. She knew that had been madness, that desire to slaughter those men. But to face them, to force them to come to her, to track them down and put an end to their stupid feud, that was something she could do and not give up her honor and pride. Killing wasn't anything she wanted to do, but she was done cowering, done hiding and letting them tell her how she had to live.

Done.

Now she'd fight back. They had no idea who they'd picked a fight with. She suspected that if they did know, they'd run like yellowbellied polecats.

No offense to polecats, which were pretty fearless critters.

Tom would be at her side, and that added to her courage. At the same time, she felt the terrible guilt of putting him in danger.

What a dreadful, life-wrecking burden of a wife the poor man had found for himself!

★ **Fifteen** **★**

Tom had rounded himself up a sweet little wife, and now he was riding out from his ranch for the first time in years.

Why, it was almost like going on vacation.

Tom had heard of such things, traveling here and there for pleasure, but he'd never taken a vacation before. Never really knew anyone who had.

True, his vacation might include a life-and-death battle with gun-wielding, back-shooting vermin, but a man couldn't ask for everything, now could he?

Smiling, Tom crossed Divide's dirt street from the general store to the sheriff's office. Zeb Coltrain's horse was tied to the hitching post out front. He opened the door and saw the sheriff, Merl Dean, and Zeb poring over Wanted posters.

Zeb glanced at Tom and picked up a poster that lay by itself on the desk. "We've found one. And I've sent out a bunch of wires. I got one back from Tennessee, someone who knows the family and is going to ask some questions to try and figure out what kind of people these Cooters are. Maybe they're a lawless bunch from way back. Maybe if they're wanted in other places, I can get lawmen interested in coming here and forming a posse and doing a roundup. If they've treated other people like they've done your wife and her children, chances are they're wanted. But I've only found one with a poster on him."

Tom took the poster. "This isn't Cord. This one's too old, and he's been around for too long." He read the name aloud. "Fergus Cooter, goes by the alias Reynolds. Wanted for murdering an Army Colonel and his wife. So he's a man that'll kill a woman. Probably came west running from the law. He looks like Cord, though, the dark hair and that white blaze. Gotta be kin."

"Never heard of him, neither as a Reynolds or a Cooter. I bet he's run afoul of the law since, but if he has, he's done it quiet. He's not a known man." Merl sighed and looked mournfully at the sizable stack of Wanted posters still to go through. "If we keep hunting, maybe we'll find more on him or some other of his family."

Merl got up and went for the coffeepot. "Want a cup?"

"Better not. I don't want to leave Mandy alone for long."

"These coyotes wouldn't come into town." Zeb accepted a cup of the black, steaming sludge that looked thick enough to float a horseshoe and hot enough to burn the skin off a man's gullet. "They're back-shooters. They'll waylay you on the trail instead."

Nodding, Tom said, "I reckon she's safe enough with Seth and Muriel in the general store, but no sense letting her wander around loose. That woman is always looking for an excuse to get that Winchester into action."

"What brings you to Divide?" Zeb sipped his coffee, grimaced, glared down at the offending cup, and then took another sip. "I thought you were gonna tighten the lookouts around your ranch and hole up. Give me a chance to catch these varmints."

Scowling, Tom considered denying the whole thing. Lying to a lawman. Better than admitting his wife had the bit in her teeth. "Mandy says she's tired of being a rabbit and she's turning wolf. She wants to strike out on the trail for Denver, find what's left of her husband's gold and do—I'm not sure what with it. She's a little vague on that, but she's sure blaming all her trouble on Sidney striking it rich."

"Is there a lot of gold she's aiming to get shut of?" Merl looked like he was willing to volunteer to take some of it.

"I saw that castle her loco husband built up high enough to scrape the sky. I wonder if there's *any* of that gold left. It had to cost a fortune. And I heard he had people come from back East, real knowing men, who built that. Took the better part of two years to finish it. No man has enough gold to throw it away like that. I'm not sure if I hope we'll ride into her Denver bank and find the money's gone or not. Will she be relieved or disappointed?"

"If the gold is gone, you're gonna have a tough time convincing the Cooters of that."

"Gray was a secretive man," Merl said. "I heard he dug until he'd found every bit of that gold he struck, then bought a string of horses and loaded them, right down to the last bit of dust, and slipped away alone. No men riding guard duty back then because he wasn't admitting yet that he struck it rich. He found himself the sturdiest vault in Denver. Then he locked his gold up without telling anyone exactly where, paid for a lot of big things in Denver, then came home with a pair of bodyguards and a lot of fancy plans, but he didn't have to ride back with so much as a speck of gold dust to be stolen. Had him some cash but no gold."

"Then he built that monument to himself." Tom shook his head. "You should see that castle. Gray stone like something you'd read in a book. It even has a tower."

"Rich folks get notional about their money," Zeb said. "And I reckon it's theirs to do with as they want."

But Sidney hadn't cared much what Mandy wanted. To Tom's way of thinking, that gold was as much hers as his. She should have had a say. "That house was dark inside. A couple of kerosene lanterns to light the whole thing. I don't think Mandy could get to town to buy more or chop the wood to keep fire going in the fireplaces. She and the three children all slept in one bedroom together. She said it was mostly because none of them wanted to sleep alone in that spooky, cold place."

"I'm surprised she didn't make you pack a string of horses to bring all her folderol down with her." Merl began cleaning his fingernails with his knife.

"Mandy didn't even bring a change of clothes. She brought diapers and her Winchester and the two horses Sidney bought from me back a few years. That's it. She wanted no part of it." Tom turned to Zeb. "So you've heard nothing from your telegrams back East about the Cooters?"

"I've gotten one wire saying they're tracking down some answers. They think this grandfather who started that whole family code of loyalty is still alive. They're going to ask him some questions. They'll let me know more when they do."

"Will talking to the old man make it worse?" Tom had decided to marry Mandy, and nothing would have stopped him. But she'd sure been right when she said trouble came riding with her. "Will he send more Cooters out here to buy into the fight?"

"Near as I can tell, things can't get any worse. The marshals I contacted have heard of this feud. The word is out for Cooters to come a-runnin' and fight for their family, and they've been doing it already for more than a year. A lot of them Cooters are missing. There's a reason they think Lady Gray is a witch. Men get swallowed up when they go after her."

"So how many Cooters are there?" Tom felt tired thinking of how long this fight could last. Would they have to wipe out the whole family before they could have peace?

"I'm just not sure. The answers aren't in yet. I've been out every day scouting the land around your cabin, and I've got a glimpse of a track here and there. I haven't caught up with the Cooters, though. Four of 'em from what I can see. I've got marshals riding in so we can cover more land. We'll get 'em, Tom. Just let me do my job."

"Well, we're trying to take the trouble with us when we ride, but hoping to leave it far enough behind that we draw the Cooters off without getting under their gun sights. Keep your eyes open, and if you see any sign of these coyotes on our trail, toss a loop on them for me." Tom adjusted his Stetson as he strode toward the door. "Now I'd better go keep watch on my wife."

★

Luther read the telegraph with grim satisfaction. Mandy was finally doing the right thing. And she'd paid for enough words to tell him she'd send a wire to her folks, too. Good.

It was too many miles into Yellowstone to get Buff, though he'd love to have his old friend at his side. He'd love even more to have Buff's tough, trail-savvy wife. And if he could get to Buff, he could get to Sally, and then they'd really be able to bring a fight to those back-shooting Cooters.

But Luther wasn't taking any side trips. He'd been hunting and trapping around Helena ever since Mandy had forbidden him to come and stay with her. Having a broken leg that was stubborn healing had helped keep him away.

But no more. He was in good shape again, and he was done listening to the wishes of a little girl, no matter how fast she was with a rifle.

He wasn't waiting for Clay either. He knew Clay would come, but not in time. And Luther didn't mean to let Mandy stand alone, not even with Tom Linscott at her side. Luther knew Tom Linscott just a bit. The man's reputation was solid.

If Mandy'd had the sense to marry a rancher to begin with instead of a greenhorn sidewinder, none of this mess would have happened. He intended to tell her that, too, but he'd soften it so she wouldn't cry or nothing.

The wire she'd sent included instructions for him to head for Divide, Montana.

Saddling his horse and packing supplies took ten minutes. He was moving down on the trail to Divide at a gallop in eleven. Too bad he couldn't talk to Buff.

★

Mandy dashed up the back steps of Bates' General Store and rushed inside, through what looked like a storeroom. She ran down a hallway to the front of the store, slammed into a cracker barrel, caught it before it tipped over, and earned herself a raised eyebrow from the whipcord-lean lady minding the place. "So"—she had to gasp for breath before she could go on—"is my order ready?"

"Yep. I'm Muriel Bates. So, you married Tom Linscott?"

Between breaths, Mandy said, "Yes."

"The man has a hot temper. I'd make it clear right from the start I wasn't gonna put up with it."

"I appreciate the advice, Muriel. I have a temper myself, so I have no room to complain. You know I'm Lady Gray. I've heard that's what I'm called." Leaving a trail was part of Mandy's plan. And this oughta do it.

Gray brows arched over a deeply lined forehead. "I've most certainly heard of you. That there was a—a—"

Mandy could only imagine what this plain-spoken woman was thinking. It seemed likely that she'd say most things that came to mind. "A witch? I live in a castle? My land is haunted?"

"That about sums it up."

"I did live in a castle, I suppose. My first husband found gold and seemed to think if he lived in a castle on a mountaintop that'd make him a king."

Muriel snorted.

Mandy couldn't help liking her. She looked out the front

200

window and saw Tom striding across the street from the sheriff's office. She almost had her breathing under control now. A quick swipe mopped sweat off her brow, but it was a hot day. Sweat could be caused by something other than running.

"So you don't want your husband to know you went down to the telegraph office?"

Swallowing hard, Mandy looked into the woman's eyes. "Uh. . .no, I'd just as soon he didn't, but I'm not sneaking to put something past him. I sent away for help. Figured his pride might get in the way if I asked permission, so I did it behind his back. I'm planning on telling him when we're a few miles down the trail to. . .Denver."

"Denver's where you're headed?" Muriel's skeptical tone told Mandy she'd caught the hesitation.

"Yep." Mandy reached for the loaded saddlebags Muriel had stuffed with goods.

"I've known Tom Linscott a lot longer than I've known you. Why would I lie for a witch?"

Mandy looked straight into Muriel's eyes for far too long. Then a grin snuck onto Mandy's face. "Because us women have to stick together?" Sort of like the Cooters, only way better.

Tom shoved open the door.

Muriel grinned back. "Good a reason as any, I reckon."

"Reason for what?" Tom walked over and lifted the saddlebags out of Mandy's hands.

"We were talking about female things, Tom. You really want to know?" Muriel crossed her arms.

Mandy hoped sneaking wasn't a female thing. She'd like to think men did their share.

"No, good grief, no. I don't want to hear it." Tom shook his head almost desperately and turned to Mandy. "Let's go. We're burning daylight."

Running her hand over her dress pocket to make sure the

directions Sidney had left her were still there, Mandy nodded to Muriel. "I'll be a good wife to him, Muriel. If I don't get him killed, that is."

Muriel closed her eyes as if she were exhausted. "Enjoy the ride to. . .Denver."

★

"I found an idler in town willing to make some money. He nosed around real quiet-like to see if anyone knows much about Linscott." Fergus eased himself down by the fire.

Cord was sick to death of standing watch on that ranch. They didn't dare get closer, within rifle range. Linscott's hands were too savvy. They'd run off a herd of beeves to see if that would clear the lookouts and draw off the men who stayed around the ranch house, but Linscott seemed to have enough hands to always keep a solid guard posted and track down stampeding cattle.

"Do you have to ride in again tomorrow to talk to him?" Cord decided he'd be the one who'd ride in. He needed to do something or go crazy.

"Nope." Fergus took a long pull on a bottle of whiskey, then corked it and tossed it across the fire to J.D., who was practically licking his lips at the sight of liquor.

"Take one long drink, and then we're hitting the trail." Fergus had a smug smile on his face that made Cord's heart beat faster.

"You found something?"

"Tom Linscott and Lady Gray hit the trail today. . .for Denver."

Surging to his feet, Cord said, "Then why are we sitting here? Let's ride."

"We're sitting here, little brother, because I trailed 'em. The man in town pointed to the trail they took, and I could make out the hooves of those big black thoroughbreds easy as if someone were holding up an arrow. And I saw their trail head northwest."

"Northwest?"

"Yep. They should be coming up the trail straight toward us. I rode hard to beat them here. We've got plenty of time to get set up. Then we finish this."

Kill a woman.

Cord didn't like it much. But Grandpappy wanted them to stick together, and that woman had killed a Cooter.

"The man also said she'd married Tom Linscott."

Cord froze. "So Linscott has to die, too?" Tom Linscott was a salty man with a lot of friends. One thing to hunt a lone man who lived like a hermit on the mountaintop. Another thing to finish his wife who had killed one of their own and who kept to herself. Cord didn't like it, but it was a blood oath, and he couldn't turn away.

But Linscott was an established rancher. Attacking Linscott could bring a whole load of trouble right down on their heads. But so what? The feud was well known, and Linscott had bought in knowing he'd joined the wrong side.

"Chances are we'd have had to kill Linscott anyway if he was riding with her," Dugger said, taking his turn with the whiskey bottle and drinking half a pint in a few gulps.

"But what if we don't get him?" J.D. asked. "He'll come after any man who kills his wife. Once Linscott's in this, we'll be fighting tough men who'll keep coming."

"We'd better be sure to get him when we get her, that's all." Cord thought he sounded confident, but it wasn't coming from his belly. This whole feud was making him sick. He'd been earning an honest living riding for Lord Gray. He'd had ambitions. He'd wanted to get his hands on Gray's gold somehow. But until he'd made that move on Lady Gray, he'd been earning the best honest wage of his life.

It had eaten at him that he rode for a man he considered a fool. Lazy, leaving his security to others, ignoring that beautiful woman and those young'uns to go to Helena and Denver and

Ogden to flash money around and spend time with dance hall girls. Building himself a mansion somewhere no one could see it, of all stupid things. Then leaving the house he'd spent a fortune on to stay in a hotel room in a frontier town for weeks at a time.

Sidney'd had everything, and Cord wanted it. All of it, right down to the three children. And somehow Cord had thought he'd find a way to end up with what Lord Gray had. If watching Gray act like a king had given Cord a little taste for acting the same, the only way Cord could satisfy that taste was to take it.

He'd goaded these others and fed them with family pride and Grandpappy's rules. Fergus had never even heard of the family rules, and he'd said, since he heard, that Curly had been killed in a shooting. Cord knew if he pushed it, Fergus would agree to go chasing off after whoever had killed their other brother. But Cord had enough to do. And chasing after Lady Gray made sense, when there was a fortune in gold at the end of the chase.

Cord had always planned to get Lady Gray under his gun sometime and, rather than kill her, make her an offer of marriage she couldn't refuse on pain of death. She was a strong woman, and Cord doubted she'd take him over death if it was only her. But for her children, she'd marry him. She'd put herself at his mercy to save them.

Yes, he'd planned it all. Even down to how he'd enjoy crushing that arrogance in her. Sidney had it, too, but it was phony, built on a foundation of gold and foolishness. But Lady Gray carried herself like true royalty. And Cord had seen how easy she was with that rifle. He'd never seen her fire it until that day at Linscott's cabin. She was pure greased lightning with that thing. But he'd always seen she was comfortable with that fire iron across her back.

The first thing he'd do was separate her from that Winchester. Then he'd teach her to say, "Yes, Cord. Right away, Cord." He'd teach her with his belt if he had to. Many's the time he'd had brutal imaginings about humbling that woman.

But all these daydreams faded with Linscott in the game. They'd have to kill them both because both would fight to the death without the children to use as leverage. And with Mandy and Linscott fighting side-by-side, the two of them went a long way toward evening the odds a bit.

Linscott had to die fast under a hail of bullets. And once he was dead, there'd be trouble because he wasn't a man whose death would be ignored, even snickered at like Lord Gray's had been.

For the first time, as Cord sat there feeling all his plotting and planning unravel, he really felt that thirst Grandpappy had bred in him—thirst for family pride, thirst for his name Couturiaux from the Old Country. The castle, Gray Towers, had been sealed off forever. The gold was locked away somewhere, and only Lady Gray could get it.

Lady Gray—Mandy, Cord knew her name well enough—was going to die on this trail, right here tonight under the Cooters' guns. They'd have to kill her hard and fast to have any hope of defeating her. And when that happened, she'd take the secret of that gold to her grave.

Years spent in scheming and Cord had nothing left but pride. He looked at Fergus and J.D. and Dugger, a sad lot, but Cooters to the bone. Couturiauxs right to that flash of white hair.

Fine, if this was all he had, then he'd fight for the family, fight for the brand. He pulled his six-gun from his holster and checked the load, and then he turned to Fergus. "What trail will they be using?"

Fergus rose from the fire with a flare of evil in his eyes. "I'll show you, and we can scout out a place to lie in wait and finish this."

Like back-shooting coyotes. Could a man take pride in that?

"Then we can head for town and get more whiskey," J.D. added eagerly as he drained the bottle.

It was all Cordell Couturiaux had.

Sixteen

W hat do you mean we're not going to Denver?" Tom followed his wife off the trail trying to catch her. He'd yelled that she'd taken a wrong turn.

She'd laughed. The little spitfire had laughed at him. Then she'd taken off to the north, through a dense stand of woods that might well stretch all the way to the Idaho border and beyond.

"Catch me, and I'll tell you all about it." Mandy looked back with a smile on her face that made Tom lean low on his horse's neck and urge it forward on the uneven ground, bent on catching himself a wife—for the second time this week.

He caught her all right and persuaded her to bed down for the night before the sun had even set. There was no talk of maps nor gold nor Denver. There was only Tom with the woman he'd wanted in his arms for five years.

Now he had her. He'd stormed through all her objections and taken her for his own, figuring himself as the sensible one of them. Smiling, he lowered her to their bedroll and let every minute of that frustrated waiting show in his kiss and his touch.

One of the very best things he liked about his wife was she seemed to have a few years of frustration of her own to relieve.

Much later, they sat by the crackling campfire in the lowering sun, Mandy in his arms, sitting between his legs, resting her back against his chest while he held her tight. "We're gonna have us a good life, Mandy girl."

And a few more children if Tom had anything to say about it.

She looked up over her shoulder with a beautiful, private smile that made Tom think of those long, lonely five years again.

Her endless white blond hair was loose and messy, raining over Tom's arms and her shoulders. It drooped over one eye, but he could see enough. She was relaxed and at peace for the moment. That look of fear and regret that always, always shadowed her face was missing right now, and Tom wished he could figure out a way to make it stay gone forever. She'd lived with fear and regret for long enough.

He wrapped one arm tight around her middle to pull her even closer, then smoothed her hair back and unwound it from his arms and her shoulders. He brushed it off her forehead. His hands were coarse and awkward, too rough for someone so beautiful, but he couldn't quit touching her. Watching the shining strands of her hair slide through his hands, he couldn't remember much in his life that was more perfect than this moment.

"I haven't had much family in a lot of years, Mandy. Having you and the young'uns is going to make my house a home."

"What about Abby, your sister?"

Tom hated to think of all his sister had been through. "I've only really known her for a few years."

Mandy twisted around to look at him. "How can you not know your sister?"

Tom wanted an excuse to keep holding her, so he decided to talk. "Abby came west with my family years ago. She was still really young."

"You didn't come?"

Shaking his head, Tom went back to caressing Mandy's hair.

He needed to learn to braid so he had a chance to touch her more. "Nope. I was a full-grown man of sixteen years. When my folks decided to go west on a wagon train, I stayed behind. I had a job and a girl and my future all laid out in front of me."

Mandy sat up straight and frowned over her shoulder. "You've been married before?"

Mandy obviously didn't like to think he'd had a wife. All things considered, this little woman had a lot of nerve to object to the nonsense in Tom's past.

"Never married her. But I was determined to when my family moved away, so I told them good-bye. I was headstrong and so sure I was all grown up."

"I suppose most sixteen-year-olds are sure." She subsided back into his arms, watching the crackling fire.

My folks had been gone about a year, and I missed them so bad, but I had my girl and my pride. I was getting by."

"What happened to her?" Mandy's hands rested on his thighs, her fingers flexed as if she were comforting him.

"I lost everything. The girl I gave my family up for found herself a rich man, leastways rich compared to me. And since I was working in her father's store, I got fired when she got herself engaged to another man."

"I'm sorry. I know how it hurts to have your dreams die, even if those dreams aren't very sensible. I was madly in love with Sidney when I married him. It took me a while learning that I didn't even really know the man."

"Yep, it hurt." Shaking his head, he added, "I was so young. I really don't blame her for picking someone else. I had no hope of caring for a wife and supporting children on the salary I was earning. I suppose I had it in my head that her pa would let me be a partner in the store, but she'd have been crazy to marry me."

He could still remember the feeling of his heart breaking in two. He'd covered it with anger and told himself he didn't really want her, but she'd torn down everything he saw for his future with a few careless words.

"She'd have been lucky to marry you, Tom. Store clerk or rancher, whatever you turned your hand to, you'd do well. You'd take good care of a wife and children."

Tom kissed her neck, just for the kindness in her voice. He could have used that kindness back then. He'd been devastated.

His arms tightened on her waist so she was pulled snug against him. Mandy lay her head back on his chest and hugged his hands wrapped around her belly. He opened one hand to lay on her stomach and wondered if maybe he'd managed to get a child of his own started with his wife. The idea was so appealing he couldn't talk for a moment.

What if she wasn't expecting yet? Tom decided he needed to do more to make sure she was. He was ready to turn her to him when she started talking again.

"So after things ended with your girl and your job, what did you do?"

He was no longer in the mood to talk about his childhood, but he found himself in the mood to be very obliging to his wife right now. "I got another job for a while, but finally pride became a lonely companion. I found a wagon train headed west and set out to throw in ranching with my family."

"But you said you haven't had much family in years."

"When I got out here, they were dead." Tom found himself in need of swallowing before he could go on.

Mandy made a sound of such pure sympathy that for a minute, Tom had a struggle to hold back tears. And that would be so embarrassing that the horror of it settled him down. "A fever had gone through and killed a lot of people, my family included. I hadn't been told. They lived a long way out from town and didn't really know anyone, so no one ever visited to see they'd died. I got here, and there were records of their claim, so I found where they'd homesteaded. I rode up there thinking they'd be so excited to see me, and I was crazy lonely for them."

The silence stretched as Tom remembered that ramshackle cabin. In bad shape because no one had done a thing to it in over a year. "I found an empty cabin. Then I found graves." Tom had thought that girl had broken his heart, but Tom knew as he stood there over those windswept graves what true sadness was. "It's the same place I live."

"Tom, I'm so sorry. But Abby was alive."

"Abby was gone. I—" His voice quit working. This went beyond grief to guilt and regret that was almost unbearable. He never let himself think about it. "I thought she'd died, too. I just assumed she had."

Mandy sat up and turned fully to face him, drawing her legs beneath her until she was next thing to kneeling between his legs. "You assumed? But where was she then?"

"A band of Flathead Indians had found her alone in the cabin, the rest of the family dead. They took her in. I didn't hear from her until just a few years ago."

"She lived with the Indians all those years?"

Nodding, Tom said, "They were good to her. She's very loyal to them. Don't act like you feel sorry for her when you see her next time because she'll pull that wicked knife and start sharpening it right in front of your eyes."

Mandy laughed. "Sorry, I'm sure it's not funny to you."

"It's just something else I did wrong. I should have been there to help."

"And died of the fever yourself?" Mandy met his eyes.

"I might have lived. Abby did."

Gently his pretty wife rose to her knees and wrapped her arms around his neck. "I'm glad you're here."

All Tom could think of for the next hour was that he was very glad he was here, too.

Finally, long after the flickering flames of their fire had turned to glowing red coals, it was time to go back to what he'd been going to ask before they'd started talking about Abby. "Why didn't you trust me with Sidney's map from the first?" He shouldn't ask when they were so content and relaxed, in harmony for once, but it had to be spoken of sometime, and tomorrow would be a long hard-riding day.

"I've always trusted you, Tom. Too much when it was the wrong thing to do. When I was a married woman."

He gathered her wildly tousled hair in one fisted hand and eased it over her shoulder. "That's not real trust. Not the kind where we talk about whatever's on our minds."

"I begged you to stay with me when Jarrod was being born. That's trust."

"You were alone with two toddlers and terrified. You'd have begged a grizzly bear if that was all the help that was to be had."

"Probably right." Mandy flashed her white teeth at him.

He was glad he hadn't gotten her stirred up and mad yet. "And yes, for anything to have happened between us back then would have been wrong. I'm not asking you why you didn't share all your secrets with me back then. But I dragged you out of that stupid castle days ago. You didn't tell me about the map until you turned off the trail a couple of hours ago. Why?"

Mandy reached her long, graceful neck up and kissed him on the side of his jaw. He was so much taller than she was, so much bigger all over. He should have worried about the delicate little lady. But she was strong. Tom caught himself hustling to keep up with her and rarely had a spare second to think of her as fragile.

He turned his head and met that kiss with his own and almost let her distract him from their little problem about trust. Almost.

He eased back and lifted one of her hands to his lips. He noticed the callus on her index finger and kissed it with special attention. It was part of what made her the most interesting woman he'd ever known.

Pulling her to a sitting position, he moved them around so the bit of glowing light made her more visible. With the starlight and his excellent night vision, he could see her well enough. "Braid your hair for me. Let me watch."

Her brow furrowed. "What?"

"You heard me." He picked up her hair, hanging nearly to her waist down along her left arm. "I want to watch, learn how to do it."

Their eyes held. More passed between them than seemed possible without words. Finally she nodded and picked up her hair. "Separate it into three parts. Like this." She demonstrated.

He helped, making it much harder but getting a feel for it before long. He'd done some braiding, he realized. Turning strips of bark into sturdy whips. Turning hemp into rope. He hadn't done it for a while, but it came back.

They worked, their hands tangled up together. Mandy watching as her braid shaped up.

"It wasn't because I didn't trust you, Tom. I just wasn't alone enough with you. I didn't want to take a chance on anyone else hearing what I had planned. I've gotten in the habit of"—she took a quick peek at him—"feeling watched, pursued. In that castle I felt like the walls had eyes and ears. It was spooky. And the Shoshone people who lived near, well, they never eavesdropped, but they were so quiet. They came and left a haunch of elk or a buffalo hide or something like that quite often. I loved them, but it added to the eerie feeling."

"So you really felt like someone was hanging around while we were alone in the house?" Tom didn't quite believe that. His house was really open. There was nowhere to hide.

"Maybe, just because it's an old habit to always feel that way. And besides, I didn't really know I was going to get my gold until yesterday. Until then I was trying only to figure out how to make it safe for the children. That day I went after the Cooter clan I could only think that I was tired of being hunted. I was ready to be the hunter. When you stopped me from that, I didn't know how else to hunt. Then I thought of the gold. I'm going to use that money for something worthwhile. Finally. I'm going to use every cent of it to buy peace."

"The real reason you didn't tell me was because you didn't think I'd go. You had your hands real full convincing me to ride to Denver. You were afraid I'd never agree to follow Sidney's map with you."

Mandy shrugged. "My hands have been real full with you."

Tom almost laughed, which would have let his stubborn little wife off the hook. "We should have given the law more time. Let the marshal work."

"I need to get to my children, Tom. They won't understand any of this. I know Belle Harden well enough that I trust her to take care of them and comfort them. But letting them stay in her care is cruel. I hate it. I—"

"You're not cruel." Tom twisted the heavy rope of her hair around his fist twice and drew her face close using the silken length. "You're smart and tough and too kindhearted for your own good. We're leaving them there because that's what's best for *my* children."

"But I need to be there. They won't understand where I've gone. They'll think I—"

He shut her up the only way that had proved to work a bit well.

And later, because they'd made such a mess of it, she had to teach him how to braid her hair all over again.

★

"Wise Sister!" Sally shouted as she strode toward the tent Buff

213

and Wise Sister lived in when they were following Sally and Logan around.

Wise Sister pushed back the flap almost immediately. Her serene eyes took in everything. The loaded horses. Sally's cowboy clothes. Logan's harassed expression.

"We'll come."

"I've got to see to Mandy." Sally looked past Wise Sister to see Buff reach for his saddlebags and begin shoving provisions in.

"Ten minutes." Wise Sister dropped the flap. It hadn't been a request.

Sally turned to Logan, fuming. "They can catch us. Let's go."

Buff came out before Sally had finished speaking, carrying two saddles. He headed for the makeshift corral behind their tent. He looked over his shoulder. "Help me." Another order.

But it kept Sally busy for the few minutes it took Wise Sister and Buff to get ready to go on a trail ride that could take weeks. It was possible they wouldn't get back to Yellowstone this season, and if that happened they'd lose everything they'd left behind. It was even possible they might die in a feud that had nothing to do with them.

Neither of them hesitated a second.

As they swung up on horseback, Buff said, "Luther know you're going?"

"Nope, no way to tell him. I heard he was trapping up closer to Mandy. No way to even send him a wire."

"He'll know." Wise Sister set a brisk pace as if she and Buff had been fighting the need to make this trip for a while. She only knew Mandy a bit, but it was Wise Sister's village that had protected Mandy all this time. The Shoshone woman never went anywhere and never seemed to have company, but somehow, if anyone had news about Mandy, it was her. If Wise Sister said Luther would know, Sally believed her.

Sally fell in behind Wise Sister, determined to push hard all the way to Mandy's fortress. She'd lead this group if they didn't move fast enough to suit her. But she could never quite catch up, which made Sally wonder if Wise Sister had reason to hurry beyond Sally's sudden fear.

Sally's hand crept to her belly.

God, have mercy on us all. God, have mercy on my baby. God, have mercy.

★ Seventeen ★

It got chilly in the Rocky Mountains at night, even in August. Mandy was only mildly surprised to wake up and find a dusting of snow covering the bedroll she shared with Tom.

It was warm as toast under the wool blankets, but an itch between Mandy's shoulder blades told her she needed to be moving. They should have ridden longer last night. Gritting her teeth against the cold, she shoved back the covers in the gray light of pre-dawn.

"Hey!" Tom woke up with a jerk as a layer of snow drifted down onto his bare chest. Mandy grinned at him as she dressed with quick, efficient movements. By the time she had a coffeepot in place, Tom had the bedroll bundled and was saddling the first horse.

"Why did I ever think marrying a city boy was a good idea?" Mandy watched Tom do all the things a man needed to do to get on the trail.

He turned to her and quirked a smile. "I reckon you needed to get up here to these mountains somehow."

"Tough way to travel, with Sidney in tow."

"Warm up some of that jerky, too. Something hot will taste

good this morning, and you can do that right quick."

"Okay, but I want to be on the trail within a half hour. The sun will be up past the horizon by then."

The dusk was already light enough that they could be traveling. Mandy knew they were lingering, which made no sense. Urgency had been riding her hard ever since they'd set out from Divide.

Turning back, she crouched beside the fire, grateful for her leather riding skirt and long sleeves. Even her ugly gray cloak. She needed to buy something in a different color, and if she lived through these next few days, she'd do it.

She'd be hot later in the day and wish for lighter clothes. She could shed the cloak, but the leather skirt and long sleeves were all she had. A woman couldn't have everything.

The goad to hurry reared up as she pulled a cast-iron skillet out of Tom's pack and tossed a few pieces of the tough jerky on to heat. It would only take a minute or two to warm it up. Then they'd chew on it while they moved down the trail.

★

"I smell smoke, Cord." Dugger pulled his horse so abruptly to a halt Cord almost collided with him.

Cord smelled it, too, now that Dugger mentioned it. Dugger might be childlike in his head, but he had better sense in the woods than any of them.

The four of them left the trail, Fergus and Cord uphill, J.D. and Dugger downhill.

Cord and Fergus eased along. The smell of smoke became stronger. Then Cord heard the crackling of flames.

Cord came to a rock wall so rugged it was tempting to just forget getting over it. But if Cord's nose told him right, that fire was set up right in front of these rocks. If Cord could get above whoever had that campfire, he could pick them off like ducks frozen on a pond. He gestured to Fergus that he was leaving his horse to climb up.

"Got it." Fergus's whisper was softer than a breath of wind. He pointed at a path that took him around the rocks, then caught Cord's horse's reins and faded back into the woods.

Cord inched his way up a pile of rounded stones that looked like a giant had been stacking massive marbles. Trees grew here and there, seemingly out of solid rock. He raised himself, silent as a ghost, to the top of the rocks, swept his Stetson off, and eased forward, an inch at a time, to see who was below him. Even if it wasn't their quarry, if the travelers had good horses and guns, it would be worth the taking.

"Let's saddle up."

The female voice froze Cord in his tracks. Whoever it was stood directly below him. But what other woman could it be than Lady Gray? A trickle of cold sweat ran down Cord's backbone as he thought of that witch woman loosing her Winchester on him.

Tightening his hands on his own gun, he knew his first shot had to take her down and the second had to finish Linscott. Even as he crouched behind the cover of rocks in the dim morning light, Cord felt like things weren't quite stacked enough in his favor.

He saw a space where two rocks were heaped together so there was an eyehole about three inches across at most, big enough for a rifle and for him to draw a bead. The opening was at the bottom of a rock. That was as safe as a man could be.

He slid his gun onto the lip of that little hole and rose up from his crouch to get a dead shot at his target. The gun was still angled upward, but as he rose the muzzle lowered and lowered, and there she was.

He remembered that witch woman all right. He'd had his hands on her once, just once. And she'd backed him off, insulted him. Now she crouched by a pack, shoving two tin cups into it. He wanted to own her. But that wasn't going to be possible, so he'd do what he had to do. His gun came lower, and he slid it forward just enough to clear the rock.

Cord smiled.

Mrs. Gray rose from her crouch to make the middle of her back an even more perfect target.

Cord smiled and leveled his weapon just slightly.

A pebble rolled from where the gun was braced.

He pulled the trigger.

★

Mandy dove sideways at the sound of that rolling stone. A gun exploded into the last of their dying campfire and sprayed cinder and ash into the air. It would have slammed into the back of her head if she hadn't moved.

Her gun was in action before she'd hit the ground, and she twisted to land on her back. Her blood turned cold and flowed like molasses in January.

Mandy spotted the exact direction where the shooting came from. She fired. A cry from that circle told her she'd hit her mark.

Firing again, she levered bullets into the chamber with a hard, whipping turn of her hand, twirling the rifle, firing, twirling, firing. Moving, she put trees and stone between her and the attacker, shooting, always shooting.

The rifle protruding fired again, but wildly. Overhead leaves shredded, hit by the erratic bullets. Then the gun muzzle was gone and silent.

In a fraction of a second that seemed like hours, she saw Tom bring his gun up and aim away from where the bullets had originated. Her eyes followed the direction he looked, and she saw two gunmen, running and dodging forward. Mandy fired at the nearest one. She had plenty of time to pick, to see which one had the best aim at Tom, the best chance of making a hit. Her bullet slammed into his gut. The gunman cried out and went down under her withering fire. His hat toppled off, and Mandy saw the white slash of hair at his temple.

Cooters.

But she'd known that already. She turned to the other man, leveled, and fired.

Tom was shooting and weaving to put trees between him and the second shooter.

A bullet from another direction spit up rock and dirt near Mandy's feet. She wheeled and fired. That gunman staggered back, and his shot went wide.

Mandy saw it all, as if the bullet inched along. This fourth man's wild shot lodged into his own kin. A Cooter killing another Cooter. She hoped they declared a feud against each other.

She fired again, and the fourth man was gone, running. She'd winged him, but it wasn't a fatal hit. Unless the bullet got septic and killed him later.

With a quick glance she saw the two gunmen down. Dead most likely. One killed by her. All she felt was icy calm.

Two had run off. She raced after them. Something hit her hard in the back. Bringing her gun around, suddenly it was swept out of her hands.

"Mandy, it's me."

Mandy made a grab for her rifle.

Tom flipped her onto her back and held her to the ground with his full weight stretched out on top of her. "Stop. They're gone."

"I can get them." Her voice sounded unnatural, guttural and savage and distant, like it came from miles away. The woods were vivid. She was aware of each leaf that fluttered in the wind. She heard the receding footsteps of two men. Both wounded, she was sure. Her blood moved like sleet in her veins as she took in every sight, sound, scent, touch, and taste. She felt all of that, but no remorse, no regret, no weight of the sin of killing.

Mandy knew she had it in her to be a monster. "We need to end this, Tom."

His weight made struggling a waste of time.

She finally gave up and let herself go limp beneath him, but inside she was still coiled like a rattler. Her heart pounded until she felt like her whole body vibrated with it. She smelled the sulfur from the gunfire, the ashes from the camp. The blood. Tom's shirt pressed on her, and in her heightened state of awareness the coarse fabric was like sandpaper under her fingers.

"You're not going after them." He sounded wrong—strange mix of fury and tenderness—when what he ought to sound like was loathing. He knew what he'd married now. "You're not running blind into those woods."

"Blind?" Mandy laughed a ragged, vicious sound she didn't understand. "I can see everything. I swear I could see through stone. What I can't see I can hear and smell."

As he held her, her eyes finally focused, not on the whole world and every detail in it, but on Tom. He was staring at her, willing her to calm down and come back to him from wherever she went when the cold-blooded murderer took over.

"Are you all right now?"

Mandy managed to nod her head. She noticed that Tom didn't let her up. The man was starting to know her.

Suddenly, Tom's head came up. "One of them's riding away but not both." He leapt to his feet, shoved her rifle at her, and raced into the woods.

Amazed he'd given back the Winchester, Mandy was on her feet running, studying the woods. Tom was fast enough that he was kneeling by a fallen man when she caught up.

The man struggled, but one arm wasn't working, and blood poured, sapping his strength. Galloping hooves faded in the distance.

Tom tossed a rifle one way and a six-gun the other.

Mandy was on her knees across from Tom just as her husband relieved the man of a skinning knife. Another Cooter, the white thatch of hair, the same glowering face, though pale. The man's arm was bleeding fast.

Tom jerked the Cooter's kerchief off his neck and tied it tight around his arm, with no regard to gentleness. "I know a U.S. Marshal who'd like to ask you some questions."

"This isn't over." The man gasped with pain as Tom knotted the kerchief. His face went gray; sweat flowed off his brow. His eyes flickered shut, but he kept talking. "Cooters will keep coming until you're all dead. We stick together."

"Real family loyalty." Tom gave the kerchief one last tug, and the bleeding slowed to a trickle. "Your kin didn't even stay to boost you on your horse. He just rode off and left you. Whoever that was is a coward, just like the rest of you."

Tom stood and jerked the man to his feet. Mandy saw the horse tied nearby and went to lead it over. Her fingers itched to do something evil to the man, but she didn't. Her sanity had returned, and she was close to normal again. As close as she got.

But she had to goad the man somehow. "Did you notice that you killed one of your own? Maybe the Cooter clan will leave me alone and start hunting you." She positioned the horse to stand beside the Cooter.

Mandy thought of the other men dead. One of them was her doing. No one could deny that. The cold in her blood receded, and guilt washed through her heart straight to her soul.

God, what is wrong with me? Protect me from what lives inside me, Lord. Protect me. Protect me. Please.

Tom was strong enough he tossed the outlaw onto his saddle. Then he bound the man's hands to the pommel and began leading the horse back to the clearing.

"Hunt to the downhill side of our camp for the other horses, Mandy."

Mandy wasn't sure if she was honored by the respectful way Tom gave her a job and expected her to do it or annoyed because he was giving her the job that kept her away from their prisoner, as if he wasn't sure whether she'd go berserk and kill this man, too.

She was pretty sure she wouldn't, but just in case, she headed for the horses.

"I'll get the other two ready to move and finish packing our gear. We'll head back to Divide, leave these men for the sheriff and marshal, and get on with our trip to..." Tom glanced at the sullen man clinging to his horseback and spoke carefully. "To wherever you say we need to go."

★

Cord felt that witch woman taking aim at the dead center of his back. He felt her tightening her finger on the trigger. Felt a bullet seconds away from slamming into his spine.

He drove his horse with a vicious continual goad of his spurs. He'd seen Fergus go down and knew J.D. and Dugger were down and dead. All three of them killed by that woman and her wild, whirling gun.

Reaching up with a shaking hand, he found the slits on his face and blood pouring down. His eye was already swelling shut.

Kicking his horse brutally, he rode and rode until his horse stumbled on a talus slide and went down hard. Cord flew over the horse's head and landed flat on his belly. He slid, twisting his body, clawing at his six-gun to aim at...nothing.

Seconds passed. No one came.

Waiting, waiting, knowing she was coming. His hands shook. The muzzle of the gun wavered.

He'd *never* seen anyone handle a rifle like that. He trembled, smashed into the dirt and rock, and waited for her to come roaring out of the woods, that witch woman with her whirling guns and deadly accurate bullets. The noise and the sulfuric smoke made him think of the afterlife and how Hades would be. The memory of how she looked grew until she was magic, pure deadly black magic.

She'd seen through rock. Aimed and hit an opening twenty yards away that was a three-inch circle. His rifle had saved his life because she'd hit it, jammed it back into his shoulder. The gun had been destroyed, and Cord had staggered back, slashed by fragments of metal and shards of shattered rock. He'd still been able to see her through that hole, stunned into frozen awe. She knew he was no longer a threat and whirled from him and unloaded that gun at J.D. and Dugger, coming from the opposite direction. He saw the bullet hit J.D. and kill him. A gun she'd had one split second to aim. Then she'd turned as Fergus had opened up from yet another direction. She was just as deadly.

Cord had been only slightly aware of Tom Linscott also firing. What Cord saw in that woman stunned him beyond noticing much else. Her Winchester seemed like a living thing with its own mind, flaring in all directions, almost at the same time. Her gray cloak flew as she turned and fired until she was a dark cloud, thunder and lightning with a Winchester.

He lay shuddering on the ground now and stared at the trail and heard her coming. His chest heaved. His hand trembled. His eyes, burning from oozing blood, riveted on the place he expected her to appear.

But she didn't.

The seconds stretched to minutes, and slowly the panic receded, and Cord realized she wasn't coming. When his blood quit thundering in his ears, he knew the pursuing hoof beats coming at him like the hounds of Hades were in his own head.

His breathing slowed. His heart rate slackened to as near to normal as he was ever going to be again.

She'd killed three more of his family. Three more Cooters dead at the hand of that witch woman.

And now he lay here on the rocky trail, crushed into the ground like discarded trash. She'd made a fool of him. Terrorized him. And his fear shamed him. So he changed the fear to hate.

Hate wasn't shameful. It was strong because it made a man do what he needed to do.

Gathering his scattered courage, he slowly rose. He fumbled for his kerchief, tearing it off his neck and sopping up the blood. His face was clawed up, but he wasn't blinded. The wounds were little more than deep scratches, and the bleeding had stopped.

The horse that had stumbled and thrown him stood just a few yards down the trail, trembling with exhaustion, its sides heaving, its head down.

Cord wanted to get on that horse and ride away, defeated, beaten into rubbish. But he couldn't quit. And he couldn't go back and face her alone. The cousins he'd sent for might be in Helena by now, awaiting him. There might well be dozens, and even Lady Gray couldn't defeat that many men.

With grim determination, Cord stalked to his horse and was astride. He didn't spur the horse this time, contented to walk. Cord was as exhausted as his mount.

He'd get to Helena soon enough. Give himself a few days to heal so the cousins wouldn't think he'd been bested. Then he'd gather his family and come back with overwhelming strength to avenge his name.

Dugger, J.D., and Fergus, all dead. That was enough to keep the feud alive. He'd use that to inspire his cousins.

But Cord's real thirst for blood came from knowing there was a woman who could defeat him, humble him, and make him fear.

That woman had to die.

★ Eighteen ★

Mandy, this one's alive." Tom's heart picked up speed. He'd seen Mandy hit this guy hard. It had looked deadly. Tom didn't want this scar on her soul, and when he saw the man's chest rise and fall, he rushed to him, hoping he could be saved. Tom knew what it had cost her to kill once before.

Mandy appeared from the woods leading two horses. Her eyes sharpened. She walked quickly toward where Tom rose from the man's side.

"I know I hit him in the heart, Tom." Mandy sounded grim.

"It's dead center on his heart." Tom swallowed hard to think of his wife's aim, in the middle of a gunfight. "But there's something in his shirt pocket. The bullet's nearly stopped by a little book."

"Nearly?"

"He's bleeding." Tom unbuttoned the man's blood-soaked shirt. "It went through. It's lodged in his chest, and I guess it knocked him cold, but it wasn't a killing shot."

Mandy knelt beside Tom. "Yes, it was." Mandy looked up from the wound.

Tom met her eyes and saw the guilt and pain and danger of

his wife. "Yes, it was. And I'm glad you're as fast as you are, or we'd both be dead. In case you didn't notice, I never hit a thing."

"You kept their heads down. You messed up their aim."

"While you finished them. And now we've got three of them in custody, and you haven't had to commit murder."

"Then why do I feel like I have?"

Tom looked at the still man on the ground. He lifted his head to study the man slouched over his pommel, apparently unconscious. "I don't think you do feel like you have."

"Yes, I do."

"No, I don't think you know what you'd feel like if you committed murder. As awful as you feel now, that would be worse, and a different kind of pain. Uglier."

Mandy's eyes went to the freely bleeding wound in the man's chest. "This is pretty ugly."

"Then be glad it isn't worse, woman. Be very glad." Tom made quick work of digging the bullet out of the man's chest and wrapping a rough bandage over the wound. The man never woke up, and Tom noticed that he had a knot on his head the size of a chicken's egg. That was the reason he was unconscious.

Tom boosted this man as well as the dead one on the horses Mandy brought. "Let's haul them to town. That's the end of this bunch, except for the one who rode away, and he's wounded. And one man alone, especially a coward like these Cooters, isn't much danger. Alone, he won't even come at us from cover."

They made a quick trip back to Divide and left the men with the doctor, who thought both could survive. Then they made a report to the sheriff.

Tom finished being questioned then went outside to find his sharpshooter of a wife.

Mandy sat on a bench outside the sheriff's office, staring into space.

Sitting beside her, Tom said, "You want to tell me about it?"

Pulling herself with visible effort out of whatever daze she'd been in, Mandy turned to look at Tom. "About what?"

"I saw you in action. That's the first time, though I've heard tell. It's somethin' to see." Tom smiled. He was careful not to touch her because she looked like she might just explode.

Pulling in a breath so deep her whole body shuddered, Mandy said, "I'll understand if you want to get me out of your life. Any man would want to—" Her voice broke. She lifted her chin and stared straight out into the middle of the street.

Tom saw the fight for control. "If a woman can't shed a tear when she's been attacked and nearly killed and forced to fight for her life, then when can she?"

Tom saw tears brimming in her eyes as she turned to face him. Her shoulders, so square, so strong, shuddered, and she threw herself into Tom's arms. "I hate what happens to me. I'm evil. I'm—"

Tom kissed her quiet right in the middle of the day in Divide, Montana. Once he thought he'd taken her mind of that "evil" nonsense, he pulled back. "The sheriff said we can leave town. One of the outlaws, the one who shot his kin, is a wanted man. The others were riding with him, and that's enough. We can go"—Tom leaned so close no one could overhear—"on a treasure hunt."

★

Mandy set a blistering pace.

They were three days on the trail and getting close to their destination, when Tom pulled up abruptly. "Tracks!" He pointed at hoof prints of an unshod pony obviously carrying a load.

Indians.

"We walk from here." Tom snapped out the order, even though he was whispering. He dismounted.

Mandy didn't even consider disobeying. She'd found it didn't suit her much to take orders from anyone, especially a man, but why bother squabbling about such a thing when the man in question was right?

"How close are we?" Tom eased off a barely visible trail into the thick woods that surrounded them.

Mandy pulled the map out in the waning light. "Close." She looked up. "I'd say it's right up at the top of that rise. Then there's a mountain valley and directions where the gold is hidden."

Tom looked at the peak. It was still miles away and only visible through the heavy forest because it was so high. He turned to Mandy. "Let's pull back, set up camp for the night, and figure out how we do this tomorrow."

Shaking her head, Mandy said, "I've already been gone from the children too long, Tom. I just can't wait any longer. Worrying about them is eating me up inside."

With a long look, her cranky, bossy, short-tempered husband seemed to take her word for it that she was telling the truth. She really was about ready to snap.

Nodding, he said, "Let's see that map."

They found a spot and sat side-by-side on a boulder.

"The trail that rider was taking looks to lead to that low spot on the mountaintop." She studied the map and the mountain. "But Sidney says the treasure is far to the northeast side of a huge mountain valley, just beyond that rim."

"Maybe we can go north and slip into that valley without the Indians knowing." Tom sounded doubtful.

"That's not what the map says to do." Mandy tapped her lips as she considered that. "In fact, the map seems to follow the exact trail of those unshod hooves."

"Your husband isn't the kind of snake who would leave a treasure map behind for his wife that would force her to risk her life to find the gold, is he?"

Mandy set that thought aside as she remembered how well the Shoshone folks who lived around her knew what went on around them, even in the dark of night. "It's possible those are Shoshone tracks. If they are, the people may know of me, even protect me. We might just be able to ride in there and tell them what we want."

"There are other tribes in the area, though. I think this used to be Flathead land. In fact, I think these might be the people my sister lived with for a few years after my parents died."

"Your sister? Abby? She lived here?"

"Yes, and they were good to her. She doesn't talk about them much but I know it ended badly. Her village was massacred by a gang of outlaws. She was left alive because she was white. Because of that, there was bad blood between her and the few native folks that survived."

"Can you speak their language?"

"A few words. My sister tends to lapse into Flathead when she's mad. And she spends a good part of her time mad, so I've had a chance to learn what some of it means."

They shared a look that stretched long. "Do we dare just ride into the middle of a Flathead village and hope they'll be friendly?" Mandy's heart sped up with fear.

"Do we dare try and sneak past a bunch of trail-savvy Flatheads and hope they won't notice?"

Mandy finally shrugged her shoulders. "How about we do both? Sneak and, if we get caught, try and talk to them."

"How about we ride back to Divide, abandon the gold, and forget this ever happened?"

Shaking her head, Mandy stared at the mountain for a long time, thinking. What was bothering her about this? "It's so far from where our cabin was when Sidney was gold mining. How did he ever find this place?"

After an extended silence, Tom said, "Is it really that far?"

"We've ridden for days, and this map starts from Divide. It's shown us every step from there."

"But how about from your castle? We rode for days south from your place to Divide. Now we've ridden west and north from Divide to here."

Mandy's brow furrowed. "We might be closer to my house than I think, but I can't be sure from this side of the mountain."

"Maybe your husband deliberately laid out a hard path, thinking no one would ever understand where he was sending them, a way to make it even harder to find his gold. A way that would lead into the heart of a hostile Indian village."

"But he left this map where I'd find it. It wasn't easy to find, but it wasn't impossible either. That would mean Sidney wanted me to never find the gold, and if I did, he'd put me in danger." Unfortunately that did sound like her husband, the sneak.

"It's possible that if we went up over that rim and across that high valley and over the other side..." Tom fell silent studying the mountain. "That stupid Gray Tower might be an easy ride from where the treasure is hidden."

Mandy's temper flared. "And that explains how my husband could get on a train, ride all the way to Denver, come home with his gold, and never let anyone see where he'd gotten it. Because he probably went up to get the gold before he even left for Denver. Sidney always was too suspicious and sly for an honest man."

"So do we walk in and try to deal honorably and directly with the Flatheads? Or do we turn weasel and try to sneak past them?" Tom turned to her, and in the fading light their eyes met and held as they weighed the possibilities.

"I think we'd better sneak."

With a smile, Tom said, "Me, too."

"And the best sneaking goes on at night."

"And there's no sense waiting for the next night when we've got a perfectly good one right here." Tom nodded. "Let's get on with it."

★

This train is crawling!" Clay wanted to jump out of the slow-moving train with his horse and storm the Rockies.

"You know we're making better time this way." Sophie rubbed his shoulders.

Beth sat across from him. Alex was down one seat with one baby on his lap and the other stretched out on the seat.

Clay couldn't believe they were taking two little children to a gunfight.

Both women were in a fury from Mandy's telegraph, but they were holding it inside. Clay struggled to be as strong.

"She's married?" Clay couldn't believe it. Finally he'd gotten up the gumption to go fetch his daughter home, and before he could get there, the girl got herself hitched to someone else who lived half a country away from him.

"Tom Linscott." Beth said what they all knew. "So she's in a little town called Divide. We can travel on the train all the way to town."

"Slow, slow way to travel."

The train labored up a grade. Clay could have gone faster on foot. "A horse can run faster than a train." He knew he was just on edge. This was the fastest way to get there. But sitting in comfort while Mandy was in danger made him crazy. If he'd been on a galloping horse, at least he'd have felt like he was doing something.

"But it can't run for as long." Sophie's hand rubbed harder on his shoulders. "If we'd had a string of horses and kept changing saddles, we might have been able to beat the train, but probably not if we ran into rain or outlaws or one of the horses came up lame or threw a shoe. It all slows things down. The train goes slow but steady."

The rubbing changed until she was almost beating on him.

He looked sideways and saw that his wife was on the brink of snapping, just like him.

The train went around a curve ahead, and for a while he could see all ten cars. There hadn't been a car to sleep in, so he and the family had been sitting up for days.

Clay knew he wasn't making anything easier with his ranting. "I'm going to check on the horses again. Make sure they're holding up."

"You're just back from checking them, Pa." Beth gave him a level look that almost settled him down. The kind of look a young woman might give to her misbehaving children.

He couldn't stand it. "Then I'll go for a walk. I need to move, or I'm going to get my horse and jump off the train and ride." He erupted to his feet and stormed toward the front of the train. He hadn't been up there, preferring to stay close to his horses. As he neared the door that would let him outside, between the cars, it slammed open, and he stepped back, thinking to let some other impatient person go through.

An old man with lines cut deep in his face stepped in. He looked cranky and irritated and about ready to jump off the train right along with Clay. The only thing noticeable about the scowling old coot was the slash of pure white in a head of hair that was turning gray.

The old man looked up, and his eyes locked on Clay's, and they stayed there, direct and defiant, like he was looking for trouble.

★

Mandy set a blistering pace on the treasure hunt.

She glanced behind her in the shrouded night woods and saw with satisfaction that Tom was keeping up. It might have been shadows cast from a full moon, but she thought he had a look on his face just as determined as hers.

He didn't want the gold. He wasn't a man to search for

treasure. He expected to work for his keep. But Tom knew this was important to her. He might even agree with her that a staggering price on the head of every member of this family of feud-loving coyotes could end this almost instantly.

She looked back at the nearly invisible trail she'd found heading for the far north end of the valley. Her map told her the gold was at the end of this trail.

Trees surrounded them, and she often was forced to slow to a walk as the trail grew steep until they were going up as much as forward. The moon was full, and that helped, but mostly she trusted to her horse to pick his way along the rocky landscape.

What critter had created this trail anyway? Mandy suspected it was a herd of mountain goats. But Tom's horses were game and strong and surefooted.

They scrambled along on the climb until suddenly the forest thinned. The trees were shorter and farther apart. Mandy saw the increasingly gnarled limbs as they moved onward, upward. They must be nearing the tree line. Seconds after she realized it, the sky opened up above her. The moon was so bright she couldn't see many stars, but there were a few, enough to tell her she was on the right trail.

She pulled her horse to a slow walk and continued forward. When she finally saw a clearing ahead, she pulled to a stop. The land became impossibly rugged. It was more rock than grass and sloped steeply upward within a few feet of the trees ending. The mountain goats might have been able to scale it, but no thoroughbred was going to.

Tom came up beside her. "We walk from here?"

Nodding, Mandy dismounted. "There's grass. The horses won't mind standing for a few hours."

"Let's see that map one more time before we go. Sidney's got it marked that he's hidden his stash on this end of the valley, right?"

Mandy secured her horse while Tom did the same. Then they

mulled over their next step.

"We'll be exposed for a while once we walk out of these trees." Mandy looked at Tom and considered, not for the first time, that getting mixed up with her might be the death of him.

"Yep. I don't see any sign of Flatheads around here, and most Indians don't hunt at night. I think. Besides, why hunt in this steep woods when there are better places to the south?"

Pointing to the land above the tree line, Mandy said, "We're going to have our hands full getting up there and over the rim. Sidney's map says it's possible."

"Your husband drew this map long after he'd found that gold. You know that, right, Mandy honey?"

"I know. He must have found the gold coming into that valley from the north. Then he scouted a trail to the south to create the map, just to keep anyone who found the map confused. Then he used the night sky as his guide. None of that made sense to me from our house. But once I studied the night sky from where we slept out the night of our wedding, it was easy to follow."

"So, you weren't really fascinated by the stars in the night like you said at first. You were trying to understand the stars well enough to find the gold." Tom studied the land, as Mandy did, making sure the coast was clear before they stepped out of the scrub pines. He looked around until their eyes met. "You wanted that gold almost as badly as Sidney did."

She hated to admit to anything that compared her to her deceased husband. "Not for the same reason, though. I always saw that gold as a way to buy freedom and safety for my children."

"Hired killers? Bodyguards?"

"Bounties, Tom. I'm going to put bounties on the white-thatched head of every Cooter I can find who's related to this bunch."

"You said that before you'd give a reward for their capture. But you've got to prove they're wanted. It's not enough for you to say a few of them pestered you and you want them all in jail."

"I know. But I think I could make things hot enough for them that they'd back off. I can definitely get the sheriff and Marshal Coltrain to name Cord as a wanted man. And they found that one Wanted poster."

"But that was for Fergus, and he's already locked up."

"We might find a few others that qualify. I can pay some people to look into it more carefully than the sheriff can. And I can raise those rewards then put out the word that anyone who bothers me can expect the same treatment, even after my death if need be. I can set a reward so high the whole Cooter clan will go away and stay away."

"It's not a bad plan." Tom looked around again. "I've got some money these days. We could probably make your plan work with the cash I have on hand."

Which was just Tom saying one more time she should trust him to protect her. "You'd break the ranch doing it, Tom. After all your years of hard work, marrying me might ruin everything you've built."

"We could make it work, Mandy. We don't need to sneak into a valley full of very smart, possibly hostile Flathead Indians in hopes of finding a treasure."

"It's got to be huge, Tom. If it isn't, it'll just make the Cooters mad and drive them to come at me even harder." Mandy took a deep breath and stared at her husband.

"Last chance, Mandy girl. Let's go home. Let's fight this out, use the law, do it right."

She knew he was right, but she wasn't turning back. "I'm going. If you don't want to, I'll understand. I won't think less of you if you—"

"Just go then. Don't insult me by telling me to leave."

Nodding, Mandy turned.

Protect me, Lord. Protect Tom.

She stepped into the clearing and almost immediately found herself scaling instead of walking. Her husband grumbled behind her, but she noticed he kept coming after her. That seemed like a real nice quality in a husband.

★

Tom had a new respect for mountain goats by the time he'd gotten to the rim of this canyon. And he'd respected 'em quite a bit before.

The sun was casting the first bit of color across the sky to the east but it was still dark enough. He grabbed Mandy's ankle, which was just an arm's reach over his head. "If that map is right, the gold ought to be just a few hundred yards ahead. We can get in there, grab the gold, and get out before the sun has risen fully."

She jerked against his hold, but when he didn't turn loose, she glared down at him. "I heard you. I agree. Now let go."

His throat went dry. "I should have talked to Abby first, asked her what to expect. She might have been willing to try and talk to the Flathead. She speaks their language and knows how they think."

'Too late now." Mandy, his stubborn-to-the-bone wife, went over that rim like she was a goat herself.

Scowling, Tom followed the she-goat into the valley of the Flatheads. When he wriggled over the rim, he found the going easier. Steep but not straight up and down like the outside of the bowl-shaped valley.

Tom couldn't see much—the rising sun wasn't up high enough to penetrate this highlands. Good, less chance of being seen. He heard water running nearby and caught a glimpse of a spate, silver in the darkness, gushing out of a rock.

"The map said there'd be a spring." Mandy kept moving.

His wife was slithering down the slope, so Tom tried to catch up and keep a sharp eye out for trouble at the same time. Though she was moving with reckless speed, he had no doubt his wife was being careful. There was just no denying that Mandy was a wily one. He'd learned she could be fast and cautious at the same time with no trouble at all.

Tom saw no sign of life. He couldn't make out too much, but there didn't seem to be a tree line inside this valley. The moonlight helped, but mostly the terrain was shrouded in darkness. He scampered down and down, afraid he'd lose his wife. She had the map after all. So, he stuck with her.

The land leveled a bit. Not real level of course—there seemed to be nothing purely level in the whole state of Montana—but better.

Tom was able to walk upright, hurrying to find that stupid treasure and get out of here before the light revealed them to a tribe of bloodthirsty Indians.

Honesty forced Tom to admit that his sister, on the rare occasion she spoke of her years with them, had always talked of the Flatheads as a gentle people. But then she'd known them as an orphaned child. Tom really didn't want to count on them being all that friendly to him.

Mandy stopped so suddenly that Tom ran straight into her. He had to get the woman some clothes that weren't gray. It was like trying to keep track of a wild cat in the dark. He wondered if her eyes would glow if he carried a lantern.

Tom caught her so he didn't knock her flat on the ground, and she hissed—another cat-like attribute. "This is the spot." She waved the map in his face and pointed at a triangular rock jutting out just to one side of that spring. "That's got to be the stone from this map."

Tom realized his wife, the sharpshooter, had eyes like an owl by night and an eagle by day. If he managed to survive marriage to her, she was going to be handy to have around.

Dropping to her knees, Mandy began pulling at a small pile

of stones stacked at the base of that triangular rock. Tom hadn't paid that much attention to the map, not the details. He'd never figured to get this close. But now he pitched in, pulling at stones sized from about even with his fist to bigger than his head. They weren't stacked in here in a natural way. It was clear that they'd been moved in to bury something. He felt a little hum in his veins thinking about finding a fortune in gold.

Gold fever, was it possible he might be catching it? He almost hoped so. Then he could blame madness on being here treasure hunting. Better to be crazy than to think rationally that this was a good idea.

They dug industriously for long minutes, the silence broken only by the tumble of stones. They cleared the rocks and found sand. Scooping with bare hands, they dug faster. Dirt kicked up. Sand flew. Tom's hands were coated with dust and gravel.

He took a quick look at his wife and saw that she must have touched her nose because her face was streaked with dirt. He reckoned his was, too. He went back to digging.

Mandy froze. "I found something."

She turned to Tom, and he realized he could see her clearly. The sun wasn't over the canyon rim, but it was pushing back the dark. Indians weren't famous for sleeping the daylight hours away. They had to get out of here.

She tugged and Tom's hand brushed against heavy leather coated with dirt and sand. She pulled hard, and for a long moment everything was frozen—the bag, Mandy leaning backward, even the dirt seemed to stop to catch its breath. Then it gave all at once with a *whoosh* of exploding sand and dirt.

Mandy flew backward. Tom snagged her in midair, or she'd have fallen into the stream that rushed away from that spring.

She sat down hard and began swiping at the dirt on what looked like ancient saddlebags. She uncovered a symbol of some kind. Her fingers ran along an indentation, looked for the edge of the battered leather. What looked like a crest appeared, with a helmet of some kind engraved above the crest.

Tom would have liked to see it better, but in the dim light there wasn't much detail visible, even without dirt.

Tom saw her hands slide under a flap on the edge of the bag. When she went to lift it, a knotted strip of leather held it in place. She fumbled with the leather thong that tied it shut.

Tom rested one big hand on hers. "Leave that until later. We need to get away from here."

Mandy smiled at him. "You're right."

He planted a kiss on her dirty face. "Are you sure there isn't anything left in that hole?"

They both dug, but the ground turned to solid rock just inches below where they'd unearthed the bag.

"There's nothing else." Mandy swiped at her forehead.

Tom saw her leave a damp trail of dirt and knew she was sweating. But though they'd been working hard, it was a cool mountain morning. The sweat came from tension more than labor.

"Sidney buried it here, probably moved it here from wherever he found it."

Nodding, Tom said, "Let's get out of here."

Mandy lifted the heavy saddlebags.

Tom heard a dull sound from the inside like something hard rattling. Gold. His heart sped up as his wife lifted the treasure.

"The solution to all my problems is in this saddlebag."

"Gold don't usually fix what's wrong with our lives, Mandy honey."

"This gold will. I just know it." Rising to her feet, she smiled. "Now I've got enough money to buy some safety, some peace, some happiness.

The sharp crack of a gun being cocked stopped them in their tracks.

★ Nineteen ★

Luther rode hard for Divide, trusting that the Cooters were busy tracking Mandy and weren't looking for him these days. It was a hard ride through about the worst that this rugged land had to throw at a man, but Luther was used to it. His horse was game, and his cause was life and death.

He pulled into the streets of the dusty little frontier town just as the sun lowered behind the towering mountains to the west. Following the instructions in Mandy's wire, he rode straight to the sheriff's office.

A stout man with knowing eyes looked up when Luther shoved open the door.

Those eyes went straight to Luther's six-gun. "You huntin' trouble, mister?"

"Nope. Not with you anyway. I'm hunting a man named Tom Linscott, and more important his wife."

The sheriff rose slowly from where he sat behind a scarred wooden desk. "Your name Cooter by any chance?"

Luther relaxed. The sheriff was clearly well informed. "Nope. But Mandy sent me a telegraph saying she'd moved here and was ready to accept some help from an old friend. So, I came a runnin'. My name's Luther."

Sinking back into his chair, the sheriff nodded at coffee steaming on a potbellied stove that was casting off unneeded heat in the summer evening. "I'm Merl Dean. Pour yourself a cup. Tom and his new wife have told me their story, and I've been doing what I can to see the Cooters brought to justice. Pull up a chair, and let's talk about what's to be done."

The door slammed open just as Luther reached for a tin cup. Luther had his hand on his Colt as he whirled to face whoever had crashed in. Then he laughed out loud. "Sally!"

He charged for one of his favorite people in the world and hoisted Sally. . .McKenzie up in the air. It was hard to get used to her new name.

"Luther, you're here. Where's Mandy?" Sally's arms wrapped around his neck. He remembered when she was just a little thing, no bigger'n a sprite, tormenting him with her chattering and tagging along, determined to out-cowboy all the cowboys.

"I'm just in the door, looking to find her. She told me to come to the sheriff's office and he'd fill me in." Luther set her down and grinned, then looked past her, and his smile faded at the sight of her husband.

Logan McKenzie. Strange man. Strange business painting for a living. Not a man's way to earn his living, to Luther's way of thinking.

Logan did make a living, though. And the wandering seemed to suit Sally. Not like the way everything Sidney Gray did annoyed Mandy.

"We'll ride out to her place together." Sally smiled then jabbed her thumb behind her. "Buff and Wise Sister are with us. They're stabling the horses for the night."

"How far have you travelled?" Luther thought his girl looked tired, and Sally was a hearty little lady.

"We're riding in from Yellowstone." Sally quit grinning. "I got such an itch to see Mandy and drag her off that mountaintop she lives in that I couldn't stand it. It hit me one morning so hard I couldn't stay still. I'm going to ride in there and drag her and her youngsters out of there."

"Mandy left that fool house Sid built, and she's married." Luther pulled the wire out of his shirt pocket.

"Married?" Sally gasped. Her eyes narrowed. "God have mercy."

Luther didn't blame the girl a bit. Mandy would have done better to let someone else pick her next husband. She'd shown no talent for it.

"Yep, and living here in Divide." Luther handed over Mandy's brief message then turned back to the lawman. "'Is'zat right, Sheriff?"

"Come on in and I'll tell you everything I know." The sheriff waved a weary hand. "We've got two men under arrest and one dead after a run-in with your sister and Tom Linscott."

"What?" Sally looked at the empty jail cell.

"They're over at the doc's, but they're expected to pull through . . .eventually."

"That sounds like my big sister." Sally wouldn't have minded a crack at those outlaws herself. She might just go ask them a few questions later. "Tell us what's going on."

Buff came in before they could get settled, with Wise Sister at his side.

Luther was happy for his old friend to have found a wife, but he missed him something fierce. It had been okay when Luther'd been around Mandy and had someone in his life. But since he'd gotten shot and Mandy had told him to stay away, Luther had hurt with the loneliness.

The two exchanged a hearty handshake and very few words; then they turned to have it out with the sheriff. "So where's Linscott live?"

"His ranch isn't too far out of town, but he and his new wife are gone."

"Gone?" Luther had to fight to keep from growling like a rabid wolf. "Gone where?"

"Just this morning they hit the trail east for Denver. They'll be—"

"We came on the main trail from the east," Sally interrupted. "We'd have met them if they were heading for Denver on horseback."

Luther looked from the surprised sheriff to Sally to Buff. "Did you see anyone on that trail who looked like one of the Cooters?"

"No, the trail was plumb empty." Sally pulled off her gloves, and Luther noticed in passing that his girl was dressed like a cowboy. She'd given a lot of that up after she'd married, but it appeared she hadn't given it up completely.

He'd have smiled if he hadn't been so worried. "Well, if there weren't any Cooters, then they can't be in too bad of trouble."

★

Mandy had her rifle aimed and pointed, her finger on the hair-trigger, before she'd seen who it was. A dozen grim, black-eyed Flathead warriors, half armed with steadily aimed guns, the rest with tomahawks and knives. All primed for trouble.

Ice cold all the way to her soul, she eased her hand slowly, carefully away from the Winchester.

God, protect me. Protect Tom.

Mandy risked a glance at Tom. He was raising his hands in a slow, steady way so as to not startle anyone.

The warrior in the center spoke something Mandy couldn't begin to understand.

Tom said some guttural words that were similar in tone to the words she'd learned trying to communicate with the Shoshone who lived around her home. None of those tones shaped themselves to being a word Mandy could recognize.

The warrior pointed his rifle at the saddlebags that had fallen at Mandy's feet.

Tom moved so slow he'd've lost a race with molasses in a blizzard, crouching, an inch at a time, to fetch the saddlebags.

"No!" Mandy couldn't lose that gold.

Every brave raised a weapon. They aimed evenly between her and Tom as if they'd planned well beforehand, given out the responsibility of who to take aim at.

Had they been watching them ever since they'd ridden into the valley? Or ever since they'd entered their hunting grounds outside this mountain canyon? After a year living surrounded by those sharp-eyed Shoshone, Mandy was ashamed of herself for underestimating any native folks.

"No help for it, Mandy girl. I've got to let them have it."

A thousand words crowded to get out of Mandy's mouth; any one of them could get Tom killed. And that was just why she'd resisted marrying him.

"If we make them real happy, they might let us out of here with our hair."

Her throat had gone bone dry, which helped her keep quiet.

Tom eased forward, the saddlebags dangling from his fingertips.

Giving it all away. All her hopes. In that second of crushing despair, Mandy knew she was a fool to put her hopes on gold, just as Sidney had been.

When had that started? She'd gotten Sidney's map and recognized the markings as from the sky. But the sky didn't make sense.

She'd watched the sky and dreamed of finding her way to that gold. But she'd also learned a lot about how beautiful the sky was, how powerful God was to create it all. She'd learned humility as she thought of the One who'd set it in motion and made such a beautiful world work.

She'd learned from her watching and from what she'd read in Sidney's books that the stars changed through the night and through the year. She'd hoped that the day would come when her map made sense and she might find her way to the gold and safety. But that hope had been vague as long as the sky didn't fit the map and there was no way out of her prison.

The Flathead brave nearest to Tom moved forward just as slowly as Tom until he reached the saddlebag and lifted it away. The brave fell back quickly, focusing on the bag. The rest of the tribe kept their attention strictly on Tom and Mandy.

Mandy was frigid inside, her senses registering every sound and smell and movement. She rubbed the little callus on her finger and knew, with cold, hard logic, that she couldn't win with all these guns. She was glad she had no possible chance of going for her rifle. She and Tom were the intruders here. To open fire on these men, who were just guarding their home, would be an awful thing to live with. Even knowing that, Mandy felt that cold, that sleet where her blood should be flowing in her veins.

She wondered, in the detached way of her chilled heart, if she saw an opening, a chance, would she grab her rifle and open fire? She hated knowing it might be beyond her control.

The warrior holding the saddlebag backed until he was at the brink of the stream cut by the gushing spring. He took his knife, so sharp it gleamed in the early morning light, and slashed through the leather thong that held it closed. He flipped open the saddlebag and pulled the mouth of it wide. Leaning down the man grunted, a sound of confusion.

Mandy had expected a gasp of pleasure at the sight of all that gold. But maybe Indians were too sensible to care about a golden rock.

A few harsh-sounding words drew two more warriors away from Mandy and Tom. Mandy glanced at Tom to see if he was considering that now, at about nine to two, this was a fight he'd buy into. A hard single shake of his head told her not to go for her rifle. Her fingers itched. Her blood ran cold, but she knew he was right, and she held off.

Suddenly the three men studying the contents of the saddlebag laughed, and the one who was the leader lifted the bag high in the air.

The gold, they'd realized what it was. They'd realized how their lives could be changed with this wealth. Mandy felt sick to think of how close she'd come to possessing it. And what a fool she'd been to think money could solve her problems.

A quick, guttural statement by the Flathead leader brought a smile to the face of nearly every man there. Then the man stretched his lifted hand to the side and stretched his arm wide until he held the bag over the fast-moving stream. And he poured.

"No!" Mandy jumped.

Tom grabbed her around the waist as she saw. . .dirt.

Dirt and stone and nothing else poured out and splashed and was swept away.

"Where's the gold?" She couldn't tear her eyes away, willing it to turn gold.

The drab gray and brown poured, dropping into the water.

Mandy held her breath, waiting, waiting, waiting for that moment when the stones and dirt would sparkle, when whatever was on top of the gold finished falling out and the gold coins followed, lost forever in that deep, rushing water.

The gold never came. The dirt and rocks quit pouring. The bag was empty.

"Nothing." Tom was behind her, his arm clamped around her waist. It wasn't lost on Mandy that the way he held her pinned her rifle to her back. She couldn't get it into action. She knew Tom well. His grip was no accident.

The leader finally tossed the now flat leather bag aside and turned to Mandy and Tom. Somehow Tom moved so he tucked

Mandy behind him. She noticed he'd left her the rifle.

Harsh, cutting words came from Tom. They were returned at about double the speed by the warrior. Back and forth the two men talked. Tension built. The other Flathead men kept their black, angry eyes on Tom. Their tomahawks and knives and guns at the ready.

The cold grew and spread in Mandy's body, swallowing up her limbs, her heart, the breath in her lungs. She wondered if the cold was of the devil and would soon swallow up her soul.

Suddenly the warriors lowered their weapons. A few more harsh words were traded between Tom and their leader. Then Tom reached his hand back, as if to corral Mandy, and began easing up the hill, the way they'd come.

"Tom, what—"

"Quiet," he cut her off. "Move."

Mandy shut her mouth and moved.

One step at a time. The Flatheads no longer had their weapons aimed, but neither did they take their eyes off their white visitors.

"Go ahead of me." Tom's voice was low, barely audible to Mandy. "Climb. Hurry."

Mandy had to quit staring at the men to watch where she was going. She began climbing in earnest. Faster, running away from danger. Leaving behind her dream of safety bought with gold.

She crested the steep edge of the mountain valley, and as she topped it and began descending she took one long second look back and saw what remained.

Nothing. The warriors had vanished as if they'd never been. All that was left was the spent, flattened saddlebag with the odd, ancient crest. "Sidney's gold. Where is it?"

"It's gone, Mandy girl."

"Gone where? We have to find it!"

"No, not gone, like it's been moved. Gone, like spent."

"Spent by who?"

"By your husband. I did my best to talk with those men, and they say no one's been in here since they took over this valley. They're sure of it. They know their land well. That means Sidney hasn't been in here for the gold in years. He may have come the first few years to get a bit more when he needed it, but building that house must have taken it all."

Mandy thought of her mansion. She could imagine that it had drained a Spanish treasure chest to construct it.

They hurried, dropping lower and lower in the full morning light now that they were on the east side of the canyon. Their feet skidded on the stony ground, kicking up dust that permeated the cool morning air.

"Then why leave the map?" Mandy glanced behind her, able to stand mostly upright as they reached slightly more level ground.

"Maybe he never intended you to find it. Maybe he made that map strictly for himself." They had only a few dozen yards to go to reach the tree line and their horses, and then ride like the wind to put space between themselves and those Flatheads.

"But we decided he deliberately marked the map to confuse me." Mandy wanted to get her hands on Sidney and shake him until he wasn't worthless.

"It made sense if he left that map for you." The land became smoother. They rushed for the trees. Tom's hand rested on the small of her back. "But I think he must've drawn it earlier. He'd have wanted to be very careful not to lose track of it."

"But why draw it so it led out of the valley to the east when he came in from the west?" Mandy could almost feel those Flatheads back there, changing their minds, getting worked up and deciding they should never have let people intrude on their land without paying a price.

"Just being sneaky I reckon." They reached the tree line, the first scrubby pines that barely reached waist high.

"He drew the map so he could understand it and no one else."

Mandy brushed hard against one stumpy tree as she rushed past. It scratched her hand and filled the air with the scent of pine.

"Makes sense. Anyone might find a streak of weasel in his soul if he'd found a treasure trove. You wouldn't want anyone finding it."

"Including me?" Mandy asked bitterly. The trees grew taller, head high. Mandy could almost breathe again.

"I doubt he created that map intending to cause trouble for you. I doubt he intended to die." Tom steered Mandy with his pressuring hand and guided them straight to where they'd tied their horses, hours ago in the pitch dark.

Mandy thought with cold satisfaction that if Sidney had tied those horses there, he'd have never found them again, the big dope. The big gold-wasting dope.

Mandy unlashed her horse from the scrub pine where it had been quietly grazing. She looked over the back of the magnificent black, into the eyes of her magnificent husband. He caught the pommel to swing himself up, but his eyes met hers, and he stopped. Between them something stretched, as if he'd lassoed her and now stood, a tough cowpony that had her completely bound to him.

A smile crept across her face as she thought of it.

"What? Something funny happen in that valley? You lost your gold. You lost your chance of buying your way out of Cooter trouble. You almost lost your scalp."

"It's not funny, but it does occur to me that I found something in there, too." Mandy wanted to be away from here, but she didn't know where to go. Back to Tom's? To Belle Harden's to get her children and bring them into the path of danger? Where in the world could she find safety?

"Nope, all you did was lose."

Shaking her head, Mandy quietly said, "I found you, Tom."

"I wasn't lost."

"I found a man who stood between me and danger."

"I've done that before a couple of times."

"A man who's going to stick even though there's no gold."

"Gettin' that gold was always a hare-brained idea."

Mandy's smile stretched. "I found a man I can respect. A man to ride the river with."

Tom's disgruntled eyes softened, warmed, heated.

"A man to love."

"You're just figuring out now that you love me?" Tom shook his head in disgust. "I knew that five years ago."

"So did I, but it wasn't something I could admit, or even let myself think."

"Nothin' stopping you now."

"Not a single thing."

If Tom would have moved, Mandy would have gone to him and let him wrap her in his arms. But a big part of why she loved him was that he had too much sense to take time for kissing and hugging when they were within spitting distance of a tribe of irritated Flatheads.

Tom swung up on his horse instead of rounding it to drag her into his arms. That made her love him even more. "Let's go home, wife."

"Home or to get the children?"

Tom picked up his reins, then frowned and turned to her as Mandy mounted up. The gaze between them held. Mandy knew he was thinking, just as she was, weighing the danger.

Finally, reluctantly, he said, "I think we need to get them and bring them home."

"The Cooters will keep coming." But Mandy was in agreement. They needed to start as they meant to go on. She was sick of hiding.

"And you need to trust me to protect you."

"You've seen me shoot, Tom. You know I'm not used to relying on anyone to protect me."

"My delicate lady wife don't need much help, and that's a fact." A smile bloomed on Tom's face. "But I'll see if I can make myself of some use."

"I 'spect you'll be right handy to have around." Mandy smiled back.

"For now, I reckon we've thinned 'em out and backed 'em up a few steps. Maybe we can have a few good days before they show up."

Nodding, Mandy said, "Then let's get the children and go home."

★ Twenty ★

"I'll take a watch, Miz Harden." Mark was sorely tempted to call her ma just to see if he could do it and walk away with his head still on his shoulders. He always had liked taking a risk.

She had to know he was sweet on Emma, and yet he was still allowed to live. It was probably because of the babies.

Belle turned, scowling, to face him. Her arms crossed, her jaw a hard line.

He sat on the ground, behind her cabin, with the boy on his lap, eyelids heavy in the afternoon sun.

Angela was busy strangling Mark from behind. Catherine talked his ear off and tugged on his hair.

Mark was kicking himself for not getting it cut recently.

Even Tanner had taken to hanging on him and was trying to yank off one of Mark's boots. Betsy, with her black eyes and riotous black curls, sat in the dirt beside him making faces at Angela as if she were encouraging the girl to torment Mark.

Why wouldn't Tanner and Betsy hang around? Mark had possession of all the Harden children's best playmates.

It didn't really make sense that Mandy's young'uns had taken such a liking to Mark, except that he'd felt such a powerful need to protect Mandy and that stretched to include her children. They must be able to tell his concern for them was real and deep.

Emma had just gone inside carrying her baby brother. They had a good chance of getting Jarrod to sleep, too. Then Emma said the rest of them would have cookies. Before that she'd been out here with him while they cared for the six best chaperones God had ever put on this earth.

"You plannin' to take all the children with you to the lookout?" Belle asked with cold contempt.

Seven best chaperones.

Now was the time to point out that he really was indispensible because of how attached the children had gotten to him. Except he feared that *indispensible* wasn't a word Belle Harden used when it came to menfolk. . .at least not when they were sparking her daughter.

"I reckon they'd be fine here with you and Sarah and. . . Emma." He had a hard time saying Emma's name right into the cranky face of his future mother-in-law. As if five children weren't enough, Belle had been a better chaperone than an army of Catholic nuns. He hadn't gotten a chance to steal a single kiss. A shame because he had a strong sense that Emma would go along nicely with the plan. She hadn't forked a horse to check the herd since Mark had arrived. He understood that to be out of the usual way of things.

"Just stay put. We're handling the lookout just fine without you."

"Miz Harden." Mark swallowed hard, hopeful Belle would hesitate to kill him in the presence of small children.

"What?" Her voice was so hard it landed on Mark like a rock.

"I want you to know I—I—" Mark fell silent. There really was nothing he could say that would ever make Belle like him. "As you know, I have asked to call on Emma."

"I believe I have some vague memory of that." That hard voice was turning into an avalanche rather than one lone rock.

"I have only the most honorable intentions for your daughter, ma'am. She's as fine a woman as—"

"She's too young."

"How old would you say is old enough?" Mark heard that tone he sometimes got that riled up schoolteachers and made men narrow their eyes at him. It was left over from the antics of his childhood. He was a sober, thoughtful man now.

"You want to stay on this ranch, you watch your mouth." Belle didn't like one bit of sass unless it came from herself. Mark made a note of that for the future.

"I'll wait until whatever age you say is old enough, ma'am." Mark had no intention of waiting. In fact, he fully planned to be living in a house with Emma as his wife before the snow fell. And it was getting on toward the end of August already. It didn't make him a genius to refrain from being fully honest about *that* part of his honorable intentions.

He hoped he and Emma didn't have to run off and get married. Would Emma protect him against her own ma?

Emma came out of the house without the baby. Mark had yet to see the day all of these tykes decided it was nap time at the same minute.

And Belle never slept.

Emma came over and crouched beside him and reached for Jarrod, dozing despite the rambunctious children surrounding him. "Let me get him settled."

Mark looked up into those blue eyes and was lost in the notion of Emma coming to lift a child out of his arms. Soon it would be their child.

Then his eyes went past Emma's pretty face and reaching arms to see Belle, her jaw so tight it was a wonder her teeth hadn't been worn down to nubs.

A spark of defiance flared to a flame Mark couldn't quite

control. "Emma, when do you think you'll be old enough to consider taking a husband?"

Emma froze. Her eyes wide. Her reaching hands not coming a bit closer. He saw her throat work as if she were gulping down something she hadn't meant to. "I—I reckon I'm a woman grown now, Mark." Those frozen eyes thawed.

From behind Emma, Mark heard a noise similar to one he'd once heard from a mountain lion that he'd startled. Part snarl, part scream, all terrifying.

A hard hand landed on Emma's shoulder and pulled her to her feet. Belle stepped between Mark and Emma.

Mark struggled to get to his feet, without stomping on Tanner or knocking any child to the ground.

"I told you she's too young, Mark Reeves. You do your talking to me, not Emma."

Emma came around Belle and hoisted Tanner into her arms. She thrust the boy at Belle. Then Emma tore Angela off Mark's back. That left Catherine yammering around Mark's knees and Jarrod asleep in his arms and Betsy jumping at his side.

Very deliberately, Emma stepped closer to Mark and faced her mother. "You've always told us we're not to let anyone force us into marriage, Ma."

"I'm not going to force you—"

Emma grabbed Mark's forearm and sank her fingernails in so hard Mark shut up to keep from yelling in pain.

"But I don't think I'd let anyone force me into *not* getting married either. You raised me to be strong enough to take care of myself, and that includes making decisions for myself."

"Not about this. Not when this polecat is acting as if he's such a good caretaker of children. He's doing it to charm you, Emma."

"I am not. I—ow!" Mark closed his mouth before he ended up with scars on his arm.

"He's taking care of these children because Mandy is an old

friend of his family, from back in Texas."

Belle's dark eyes slid from Emma to Mark. "First I've heard of that."

Mark glanced at Emma to see if she was going to let him talk. Her nails retreated from his skin a bit, so he took that as a good sign.

"I didn't speak of it at first. Tom Linscott and everyone with him saw that we knew each other. I didn't hide that. But I didn't tell about where we'd met. I wasn't sure how Mandy had ended up there on that mountaintop, with the name of Lady Gray. When I saw her—" Mark looked at Emma. He'd already told her that Mandy was important to him, but not in the way Emma was. He hoped Emma knew that.

He hoped Belle did, too.

"I just—I hadn't seen anyone from home—" Mark thought of how hard it had hit him, to see all the trouble that had landed on his old rival. How it made him feel when she launched herself into his arms and started crying.

"Mandy and Tom had to send the children to safety. I couldn't help Mandy. Tom was doing that." Mark's throat ached at how badly he'd wished he could do more for Mandy.

"But the children needed someone. I think they can tell I care about—" Mark's voice broke. Horrified, he quit talking and crouched down and got real busy gathering Catherine into his arms, keeping his head down, and taking far too long to shift Jarrod to one side. His pa would be shocked. His brothers would torment him forever. A man didn't *cry*.

Emma's hand on his arm slid away as he crouched. He got the burning of his eyes under control, and the embarrassment of it all eased the thickness of his throat, but now his cheeks burned as if he'd turned ten shades of red.

This was *not* how he'd planned to court Emma, by arguing with her ma and showing himself to be a weakling in her presence.

He squared his shoulder, braced for the sneer he'd see on Belle's face and the disdain on Emma's.

He looked at Belle first because he couldn't help himself and saw. . .kindness.

He almost dropped Catherine.

"Let me take Jarrod." Belle relieved Mark of one of his burdens. She now held two children in her arms without looking overly burdened. He shifted so Catherine was on his right hip.

Then he dared to look at Emma. Her eyes shined right into his, and there was only softness and sympathy.

Could crying possibly be useful in attracting women? Mark had never considered such a thing before. He wondered if he'd be able to learn to do it on command.

Emma moved Angela to her left side and rested her arm on Mark's back, not even looking at her mother and not a fingernail to be found anywhere. "I think it's wonderful that you've been so good to Mandy's children. Wonderful."

Mark wished like crazy that Belle Harden would just take these children and go away. In fact, he wished it so bad, he turned to her. "I want a private word with Emma, Miz Harden. We won't go far, and we won't go for long, but if Emma's agreeable—"

"I am."

He snuck a quick look at Emma when she said that. And liked what he saw.

Turning back to Belle, he was having a little trouble even being scared of her, which was just pure down-to-the-bone stupid. "Please."

Belle's kindness faded, but she replaced it with worry and just a hint of sadness, which made Mark feel like a worm. The woman was just trying to protect her daughter. Here Mark stood with all these children, children he'd die to protect. He could feel exactly what Belle did, only her feelings had been going on all Emma's life. His had started when he'd met these children a few days ago.

"Betsy, help me get the children inside." Jerking her head toward the cabin, she added, "Let's go get some cookies."

Angela raced for the house with Betsy on her heels. Catherine started wiggling, and Mark let her down to run for the promise of sweets.

Tanner started squirming and tugging on Belle's hand to get loose. He yelled, "I want a cookie!"

Belle let him go, which left her with a sleeping baby and a scowl. "Don't be gone long." Belle turned and stomped toward her cabin.

Mark could barely breathe as he reached out to Emma and she caught hold. There were lookouts everywhere. Mark couldn't think of anywhere he could possibly be alone with her.

Emma dragged him straight for the barn. She pulled him inside, swung the door shut, and turned.

He tried to work up the nerve to say what was in his heart.

Emma launched herself at him and wrapped her arms around his neck.

He laughed, caught her around the waist, and lifted her right off her feet. The words wanted to all get out at once, and for a moment Mark wasn't sure he'd be able to say anything. "I've homesteaded some land only a couple hours' ride from here. I'm planning on having a cabin built before the snow falls. Will you—"

"Yes!" Her smile was blinding bright.

"Marry me." Mark said the words, but he didn't need to hear more. He laughed, spun his woman around in a tight circle, then set her on her feet, lowered his head, and kissed her.

It was his first kiss. He'd have taken one a few times before, but he could never convince the girls to go along. He suspected, considering Belle's extreme watchfulness, it might be Emma's, too.

They were both fast learners.

Mark pulled away reluctantly. "I can get the cabin built fast, but it won't be much at first." He ran one hand over Emma's beautiful hair, pulled back in a no-nonsense braid that reached down to her waist. He wanted to see her hair loose. He wanted to have the right to ask her to leave it swaying around her shoulders, just for him.

"I don't want to wait until spring." He kissed her again. He desperately didn't want to wait until spring. "But what I'll have up by the time snow flies will be a humble home. We'll be able to stay warm." He had no doubt of that. "But—"

"Can we ask my pa to help build it?"

"Your pa?" That got Mark's attention. He frowned. "I don't want him to think I can't provide for you, Emma. I wouldn't ask you to marry me if I couldn't. We'll be okay."

"He helped build Lindsay's first house when she got married." Emma was a tough Montana pioneer woman, and Mark knew that. But she was acting purely female now, with a coaxing smile and her hands brushing across his neck.

He was sorely afraid he'd agree to anything. "I'd love the help, but—"

"It don't matter. I'm not sure you can stop him."

"Truth be told, I'm mainly worried about your ma." Mark could almost feel Belle Harden burning a hole in the barn with her eyes.

"She let us come in here. That means she's going to be okay. She might not ever admit it. And she might threaten to kill you from time to time, but that's just tough talk."

"Tough talk?"

"If she really gets mad, you'll never see her comin'."

Nodding, Mark slung his arm around his brand-new promised-to-be wife. "Well, let's go give her the good news. Right now. Before Mandy's young'uns figure out they don't need me and your ma can run me off her range."

Emma laughed and slid her arm around his waist. "You'd better let me do the talking."

"Don't you think your ma will judge me a coward for that?"

"Nope, I think she'll be impressed with your good sense."

Mark walked out of the barn holding on to Emma, trying to figure out just what kind of family he'd be joining. And not caring one whit, because he'd be getting Emma. As for making her ma like him, well, he'd figure that out later.

When he stepped outside, he saw Belle and Silas. Silas looked grim. Belle had her six-gun tied down.

★

The first thing Cord saw when he rode into town was a man with a streak of white in his hair. And he wasn't alone. He found a new passel of Cooter cousins waiting for him in Helena.

Striding up to the first man he saw with the odd hair tuft, he thrust out his hand. "You're a Cooter, aren't'cha?" He saw a small army of men standing behind this one. Not all with the family hair. Maybe time in America was breeding that out of the Cooters. Cord hoped so. He hated that hank of white.

"Yep, we're from all over the country. We've been gathering for weeks waiting to hear from someone."

Another man from the group said, "We heard a Cooter'd been gunned down, and we're here to see the killer pay."

Cord didn't want to explain the whole truth. When it had been only a single woman against the Cooter family it had been a little bit embarrassing. But now they had someone to war against. "Tom Linscott has a ranch about three or four days' ride south of here. He's just killed three more of us." Cord was pretty sure Lady Gray had killed them all. It stung bad that a woman could be so salty.

"He even got my brother Fergus, and they almost got me." Cord knew the scratches still showed on his face. He was glad they did because it helped stir up his family.

Another of the nearly two dozen men standing in the crowd

pushed himself forward. "I rode with Fergus a few years back. Anyone who killed Fergus is going to pay."

Cord wasn't absolutely sure Fergus was dead. After that terrible racing panic had eased, Cord remembered that Fergus had been running away just a step behind. What had happened to his brother? Cord wasn't about to admit he'd run and left a wounded brother behind, not when he'd been the biggest talker when it came to sticking with family.

It didn't really matter, except Cord didn't want his kinfolk to find out he'd left Fergus behind. For a man crazy to stick with his kin, Cord was surprised how little he cared about his brother. They'd only met a couple of years ago. It wasn't like they'd grown up together.

Cord took in the look of the group. A shady crowd. He knew there were poor Cooters, rich ones, honest ones, and outlaws. This group looked like a poor band of outlaws for the most part. Worn clothing, battered saddles. Weary-looking horses and boots that were down-at-the-heels. Probably no-accounts. He suspected they hadn't all ridden here on a train, because the tickets were too expensive.

"We need to end this now," Cord said. He heard the grumbling of agreement. Good. "And we've got enough men that we can attack hard and fast and finish Linscott and his men all at once."

And his wife.

Again Cord kept that to himself. Cord would see to Mandy Gray personally. Even that wicked shooting iron couldn't stand up to this many men. "Let's saddle up and ride."

They headed straight for their horses, mounted up, and were galloping before they'd reached the edge of town. As his kin thundered along beside and behind him, Cord's throat swelled with pride. His family was here. Enough men to start a war. Now, with all of them thrown in with him, and that cursed land around Gray Towers not haunting them, the Cooters finally had a real chance to show the world they were a family to be reckoned with.

Cord counted down the hours until they could finally make this right. With luck, if they pushed hard, they could rain down like fire on the Linscott ranch in three days.

★ Twenty-One ★

We'll be three days getting to the Hardens if we stop for the night. We are *not* stopping."

Tom reined his horse to a stop. "Yes, we are."

"You said it's only about four more hours. We can keep going that long. And we'll be at Belle's house when the children wake up."

Tom was careful to roll his eyes before he turned to face his nagging wife. Once he was looking at her, he did his best to be real respectful of the battle-ax he'd married.

"I am not riding up this trail in the dark." He caught her reins and thought he might catch a fist in the face.

But despite her protests, her endless protests, her endless cranky protests, he was pretty certain Mandy was ready to stop for the night. It just seemed weak to her, so she was fighting it. And him. "I've ridden a lot of hard trails in my life."

For an observant woman, Mandy didn't seem to notice that he was tying her horse up, alongside his, and stripping off his saddle. He might have to strip hers off with her still sitting on top of it. "Come on down. That trail is a killer in the full light of day. I'm not riding up it with exhausted horses and exhausted riders. We'll set out the minute the sky lightens in the morning."

Tom knotted her horse's reins tight enough she'd have to dismount to untie it. Once her feet hit the ground, he'd steal her saddle, and then he'd have her. Watching for his chance, he started building a campfire.

The growling behind him continued, but finally she got down. Ready to lunge, he was pleased to see her working the cinch loose. He went back to setting up camp, glancing up occasionally to make sure she hadn't stolen the horse and run for the upland trail. He relaxed when she took to rubbing down the black mare she was riding. He had a fire crackling before she was done.

She grabbed a small pot and filled it with spring water for coffee.

"There are talus slides on that trail." Tom wasn't opposed to talking sense to his wife. Being reasonable, explaining his actions. It just proved to be a waste of time up till now. "It winds around like the great-granddaddy of all timber rattlers. I haven't been on it in years. There are spots that cave off and drop away for a hundred feet."

"If it's so bad, we might not even be able to get through that trail into the Harden spread." Mandy set the coffee on to boil and pulled fixings for supper from her saddlebag.

"We'll get through. We might have to pick our way, lead our horses, and clear the trail in spots. We can't do all that in the dark."

She grunted but quit her nagging. Tom thought the quiet sounded like a slice of heaven. They worked quietly side-by-side setting up camp and getting supper.

"What are we going to do to keep the children safe? We should have—"

Closing his eyes in near physical pain, he knew she thought of something new to complain about. But she was upset. Tom didn't blame her.

While she fretted, they finished their quick meal. The coffee was black and hot. Tom poured them both a cup in the cool mountain night then edged back from the fire to rest his back against a nearby log. Even in August it got mighty cold at night in the mountains.

With a sigh of contentment, he took a sip of the wicked brew and sighed again when his brand-spanking-new wife sat down beside him. "I'm sorry we couldn't get there tonight, Mandy girl. You know I'm right."

Mandy grunted. Which was an improvement over the nagging. Tom thought he could handle the racket, though. He wanted a wife with her own mind.

"And I know how much you want to get to your young'uns."

Mandy took a long sip of the slowly cooling liquid then sighed deeply. "They'd be asleep when we got there anyway." She looked sideways at him.

In the flickering firelight, he was reminded of the first night he'd seen her. Well, the first night since he'd gone to drag her out of that tower she lived in. Her hair loose and white, her clothes as gray as the stones that surrounded her. The blue in her eyes washed gray by the firelight. Her eyes glittering—spooky. Beautiful.

"I'm just so crazy to get to them. I should never have—"

His lips stopped the beating she'd been giving herself all day. He pulled her coffee cup out of her hand and took that stupid rifle off her back and eased her sideways until they lay on the ground, between the log and the fire.

"Stop, Mandy. Please." He ran one hand deep into her hair. "You thought long and hard before you left them."

"No, I—"

Silence again reigned. Tom was almost starting to like her criticism of herself. Better than him. Besides, it gave him a great excuse to distract her.

When he eased away from her pretty lips, they were stretched out on the ground. "Enough. You're too smart to waste this much energy fretting about something you can't undo."

With his body blocking the fire, he couldn't see her eyes anymore. Her hair flowed like milk over her arms and chest, and he realized he'd pulled the leather thong away and let her braid loose. He caressed the silken weight and wished it were full daylight so he could read her expression better. As if she was making any secret of how she felt.

"I know. And you're right. It's been an exhausting day. If that trail's half as treacherous as you say, we'd be lucky not to kill ourselves or our horses. We have to stop. I'm sorry I've been fussing at you, Tom." She smoothed his forehead with her fingers. It was the sweetest touch he'd ever known.

He wasn't much in the mood for sweet right now.

She closed her eyes and rolled so her back was to his. "We need to get some rest and get an early start tomorrow. Good night then."

He caught her shoulder before she could get comfortable and rolled her flat on her back. "Not quite yet."

"What?"

"You've been worrying about your children, and I know they're mighty important."

"Important? Well of course they are. They're the most important things in my life."

"I suppose that's fair, but a husband ranks right up there, doesn't he?" Lowering his head, he said, "I think you need to worry about me for a little while."

He kissed her and didn't stop until she was thinking only wifely thoughts, and plenty of them.

"This doesn't worry me one bit." She slid her arms around his neck and smiled.

Laughing softly, Tom said, "Well, maybe I'm not doing it right then."

★

Mandy came awake slowly, feeling as if she were wrapped in

comfort. Feeling safe. Strange, unfamiliar feeling. She looked skyward and remembered how the stars had almost seemed to speak aloud to her the first night she and Tom had spent in each other's arms. She'd been lying just like this.

At peace, even in the midst of the madness of her life, and the stars had hinted that there was a way to read them so Sidney's map made sense.

They weren't talking now, but then Mandy had learned what that map and those lights in the sky had to say already.

Instead she wondered how long she'd slept. Her head was fuzzy, but it wasn't heavy with exhaustion. The stars told her dawn wasn't far away. Tom was warm and solid beside her, letting her use his shoulder for a pillow.

They should get up. By the time they'd built up the fire and warmed up what was left of last night's coffee and eaten a biscuit or two, the sun would light their way.

She felt Tom stir beside her. Though she hadn't moved, she'd obviously disturbed his sleep. Or something else had disturbed them both.

Mandy listened, but nothing alerted her, and she trusted her wood-smarts.

"Let's get moving." His voice was scratchy and gruff. It stroked something deep inside her, almost an ache but not really. Too pleasant for that.

Mandy rolled up on her elbow so she looked down on her new husband. The moonlight lit his eyes. "I'm sorry I've brought trouble to you, Tom."

"Now, Mandy girl, don't start that again."

"But trouble or not, I wish now I'd come storming out of that stupid castle the minute Sidney was dead. That sounds awful and so unloving, but I wish I'd packed up the children and come running straight to you. I knew I could. I knew you'd take me in. But all I could think of was the trouble I'd bring." She knew the sun was coming close to rising because she could see the surprise and satisfaction on his face.

"I wish I'd been married to you for a year already." She leaned down and kissed him.

His arms were hard, as strong as oaks. Strong enough to protect her. Maybe her constant prayers for protection had garnered her the lightning speed with the Winchester, and now God had added a tough-as-nails husband.

"We'll get the children today." Tom stroked the hair back off her forehead. "We'll take them home and start living our life tomorrow. We'll be on guard, and the sheriff and the marshal will do their jobs. Worrying day and night about survival isn't going to be your life from now on, Mandy. We'll find a way to live in safety and as much peace as a body gets in the Rocky Mountains."

Smiling, Mandy nodded. "We will."

They were in the saddle soon after and riding out in the gray light of pre-dawn.

Before they'd ridden a hundred yards up the trail, they were stopped by a slide.

"This is awful." Mandy led her horse around the worst of it. Tom was in the lead, so he pushed rocks off a steep cliff on their left when necessary. They'd mount up and ride, then have to stop and lead their horses again. By the time they reached the top of the trail, the sun was fully up. But Mandy's nerves were strung tight from the mean, twisting trail.

"Glad we waited until we were rested?" Tom looked over his shoulder and gave her his usual "I told you so" smirk. She was almost starting to like it.

Mandy rode up beside him when the path widened enough to allow it. "I'm learning something about marriage from you, Tom."

He aimed his horse down the much more civilized slope that must lead them to the Harden ranch. The bottom of the trail was visible, and it seemed to end in a lush, grassy valley. There was no sign of a ranch house. Mandy had never been here before, but Tom seemed to know where he was going.

"What's that?"

"When you're married to a man you respect, it's a lot easier to let him lead. I know a man's supposed to be the head of the home, but with Sidney I never trusted him enough to even consider letting him take charge of much."

"You mean you built that castle?" Tom's lips quirked, so Mandy knew he was only teasing.

"Nope, that was all Sidney. But I didn't let him take care of the children. I never trusted him to find food or chop wood. Maybe he'd have done it if I'd let him get cold and hungry, but my children and I would have had to get cold and hungry, too, and I wasn't willing to trust him enough to leave it to him."

"But you might let me do important stuff?" Tom's smiled bloomed fully.

"I very definitely might."

Laughing, Tom said, "I am fully honored, Mrs. Linscott, that you might let me run my own household."

"Well, you oughta be."

Tom reached a smooth stretch of the trail with no rocks to roll beneath the horses' feet and kicked his horse into a ground-eating trot. Mandy kept up, eager to see her children. As they rode, she remembered the last time she'd felt this excited about life. It had been the day she'd married Sidney and had gotten on the stagecoach to leave Mosqueros, Texas, and start her new life with him.

And look how badly that had turned out.

★

"Look who's here." Mark lifted Angela off his lap and stood, turning to face Mandy and Tom. "Your ma's back."

He looked from Angie to Catherine in Emma's arms. Emma

was watching the oncoming horses. Jarrod was taking a mid-morning nap. Mandy was still a ways off, but Angela howled and reached for her mother and started crying her head off. Catherine joined in at once, though Mark didn't think the little girl knew exactly why she was crying.

"I guess I should've waited to mention it." He looked at Emma.

"I reckon." Emma had to shout to be heard over the wailing children. She rolled her eyes at him.

He smiled to think of a lifetime of Emma and her sass. "Let's walk out to meet them. Maybe if we act like we're hurrying it'll stop their crying."

"I'll tell Ma they're coming first." Emma hurried to the ranch door and was back in a trice.

The oncoming riders had goaded their horses into a gallop and were closing in so fast Mark didn't bother walking toward them. Instead he fussed over Angela, teasing her out of her tears with nonsense.

Emma reached his side with her own fretful child just as Mandy and Tom rode up.

Mandy was off the horse and running the few feet to her children before her horse had come to a full stop. Mark looked over Mandy's head to see Tom dealing with the horses. Belle came out of the house carrying a sleepy Jarrod with several more children on her heels. Mark and Emma both set their wriggling girls free to run to their mama.

Her arms full of crying children, Mandy hugged and kissed and comforted her girls. Mark heard her apologizing repeatedly.

Tom came up and said, "Got a howdy for your pa?"

Angela looked up, quit crying, and stretched out her arms. "Hi, Papa."

Tom scooped her up and tossed her into the air. The tears were forgotten as Angela giggled and Catherine yammered for a turn.

Mark whispered to Emma, "You don't think he's really their pa, do you?"

"Of course not." Emma shook her head. "Mandy's a proper, decent woman."

There wasn't a real strong sense of assurance in Emma's voice, even though Mark thought she was right. Probably.

Mandy reached for Jarrod when Belle got close enough. His legs were pumping as if he were running toward his ma, even though Belle still had him in her arms. Smiling, she handed the boy over. Then Belle gave Mandy a hug, even though the children were in their arms.

When the riot calmed down, Belle said, "Come in and sit a spell."

"We need to get back to the ranch," Mandy said.

There were tears in her eyes. Mark couldn't get past how fragile Mandy McClellen had become. It stirred him until he wanted to fight someone just to take the pressure off his gut.

He went to Mandy when Belle turned loose of her and pulled her into his arms, children and all. "Are you all right?" He pulled back so their eyes met. So much passed between them.

"You have never been nice to me a day in your life, Mark Reeves." Mandy's eyes were watering, but he saw her spunk. She was in better shape than when Tom had first brought her to his ranch.

"You didn't deserve nice. You were bossier than my parents and the teacher combined, you pointed out more of my sins than the parson ever did, and you never quit nagging me for a minute." Mark grinned.

"And you tortured perfectly nice teachers and disrupted the school, and you earned every sharp word I ever spoke."

Mark caught himself before he dropped his head and kicked at the dirt in the sullen little boy way he'd had whenever his pranks had caught up with him. Instead he stepped back and said,

"I believe you said on a number of occasions that I was born to hang."

"And yet here you are walking around." Mandy's tears eased and she smiled fully. "A testimony to years of desperate prayers your mother sent heavenward."

Mark glanced behind him and saw Emma watching him with narrow eyes. He made a quick move and snaked his arm around her waist—right in front of Belle Harden—and pulled her to his side. "And now I've got another good woman with her work cut out for her."

Mandy looked from Mark to Emma. Mark noticed a faint blush on Emma's tanned skin.

"Well, since she didn't slam the butt of her six-gun into your skull, it must be true." Mandy looked at Emma, who nodded. "Emma, we've got to find a time to talk privately. I know all the best ways of punishing Mark when he's up to no good."

Emma smiled. "Have you got things straightened up? I thought you were on your way to Denver. We didn't expect you back for days and days."

Tom came up to Mandy's side and hoisted Catherine out of her arms. "We let everyone think we were heading for Denver, but that wasn't our goal. We've done what we set out to do."

Mark had no idea what that meant exactly. Tom definitely wasn't telling all he knew.

"Now we're going to go home, make sure the ranch is secure, and let the law handle the Cooter clan." Tom looked down at Mandy.

Mark thought he saw just a hint of warning in Tom's eyes, a bit like what he'd seen in Emma's. Maybe Mark had oughta quit hugging married women.

Then Tom glared at Mark. "Are you coming with me, or are you staying here with the Hardens?"

"He's going with you." Belle stepped up close. "Let's get you something hot in your stomachs. Trail food gets old after a while."

They turned to the house. Mandy and Tom walked ahead with all three children, still clinging.

"Have you talked with your family, Mandy?" Mark might be wise not to hug her, but he couldn't help wanting to protect her. "Do they know what's going on? I didn't send a letter or a wire. I wasn't sure if I should."

Mandy looked back, frowning. "Are you coming back to Tom's place?"

"*Our* place, Mandy girl," Tom said.

"Our place." Mandy smiled at Tom a private kind of smile that made Mark restless to have his very own wife.

He reached out to pull Emma close, and Belle was there. She knocked his hand aside. "Let's get inside."

"You know I'm really starting to like you, Ma." Mark braced himself to take a fist to the jaw.

Instead Belle smiled. She wiped the smile away quick but not quick enough.

"I saw that."

She scowled, and Mark didn't push his luck. He headed after Mandy and Tom. He needed to ask his boss about the cattle he had coming for pay. He needed to get on with building a house and arranging a wedding.

If he had his way, he'd get it all in order by the end of the week.

Mark saw Charlie riding in from his stint standing watch. Charlie had done his best to sneak a word or two with Sarah, but it'd been a challenge.

Silas rode alongside him, and the two were talking. Silas looked plumb depressed.

It occurred to Mark suddenly that Charlie was talking to the man of the family. Why hadn't Mark thought of that? It was the proper way, and it had the advantage of going around Belle instead of through her.

Silas swung down off his horse and handed the reins to Charlie, who started leading the animals toward the barn.

Sarah stepped to the door of the cabin. "I've got some stew heated up."

Her pretty voice drew Charlie's head around, and he stopped in his tracks.

"Let's get inside now," Belle ordered.

Silas came up to Belle and said something in a voice too low for anyone to hear.

Belle shook her head and looked horrified.

Tom and Mandy went inside along with the children.

"Sarah, come out here." Silas's voice was hard and cranky. Belle's jaw was so tight he doubted she was capable of speech.

Sarah had backed into the house as the crowd moved in, but she came back out so quickly Mark knew she'd been paying close attention to what went on outside. She headed for her parents, but her eyes went to Charlie as if they were beyond her control.

Charlie turned back from the barn, and Mark said to Emma, "I'm going to see to the horses. I'll be right back."

Emma looked past him and saw Charlie walking toward her ma and pa and Sarah, and her eyes went round with surprise.

"We can live next door to 'em if you want. There's another nice stretch of land close to mine that will suit my cousin." Mark paused as Emma sorted all of that out. Then he added, "And your sister."

Emma whispered, "See to the horses. I'm going to say a prayer for Charlie."

Mark nodded and made quick work of taking the horses to the barn, leaving his cousin to his fate.

Twenty-Two

I can't seem to get my breath." Mandy looked behind her at the receding gap they'd just ridden through. "That place seemed safe. Now we're out here, exposed. We need to ride hard for your ranch, Tom."

Angela was asleep sitting in front of Mandy. Catherine was asleep in Tom's arms. Mark had Jarrod on his back. Six cowhands rode strung out behind them. Including Mark Reeves, though Mandy had wondered for a while if he'd agree to go.

"You're looking at it wrong, Mandy girl."

"How so?" She kicked her horse to up her speed from a ground-eating canter to a flat-out gallop.

"You're still thinking like a rabbit. Running from hole to hole. Your stupid Gray Tower was safe, Belle's was safe, my ranch is safe."

"Well, they are." Mandy felt her heart pound hard at the wide open spaces. She looked at the cragged hills and thick forests. Well, not wide open exactly.

"We're not going to live like that. We'll be cautious, but we are not going to run into my house and pull that heavy door shut behind us and hide."

"Yes, we are."

"We're going to live." Tom reached over and caught Mandy's reins and slowed her horse. "We can't keep up this pace all the way home. The horses can't handle it. Settle down."

Mandy wanted to knock Tom's hands away from her horse and spur the animal faster. Of course she had no spurs, but she'd manage to wring speed out of the poor critter. And she wanted it so badly, so desperately that she suddenly knew Tom was right.

She was thinking like a rabbit. Half rabbit, half rabid swamp rat.

With a sigh, she quit fighting over control of her horse, and when she quit, Tom let go. They settled into a fast, steady walk that the horses could keep up all day.

"I can feel them out there, Tom. I can feel them drawing a bead on my back."

"I've got good men with me, and I know these hills. There's nowhere to lay in wait along here. The trail is too rugged. There aren't good overhangs. Farther down the trail toward the Double L, I'll have the men split off and make sure no one's around, but for now we're fine."

"We're not *fine*, Tom. We'll never be fine as long as one Cooter is still living."

Mandy settled in to rail at her husband for the rest of the long ride home when a wider spot in the trail allowed Mark Reeves to ride up beside them. Mandy clamped her lips shut and glared at Mark. He grinned back. Mandy suspected she looked a lot more like his old enemy when she was glaring.

"Can I talk to you, Boss?"

Mandy waited for Tom to tell Mark to beat it so they could discuss important, life and death things.

"Sure, what do you want?" Tom didn't even look at Mandy.

She wondered if maybe she'd done a bit too much nagging. It didn't seem to be having much good affect.

"I've asked Emma Harden to marry me."

Mandy gasped and looked sharply at Mark.

"Any reason that's a bad thing, wife?" Tom's voice sounded a bit too harsh.

"Yes, of course there's a reason. I've got to warn Emma to run for her life."

Tom's harsh tone was lost in a quick laugh.

Mark scowled at her, but there was a twinkle in his eyes. "Too late."

"Maybe I'll talk to Belle, then."

"She's already given her blessing, or as close as she's ever apt to get when a man comes courting her daughter."

"How close?"

"She hasn't threatened to shoot me for nearly two days."

Tom laughed again, and Mark joined in. Mandy closed her eyes then was helpless not to laugh, too. "Well, if Belle's given you her. . .sort of. . .blessing, then who am I to oppose poor Emma signing on her future with you."

"Silas is Belle's fourth husband. The rest were a worthless lot. I think Emma will be okay with me because she's had some terrible men to compare me with." Mark grinned.

Mandy was tempted to swat him. He wasn't quite close enough, though. And that might not be accidental.

"So are you telling me you want to draw your time?" Tom reminded Mandy that Mark had started this for a reason.

"You said you'd pay me in cattle. I've homesteaded on a holding up in these hills." Mark pointed straight at a bunch of trees no one could begin to see through. "There's a nice mountain valley I scouted out a few miles to the north of Belle and Silas's. It turns out Emma's sister lives to the north. Belle knows the place I picked and seems to be pleased with it. I'll need the cattle. I'll work as long as I can, but I want to get a cabin up before first snow, and I—"

"I'll send some men with you to put up the house." Tom

looked at Mandy. "In fact—"

"You don't have to do that," Mark interrupted before Tom could go on. He had a tinge of pink on his cheeks as if his temper was up. "I can take care of my own wife and build my own cabin."

Tom glared at Mark. "Neighbors help each other out here. You think I built my house single-handedly? And maybe Mandy and I could come, camp out with the young'uns. Get away from the ranch for a while. Let the Cooters hunt around for us."

"It wouldn't be hiding, and yet they'd have a hard time figuring out where we went." Mandy liked the idea real well.

"But I thought I'd work another month or two. I figure I've earned five or six head of cattle. I'd like to add a couple more, get a better start for Emma and me."

"I'll make it ten—nine cows bred Angus and one young bull."

Mark jerked a little and looked surprised and delighted.

"We'll have to camp on the trail tonight. But we'll get home midday and leave as soon as we can, maybe tomorrow if I don't run into anything at the ranch that slows me down. I have to get in to Divide to talk to the law, but we can swing through there on our way to the building site. We'll take all the men the ranch can spare and get the cabin up and finished while the sheriff and marshal do their jobs." Tom looked satisfied.

Mandy liked it, too. It wouldn't be hiding. She wasn't a rabbit if she was helping a friend build a cabin.

"Well, I suppose—"

"It's an order. And go back right now and tell Silas about it. He'll need to come along with Emma, and he's a good carpenter." Tom shrugged. "No, forget that. Just tell Emma you want her to have say in how we build the cabin. Don't even bother telling Silas. He won't let his girl ride away from his place with you. He'll come whether you ask or not."

With an expression that made Mandy wonder if he was dizzy from his life being planned for him, Mark said, "I'll go back and talk to her, then catch up with you wherever you camp." He wheeled his horse.

"Wait a minute," Tom ordered.

Mark turned back instantly.

"Leave Jarrod with me." Tom shook his head as if Mark didn't have possession of a lick of brains.

Grinning, Mark said, "I've gotten used to him." He slung the pack off his back, and Tom donned it. Then Mark headed back in the direction they'd just come.

Tom gave a firm, satisfied jerk of his chin then headed for home carrying two of Mandy's babies. He was protecting them. And Mandy. She'd brought terrible danger into his life, but he was strong enough to handle it all and build a house for one of his cowhands in his spare time. "The horses are rested. Let's put some miles behind us." Tom sped up, and Mandy fell into a gallop, keeping up with Tom's fast pace toward home.

He was carrying more than just her children. He also had her heart.

★

Cord crested a high ridge in the trail and pulled up. "Look down there." He pointed at a spot to the west of the Linscott ranch.

There was room for several of his cousins to come up beside him. "What're ya lookin' at, Cord?"

"It's Linscott. I recognize his black stallion. I'd know that big beast anywhere." It was getting on toward noon. They'd ridden late last night. Then one of his cousins had produced a bottle or two of rotgut, and they'd stayed up late playing poker and talking.

Cord knew they needed to push hard, but he'd enjoyed the whiskey himself and had needed the sleep this morning.

"You said his ranch was to the east of here." One of the cousins was a whiner.

Cord could taste the victory, and it would cost far less than he'd planned. A direct assault would have brought a lot of Cooters down. Cord had been ready to do it, but now he saw a way out. "He's heading for Divide. He's got a few men riding with him, but he's not barricaded like he'd be at the ranch."

And he had Lady Gray with him. With cold pleasure, Cord focused on her white braid. He saw a toddler strapped on Linscott's back. Cord suspected the other two children were on someone's horse, but he couldn't see them from this distance.

Thinking of that, the children, twisted his gut. This was a blood feud, and those young'uns had bought in just by being born. But he hadn't really thought of bringing those little ones under his gun. Unless he was killing mad, he didn't think he could do it. And he was sure the rest of his kin hadn't given it much thought.

But how could he spare the children if he was raining fire down from an overlook? If he tried to be careful of them, he'd miss his chance to finish Lady Gray and Linscott. He settled it by nursing his grudge and letting the need to avenge his family turn his mind from an act even he couldn't stand to think about.

He glanced at his kinfolk. "We can take the high trail right here, instead of going down. We'll get ahead of Linscott and cut him down where he stands." He studied the landscape then pointed to a high outcropping of rock. "That looks like it looms right over the trail. A perfect place for an ambush."

A lot of heads nodded, and more than a few seemed relieved. They hadn't complained, but Cord sensed they weren't eager to launch a frontal attack on a well-defended ranch. He wondered what flowed in the blood of the Cooter family that made them inclined toward back-shooting. He preferred it himself.

He turned his horse, not half the animal Linscott's stallion was, and headed straight north on the highlands. He didn't know the country around here, but he knew the woods, and there was a faint but clear game trail. These were mountain-bred horses—at least his was. If a deer or a mountain goat could leave a trail, his mustang could follow it.

"This is gonna be over in a couple of hours." With renewed energy, his family followed him to the final showdown.

★

Tom set a blistering pace. He wanted to talk to the marshal and Sheriff Dean then do his best to get into the highlands before nightfall. They'd find the place where Reeves's cabin would be built and have themselves a few days of hard labor, in complete safety.

He loved his ranch, but the whole time he'd been there this morning it'd itched at him that the Cooters would be coming. They were pure weasel, but they were dependable.

Without slowing up, he hollered back, "Reeves!"

Mark came up beside him. "Here, Boss."

"There's a narrow spot in the trail ahead. It's the only place where someone could get a good shot at us from cover. We can't scout the trail without it taking half a day, there's just no way up to those rocks." Tom pointed at an overhang in the distance. Then he glanced back at Mandy and met her eyes.

She nodded, taking in every word.

He made no attempt to keep anything from her. After what he'd seen of her in action, there was nobody he'd rather have fighting at his side. She might be worried about becoming a killer, but Tom wasn't overly. He suspected he could keep her from hiring out to settle range wars if he watched her close.

She was trailing him, but only because it was too narrow to ride three abreast, especially at a gallop.

"What do you want me to do?" Mark asked.

Tom tried his best, but he was having a hard time getting really mad at this little punk who'd known Mandy for so long and had such a deep connection to Tom's children. "Drop back and tell the men we're going through hard. I'll signal you when I'm ready to pick up speed." Tom shifted his grip on the reins so he held them in his left hand, which was busy holding Catherine on the saddle. He raised his right hand in a fist. "That'll be the sign. I don't want to yell and wake up the children. Tell the men to ride low to their horses until I signal you to stop. We'll make it. The Cooters wouldn't have any way of knowing where we are. My men have been scouting around the ranch, and there's no sign we're being watched. But even so, we ride hard, keep low, and be ready for trouble. Tell 'em."

A firm jerk of Mark's chin was the only response before Mark let Tom ride on ahead.

That tight stretch in the trail was still a ways ahead. Tom had ridden this trail a hundred times and knew it right down to the trees and game trails. Within the hour they'd pass through what felt to him like a death trap all of a sudden. Rugged rocks rose high on the right side and dropped away on the left. Swallowing, he realized he'd never given it much thought before. Despite the hard life, most of the danger out here came from rattlesnakes and grizzlies and blizzards, not gunmen. Even the outlaws tended to run off a few head of cattle and avoid coming under anyone's gun.

Being married was going to be tricky, what with Mandy always halfway ready to run away, thinking to protect him. He looked down at Catherine, deep asleep in his arms. He'd have to guard the children to keep their stubborn mother in line. She wouldn't run off without them. Then he realized she already had once.

Hugging Catherine close, he felt the weight of Jarrod on his back and thought of what would happen if dry-gulchers opened fire on him or Mandy. The children would be right in the line of fire.

Tom's fury tightened his whole body, and Catherine shifted in her sweet sleep. Forcing himself to relax, lest he squeeze her until she woke up, Tom set his jaw and looked ahead. One more hour and they'd be through that narrow stretch of trail and likely be safe.

His big hand nearly covered Catherine's tummy, and he wished his hand were iron, a solid barrier for the little girl.

One more hour.

★

"We'll be down there in less than an hour." Cord pointed to the outcropping of rock that loomed over the trail the Linscott party was traveling. "We'll have time to set up and be waiting for them."

A grumble of satisfaction from behind pulled a smile onto Cord's face. This was all going to be over. He thought maybe he'd move to California once this was done. He was tired of the Rockies in winter. He had no taste for homesteading or ranching. Maybe he could work for someone like he'd done for Sidney Gray. That had been the best job he'd ever held. Easiest, too. With a smirk he thought of how that fool Gray had ended up dead at his hand.

It flickered through his head that if he hadn't mistreated Lady Gray and gotten himself fired, he might have instead continued to protect Sidney. Sidney might still be alive, especially since Cord had killed Gray personally.

For one second his whole world tilted as he considered that he had set all of this in motion. He had lost the best job he'd ever had through his own behavior. Now he daydreamed about getting a job just like that again.

Shaking his head to avoid the unsettling notion, he remembered when he'd gone up behind Lady Gray and put his hand on her shoulder. Offering her protection and...male companionship. She should have been honored. Cord knew the way Sidney treated her. She should have jumped at the chance to be friendlier with Cord. Instead she'd been offended and had him fired. Gray had acted like it was about the gold, but Cord knew the truth. Mandy had spoken to her husband, and Cord got booted out of his job. The sting to his pride was still there.

He looked down the tree-covered slope to the trail where he'd seen Linscott. It was hidden from sight, but Cord knew it was there. He knew Lady Gray was there. He'd teach that woman a lesson.

Then he touched his face where she'd nearly killed him. She'd hit, near as Cord could tell, his rifle right in the muzzle. As good as sent her bullet straight up the barrel of his gun. If she'd really been aiming for the muzzle, then she'd hit a target less than an inch in diameter. And she'd done it while she was moving, ducking, diving. Shaking his head, Cord knew no one was that accurate. Lucky shot. But Cord couldn't deny she was greased lighting with that Winchester. Well, he'd see how she did against two dozen hardened men.

He also decided he'd take his pick of spots. Even with him high above in a surprise attack, she'd get her rifle into action. He suspected she'd keep firing even if she were dying. It'd take a well-placed bullet to bring her down, and if they didn't place the bullets well, it'd take a hail of them.

The first bullet out of Cord's gun was already marked just for Lady Gray. He saw the game trail he was following narrow, which was next to impossible because it was already so narrow it was little more than a rabbit track. It curved downward sharply, and Cord had to slow his horse. Tree branches reached out and would have knocked a man off a running horse. Keeping low, Cord wondered if they'd have to end this on foot. Could his horse even get down to that overhang?

He wished he could see the Linscott crowd, but they were out of sight. That lone stretch of rock topped by the outcropping would be the only place they'd have a clear shot. They'd gained ground. Cord suspected they'd pulled well ahead of the Linscotts.

Now they just had to get into place and bide their time, patient as hungry cougars.

Cord liked that image. He was coiled and ready to spring. All he needed was a rabbit to pounce on.

★ Twenty-Three ★

For the first time in years, Mandy didn't feel like a rabbit being stalked by a pack of coyotes. She followed Tom's broad shoulders, feeling like he could block the whole world for her. Hating that she'd put him in danger, but still glad not to be on her own anymore.

And they were nearing Divide. Somehow getting to town seemed like the end of all the danger. They'd consult with the marshal, find out hopefully that they had the situation with the Cooters under control, and then make tracks for Mark's homestead.

If they needed to build Mark an eight-bedroom mansion, they'd do it and stay at that homestead until the Cooters were arrested and no longer a risk to anyone. If her husband would just agree.

Tom looked back over those broad shoulders. "We're almost to that narrow stretch."

He spoke softly, so as not to wake the children. Trying to smile, she barely managed a brief upturn of her lips and a terse nod.

Tom wasn't fooled. He knew her very well considering how short was their acquaintance.

Looking ahead to the tapering trail, Mandy swallowed hard and held Angela closer. The trail twisted and climbed. They could only see a few yards ahead. It led to a woodless rocky stretch. The whole trail was narrow and heavily forested, except this one stretch. For a few yards, it would be so tight it almost grabbed Mandy by the throat. They just needed to get through it, and the mountain on the right dropped away. There was nowhere to ambush riders on the trail after that one spot. After that was a fairly safe route to Divide.

They'd be passing through it in minutes. Mandy was scared right down to the ground, but at least, finally, she was no one's rabbit.

★

Cord didn't speak a word. They were too close. Chances were the heavy forest would drown out any sound, but he wasn't taking a chance. The trail was so sheer now his horse took a single step at a time. They were cutting it close, but they'd get there. A trail had to go somewhere after all. And though Cord wasn't familiar with this area, he was dead certain that this trail led straight to that rocky knoll.

He caught a glimpse of a rider far below, still well behind the Cooters. All he had to do was reach that stack of boulders, and that was only a few hundred yards ahead.

Salivating, Cord could taste the victory. He'd like to get his hands on those beautiful black horses of Linscott's. He'd like to get his hands on Lady Gray's gold. He'd like to get his hands on Lady Gray. He doubted he'd manage any of that because he was going to come down on that party like iron fire raining from heaven. Lady Gray was too fast and too accurate to risk leaving her alive or aiming carefully to spare those horses. The horses were too well-known anyway. Someone would identify them as Linscott's, and that would tie the Cooters to their deaths. He was content with just finishing this business and riding away with the slate wiped clean, the feud settled.

He reached a sudden drop-off in the middle of the trail that forced him to stop. He could clearly see tracks. Deer and mountain goat, heading down, straight for that overlook. But his horse had finally reached the limits. It balked and wouldn't go another step. What's more, Cord knew the horse *couldn't* go another step. It couldn't handle this sheer descent. But a man could.

Grimacing with anger, he looked back at his kin. "There's no trail from here on, not one a horse can handle. We've got to go on foot."

His family grumbled, but they all knew there was no time to hash out a new plan.

Swinging down, they tied their horses to the nearest limb, and there was an abundance of them. Cord looked again at that drop-off. Easy enough on foot. He'd just have to jump. It might have been twenty feet of sheer rock, but Cord could swing down, hanging on with his fingertips, then drop the last bit. He checked that his six-gun was firm in his holster and took his rifle. He'd need the long gun to make that shot. Even from where he wanted to lie in wait, it was a long shot to make a hit. But he had no doubt he and his cousins could do it.

From up here they were out of rifle range. There was no chance to even draw a bead on the Linscotts because the trees blocked their line of sight. Which was fine. That let the Cooters get close without being detected.

Cord slid his belly over the drop-off and, with his rifle in one hand, hung for a second from the other, then dropped. Simple.

He looked up into the eyes of one of his cousins above, nodded, and turned. They still had plenty of time to set up at that overhang, take aim, and fire.

★

"Reeves!" The trail was too narrow to ride two abreast, but for a few seconds, if they were careful, they could manage it.

Mark eased up beside him.

"Take Catherine." Tom slid the boneless, sleeping girl into Mark's arms. "I don't want Jarrod on my back when we ride through there." Tom swung Jarrod around front and held the sleeping toddler, sheltering him as well as possible.

Mark jerked his chin and dropped back. A glance told Tom he fell behind Mandy, too. Guarding her from the rear along with six more men behind Mark. Good men, men to count on in a fight. None of that would protect them if lead started raining down on them from overhead.

They'd be in that tight neck and out before those Cooters could take aim. And, considering that the Cooters weren't even there, it'd be fine.

Still, Tom saw no reason to hope for the best. His eyes rose to that overhang of rock. Perfect cover for an ambush.

Tom asked everything of his horse, himself, and his God as the trail narrowed.

★

Sliding more than walking, Cord didn't try and stop his descent. He needed to get down there in time to take aim, and all his cousins with him.

From behind he heard all the men coming. Dust and small rocks dislodged under his boot heels, and a few clattered down on his head kicked from above. The dust rose up until a small cloud formed. Was it visible to riders below?

Cord clung to his rifle and kept heading down.

Tom pulled Jarrod close to shield him, then raised his fist and spurred his horse.

Teeth gritted together with rage, he hated to think those

coyote Cooters were so bent on their feud they might kill one of Tom's children—and they *were* Tom's children. Whatever their father's name, they were *his*, and they were Linscotts to the bone because Tom decided they were.

He pushed ahead fast without checking those behind him. The men were solid. Mandy was as dependable as the sunrise. They were right where they needed to be.

The trail continued to rise, and it was more narrow by the stride. His horse was game, though, and it didn't falter as it raced for a stretch of trail that could become a death trap.

★

With a tight hold on his rifle, Cord hit a slightly less treacherous stretch of the trail. It still slanted sharply downward, but he was on his feet now instead of his backside. He ran flat out. Closing the distance, listening, hoping he didn't hear the sound of oncoming hooves.

Not yet. He threaded his way through a clump of aspens, hitting one with his shoulder and setting it to quaking. The shiver of the tree startled a deer out of the brush slightly down the trail. Running, the deer vanished into the trees, but his direction went right along this trail.

"We're on the right track." The deer was leading them, proving this was an established trail. He chanced a quick look back at his family, all racing along after him. His heart pounded hard, as much from excitement as from exertion. All these Cooters working together. He was proud of his family. Proud of their loyalty to each other. Lady Gray was about to finally realize just how foolish she'd been to aim her rifle at a Cooter.

With his eyes squarely on the path ahead, Cord risked a smile. All they had to do was get there in time.

★

Trees on both sides slapped at Mandy's shoulders. Galloping as they were, she ducked a branch and still took a swipe in the face from whipcord-thin branches of aspen.

The aspens grew more up than out, which told Mandy just how narrow the trail was. If they'd wanted to turn around, they'd be hard pressed to manage it. The horse could rear and wheel around probably, but it would be difficult and slow, especially with so many riders packed tightly and traveling fast. They were as good as forced to go forward.

Tom rode this trail every time he went to Divide. He should have widened it. Cut trees for his cabin from this spot. She'd spend awhile nagging him to do just that as soon as he'd worked out all the other trouble that came along with marrying her.

Pine trees occasionally replaced the aspen and clawed her. She focused on speed and protecting her little girl. With one hand busy blocking blows to Angela's precious face and the other guiding her horse, she wasn't able to spare herself.

A ponderosa pine nearly unseated her. She crouched lower, using her shoulders and her stinging face to protect Angela the best she could.

She'd ridden this trail once with Tom, the day they'd gone to town. They had come from another direction when they'd ridden in from Gray Tower and from yet another way when they'd come back from the Flatheads' valley and the Harden place. This tight passage had been hard to endure on the earlier trip when she *didn't* feel like she had a gang of outlaws on her trail.

Now, knowing the Cooters might have regrouped and come back, it was a hundredfold worse. Every breath she drew was a struggle as her throat tightened with fear. She felt the cold creep into her blood, her muscles, her nerves.

Surely Cord, the only one of those last four men unaccounted for, hadn't found more cousins already. But Mandy and Tom had taken three men into the sheriff, one dead and draped over his horse. They'd ridden to the Flathead village and back.

A good chance he couldn't gather any help in that time, but Cord could be up there alone. And he could do terrible damage from that overlook.

Mandy desperately looked forward to getting through this gauntlet.

★

Cord saw the deer ahead of him. Then he saw it leap gracefully over. . .nothing. Straight ahead he saw the end of the world.

He threw himself flat on his back.

"Stop! A cliff!" A strangled yell of warning was all he had time for. His shirt tore on a projecting scrub pine and he felt his back being cut and scoured by the rock and grit of the mountain. He slid to a stop just inches from the ledge.

A cousin came sliding fast. Cord grabbed at him. His cousin stopped with his legs hanging out over. . .Cord wasn't sure what.

The next few seconds were a fur ball of tumbling and grabbing and muffled shouts. But when the dust settled, no one went over the ledge. When they all lay, scattered like battered branches after a wind storm, Cord finally had the time and gumption to lean forward and see the pit he'd almost gone flying into. There was nothing but a huge crack in the mountain.

Straight across the crack stood the deer that had led them this direction. It had jumped, probably without giving it a thought. The deer arched its neck, and a rack of proud antlers rose as the animal seemed to sneer at Cord. Then it whirled and ran straight to that outcropping of rock and posed there as if it was the king of this whole mountain. Then it vanished into the woodlands beyond. Of course this trail worked for a deer.

Cord looked down. This crack dropped into a pit so deep Cord couldn't see to the bottom.

Heart pounding, gasping for breath, Cord's stomach clenched so hard at the near miss he thought he'd toss his breakfast right

293

into the depths. He fought that off and then had time to really look, up the mountain and down. If they could get across, that outcropping of rock that overlooked the trail was only a few dozen feet on the other side of this split in the earth.

It might as well have been on the moon. The crack stretched as far as the eye could see up, and on the downhill side looked to go all the way to the trail Linscott was on.

He could just faintly see where Lady Gray and her guards were riding through the trees far below. And he wouldn't have known he could see it at all if he hadn't watched riders, visible for fleeting seconds, passing.

"We missed them." Cord's terror twisted into fury. But they wouldn't miss them for long. "Let's get down there and finish this." Cord turned, ignoring his kin, and charged back up the slope, twice as hard and half as fast as he'd come down.

He heard his family grousing, but he didn't wait. The Cooters would come. He knew the kind of men they were. They'd bellyache maybe, but they were loyal. They were men who understood what was important.

In the end, Cooters stuck together.

★

"Did you hear something?" As they cleared the narrow stretch of trail without incident, Mandy rode up beside Tom.

"Nope." He lifted his head and listened with keen concentration for a few seconds, then looked up and behind him as his horse moved along at a gallop. "Smells like dust or something." Tom shook his head and pulled his horse to a fast walk. "Probably kicked up by the horses. Who knows."

Looking over her shoulder, Mandy saw a magnificent mule deer with a huge set of antlers step up on the rocky overhang as if he were their lookout. As if he ruled the world.

"That must be what I saw."

Tom looked back just as the deer turned and darted away. "Well, no one up there, or a deer wouldn't be hanging around."

Mandy felt the chill recede as she accepted the movement and slight sounds of the deer as the reason why she'd felt so itchy. For a second she'd been ready to reach for her rifle, and she already knew exactly where she'd have aimed and fired. And Mandy was one to trust her instincts.

"We made it through that gap. There's no real good place to stake out the trail from here on in." Tom's horse emerged from the heavily wooded stretch into a flatter land, grass and some scrub brush but no highlands edging the trail. And no trees big enough to hide behind.

"Those back-shooting Cooters won't face us head-on, so with that bad stretch behind us, we'll be fine now." Tom smiled then looked down at sleeping Jarrod. "Can you imagine feeling this safe?"

Mandy reached across and brushed the flyaway brown hair off of Jarrod's forehead. "I think I already knew how to load Ma's rifle at this age. Definitely by Angela's." She tightened her grip gently on the child in her own arms. "And Sally could already rope a moving calf from the back of a good cowpony when she was just a bit older."

"We can get started training the girls to rope and shoot as soon as we get done building Reeves's cabin. Get 'em their own rifles."

"Tom, I don't think—" Mandy looked up and saw the sparkle in her husband's eye.

"Maybe we wait a little longer, huh?" He chuckled.

"Maybe just another year or two." Shaking her head, Mandy smiled. "Let's get to Divide. I'm going to be mighty glad to be done with this trail."

They walked awhile, the heat of the summer, the scent of the pines at their backs, the jagged white peaks all around them, the soft clop of the hooves.

Mandy dropped back when Angela woke up and started chattering. Her horse was inclined to move along following Tom, and it required almost no effort from Mandy. Jarrod riding on Tom's lap was chattering, but the boy wasn't a big talker yet. Mandy heard Tom's deep voice—probably going over and over that the boy was to call him Pa. The thought made Mandy smile, and it eased her tension. She looked back and could see Catherine sitting with relaxed contentment on Mark's lap.

Mark smiled at Mandy and gave her a reassuring nod. A world where Mark Reeves was mature and helpful just made no sense to Mandy at all.

When the horses were rested, Tom picked up the pace, and it wasn't long until they rode into the sleepy little town of Divide.

Mandy had told herself she was safe before, but now the weight that lifted off her shoulders told her she hadn't really believed it.

"I want to see Sheriff Dean first thing," Tom said to Mandy. Then he turned to his cowhands. "See to that list of supplies. Mark, do you mind keeping Catherine? We can take her."

"I'm fine." Mark smiled down at Catherine as if to ask her if she was happy. Catherine giggled.

Mandy was a bit surprised at the way Mark accepted the children's attention. He'd never shown much patience as a child. Though his little brothers had begun popping up in school before Mandy had grown up. And he'd always included them in his nonsense. Mandy had considered him more a bad influence than a caretaker.

Tom rode straight up Divide's single dirt street for the jailhouse, and Mandy followed.

She'd only been in town briefly, but she was struck by how quiet it was. No tinny music coming out of the Golden Butte. No wagons or horses on the street. Not a single soul anywhere.

Tom swung down, carrying Jarrod as if he didn't weigh an

ounce. As Mandy's feet hit the ground, the sheriff's door burst open, and she saw—

"Sally!" Mandy ran and threw herself into her sister's arms.

Angela was between them, but Mandy didn't let that stop her from hugging Sally tight and long and deep.

★ Twenty-Four ★

Luther came next. Tom remembered him and Buff and Wise Sister. They all poured out of the sheriff's office, talking a mile a minute.

Well, at least Mandy and Sally were. Sally snatched Jarrod out of Tom's arms. Tom didn't even try to keep up with the chatter. She might have asked nicely for the little boy.

"Mark Reeves?" Sally shouted the name, sounding stunned.

Tom saw Reeves, carrying Catherine, turn, flash a smile, and come back at a near run.

It burned a little. Tom had told the men to lay up supplies. But there were more than enough men for that. He just hadn't wanted the whole bunch of them crowding into the sheriff's office.

Mark swept Sally up in his arms just as Logan McKenzie came out of the sheriff's office. . .and started scowling.

Tom hadn't seen any of these folks since Jarrod was born, and then he'd met them once and not for very long. But he felt an instant brotherhood with any man who didn't like Mark Reeves hugging his wife.

Tom reached out a hand to Logan and drew his attention. "We're brothers now, I think."

"Why, because you don't like that guy touching my wife either?" Logan didn't take his eyes off Sally.

"No, because I married Mandy. We really are brothers."

Logan's brow smoothed, and he smiled. "You finally got Mandy to marry you, huh?"

For some reason it gave Tom fierce satisfaction that someone else had known how he felt about Mandy. And how much sense it made that they'd be married now.

"That kid with his hands all over your wife is one of my cowhands. He knew Mandy—Sally, too, it looks like—back in Texas."

"Hmm—" Logan's smile faded.

"All those years I told everyone you were born to hang, Mark Reeves." Sally grinned and slapped Mark's shoulder. "Guess I owe Beth five dollars. I bet her you'd never live to be an adult."

"It's not ladylike nor Christian to wager, Sally." Mandy looked stern, but Tom saw the twinkle in her eye.

"You're right. But with Mark I never figured it for any kind of a gamble."

Mark laughed and slid an arm around Sally's waist, and she let that arm stay right where it was.

"That's how Mandy talks to him, too." Tom drew Logan's eagle eyes away from the little group. "In fact, she called him her childhood enemy. I've decided he's no threat."

Then Mark put his other arm around Mandy, and Tom wasn't feeling quite so charitable.

"Still don't like it," Logan muttered.

"I'm planning to fire him." Tom nodded.

Luther bulled his way into the reunion and had Mandy in a bear hug.

Tom waited until the fuss had calmed down, not that hard considering Luther, Buff, and Wise Sister barely spoke, and Logan was busy glaring. It boiled down to Mandy, Sally, and Mark, who were talking like magpies, and Mark was touching them again.

Finally Tom reached for the sheriff's door. "Let's go see what Merl found."

"He's not there." Logan shook his head.

"He left the door unlocked?"

"Yep, he rode out this morning to check on some cattle rustling in the area. He said he wouldn't be gone long."

Looking around, Tom realized there wasn't a single horse tied at a hitching post. Not a single man walking down the street. No music coming from the Golden Butte.

"What's going on? Divide's a little town, but this is too quiet." Tom frowned. He'd thought that a town full of rough Western men meant safety.

"A cattle drive came through the other day hiring and paying top wages. Took every able-bodied man in town. Even Seth and Muriel at the general store hired on as camp cooks. Thought it'd be fun to get away for a couple of weeks. They left one of the few women in town to run things."

"How long have you been in town?" Tom asked Logan.

"Just a few days. Sally decided she wasn't going to put up with Mandy living on that mountaintop anymore. We came through Divide on our way north and met Luther here, just coming from Mandy's castle. The sheriff told us you weren't at the ranch, that you'd headed off for Denver. But we knew you hadn't gone to Denver because we came up that trail. He told us to wait here for you."

Belle Harden chose that moment to ride into town with Emma. She came from the west, crossing the train tracks that bordered the town on that side.

"Reeves!" Tom had to yell to get Mark to quit with the girl talk. Maybe if the halfwit didn't have the sense to keep his hands off his boss's woman, he'd figure out he shouldn't be hugging his boss's woman in front of his fiancé. When Mark looked up, Tom jabbed a finger toward Emma.

Mark wheeled around and smiled a greeting.

"What are they doing here?" Tom asked Logan that question, but it was clear with one glance at Logan's expression that the man had no idea who these newcomers even were.

And as the Hardens dismounted and Mark rushed to her side and slipped his arm around Emma, one more crowd rode in. Red Dawson with his wife and three young'uns, along with Silas Harden.

From yet another direction, Tom saw his sister coming in with Wade. And they'd brought their two children with them.

"I sent a rider out to tell them we were going to build a house," Tom told Mandy. "Abby wants to help. She thinks white people build unwisely at times."

"Unwisely?" Abby had ridden close enough to overhear the remark. "I think my exact words were that white people are fools who would try to close the whole world inside." She swung off her bareback horse in a fluid leap that always drew Tom's admiration.

"White people?" With one brow arched, Sally looked from Tom to his blond sister.

"I'll explain later," Mandy whispered.

Mark and Emma were talking fast, and a grin spread so wide on Mark's face, Tom thought the boy's head would split in half.

Then Mark gave a yell that'd make a wild Indian back down. He lifted Emma in his arms and whirled her around. "We're getting married," Mark announced at the top of his lungs.

Belle must have given her the go-ahead and sent Silas for the preacher.

"Well, we were going to build them a house," Belle muttered, glaring at Mark. "Emma decided she wanted to get married and live in it."

They all gathered in a circle to discuss the details. The loud click of a gun being cocked whirled them around to face two dozen heavily armed men.

Most of them bearing white streaks in their hair.

Tom had his gun drawn, but he froze at the sight of all that firepower, aimed right at them. His first thought was that his children were in the middle of this. Red Dawson's children, Abby's children. And too many women. The Cooters didn't open fire. But it was clear from the fanatic hate gleaming in Cord Cooter's eyes they'd come to finish their feud.

Today they weren't back-shooters. Today they planned to face this feud as men. Men who'd put children and women under their guns.

Tom's opinion of the family didn't improve. "Let the woman and children step away from us," Tom ordered. As if these coyotes obeyed any civilized law.

"All but Lady Gray." Cord's eyes went straight to Mandy. "She's part of this, and she's not going anywhere."

Sickened, Tom looked at Mandy, knowing she'd never back down anyway. She had her rifle in her hands. With one look, Tom could see the cold in Mandy. She was detached, ready to fight and keep fighting. Fire that Winchester until she won or died.

He hated that for her. He knew how that scared her, that part of herself. He'd hoped to give her a safe enough life that she never had to let that cold flow in her veins again.

It's a wonder she hadn't just started mowing down Cooters the second she saw that white streak. Only about half of them had it, Tom noticed. Maybe, if they could breed that streak out of a man, they could breed the evil out of him, too.

"Let 'em go, Cord." There was grumbling from behind Cord. "I'm not shooting women and children."

Cord nodded.

"The little ones and all the women but Lady Gray can go," Cord agreed quickly.

Tom realized that even a snake like Cord Cooter didn't have a belly for shooting children.

"I'm not going." Belle Harden had her six-gun drawn.

In the distance, a sharp, high whistle blew. The train, which came through once a week on a good week, would be in town in a matter of minutes.

"I'm staying." Sally had her own rifle. She'd pulled it from a sling around her back just like Mandy had.

"Cass honey, you take the little ones."

"No, Red." Taking his eyes off the Cooters for only a second, Tom saw the tension on Cassie Dawson's face. She wanted to stay just like the other women, but her eyes went to the children, and Tom knew she'd do as she was told to save them.

"Please, Cass honey, take 'em and go. Get 'em out of here."

"This is madness." Tears brimmed in Cassie's eyes, and Tom knew she had the right of it.

"I know, Cass. Please. Stay in the church until this is over and get down. Flying bullets don't respect even a house of God."

"Yes, Red." Reluctantly, Cassie started shooing children. Cassie Dawson was inclined toward obedience.

"Go with her, Emma." Mark Reeves sounded real bossy for a man who didn't have a prayer of getting his way.

"I'm staying." Emma wasn't so much inclined.

Tom knew better than to even waste his breath ordering any of the rest of these women around. Mark'd learn that soon enough. But a wild country wasn't settled by weaklings. It figured a lot of Western women would buy into a fight someone brought to their doors. Not that Cassie was a weakling. She was just a sweetheart, and she couldn't seem to stop herself from minding her husband. And someone had to get these children out of here.

Tom felt a moment of pure envy before he stepped closer to his wife. Then he focused on those drawn Cooter guns and felt sick. They needed to stop this or a lot of people were going to die. When had the Cooters stopped being dry-gulchers? Why'd they pick today of all days to grow backbones?

"I'm a man of God." Red Dawson stepped forward as Cassie herded the children out of harm's way. "I'm telling all of you men to stand down. There's no reason for this. What is your purpose for coming at us with guns drawn? What is calling you to such a terrible sin as shooting at honest folks, including women?"

The train steamed closer. Tom saw a blast of black smoke belch out of its chimney and heard the first squeal of the brakes.

"It's a feud, Preacher-man. It was started by Lady Gray." Cord gestured at Mandy with his pistol. "Today it'll be finished by Cooters. The minute she shot one of our family, she drew this onto herself. Cooters stick together, and that's why we're here. When we're done, no one in the West will dare to pick a fight with one of us. We'll have a name to be proud of. A name to fear."

"There's no pride in this." Red's voice was kind. Tom didn't know how he managed it when talking to scum like this. "And now with the train here there are witnesses."

"We *want* witnesses," Cord sneered. "We want everyone to know, and be afraid."

"It's murder. A waste of lives. And the folks on that train will know, and those of you who live through this will be brought to justice."

"Those of us who live will remember every one of you who stood by Lady Gray. Our feud will be against all of you, and all your kin."

There was a shifty look in the eyes of several of the two dozen men who faced them. Tom suspected that given half a chance they'd back down.

Tom stepped up beside Red. "We're wasting time. These men don't know a thing about right and wrong. They only know revenge and hate."

Tom saw Cassie get the last of the children inside the church. She gave one last long look back. Even from here, Tom could see tears in her eyes.

"I reckon you're right, Tom. But I had to try."

"You step out, too, Red. It's not fitting that a parson be involved in this."

The train pulled up, and the engine passed them, slowing, the brakes squealing.

"I'll stay. I won't let it be said I backed down and let the evil happen without fighting back."

"Enough of this." Cord raised his gun. "We end this today."

Feeling sick, Tom exchanged a long look with Mandy. She was standing in the front, far too many of those guns aimed right at her. She wasn't going to live through this no matter how fast she was. Tom braced himself to jump in front of her.

An elderly man jumped off the still-moving train with surprising agility and strode straight for the standoff. "Hold your fire!" He was an elderly man with a wide white streak in his hair.

★

"Grandpappy?" Cord lowered his gun.

Mandy looked past the old man and saw her pa getting off the train. Even better, her ma. Mandy had to fight every reflex in her body to keep her rifle aimed and not run to throw herself in her mother's arms.

Pa was walking just a pace behind the old man. Grandpappy Cooter, who'd laid down the rule that Cooters stick together. If there'd been a chance the Cooters would back down, that was over. The man behind all their feuding was here to lend them his backbone.

The train bumped to a haut, and a crew of men jumped off the train, ignoring the goings-on in town, striding down to what looked like a cattle car that was dead even with the Cooter clan.

Grandpappy walked smack into the middle of space that would be filled with flying lead in just a few seconds and stalked right up to Cord.

As if time suddenly slowed to a crawl, Mandy braced herself.

"Protect me, Lord. Protect all of us." Mandy didn't see how even God could protect them all.

"God, have mercy." Mandy heard her little sister behind her, praying, maybe dying today because of Mandy.

"Lord, help me." That was Ma, striding right into the middle of this madness.

Her throat swelled when she saw Beth step off the train. Beth took in the nightmare in a single glance, walked straight toward the worst of the trouble praying, "Give me strength."

Sally stepped up beside Mandy on the left, Beth on the right. The gentle-voiced doctor in petticoats, who'd been back East to medical school and dedicated her life to healing, had her rifle leveled. Ma was there, ready to fight for her daughters, as she always had been.

Belle Harden shoved between Sophie and Tom. Tom's eyes were narrowed and ready.

If her blood hadn't been so cold, Mandy would have wept to think she was bringing death to the people she loved so well. But the tears were frozen solid behind her eyes.

Silas was between Belle and Tom, back a step just because Belle wouldn't have it otherwise, but he was ready.

Pa was there, too. Farthest away, with Luther and Buff at her side, Wise Sister stood with her bow drawn. Abby had a knife in her hands that gleamed in the sunlight. Red Dawson, a man of God who didn't want this but wouldn't stand by while evil men killed the innocent. Mark Reeves with Emma at his side. There were cowhands from Tom's ranch, too.

But even with all of these, there were more Cooters. They were outgunned, but they'd make a fight of it.

Mandy's cold blood chilled to frigid, solid ice as she waited for the old man who had started all this with his rules and twisted sense of pride to turn and fire.

He reached up a gnarled hand and. . . "What are you buncha no-accounts doing?"

He knocked Cord's gun hand aside.

"Uh, that woman over there shot a Cooter." Cord suddenly looked about ten years old as he fumbled with an explanation.

"Why?"

Two men started opening the wide side doors of the baggage car. The scrape of those doors was the only sound in the whole town.

Mandy, with her sleeted nerves, seeing everything, hearing everything, noticed other people getting off the train, a man carrying two little children.

"Why what?"

Mandy wondered, too. Why had they waited so long to kill someone who'd harmed a Cooter?

"Well, 'cuz her husband's guards shot Amos and a bunch of others."

"And what was Amos doing when they shot him?"

Cord got a mutinous look on his face. "It don't matter what he was doing. You're the one who said Cooters stick together, Grandpappy."

"Yep, I said that all right. They stick together to uphold the family honor. There's no honor in this."

Pa reached Mandy's side. "Lower your gun so I can give you a proper hug."

"Not now, Pa. Not until this is over." The ice in her veins began to thaw when Pa touched her arm, but she was still cold, unnaturally calm, and ruthless and ready. Maybe that old man could stop this, but she wasn't trusting him. Not yet.

"I rode on the train with that man. He's the head of the Cooter family. He said the law came to him back East and asked about this feud. As soon as he found what his kinfolk were up to, he set out. We've been riding the train together since Denver. He's going to put a stop to this right now."

Mandy heard that wavering, elderly voice ranting and raving at the Cooters. She started to believe it might really end without gunfire. But she remembered the hate in Cord Cooter's eyes and kept her rifle leveled.

More passengers got off the train. Mandy saw Sheriff Dean ride into town from the north. The baggage handlers shouted as they rigged a ramp from the side of the train and, using wooden poles, carefully controlled a huge wooden keg rolling out of the car's belly.

Cord had a burn of red on his cheeks. His head was bowed like a chastised child. Grandpappy was yelling. All of the Cooter guns were lowered.

The keg reached the ground and was pushed to the side to unload a second one. Mandy saw the word MOLASSES stamped on the side of the keg. Supplies for the general store.

"I'm ashamed of all of you, do you hear?" Grandpappy waved his arms wildly.

Cord's eyes rose. Mandy didn't like what she saw. Cord wasn't a boy any longer, and being scolded clearly didn't sit well.

"All my life I've fought hard to make the Cooter name stand for something, and now you run around like a pack of yellow dogs chasing one woman. She's made you look like fools. She's shamed you, and you've shamed the Cooter name."

Suddenly, at the word "shame," Cord snapped. Mandy saw the second it happened. The sleet in her veins lanced through every part of her as Cord raised his gun, his eyes straight on hers.

"Look out!"

A shout from the train didn't pull Mandy's eyes away from Cord and his gun. She was busy raising and aiming her rifle.

Then just as Cord's eyes told Mandy he'd fire in the next instant, the runaway keg slammed into the whole crowd of Cooters. They began to tumble like tenpins, knocking one into the other until they went down in a heap, Cord at the bottom of the pile. The stack of Cooters groaned and shouted and shoved.

Grandpappy Cooter missed being bowled down by inches. The keg split open, and molasses poured out over all of them.

The sheriff jumped off his horse and waded into the mess, plucking guns out of molasses-coated hands. The men were too busy howling in disgust to resist.

Grandpappy helped disarm them.

Wondering what molasses did to a fire iron, Mandy's gun lowered. She clearly saw that the danger was past, but she was still as cold as death inside.

Until Tom had his say. "I guess what Cord said is right."

She turned to him. Just seeing him brought her back from that arctic place. As their eyes met, the heat in his look made her feel alive and warm and hopeful. "Cord was right about what?"

"Those Cooters really do stick together."

★ Twenty-Five ★

Just because Mandy no longer wanted to hide didn't mean Mark and Emma didn't need a house.

Mandy introduced her family to Tom while the sheriff locked up so many Cooters it was likely the whole western half of the nation had been stripped clean of them.

Grandpappy told names and, angry at this blight on the family name, pointed out any he specifically knew were wanted men. "There are lots of honest men who bear the name of Cooter. I'll not have the family shamed by defending vermin just because they've got streaks of white in their hair and share my name."

The sheriff groused about the molasses ruining his jail cell, but in the end, all the right folks were on the business side of a door with iron bars.

"So, Tom"—Pa had that old look in his eye, the one that had run off so many men over the years—"you got the means to take good care of my girl?"

Tom smiled. He winked at Mandy then said, "Come and look at my stallion."

Jerking his thumb at the black thoroughbred, Pa's interrogation was diverted, and he went with Tom to study the horse more closely.

"And I'm running a herd of Angus beeves."

"Black cattle?" Pa ran his hands along the stallion's front shoulder, clearly admiring all that muscle. "Not longhorns? How do they handle the cold weather?"

Mandy would have stayed in her ma's arms all day except she had to keep taking turns hugging her sisters. And there was Alex to meet and all the children to fuss over.

Ma shocked all her girls by crying over Mandy's three little ones. Mandy, Beth, and Sally created a little circle around Ma as she crouched to hold Angela in her arms, hoping to block the sight of tears from Pa.

Alex and Logan did their best to act interested when Tom and Pa talked ranching. Mandy knew neither of them had much to do with it. But they must have figured out something to talk about.... Maybe McClellen women in general, because they seemed to be having a good time.

The talking went on for a solid hour until Belle Harden snapped, "Red, you gonna perform this wedding ceremony any time soon?" Belle Harden couldn't exactly sound excited about the wedding, but she sounded impatient with life in general, so scolding Red seemed to suit her.

"We get on with this, or I'm taking Emma back home." She'd seemed okay talking to Abby and Cassie, but apparently she'd been faking her agreeableness.

Mark flinched. Silas broke off talking with Red and Wade. Emma grinned and went to stand by Mark.

They had the wedding in the little Divide church then headed out for a house raising.

★

With all these knowing hands, Mark and Emma had a nice roof within a few days.

Better'n he deserved, Mandy thought, though she was having

trouble hating the kid like she'd once done. And she'd fallen in love with Emma...the poor thing.

Mandy spent so much time crying she thought maybe, just maybe, her pa actually got kind of comfortable with tears.

Tom seemed to have the time of his life with Pa, Ma, and Belle Harden talked together for hours.

As they worked on Mark's house, Mandy learned everything that had gone on with her sisters and her ma for the last few years.

The cabin was a good-sized one, thanks to an abundance of hardworking men. But not *too* big thanks to Abby.

Belle had stocked the larder for a long winter, along with providing cattle and horses and so many wedding presents Mark had taken on a permanent irritated scowl.

Except when Emma stood beside him and whispered in his ear. Then he got purely cheerful. Mandy decided Mark Reeves had found the perfect woman to tame him.

The last day of building came. One family at a time—the Sawyers, the Dawsons, and the Hardens—packed up and headed home. The McClellens were leaving soon to spend a few days at the Linscott ranch.

The women were hanging curtains in the house while the men finished some work on the front porch railings. Emma and Mark were taking their turn watching over Mandy's and Beth's children so the work could be finished in peace.

Tom came in with a cupboard and carried it to a spot where it would hang on the kitchen wall. "Mandy, can you lend a hand here?"

Mandy went eagerly. She'd barely spoken to Tom in days. And certainly she'd had no time alone with him.

The only ones allowed time alone were Emma and Mark, which rankled Mandy a bit since she and Tom were almost as much newlyweds as those two. She wouldn't have minded getting Tom off by himself.

He adjusted the cupboard carefully. "I want to fasten it on tight. I've got the weight on the pegs I hung earlier, but I want to level it." He moved it one way and then another until he was satisfied. "That's good. Hold it steady."

He glanced at her, standing very close, her hands on the shelf, her eyes on him, her mind not on her work at all.

Tom read her mind and closed the distance even more. "How long are we gonna have to build this stupid house? I want to take you home."

She shivered under his heated words, and it wasn't the kind of cold that worried her one bit. She hadn't felt so much as a twinge of the coldness that she often feared would come one day and never go.

She was so distracted by his words and the intent in his eyes that she forgot what she was doing with the cupboard and let go to wrap her arms around his neck.

The cupboard dropped, and Mandy jumped back to catch it. A rough edge jammed a splinter right into her index finger. "Ouch!" Mandy saw blood welling up and an ugly shard of wood protruding.

Tom steadied the cupboard. Not level, but it would stay up. He turned to her finger and bent his head low over it. "Let me get it out for you."

With his head bent so low, Mandy was almost nose to nose with the man. Lip to lip. He smiled then turned to his doctoring. Mandy never for an instant considered calling for help from her doctor sister.

With his strong white teeth, Tom bit into the nasty piece of wood and pulled it out of her finger.

Red blood oozed from the wound, and Tom murmured sympathy. With the splinter gone, Tom pressed her fingertip into his mouth to soothe the pain.

It worked because instead of pain she felt a tingle that started where his mouth touched her and spread up her arm until it reached all the way to her heart. "I love you, Tom." Mandy tried to remember what it was like living on that mountaintop with no one to care for her. No one to share any burdens with her.

When he raised his head next, her finger looked raw. The bleeding had stopped, but that warm tingle had gotten far worse. Somehow it pushed out the cold so completely that Mandy couldn't even worry about it returning. She knew now that if it did, it would never be who she truly was, never take over and not recede. Not with all the warmth of love Tom brought into her life.

"I love you, too, Mandy girl." He smiled then studied her finger again. "Hey, look."

Mandy followed the direction he was looking, to her wound.

"The callus." Shocked, she looked closer. "It's gone."

Nodding, Tom kissed her finger again. "I live a pretty quiet life at the Double L. I reckon we'll never have enough trouble for you to grow in a new one."

"Maybe, or maybe now that little sore on my finger will scar over, and I'll be stuck with a tough spot on my trigger finger for life."

"Don't matter none." Tom kissed her palm then her wrist. "I want you to be just who you are. That means you're fast with a rifle. I'm proud of that. I'm proud of you."

"I doubt you'd have married me if you'd known how fast I was. I'm told it's a pretty scary sight."

"Well, I've seen it, and I love you as much as ever. As much as a man can love a woman. I think I've rounded up the best little ranch wife a man ever had."

"You might as well think it because you're stuck with me." Mandy couldn't stop the silly tears she'd found such a talent for since she'd married Tom. As the first one trickled down her cheek, she felt Tom flinch, but he stayed close.

A strong arm slid around her waist. He drew her into his arms and lifted her clean off her toes, then raised his head and froze.

Mandy twisted her head to see her sisters standing nearby, watching her, crying.

She looked past Sally and Beth to see her ma turning from the curtains and her pa coming in the cabin door, with Alex and Logan just behind him.

"What's going on here?" Pa sounded panicky.

"Sorry." Mandy sniffled. "I'm just so happy."

"That is a pure waste of salt and water, Mandy. You know better'n to cry." Pa looked behind him as if to check to see if the coast was clear. He didn't run, but Mandy suspected it was a near thing. "Sally, not you, too?"

Sally sniffled, and Logan went to her side.

"You've raised yourself up a nice brood of daughters, Sophie and Clay." Tom turned so Mandy could see her sobbing family better. "But I think I got the best of the lot."

Alex and Logan shook their heads, but they didn't stop smiling.

"I don't care how fast you shoot, Mandy," Pa fussed. "Or how well you doctor, Beth. Or Sally, how good a hand you are with cattle. You girls have gone soft since you've grown up."

The waterworks had turned loose, and there was no stopping them. When Ma started crying, Pa sighed and went to pull her into his arms.

There was a long, sweet, quiet time while the women in the McClellen family ignored Clay's Rule Number One for about the ten-thousandth time.

ABOUT THE AUTHOR

MARY CONNEALY is a Carol Award winner and a Christy Award finalist. She is the author of the Lassoed in Texas Trilogy, releasing in the fall, which includes *Petticoat Ranch, Calico Canyon,* and *Gingham Mountain.* Her Montana Marriages series includes *Montana Rose, The Husband Tree,* and *Wildflower Bride.* She has also written a romantic cozy mystery trilogy, *Nosy in Nebraska*; and her novel *Golden Days* is part of the *Alaska Brides* anthology. You can find out more about Mary's upcoming books at www.maryconnealy.com and www.mconnealy.blogspot.com.

Mary lives on a Nebraska ranch with her husband, Ivan, and has four grown daughters: Joslyn (married to Matt), Wendy, Shelly (married to Aaron), and Katy. And she is the grandmother of one beautiful granddaughter, Elle.

Mary loves to hear from her readers. You may visit her at these sites: www.mconnealy.blogspot.com, www.seekerville.blogspot.com, and www.petticoatsandpistols.com. Write to her at mary@maryconnealy.com.

If you enjoyed

Sharpshooter in Petticoats,

then read:

LASSOED IN TEXAS TRILOGY

THREE HUMOROUS WILD WEST TEXAS ROMANCES UNDER ONE COVER

This jumbo volume encases three beloved novels by Mary Connealy. Wild West Texas romance begins on rough footing when a self-sufficient woman meets her rescuer, a prim and proper teacher is roped into marrying a rowdy rancher, and a nosy schoolmarm accuses a cowboy of exploiting orphans.

978-1-61626-216-7

$19.99

Available wherever books are sold.

Other Books by Mary Connealy

Sophie's Daughter series

Doctor in Petticoats
Wrangler in Petticoats

Lassoed in Texas series

Petticoat Ranch
Calico Canyon
Gingham Mountain
Now all three books in one—*The Lassoed in Texas Trilogy*

Montana Marriages series

Montana Rose
The Husband Tree
Wildflower Bride

Cowboy Christmas
Nosy in Nebraska (a cozy mystery collection)
Black Hills Blessing (a 3-in-1 contemporary collection)